STORM

David Simpson

MAX MEDIA PUBLISHING LTD.
www.maxmediapublishing.com

First published in Great Britain,
2021 by Max Media Publishing Ltd.

A CIP catalogue record for this book
is available from the British Library.

Typeset and arranged by Simon Meakin of In House Design,
and Adele Dolloway of MMP.
Cover design by Andrew Dolloway.

ISBN 978-1-9169011-0-0

Printed in Great Britain by
Max Media Publishing Ltd.
Mansfield

STORM CLOUDS

Dedicated to my wife Rita.

Once again, thanks to Kath, for putting in the hard yards.

Special thanks to Andrew and the gang at Max Media Publishing.
Good work guys.

David Simpson
June 2021

Chapter One

Dubai: United Arab Emirates

The view from the Penthouse Suite was spectacular. The beautiful azure coloured seas seemed to be studded with a myriad of diamond clusters fired by the sun. The hotel stood on an enviable beachfront location, set amidst lush gardens and mature trees. The front of the building faced the sea with its own sandy beach, brought in at great expense. The sides and rear of the building were dwarfed by more modern and much higher hotels.

The land had been purchased in the 1960's when nothing more than two storey houses, a thriving fishing village and a port could be seen. Electricity didn't arrive until 1961, mains water had to wait until 1968, but nevertheless Omar Mohammed Hussein had seen the potential of its location and set about buying up a large area of prime real estate.

It was Omar's vision that had a geologist flown in to survey the land to see if it was feasible to construct a high rise building without it sinking into the coral limestone, which was mainly what Dubai's soil was made up from.

Once the area was proven to be sound, he had a young architect to design and supervise the construction of the building and the surrounding grounds.

At the time of construction many of the locals thought that Omar Mohammed Hussein had been touched by too much sun, but once the building was completed even they had to admit that it was impressive looking. Omar liked to portray himself as a simple man; a man of the desert. In fact there was nothing simple about Omar at all. He inspired the imaginations of both young and old alike.

The wealth came by way of oil of course. The area was awash with it and Omar Hussein was drowning in it. His foray into the hotel business had begun in his native Jordan. Two hotels had been built in the capital Amman, both were successful and doing well. His entrepreneurial skills didn't end with the building of hotels, Omar liked to visit London, England and during the sixties he bought up a wide range of old buildings and properties relatively cheaply with a view to letting the land that they occupied appreciate in value.

Once Omar's son Mohammed 'George' Hussein was deemed capable of running the business Omar allowed him to do so. It was a wise move and George took to it with a passion, adding greatly to the Hussein portfolio.

Mohammed George, known to his Western friends simply as George, was more liberal than his father favouring friendly cordial relations with the West. He spent much of his time in both London and Paris and it was rumoured, though quietly, that he had a mistress in both capitals, whether this was true or not he managed to sire first a son,

Ali, and then a daughter, Yasmin to his Jordanian wife.

Ali remained in Jordan, preferring the company of his grandfather, Omar. He has been influenced greatly by his grandfather's beliefs and teachings and grew up hating the west and all that it stood for.

Yasmin, at an early age, was brought over to London and educated in a private school for girls. When she was older she spent two years in Paris before returning to London to finish her education. This pleased Yasmin just fine as she now regarded London as home.

When Ali and Yasmin's father George had been killed recently in an automobile accident, though the circumstances were shrouded in mystery, it fell to Ali, as the male heir, to assume the responsibility of running the Hussein Empire.

All this had been playing on Ali's mind when his reverie was interrupted by Abdul Rahman, seated at the head of the table,

"Do you wish to ask anything Ali?" said Abdul.

"No, carry on Abdul," all eyes were directed in Ali's direction when he said this, but the truth was he hadn't been listening and didn't know what had been asked of him.

At the head of the table in the Penthouse Suite sat Abdul Rahman, an Egyptian by birth. He had asked for this meeting in order to account for the distribution and spending of Ali Hussein's recent very generous donation to their mutual cause. Something you would have thought Ali would have been most interested in, given the size of the donation.

To Rahman's left sat Ali Hussein, their host for the duration of their stay in Dubai. Next to Ali sat Mehmet Yafai, Ali's new head of security and both were Jordanian by birth.

Next to Mehmet sat Khalid Maliky and next to him was

Vkass Mohammed Hussein, both Saudi's and very wealthy.

Opposite both the Saudi's and with very good reason sat Azad Hassan and Masud Fazel, both Iranian by birth and traditional blood enemies of the Saudi's.

The Saudi's were mostly Wahhabi, a branch of the Sunni sect and natural blood enemies of the Shia sect, who were mostly Iranian.

It was down to Abdul Rahman's sheer personality and persuasive abilities that had brought about this uneasy alliance. It had not been easy, not by any means but so far bloodshed in the boardroom had been avoided.

The reason that the alliance was still holding were the mutual gains and aims of the group that had been realised by the money that Ali had recently brought to the table, which did much to cool the blood of the warring factions.

Three separate training camps, spread throughout Iran, had been set up and fully equipped with weapons, supplies and vehicles. They were manned by dedicated volunteers who were eager to be unleashed against the West.

The Saudi's had also contributed generously and their wealth had been spread throughout Europe in the form of a hundred small groups, known as sleeper cells. They too had been armed and were waiting to be activated. They had been trained to work independently or in tandem with other cells. Recent attacks in London, Paris, Belgium and Germany had been the work of these sleeper cells.

Abdul Rahman summed up by adding his own personal contribution, "The Egyptian tourist economy is still struggling to bounce back after the attacks by our brothers on the foreigners. We have hit them hard and will continue to do so as and when it becomes necessary. Tunisia has suffered greatly since our attacks on the beaches. Foreigners are no longer willing to risk their lives merely to lie in the sun; their economy had been hit hard and lies in ruins."

There were murmurs of assent from around the table but Abdul hadn't quite finished, "I am satisfied with the progress that we are making but feel that another lesson needs to be administered to our friends in Turkey. I am organising a major incident designed to bring them back to the brotherhood as they have become too close to the West of late."

Nods of approval met Abdul's words; all were in agreement.

Before bringing the meeting to a close Abdul asked if anyone wished to address the group. Everyone seemed satisfied, so it was left to Abdul to close the meeting. He was careful to bid each one goodbye in equal measure lest it be construed that he favoured one more than the other; it was a fragile alliance that could so easily break apart over something so seemingly trivial. Thankfully the parting met with everyone's approval and Abdul came back to sit at the head of the table once more.

Ali and Mehmet had remained seated and waited for Abdul whilst he settled.

"So Ali, have I spent your money wisely?" asked Abdul.

"Yes, I am very pleased, but it must have taken incredible organisation," admitted Ali.

"Thank you Ali, for acknowledging that, but believe me when I tell you that it was far harder trying to keep the Iranians from killing the Saudis. Why can they not see that we are trying to achieve the same goal? They are acting like children, perhaps I should just bash their heads together," mused Abdul, "forgive me, I'm rambling."

Abdul reached down for his brief case and placed a red folder on the table. Indicating the folder Abdul explained, "Information about your sister from my source in London."

Ali was suddenly very alert and eager to know the folder's contents.

Opening it Abdul began reading aloud what was written. "Alright let's get to it. We gave the contract on your sister to two of our best operatives, Asif and Waleed Ali. They have never failed us before but it seems both operatives were killed whilst carrying out the contract."

"How were they killed?" interrupted Ali.

Abdul read down, "Apparently they were killed in a collision with the target vehicle."

Ali interrupted again, "And my sister?"

Abdul had to read down a bit, "Shot, but only wounded, it says that the bullet had passed through cleanly without any major damage and she is expected to make a full recovery."

Ali slapped the table in frustration making Mehmet jump in the process. "She's always had the luck of the devil, clearly she still has it," thundered Ali, exasperated.

"Calm yourself Ali. We have an army of people at our disposal and we can try again," soothed Abdul.

This seemed to perk Ali up a bit and his whole demeanour changed to one of optimism, "Yes you are right of course Abdul, now onto the other matter, did you do as I suggested regarding the security breach at your home in Jordan?" asked Abdul.

"Yes, Mehmet here has been most thorough. I'll let him tell you himself," offered Ali.

Mehmet began by ticking off what his investigations had uncovered. "At first I thought the breach had been contrived by someone on the security detail. The obvious choice was the young guard stationed on Miss Hussein's corridor; the thinking was that she may have seduced him into helping her leave the compound. After very robust questioning this was soon discounted. He maintained that his attacker was tall, white and a westerner. He also mentioned that Miss Hussein knew him.

"Did she call her rescuer by name?" asked Abdul.

"Yes but the guard couldn't remember what it was; he had just been hit with a charge from a stun gun. We found it by the way, it was of Chinese manufacture. All the security staff were questioned and eliminated from blame, also all the household staff, especially the ones who had daily access to Miss Hussein. I wanted to know if she had access to either telephone or computer; which she didn't. Could she have got someone to smuggle a letter out and post it in the city? After extensive questioning I was no nearer to finding out how she had contacted someone on the outside. Then by accident I'm ashamed to admit, we realised how she must have gotten a message out. Once a month, Mr Hussein corresponds with his lawyer in London, in the form of a sealed folder, which is flown out by Mr Hussein's private jet. Anything needed to be returned comes back the next day. At some point while she was there she must have had access to the folder and simply put a note or a letter inside amongst the paperwork."

"So by deduction Ali, that must mean that your lawyer received either a note or a letter from Yasmin," mused Abdul.

"It appears so", replied Ali.

"Yes, but the question is, who was it addressed to?" said Abdul, "I think we need to find out!"

"Do you have someone in mind?" queried Ali.

"Yes I do, but tell me Ali, is your lawyer someone you would miss if he were, say, to have an accident?" asked Abdul.

"No I would not miss him at all, especially now I know that his loyalties lie with my sister," replied Ali.

“That’s what I thought,” mused Abdul, “but we need to find out who your sister wanted him to contact before he has his accident, yes?”

“Yes, agreed,” replied Ali.

“Good, I will set the wheels in motion then, no time like the present,” said Abdul reaching for his mobile.

Chapter 2

The Chameleon

The telephone call, when it came, had been a surprise; it must have been three years since Lars had been in contact with Abdul Rahman, but being the total professional that he was, he listened with interest before accepting the contract. Payment was in the usual way; half now and half when the contract was completed. This particular contract had an extra little twist, the answer to two questions was required, a name and an address? This piqued Lars' interest but he was certain that one way or another he would learn the answers.

Lars Thorkyld travelled to London Heathrow via Amsterdam where he had been living for almost two years. The place suited him admirably; it was crowded, which he liked and he got to rub shoulders with all nationalities. He claimed to be Danish which he spoke fluently and his Danish passport seemed to back up the claim but there the deception ended for he was neither Danish nor Dutch, for that matter, and his name wasn't Lars Thorkyld.

He stood five feet six inches tall in his stockinged feet, blue eyes and of slim but wiry build. His skin was light and he could easily pass for Caucasian, again this was a deception as in actual fact he was Egyptian and had been abandoned as a child to fend for himself in the hell hole that was Cairo. He had been reduced to stealing every day just to survive. The streets of Cairo became a battleground, it was survival of the fittest; dog eats dog, brutal and ugly, never enough to eat, just existing day after day. Paedophiles here in the gutter were both predatory and vicious with it. He did well to evade them and gradually gathered around him a few allies and fellow rejects of humanity, seeking safety in numbers. It was simply to survive, nothing more. They had become brutalised by the very streets that they now called home.

They lived by stealing and just like lions or wild dogs, overwhelmed their victims by sheer numbers. He quickly gained a reputation for viciousness and never backed down. His small size was no impediment, his speed with his fists was legendary and anything else that came to hand marked him out as someone to be avoided. Bigger boys in the gang would not challenge his leadership and deferred to him as boss. Eventually he became known to them as 'Rat'. A term he despised. He didn't like the name but gradually accepted it as a mark of respect. He made his first kill at the age of thirteen, or thereabouts. He didn't really know his true age.

The gang, as they lay asleep one night in an alley way, on the card board boxes they now called home, that they thought was reasonably safe, were unaware of a predator in their midst.

Rat suddenly awoke to someone fondling his penis.

At first he had thought he was dreaming but now, coming fully awake he realised that someone was leaning over him. Instinct now took over and feeling around in the darkness his hand brushed against the neck of a glass bottle. Smashing the bottle on the floor Rat aimed the jagged remains of the bottle, at what he thought was his attacker's face severing the man's jugular vein more by luck, depending on your point of view. The feral pack now came awake, alerted by the man's struggle to staunch the spray of arterial blood. Rat watched the man, fascinated by his attacker's final moments. He didn't feel any revulsion in what he had done, in fact he felt justified by his actions. It was his first kill and in truth had not been intentional, it had been messy and had resulted in a very large piece of evidence; a body. He vowed to himself there and then that he would learn from his mistake, now knowing what his chosen profession would be.

Thirty years later he was at the top of his profession and could pick and choose which contract to take or reject, but that first kill still excited him, he remembered it in detail like it was yesterday.

Now, in London, he followed the instructions carefully. Go to the newsagent near to St Paul's, buy a copy of 'Hello' magazine and at about 11:45am cross the road to the pavement cafe, purchase a drink and sit at a table with the front of the magazine in full view. At approximately 12:00pm someone will approach you and ask, "Have you finished with the magazine?"

You will say, "Yes, by all means take it," and in exchange you will be given a package.

Now seated at the pavement cafe table, nursing a large strong black coffee Lars waited as instructed, the front of 'Hello' magazine in clear view. A young woman, coming from the direction of St Paul's seemed to study him overly long. He wondered if this was his contact but she passed on by and disappeared into the main street. No one else approached him and by his watch it was just after 12 o'clock.

This didn't worry him unduly the handover stated that it would take place at approximately 12 o'clock. His patience was rewarded as his attention was aroused by the return of the young woman who had passed by earlier.

Approaching his table he noticed she had a carrier bag in one hand, which he remembered she hadn't had before.

She asked, "Have you finished with the magazine?"

Lars answered, "Yes by all means take it," and the exchange was concluded.

Both parties knew that if the correct wording had not been adhered to the exchange would have been aborted. It would have meant that one or both of them had been compromised and was a clear signal to walk away.

The exchange now made, Lars remained seated whilst watching the young woman return towards St Paul's. He hadn't been in his line of work for this long without becoming cautious. He wanted to be sure that she hadn't been followed and remained vigilant for a further five minutes, long after she had disappeared from sight.

Lars Thorkyld once known as the 'Rat,' drank down the dregs of his now cold coffee with a grimace, and headed away from the pavement cafe towards the crowded streets of London. He moved amongst the pedestrians as if invisible, which in a way he was. No one seemed to notice him as they flowed around him, as though he was as insignificant as a leaf, ordinary and not worthy of notice. So ordinary in fact that he became part of the back ground and now no longer on anyone's radar, was not perceived as a threat.

That was his strength, the ability to blend in and be

perceived as someone unimportant. It was a skill that had had to be learned and once learned, honed and perfected. He had mastered the technique perfectly and had graduated with honours.

Once known as the 'Rat', a name he had despised because it had been picked for him, and was a derogatory name in his opinion, the code name 'Legend' as it was known in his line of work, he had picked for himself, felt more comfortable to him. He had used the 'Legend' for many years, tried it on for size and liked the fit. Now, no longer the 'Rat' he had been transformed and become the 'Chameleon'.

Chapter 3

Istanbul, Turkey.

The siren could be clearly heard in the distance above the noise of the traffic in Istanbul's fume laden streets. As with most societies around the world drivers here were accustomed to pulling over at the earliest opportunity to allow the emergency services through, in this case an ambulance; its lights flashing seemingly out of sync with its siren as it progressed through the congested streets.

At the International Hotel, some distance away, the pavements were crowded with pedestrians, both native and foreign. It was a lovely sunny day and people were going about their business happily buying or simply window shopping, content to just bask in the sunshine.

The siren got louder and the ambulance lights could now be seen quite clearly. People began to stop and take notice of the ambulance's approach wondering, as people do, what the emergency was.

The ambulance pulled quickly onto the International Hotel's forecourt, coming to rest in front of the main entrance. Obviously someone at the hotel must be in need of medical attention, was the general opinion of the now-curious bystanders. Now no longer interested in walking by they were content to stand and watch the drama unfold. Strangely no one thought it odd that the driver of the ambulance, now out of the vehicle, was seen to quickly walk away and thirty seconds later the lovely sunny day was eclipsed by a tremendous explosion and a fireball that ended most of the bystanders' lives. The front of the hotel up to the eleventh floor was simply ripped away like cardboard, exposing the interior of the rooms for all to see.

The people who had been closest to the ambulance, and there were many, were shredded; arms, legs, heads, and torso's were strewn in all directions for fifty metres, landing like some obscene collage, constructed in hell. Being further from the blast offered no protection and brought no relief from this human slaughter house. Anyone still lucky enough to be alive had suffered appalling injuries, loss of limb as well as multiple wounds from shrapnel.

The lucky ones, the ones reasonably able to count themselves fortunate for having survived initially, would eventually die in the weeks to come, from the wounds inflicted by the shrapnel and debris or from infection. This accounted for the casualties on the street but the hotel had also suffered its share of deaths and injuries, as the first responders to enter would discover. It proved a logistical nightmare for the emergency services, too many dead and seriously injured but not enough ambulances, not enough doctors and medical staff to treat the hundreds of casualties. The nearest hospitals couldn't cope and more worryingly, soon ran out of blood supplies. Inevitably people died from lack of something or other; altogether it proved to be too much.

The first T.V. crews to arrive were un- policed and as a result beamed live pictures, uncensored, around the world sparing no-one the gory details. Later the authorities would step in and edit what was broadcast but for now it was out there in vivid colour.

Meanwhile the orchestrator of this atrocity Abdul Rahman had been in contact with the Turkish government in Ankara claiming responsibility on behalf of the Islamic Brotherhood of which he was the head. By proclaiming himself openly as the head of the Islamic Brotherhood Abdul knew that his days were numbered, already with a price on his head, he would now be marked for assassination by the western powers.

He no longer cared, he was willing to die for the cause, just like his brothers, the only difference was he planned on further attacks against the West before his death. Abdul believed, with every fibre of his being, his 'Jihad' with the West was just and inevitable, something that westerners couldn't comprehend.

The government in Ankara had seen the graphic scenes of death and destruction in Istanbul, now they were watching a recording made by Abdul Rahman warning them of more attacks to come if they didn't follow his instructions.

It amounted to this: the expulsion of all foreign military personnel from Turkey, the cooling of relations with the western powers and a return to the beliefs and teachings of Islam.

Some of the viewers looked at the face of this man, who had just ordered the murder of many of its citizens with loathing. It would have surprised them to learn the thoughts of others, who didn't think his demands were unreasonable and actually agreed with him.

The actual death toll in Istanbul would not be known for several weeks but once they were totalled up it would stand at 279. The injured would amount to 711. It was a callous and cowardly attack on innocent civilians brought about by one man and a few acolytes. It was a sobering thought and a frightening one too, to think that spread across Europe was not just the odd like-minded individual but thousands of them all waiting for the order to strike.

Chapter 4

Claire

I was sitting on the floor playing with Adam and looking out through the patio doors watching Luke and Steve working on the new decking. The house inside was mostly completed weeks ago, just the odd cosmetic touches now needed doing to finish off what had been a labour of love. I had been worried about the security of the rear garden and had managed to convince Luke to bring in a company who could complete what was required in a relatively short time.

Steve had suggested a small company who specialised mainly in fencing but who would be willing to level the garden off as well as make it secure. It had taken just over two weeks for them to install concrete posts and plinths and insert welt-made wooden panels that had been dipped in dark green coloured preservative. A well-made gate with a central lock and heavy bolts to the top and bottom gave entry and exit from the bottom of the garden. They levelled the garden as required, taking away surplus soil and rubble and then I had them bring in decent top soil which was laid level. I had planned on having shrubs and -plants growing so wanted to give them a decent start and make a proper garden. The area was now enclosed to a height of about seven feet and it looked reasonably secure to me and it was only now that I felt comfortable letting Adam loose in it. We had planned on having decking to the rear and Steve was confident he could deliver a professional job, provided that Luke was willing to give him a hand.

Luke wasn't sure at first, but as the work progressed he grew more confident and actually began to enjoy working with his hands. They had worked well together and the last two pieces of decking had been cut ready to screw down.

I placed Adam in the security of his playpen whilst I went to make the workers a mug of tea. Adam could still see his dad in the garden so didn't protest in the slightest; if he could see his dad then Adam was content.

I knew there was a definite link between Luke and Adam, for instance if Luke stepped out to fetch a newspaper from the corner shop Adam would look to the front door three seconds before Luke walked back in. I wasn't worried about it, in fact I was relieved when he started showing signs of this behaviour as it meant, in my eyes, that Adam had inherited some of his dad's skills.

The television was on but turned down low when I called them in for a tea break. Glancing at the T.V. it was showing the first televised pictures of the bombing in Turkey. Reaching for the remote I turned up the sound to hear what was being said. We watched open mouthed as the details of death and destruction were being played out in our living room. The camera panned to the hotel revealing the devastation that the bomb had caused to the building.

Thankfully pictures of the dead and injured had been deemed too horrific to show, but the final toll was thought to be in the high hundreds.

It seemed that everywhere in the world some type of atrocity or other was being carried out by some faction of religion or sect. I didn't believe any of that bullshit, I just thought they were murdering bastards, and cowardly ones at that.

In a few days' time Luke and I would be getting married, surrounded by all our friends and family. It was something to look forward to. It was now sobering to think, looking at the aftermath of the explosion, that for many there would be no tomorrow, their dreams and aspirations blown apart in an instant, pawns in someone else's sick ideology.

Turning off the television we sipped our tea in silence lost for words and numb from what we had just seen. There was genuine evil in the world and it was being played out before us via television.

Chapter 5

The Chameleon had meticulously laid out all the information and photographs on the bed. He studied the photographs of his intended target and the target's wife. The information was extremely thorough and answered everything he needed to know, the man was quite small, even smaller than the Chameleon, at five foot six inches and a little overweight. His wife was about the same height and definitely over weight, married for close on forty years, no children, unfortunate thought the chameleon, as he read on. It said that he had been the Hussein's family lawyer in London for most of his working life. He read on and deduced that somehow the target must have fallen out of favour with the Husseins to warrant a contract being invoked.

Still, that wasn't his problem, he had accepted the contract and half the money had been paid; he was honour bound to see it through. Examining the photographs of the target's house in minute detail he worked out his plan of approach. The house itself was a beautiful, detached brick mansion set back from the roadside and surrounded by well-tended gardens to either side. "Mmm obviously they have a gardener to keep them looking so neat, mused the Chameleon, still that shouldn't be a problem."

The gardens at the rear were completely enclosed with a high fence and looked to be the best means of getting into the garden. There was a single door at the rear of the house, the top half of which was glass. This looked to be the best means of entering the house as patio doors opened onto the grassed area, but he dismissed entry through these in favour of the half glassed door. Having decided on his mode of entry the Chameleon now turned his attention to the target's daily routine. It seemed from the information, that he was fairly punctual in his working practice and tended to be a bit of a workaholic, arriving home usually around 6 p.m.

The Chameleon actually began to feel sorry for this man, who by all accounts was hard working and good at his job, loyal to his long term wife and whose only crime, as far has he could ascertain, was to fall out of favour with Ali Hussein. Well, bad things happened to good people every day, tomorrow it would be his turn.

Gathering up all the information spread out on the bed, he placed it all in the carrier bag ready for disposal later.

Now he turned his attention to the handgun. He had asked for and received a colt .45 automatic pistol, in his opinion one of the finest and most reliable pistols ever produced. Made originally from a design by John Browning the colt automatic had a magazine holding seven rounds in the grip. He began to meticulously check and clean the weapon until satisfied that it met with his standards.

Now, all he had to do was to wait for tomorrow to put his plans into action.

Chapter 6

In the early evening light, the detached brick house standing back in the lovely setting from the road, with mature trees and shrubs framing it, was obviously well maintained. The Chameleon had already done one slow walk by to see if the gardener was working today. There was no sign of him but it was possible he was working in the rear garden.

His plan of entry was through the backdoor so he took the risk and headed towards the side gate. He unlatched it and went through, if the gardener was in the back he would have to be eliminated and treated as just a casualty of circumstance; wrong place, wrong time. Standing by the side of the house he carefully scanned the well maintained gardens checking the shrubbery for movement. After several minutes he judged it empty and safe to proceed; it proved to be a lucky day for the gardener.

Approaching the back door he listened and watched for

movement through the glass top half of the door. Hearing nothing, and seeing no signs of movement from within, he fished the thin rubber gloves out of his pocket and carefully eased them on. The gloves were almost at thin as those worn by a surgeon and would remain on his hands for the duration of his time in the house. He was about to select his picklocks when on a whim he decided to see if the door was unlocked. The handle moved easily and the door cracked open; he was in.

Closing the door behind him he locked it and stood for thirty seconds just listening. As his ears became attuned to the house he could hear the muted sounds of a television in another room. Heading towards the sound he arrived at a door not fully closed. Looking through the narrow gap he could see the television in what he assumed was the living room at the front of the house.

He couldn't see anyone, but from the position of the television screen he thought it most likely that whoever was watching it was lying down on the large settee. Now holding the gun in his hand he quickly made his way to the settee. The floorboards groaned beneath his feet making a mockery of his stealthy approach, a woman's surprised face lifted and registered the stranger just a few feet from her.

He saw the eyes widen in fear and was moments away from a scream. Pointing the gun at her face he said,

"Be quiet or I will be forced to hurt you."

Her lips quivered in terror as she asked, "Who are you? What do you want?"

Angry now he said, "Be quiet woman or I will really hurt you."

This time the threat registered with her and she nodded her head in compliance.

Lifting a heavy wooden chair away from the expensive

looking dining table, he placed it in the middle of the carpet facing towards the front entrance. Once this was done he indicated with the gun that she was to sit on it. He could see that she was absolutely terrified of him and doing her best to comply, well that was good, it would make his job easier.

Earlier he had stopped at a hardware store and bought some clothes line and a roll of duct tape. He had cut the clothes line into three equal lengths and now used it to tie her to the chair. It was now that, had she chosen to, she could have caused him a bit of trouble as he needed two hands to secure the clothes line and had to temporarily pocket the gun.

She must have been too frightened to realise, but it no longer mattered as she was now securely fastened to the chair and in his control. He pocketed the gun once more and sat in one of the armchairs facing the door, readying himself for her husband's return.

They sat in silence for a good ten minutes before nervous energy began to get the better of her.

"Please, what do you want?" she pleaded.

He said nothing, content to let the time tick by.

Emboldened she told him, "If its money you need we keep a little in the house, you would be welcome to it."

Looking at her sideways he said, "Please do not insult me, I am not here to steal your money. Once a long time ago I was forced to steal just to survive. Now I prefer to earn my money, but in answer to your question I am waiting for your husband to come home. He has information that I need, once I have it I will leave you in peace. Now please be quiet."

Some twenty minutes later she again tried to reason with him saying, "I really need to go to the toilet."

This time he got up and ripped a piece of duct tape from

the roll placing it firmly across her mouth before returning to his chair. If she needed to go to the toilet so what, in his line of work it always ended in piss and shit anyway.

As it got nearer the time he brought the gun out once more and sat with it in his hand. At a little after 6 p.m. he saw the car arrive home and heard the front door open.

When Mr Almeda walked into the living room he was faced with his worst nightmare, his wife of nigh on forty years tied to a chair with a gun to her head.

The Chameleon greeted Mr Almeda cordially, "Welcome Mr Almeda, I have been waiting for you, with your lovely wife of course."

"Please, whoever you are, don't hurt my wife I beg you," pleaded Mr Almeda.

The Chameleon knew from his tone that he genuinely cared for his wife, good it would make this easier.

"First, place your briefcase on the floor, that's it, right. Now, slowly kneel down beside it," ordered the Chameleon.

It was with difficulty that he complied, his knees cracking audibly and painfully.

"Please, what do you want?" asked Mr Almeda, obviously now in some discomfort.

"Information Mr Almeda," replied his tormentor.

"What information?" gasped Mr Almeda, wincing at the pain now building in his knees and lower back.

"Alright, let us begin," said the Chameleon, placing the gun against Mrs Almeda's knee, "but if you lie or try to deceive me your wife will suffer the consequences."

"Don't hurt her, I will answer your questions, please just ask and I will answer," pleaded a broken Mr Almeda.

The Chameleon knew the time was right, the poor man was so frightened for his wife, he would have answered anything in order to protect her. He wasn't so sure she would have done the same for him, but that was irrelevant, it was time for answers.

"Whilst Yasmin Hussein was a guest of her brother you received either a note or a letter from her is that correct?" fired the Chameleon.

"Yes, a letter," stammered Mr Almeda.

The speed at which he had answered confirmed to the Chameleon that he was telling the truth.

"Good, very good, Mr Almeda. Just two more questions and I will leave you and your wife in peace." He saw the hope flare in the kneeling man's face as he produced a small notebook with a pencil down the spine, from his pocket. He threw the notebook towards Mr Almeda but it fell short and he had to watch as he painfully moved forward to retrieve it.

"Who was the letter addressed to?" Mr Almeda.

He saw him swallow and recognised that even though he was under duress and fearful for his wife, he was considering withholding the name. "The name Mr Almeda, or on a count of three, I will shoot your wife's knee."

He had no choice; Mr Almeda gave up the name in defeat. "Claire Wilson, the name on the letter was Claire Wilson."

The Chameleon nodded, though in truth, he had expected the name of a man. "Please write it in the note book."

Watching as he wrote the name down.

"Now just one more question and we are done, please write down the address," ordered the Chameleon.

Again Mr Almeda complied and nodded that it was done.

"Now throw the notebook over here, carefully," prompted the Chameleon, "we don't want any accidents now do we?"

Again Mr Almeda complied and the Chameleon stooped to pick up the notebook. Leafing through until he came to where Mr Almeda had written Claire Wilson, Flat 4, Walpole Court Gardens, London.

He read out what Mr Almeda had written failing to see the change in his victim's expression as he did so.

What Mr Almeda had just realised was that in his agitated state he had written down Claire Wilson's name and address as of the time he had received Yasmin Hussein's letter. Claire Wilson had since moved and someone else now occupied Flat 4, Walpole Court Gardens, London. Mr Almeda now faced a dilemma, should he tell this man or not? He bravely chose not to.

Pocketing the notebook the Chameleon seemed satisfied with the outcome and made ready to leave. Walking passed Mr Almeda he gave him a wide berth, people did silly things when stressed. Turning suddenly he picked a cushion up off the chair pressed it to the back of Mr Almeda's head and fired the hand gun in one fluid movement.

Moving swiftly he approached Mrs Almeda her eyes wide open in terror, using the same cushion as before he pressed it to her face and fired through it once. Both were clean kills and the cushion had absorbed most of the sound so he was reasonably sure the shots had not been heard from outside. Picking up the ejected shell casings he pocketed them and reflected on his actions.

He had killed Mr Almeda first,to spare him the pain of watching his wife's death. The Chameleon had given him this small mercy because he saw him as an honourable man, not once had he pleaded for his own life but he had asked mercy for his wife's constantly. That act alone gave testament to the kind of man Mr Almeda was.

The contract had been completed and he pressed the pre- programmed number into the mobile phone he had been given. It was answered by a voice he didn't recognise but that didn't worry him unduly. He confirmed that the contract had been completed then read out the name and address he had been given, to the listener.

The voice at the other end thanked him for his service and confirmed that the final payment had been transferred into his account, then the call was ended. One final check of the room and then the Chameleon made his way to the front door. He left it locked behind him and quickly walked away noting with some satisfaction that there was no one in sight.

All the evidence would be disposed of separately. The gun last of all and in pieces. He had fulfilled his contract; it was time to go home.

Chapter 7

Claire's House, London, Tuesday 10th May

"Luke, can you get the front door, it's probably the caterers and I've got my hands full with Adam?" Claire shouted down the stairs.

"On my way," shouted Luke.

It was true Claire really did have her hands full with Adam. Ever since he had learned to pull himself upright with the furniture and could stand, she needed eyes in the back of her head and two pairs of hands. He had only just been bathed and was trying his hardest to crawl away from his mum.

He was content being naked, and was doing his best to remain that way.

Claire caught him and scooped him up eliciting an excited squeal from Adam who clearly thought this was great fun. She was delighted with his response, mock chiding him, whilst wrestling him into his clothing and not for the first time Claire realised how lucky she was having such a happy baby.

Meanwhile downstairs, Luke was directing the caterers where to put the food. Two trestle tables had been set up in the kitchen and covered with white linen cloths ready to receive the food.

Stacks of canned beer, both bitter and lager, covered one side of the kitchen work surfaces, bottles of spirits, wine and soft drinks were neatly arranged on another work surface. The one nearest to the kettle was covered with ranks of white mugs. The table belonging to the kitchen was covered over with a white cloth also and rows of gleaming glasses.

Claire came downstairs with a suitably clothed Adam and as soon as he saw his dad he squealed with delight holding out his arms.

Luke happily took him from Claire knowing that she would now rearrange all the trays of food more to her liking. He wasn't offended in the least, Claire had a flair for this sort of thing and he played with his son whilst she put the trays of food where her ordered mind dictated they should be.

Carrying Adam over to the patio window they looked out over what would eventually be a proper garden. At the moment it was bare of both shrubs and plants but the plan was to create a lovely garden that they all could enjoy. It had rained sometime in the night and the newly completed decking was beaded with droplets of jewelled water. Luke had brushed the preservative onto the decking as instructed on the tin and by the look of it, it was doing its job. He gave himself a pat on the back, it was true that Steve had done the lion's share of the job, laying the actual decking, whilst Luke fetched and carried, but he had brushed on the preservative and he allowed himself a moment to feel smug now that it seemed to be working.

Claire broke into his smugness by putting an arm about his waist and saying, "It looks good, you have made a good job."

Luke now felt guilty, he knew that Claire was only stroking his ego, and he knew full well that she had witnessed Steve putting in the hard yards to finish the decking; still it was nice to have a little praise now and again, even if he hadn't really earned it.

"I'm going to make some tea Luke, would you like one?" offered Claire.

"Yes please," smiled Luke as Adam twisted in his arms clearly wanting to be passed to his mum. "Sorry young man your mum is going to be busy for a few moments so I'm afraid you will have to stay here with me."

Adam seemed to comprehend what Luke had said, and stopped struggling, content to wait for his mum to return.

They were a close knit family unit and if either Claire or Luke was missing from Adam's sight it seemed to bother him.

Today would be an emotional one, most of Claire's friends and family would be gathering here. Even now some would be en-route, travelling down to London to help Claire and Luke celebrate the long awaited happy union.

Claire reflected that it was sad that Luke had no family or relatives to witness their marriage tomorrow, but then how could he have? Still, having their own son present was family enough for Luke, and Claire's own friends and family were now Luke's anyway. They all genuinely liked him, what wasn't to like?

Later on, a telephone call to the Premier Inn, Blackfriars, confirmed that some of Claire's guests had arrived and had checked in. Claire breathed a sigh of relief as she had been on tenterhooks whilst awaiting their arrival. Uncle Tony and his son Chris would come when they were ready; they had some catching up to do!

Yasmin and Frank, their close friends, would probably be on their way here now, they regarded this as their second home, and us as family, which just left Steve, Frank's army buddy and the person who was responsible for turning a once shabby house into a lovingly restored home. Steve had recently met a young woman and was bringing her with him. We couldn't wait to meet her and give her our seal of approval, we regarded Steve as a friend after all the hours he had put in working here.

I had changed Adam and just finished feeding him when I heard the doorbell sound. It was a given that it would be Yasmin and Frank that Luke had just let in. Coming downstairs Yasmin, now relieved of her coat, came to meet us.

Adam saw her and automatically held out his arms to her, eager to be free of me. It didn't bother me that he readily went to her on sight, Adam merely saw Yasmin as an extension of me and in a way, I suppose she was. Ever since Adam's birth, at less than one hour old when Luke had placed him in Yasmin's very reluctant arms, she and Frank had become a very big part of his life.

This lovely young woman, now holding my son was destined to become a mother herself, it would be a crime if she didn't. Now relieved of Adam I embraced Frank kissing him lightly on the cheek, Frank gave me a bear hug in return, then followed Luke into the kitchen. It seemed a focal point for anyone visiting our home. Yasmin automatically went to the patio windows looking out at our bare garden. Soon tiring of seeing this waste land Adam twisted in Yasmin's arms searching for me. I had to smile to myself, yes! I was glad that Adam loved Yasmin and vice-versa but was still pleased to see that Adam grew anxious if I was out of sight. The mother-son bond was strong and I was glad of it.

Yasmin and I were keeping Adam entertained when the doorbell announced visitors. This time I went to greet leaving Luke and Frank in the kitchen and Adam in Yasmin's capable hands.

Opening the door revealed my sister Maureen, her husband David and a very good looking young man who had shot up beyond all expectations, named Michael, their son and my nephew. Time could be so cruel, it had gone by so quickly. Michael was on the cusp of becoming a man and I had only seen his life through a series of photographs. I knew virtually nothing about him and he was an extension of me, family. It was an awful truth to realize how estranged our once close family had become and even worse how easily we had accepted it.

I embraced them all warmly, welcoming them into my home. Indicating where to hang their coats I brought them through to meet Yasmin who had stood to greet my guests, holding a wriggling Adam. I introduced Maureen to Yasmin as my sister. She shook hands formally with Yasmin, mesmerised with the bundle of humanity she was holding. "And this young man is Adam, my son."

Maureen seemed really taken with Adam and commented on how big he was.

I introduced David to Yasmin and he seemed to approve of her whole heartedly, shaking hands and smiling at her warmly. Michael introduced himself, obviously pleased to be meeting such a lovely looking woman Luke came out of the kitchen, shook hands with David and said, "Hello." Embraced Maureen, who returned it with warmth as they said, "Hello" to each other.

Maureen introduced Michael to Luke, who, like Claire, marvelled at how much he had grown. They shook hands formally like men, weighing one-another up. Both let go satisfied with the grip and Luke introduced Frank to Michael who seemed most impressed with this young man. Whilst Michael was homing in on the tables laden with food Luke introduced Frank to Maureen and David.

Now that introductions had formally been made and people began to relax around each other I told them to help themselves to food and drink and not to be shy about it either.

Maureen had yet to hold my son and knowing Maureen, I knew she wanted to. I relieved the awkwardness by lifting Adam out of Yasmin's aching arms and placed him in my sisters. Turning to Yasmin I whispered, "Please give us a moment," then louder, "go and get yourself some food Yasmin, there is plenty."

Yasmin took my cue and disappeared into the kitchen. There was an elephant in the room and it needed addressing.

"Alright Maureen what's wrong?" I asked.

"What do you mean? Nothing is wrong," retorted Maureen.

"Come on, we are like strangers tip toeing around one another, this is me, Claire." I said.

She seemed to chew that over for a while then ... "We are strangers, we don't see one another from one year to the next. Michael is growing up and you hardly know him and now you have Adam, it just seems like I will miss him growing up too."

Maureen was right, of course she was, there was no

excuse for either of us not visiting each other; life is too short.

I said, "I'm sorry, you are absolutely right. I have no excuse for not visiting it's just laziness on my part."

I could have looked for an excuse if I really wanted to but there wasn't one; families grew apart for many reasons, but laziness, that really was a poor one.

Maureen shouldered some of the blame admitting to her part in the distance that had grown between us. We resolved to be better sisters and hugged, trapping Adam between us. He squealed in delight thinking it was a great game, making us both laugh at the same time.

The doorbell went again I asked Maureen if she was okay with Adam. She smiled and nodded. Opening the door I saw this vision from my past ... bloody Sheryl.

I squealed like a kid, she squealed like a kid, and we gripped each other in the mother of all hugs. After what seemed like an age we parted, my eyes streaming with happy tears, Sheryl's eyes streaming with happy tears and poor James as usual waiting by her side.

I brought James in for a group hug, kissed him on the cheek and said, "Hi James, great to see you," wetting his face with my tears.

"Hello Claire," answered a grinning James.

Bringing them through, Sheryl and James said, "Hello" to everyone and then, "Hello," to Maureen.

Maureen said, "Hello," back. They were mesmerised by Adam, Sheryl for once struck dumb.

Maureen, knowing that Sheryl and James had been trying unsuccessfully for a baby for years, offered over an eager Adam.

She brought him into her arms looking at him in wonder and awe. This for Sheryl was the Holy Grail, her whole reason for being.

Leaving Sheryl alone with James we went into the kitchen in search of food. Yasmin sidled up to me and mouthed, “everything alright?”

I nodded and quietly said, “Yes it is now,” that seemed to satisfy her and I introduced her to James.

They shook hands warmly and spoke for a while, and then I guided her away to go and introduce her to Sheryl, holding a now wriggling Adam, who just wanted to go to Yasmin, but still successfully managed to shake her hand and transfer him over without mishap.

I put my arm around Sheryl’s waist, it felt good, I really missed this girl, and we watched Adam who in turn looked around and watched us. The door bell sounded once more and led me away from my friends.

Steve and a lovely looking woman were waiting at the door. I smiled at Steve waiting for an introduction to his friend. He introduced her as Miss Antonia Frasier and we smiled politely and shook hands. Steve took the lead helping his friend off with her coat and hanging it beside his own.

I brought them through introducing them to Sheryl and Yasmin, although Yasmin knew Steve quite well. Yasmin offered up Adam to me and he came willingly and said to Antonia, “I believe I know your father, Clive Frasier, the well-known London barrister.”

“Yes that’s right, “replied Antonia.

I looked at Yasmin and decided to get the gossip on Antonia when we were alone.

After a round of introductions I told everyone to dig in and help themselves to food and drink. That left just Uncle Tony and Chris to make an appearance.

I went to sit down with Adam, Sheryl beside me,

looking on in wonder.

Sheryl spoke after a while, "Not bad for someone unable to have children is he?"

I held Sheryl's hand knowing what she meant,"No he's not bad at all," looking into my son's puzzled eyes.

"What was it like, child birth I mean?" asked Sheryl.

"Bloody painful and totally worth it," I answered smiling, "the most terrifying thing," I reflected, "was finding out that I was pregnant, and then forever expecting something to go wrong, especially after being told it was unlikely that I could have children, I just thought with my luck something bad was bound to happen." Claire shook away the despondent thoughts saying, "but something bad didn't happen did it my little man, Adam happened," cooed Claire.

"Well you seem to have got the hang of motherhood Claire, he's a lovely baby," agreed Sheryl.

Just then I heard a knock at the door and Chris and my Uncle Tony walked in. Chris came by and said, "Hi Claire is the food through here? I'm bloody starving!" Uncle Tony made a bee line for me and I stood up to greet him. He hugged me lightly and pecked me on the cheek, careful not to frighten Adam, "Hello Claire, you all set for tomorrow?"

"Hello Uncle Tony, yes everything is arranged, all we have to do is turn up." Adam looked up wide-eyed at the stranger. I said, "This is my uncle Tony Adam, would you like to meet him?"

My Uncle Tony was gobsmacked when Adam held out his arms to him. His shock soon disappeared as he held my son for the very first time, looking one another squarely in the eyes. "He's a fine baby Claire," he said handing him back to me.

"Yes he is," I replied, "and he's a stinky young man in

need of changing and feeding, in that order, and then bed. It's been an exhausting day for him."

Sheryl, who knew my Uncle Tony, took him through for food and drink. I went upstairs to see to Adam. I left it up to Uncle Tony to introduce himself around, I hope he didn't think it rude of me but

Adam was my priority now, he had been passed around enough for one day and now it was mother and son time, our quiet time.

I washed, powdered and changed him marvelling at this bundle of humanity that Luke and I had created. He really was a good baby; we had hardly had one sleepless night since his birth. He still liked a bottle before bed but had been on mashed solids for a while now.

I watched as he drained the last drops from his bottle then was careful to wind him, I was always worried about him being sick and choking on it. Placing him in his cot he was still wide eyed looking at me and then his mobile that Luke had bought him. It was a miniature version of our solar system and it seemed to fascinate Adam immensely. I spun it around slowly and he watched it, delighted to see it moving. I almost missed it when Adam said, "Dad."

"What sweet heart?" I said, unsure if I had heard him correctly or imagined it. Adam said, "Dad," again, confirming that I hadn't imagined it.

Just then I turned to see Luke standing in the doorway, "Luke, did you hear Adam say dad?" I asked.

"Yes I heard him," answered Luke. Smiling like a loony.

Looking at Luke I asked, "How long have you been standing there?"

"Just a couple of minutes I guess."

"Adam must have known you were there Luke, but how, he couldn't have seen you from here." I said, then,

"Are you connected psychically?"

"Yes, I think we are, in fact I've thought so for a while. It doesn't worry you does it? I mean we both thought he may develop some of my skills," said Luke.

"No it doesn't worry me, but I didn't think they would show themselves so soon," admitted Claire.

Now that Claire and Luke were here beside his cot Adam had closed his eyes and drifted off to sleep. He looked so peaceful lying there, but now he had said his first words, Pandora's Box was well and truly open.

Yasmin met us at the bottom of the stairs asking, "Is Adam asleep?" We both said, "Yes," in unison like some corny double act, grinning as we said it.

"Well come on then, it's time to join your party," chided Yasmin, "Chris is eating all the food."

Chapter 8

The Hussein Residence, on the outskirts of Amman, Jordan.

Ali was working at his desk in his private office when his intercom attracted his attention. Pressing down the communication button he asked, "What is it Mehmet?"

Mehmet Hussein, Ali's newly appointed head of security, answered, "Telephone call sir, I've put it through to your private line."

"Thank you Mehmet "replied Ali, picking up the telephone, "Ali Hussein speaking."

"Ali, it's Abdul, just ringing to let you know the results of what we decided at our last meeting, I must be brief, the airwaves are no longer safe, you understand."

Ali did indeed understand, the price on Abdul's head had now risen to $5,000,000 dollars since the Istanbul bombing, "Yes I understand," replied Ali.

"Firstly, your lawyer in London is now out of the picture. Second, the name of the person was written on an envelope and received by Mr Almeda, just how your head of security had deduced. Surprisingly the name was a woman's, a Miss Claire Wilson.

Ali too, was surprised it had been addressed to a woman, he had expected it to be addressed to a man and most annoyingly he didn't know this Claire Wilson, "And the address?" prompted Ali.

"Flat 4, Walpole Court Gardens, London," replied Abdul. He heard Ali's intake of breath and asked, "You know this address?"

"Yes! Unfortunately I do, the building belongs to my sister Yasmin Hussein," hissed Ali, pure venom in his voice.

"I see," said Abdul, unsure whether this changed things.

Ali seemed to have grasped the situation perfectly stating the obvious, "So we still need to know who this Claire Wilson spoke to, that affected an invasion on my home. Could your asset visit Miss Wilson and extract the information from her, Abdul?" asked Ali.

"I'm already ahead of you Ali, I hope I haven't been too presumptuous in assuming your way of thinking? Unfortunately our asset declined the contract for some reason he didn't want to share, but rest assured the contract has been picked up by someone actually based in London. I hope to have the information for you soon. I'm going to have to end the call Ali, I've been on the airwaves for far too long."

Ali listened until the connection was broken replacing the handset with absent minded care. These small steps were annoying but if he was patient and determined they would eventually lead to the people responsible for violating his home, it would just take a little longer that's all, but at least one traitor had been dealt with he mused and that lifted his spirits for the rest of the day.

Chapter 9

Deep in the bowels of M.I.6., James Martin was sifting through the reports and intelligence that had been gathered on the Istanbul bombing. Abdul Rahman's photograph looked back at him from the cork board opposite. It seemed to be half smiling, taunting him, almost daring him to catch him if he could. He was doing his best with the information he had been given but it wasn't enough, the bugger didn't stay still long enough to catch and the trail had grown cold.

The bounty on Rahman's head had been raised significantly since the latest bombing, which might eventually lead to his capture or death, but the truth was, no one was willing to give up his whereabouts and until there was a breakthrough they were up shit creek without a paddle.

Doug Simons knocked and stuck his head around his boss's door.

Martin looked up hopeful, "What is it Doug?"

"Some intelligence from G.C.H.Q. concerning Ali Hussein boss, you said you wanted it as soon as it was translated."

Doug handed over two sheets of paper.

Martin read the transcribed telephone conversation to Ali Hussein and immediately felt a buzz of excitement coursing through his veins. He retrieved a sheet of lined paper from his desk drawer and wrote down a sequence of sentences that his ordered mind had gleaned from the telephone conversation.

Doug Simons watched while his boss cut through the less important shit, and wrote down the relevant facts. Many of the people who worked with James Martin and that included Doug, thought he was an arsehole but saying that, it didn't mean he wasn't good at his job. James had a first class mind, a firm grip on what was needed to do his job and the patriotic will to see it through.

Martin dotted the last letter with a flourish, then sat back to digest what he had written. Looking at Doug he said, "Fucking hell Doug, this is a telephone call from non-other than Abdul Rahman. If I read it right, Ali Hussein with the help of Abdul Rahman, has admitted to ordering the murder of the Hussein's family lawyer here in London. It goes on to say that a Miss Claire Wilson is privy to information that Ali Hussein needs, and has ordered a hit man to get whatever this information is and then no-doubt kill her. It gives Miss Wilson's address as Flat 4, Walpole Court Gardens, London, and I've just realised that is Yasmin Hussein's address too."

"Do you think she is involved as well sir?" queried Doug.

"I'm not sure," admitted Martin, "but I'm not ruling anything out. Look this is dynamite and I need to see the boss. Where did the telephone call originate from?" asked

Martin.

"Islamabad," replied Doug.

Martin thought for a moment, "So the Rat has returned to its nest, I think our American cousins need to be brought into this, perhaps this will be our lucky day, well done Doug."

Praise from James Martin was almost unheard of, but this time it was warranted and it felt bloody good to Doug, and brought a smile to his face.

Chapter 10

We were lying in bed-facing one another, the afterglow of our love making still sending ripples of pleasure through our bodies. Even after all these years, I still found it amazing that this one man, could give me so much pleasure, and it felt so damn good!

Tentatively I asked, "So Mr Henderson, do you still want to marry me?"

Luke seemed genuinely surprised by my question replying, "Of course I still want to marry you, more than ever."

"Good, just checking," I said smiling, and kissed him on the mouth. I knew it was a mistake as the moment we physically locked lips, it was like electricity surging through my body and I wondered if we had time to make love again before Adam required my attention. At that precise moment we heard Adam squealing with delight on the baby monitor beside the bed.

I couldn't help smiling, something was obviously amusing our son. Naked, I got out of bed and slipped on my silk robe. I padded quietly to Adam's room peeping through the gap between the door and frame to try and see what was amusing him. The curtains at the window weren't quite shut and a single ray of morning sunlight was shining through the gap and playing on Adam's mobile. It seemed to be sparkling and was giving off a truly magical display until the sun moved position and again as if by magic the special effects were turned off.

I continued to watch Adam for a few seconds to see what he would do. I should have known really, Adam had known I was there all along and was holding his arms out to me even before I entered his room. It promised to be a lovely day and I took Adam to see his dad.

Straight away Adam reached for his dad saying, "Dad." It annoyed me that Adam was regularly saying dad to Luke, yet failing to call me mum. I knew I was being irrational and a little jealous, but it still rankled. I just had to be patient; it would happen when Adam decided he was ready, but I was ready now and wanted to hear Adam call me mum.

Later when Adam was clean, buffed and dressed, Luke set about feeding him whilst I went for a long hot shower. I came downstairs in my silk dressing gown, clean and in Luke's words smelling uniquely of woman. Luke was spooning in the last of Adam's breakfast, then wiped up the surplus surrounding his mouth.

Sitting at the table with them Adam reached for me still refusing the mum word. Adam looked at me, then Luke, then back to me, he knew something was going on, especially after yesterday's bewildering avalanche of people, but he didn't know what.

We were going to be married in a hotel complex in

the Bloomsbury area. The hotel catered for the whole thing; ceremony, sit down lunch for the guests, evening entertainment and buffet for further friends invited at night. We had decided to stay the night at the hotel with Adam in our room. This may have been seen by some as most unconventional but we didn't care, since Adam's birth we had never been apart and weren't going to start now.

Luke went upstairs to shower and shave whilst I entertained Adam. We had decided beforehand that Yasmin would come with Frank to help me into my wedding dress which she was bringing with her and which Luke still hadn't seen. He on the other hand had bought a three piece silver grey suit, which unfairly, I had both seen, and mightily approved of.

The plan was for him to dress casually and take his suit and accompanying clothing along with Adam and his 101 things needed for the day, and to get ready at Frank and Yasmin's apartment.

Then when Yasmin had helped me to get ready, Frank would come back for Yasmin so that she in turn could also get ready. It sounded more complicated than it was, but it was what we had decided on.

Once Yasmin was ready the plan was for them all to travel to the hotel in Yasmin's car. I was being given away by Uncle Tony and was being chauffeured to the hotel by Tony's son and my cousin Chris.

Yasmin's night club owned a twelve seater mini-bus which was usually driven by Edward Burns, Eddie to his friends.

When asked by Yasmin if he fancied the work of ferrying mine and Luke's family and friends both too, and from the hotel, Eddie had jumped at the chance. It was a well-paid job and he needed the money. He was honoured to be asked.

My sister's family and Sheryl and James would arrive at the hotel courtesy of Eddie and the club's twelve seater mini-bus.

The wedding party guests would number just nineteen people, including Luke, Adam and me. It was a ridiculously small number for anyone's wedding but it encompassed everyone who mattered to us. The evening buffet and disco was another matter; most of the staff employed at the club had been invited and from all accounts, were eager to attend.

Later when Yasmin had helped me into my dress and given her seal of approval she called Frank to come and pick her up so that she could get herself ready. Once she had gone I stood nervously looking in the mirror, both apprehensive and excited. It had been a long time coming this day, but finally it was here and I was ready. I didn't know how long I had been standing there when Uncle Tony knocked and entered. He gave me a long up and down look nodding in approval and said, "I wish your mum could have been here to see you Claire, you look bloody lovely."

Just then my eyes brimmed full; he had broken my waking dream. I reached for the tissues before tears could spoil my make-up, just managing to mop them up before disaster struck.

Uncle Tony said, "Sorry love, I didn't mean to upset you, I didn't think, me and my big mouth."

"No it's alright Uncle Tony, I had just been thinking about mum myself, just before you arrived. Great minds eh!"

Managing to compose myself I said, "Right let's do this!"

"You sure you are ready, it's fashionable for you to be a little late you know," offered Tony.

I smiled at that saying, "No I've kept Luke waiting long enough, let's go."

Chris was smoking a cigarette when we came out, clearly not expecting to see us so soon.

"What's the matter Chris, cat got your tongue?" I asked.

"WOW, Claire you don't half scrub up nice, that Luke is one lucky bugger," said Chris with feeling.

"Why thank you Chris, but I already know that," I quipped back at him.

Uncle Tony helped seat me and my dress on the back seat of the car, then carefully got in beside me. Chris got in behind the wheel, started the engine and we were on our way.

As we were driving through London's busy streets, it was a lovely sunny day and I had the strangest feeling, I felt like the queen riding past her subjects and had the urge to wave to the people. It must have been nervous tension, but it made me smile all the same.

Arriving without mishap, I could see Yasmin waiting with my bouquet, but was in no hurry to leave the car, needing to compose myself, calm my nerves.

Uncle Tony helped by saying, "Take your time love, when you're ready."

Taking one final calming breath, we exited the car. Yasmin handed over the bouquet and gave my dress a few final touches before rushing off inside.

Uncle Tony proudly stepped into his appointed role and we headed off inside, Chris bringing up the rear.

I vaguely heard music, probably here comes the bride, though in truth anything could have been playing I wasn't really listening; my eyes were locked on Luke, his eyes shining, already waiting and looking back at me. Frank was beside him also looking at me and smiling. I wondered, rather stupidly I must confess, what it was that was making them look at me that way, then it suddenly dawned on me, of course it's the dress, neither Luke or Frank had seen me in it before today obviously both approved.

At last I stood beside Luke grateful for the fact I hadn't tripped up on my short journey to his side. Uncle Tony moved away, Frank moved away and the woman celebrant began the marriage ceremony that would finally join us in matrimony. We both said our words strongly, without faltering, this was for keeps and we wanted to get it right.

It was over all too soon, we exchanged rings signed the register, our witnesses signed and we were married.

Throughout the ceremony Adam had neither cried out, nor created a fuss, testament to my sister's good ministrations. Letting Maureen look after Adam during the ceremony was a start at building the bridges needed to bring us closer together as a family once again.

We had hired a newly qualified young woman photographer, to capture us on film. I believed in giving someone just starting out in business a chance, it could have been viewed by some as risky being as it was our special day, but nevertheless she was working like a pro and putting us through our paces. Everyone else was snapping away all around us and it was as this moment that I realised our already small wedding party was missing two invited guests.

As soon as the opportunity arose, I mentioned to Yasmin that Mr and Mrs Almeda had not shown up even though they had accepted our invitation and professed to be looking forward to attending the wedding.

Yasmin said, "I'll give him a quick ring," but when she tried their number there was no answer. "I will ring him again tomorrow to make sure that they are both alright," as it was most unlike Mr Almeda, being the fastidious type of person that he was.

I thanked her, feeling rather guilty at not realising that something like illness could have prompted their non attendance. I made a mental note to be more forgiving and less judgemental of people in future.

Later, being only a small party we made our way into the room prepared for the meal. One long table, beautifully laid out with carefully hand written cards for our guests, that had them searching for their designated seats. Luke and I were seated centrally with a high chair for Adam next to me. Family and friends were seated to both left and right; two seats at one end made out to the Almeda's were conspicuously empty. I felt uneasy about it and I couldn't explain why.

Everyone had no sooner sat down when our glasses were filled with sparkling champagne. Uncle Tony had them all upstanding and toasted us with the words, "To the bride and groom."

Everyone echoed his words saluting us with their glasses then sat down to await the meal. Luke had picked up on my mood, asking if everything was alright. He obviously hadn't noticed that the Almeda's were missing. I should have realised that Luke missed nothing; he had noticed straightaway that the Almeda's hadn't arrived, but hadn't mentioned it, not wanting to worry me. We both wanted to spare each other the worry, and ended up worrying about it anyway. Yasmin would get to the bottom of it tomorrow, but for now, it was time to eat.

After the meal the hotel staff wanted to get the room ready for the disco and buffet, so asked us politely if we would move into a small, but very comfortable lounge side room. It had a bar and on its surface were a couple of trays, one filled with champagne and the other with Bucks Fizz, compliments of the hotel, which I thought was nice.

Everyone helped themselves, and hefting Adam, I made a beeline towards Sir Ian Clayton and his companion, who I assumed was his daughter. I said, "Hello," to Sir Ian and leaned in to kiss his cheek, almost squashing Adam in the process.

Sir Ian replied, "Congratulations on your wedding Claire, or should that be Mrs Henderson now?"

"Claire is fine, I think Mrs Henderson seems rather a mouthful at the moment," I replied trying it out for size.

Sir Ian brought his lovely companion forward and introduced her as his daughter, Seline.

She seemed to weigh me up and I her, before saying, "Hello Claire, so you've finally managed to capture Luke."

It was like two cats psyching one-another out, but I was up to the task and parried, "Oh I think this chap had a lot to do with it, didn't you Adam."

Sir Ian said nothing, but seemed amused by the interplay between his daughter and myself.

"Yes, I can understand how Adam could influence the outcome," she purred.

Taking charge I asked her, "Are you always so forthright."

"Yes" she replied, without hesitation.

In a similar vein I replied, "How refreshing, I'm very pleased to meet you Seline. I hope you will both be staying for the entertainment; it promises to be a lively evening!"

"We wouldn't miss it for the world," she replied, smiling.

I turned to talk to my other guests. It had been my first encounter with Seline, but I couldn't help but like her. Of course Luke had known Seline for many years through his business dealings with her father. He had been brutally honest when he had told me he almost had to fight her off with a cattle prod; she had wanted him so badly. Now that I had seen her in the flesh I was amazed that he hadn't succumbed to her charms, she really was a good looking woman.

I caught up with Luke gliding my free arm around his waist in ownership. Adam looked up settled between us and I told Luke of my encounter with Seline.

"Oh, how was it?" he asked.

"One all I think, though Adam might have just tipped it in my favour a tiny bit." I replied, sardonically.

"Yes he is hard to ignore isn't he?" smiled Luke. "Do you want me to take him, he must be ready for change of underwear by now?" offered Luke.

"Are you sure?" I asked. "I can take him to our room if you like."

"No you mingle with our guests, I'll take him." Luke said, brushing my lips with his own and hefting Adam at the same time. When Adam had been spirited away by Luke, I gate crashed a table with Sheryl, James, Steve and Antonia sharing a joke. They made room for me, congratulating me, and asked where Luke and Adam were, all at the same time.

I explained that Luke had gone to change him, and would be back shortly. Sheryl put her arm across my shoulder giving it a reassuring squeeze and James, rock solid James, asked if I would like him to get me a drink.

I nodded thanks, realising that I was the only person without one and asked for a Bucks Fizz. Antonia Frasier must have been brought up to a life of relative luxury and privilege, yet it hadn't escaped my notice that they both had sought out, and were actually enjoying the company of my two oldest friends. That in itself spoke volumes in favour of Antonia's true character. This girl could well become a permanent fixture in our small circle of friends.

When Luke came back with a sweeter smelling Adam, we did the rounds as a unit and I noticed that Chris had turned his charm offensive on to Seline. I nudged Luke and voiced my opinion, feigning concern.

"Don't worry about Seline, she is more than capable of looking after herself, voiced Luke.

"It wasn't Seline I was worried about," I replied, which bought a smile to Luke's face.

Uncle Tony was in his favourite position at the bar. He was in conversation with Jimmy Small and we nudged our way between them, much to the delight of Jimmy. He was a giant of a man and a good friend to us both. He engulfed me in his arms and said, "Hello love, how are things?"

Once untangled I said, "Fine Jimmy, here meet my son Adam," indicating to Luke to hand him over.

Luke offered him over and Jimmy sat Adam on the bar top, carefully holding him safe. Jimmy formally introduced himself to Adam who replied with an infectious giggle that raised smiles all round. This gentle giant had a way with kids and vulnerable young women that I could attest to. I had been a very naive young woman when Jimmy Small had been tasked with teaching me the bar trade. Jimmy was a very hard worker and anyone working behind Jimmy's bar, that was literally how he saw his bar as belonging to him, did things his way or it was the highway, simple as that.

I had done my time under Jimmy's strict but fair tutelage and passed fit to be in his company behind his bar. Now I was in semi-retirement learning a new job; full time mother, but Jimmy would remain a friend and one of my favourite people.

Uncle Tony gave me a hug watched by Adam wide eyed and obviously wondering why all these strange men were lavishing attention on his mum. Luke shook hands with Jimmy and Uncle Tony and we moved on.

Yasmin and Frank were sitting in Maureen, David and Michael's company and it was obvious even from a distance, that young Michael couldn't take his eyes off Yasmin. I could understand it, teenage hormones raging, a beautiful young woman, a young man on the cusp of adulthood, hanging on her every word, hoping for just the merest sign of acceptance.

I could have told him of course that Yasmin had eyes for only Frank. I could have, but it wasn't my place and I certainly didn't want to embarrass Michael by pointing out that Yasmin lived with Frank, it could all end in heartbreak, I suppose, but hey that was life.

Adam upon seeing Yasmin held out his arms to her and I passed him over, noticing the flicker of annoyance that crossed young Michael's face. Perhaps my sister had been right, too many years had passed between us, Michael was no longer the loving little boy that had once clung onto my legs but was now an angry testosterone filled teenager, obviously annoyed at my interference.

I felt a little awkward and surprised that no one else had picked up on the tension between us. Maureen asked, "Are you going to get changed into something else or keep your wedding dress on?"

I told her that I was keeping my wedding dress on as it was the only time I would be wearing it, and that seemed to satisfy her.

After a while of watching Michael fawn over Yasmin I thought, to hell with it, Yasmin was my friend and she needed someone to warn her of Michael's massive crush.

As carefully as possible I managed to attract Yasmin's attention without alerting the others. Indicating for her to follow me, she handed Adam back to his dad and followed me to the ladies' rest room.

I was waiting for her inside leaning against one of the sinks. Yasmin picked up on my unease and asked worriedly what was wrong.

I said, "Its Michael, he's got an almighty crush on you and I thought you needed to be made aware of it."

"Oh Claire, I hadn't realised. I'm so sorry," apologised Yasmin.

"No, don't apologise, you've done nothing to be sorry for, it's just a teenage crush on Michael's part, he just sees a beautiful woman who's lavishing attention on him and he's mistaking it for something more. I bet he hasn't even registered the fact that you are with Frank, he's so blinkered looking at you. I would have said something to him before, only he's showing so much hostility towards me I was afraid to say anything in case Maureen came to his defence and we end up having a row." It was a mouthful and I needed to come up for air.

"What do I do?" said Yasmin, "I've never been in this situation before and I don't want to hurt anyone's feelings, especially Michael's."

"Look, Luke and I are going up to our room to change Adam and settle him down for the night. The hotel has agreed with us that one of the waitresses can stay in our room to babysit Adam. It's already been arranged and we have agreed to pay her cash in hand for the service. I know from my days waitressing how poorly paid it is so one of the girls jumped at the chance of earning some extra cash."

"Yes that sounds an excellent solution" agreed Yasmin, "but how do I diffuse the crush situation with Michael?"

"Well the disco will be starting up in about ten minutes time, wait until Luke and I have gone up, then, very much as a couple make your excuses to Maureen and mingle with the other guests. Once Michael sees that you are with Frank he should begin to realise that you and Frank are together and hopefully that will help to cool his ardour," I replied.

"That sounds excellent advice," agreed Yasmin. I washed my hands and together we left the ladies rest room to put the plan into action.

Once in our room I told Luke about our conversation.

Luke asked, "Do you think Michael might cause trouble?"

"Truthfully, I don't know, but I hope not anyway."

We had just got Adam changed and settled down for the night when there was a knock on the door.

Luke let in a young woman I remembered from serving us the meal earlier, called Christine.

I said, "Hello, Adam has just been changed and settled so he will probably be out for the count as it has been a big day for him. If for any reason, you need us, ring down to reception and have them come and find us. You are okay to watch television, it doesn't bother Adam, in fact it helps him sleep better. Oh, and we will send some food up from the buffet later on if you like?"

Christine said, "Okay," and for the very first time, uneasily, we left our son's welfare in a stranger's hands.

When we arrived back downstairs in the reception room the disco was in full swing. Luke and I were quickly mobbed by old friends and work colleagues of mine, from before Adam, as they arrived. Luke was still actively employed at the club so I got the lion's share of the kisses and hugs. Everyone admired my dress which pleased me immensely and for the next hour or so we were constantly greeting friends and colleagues.

Everyone had been encouraged to bring along their partners and most of them had. It made for a very busy night and the bar was doing a roaring trade. The dance floor was doing okay too and I spied Sheryl and James making some shapes.

Just then the tempo of the music became more upbeat and I turned to see Chris, still with Seline at the turntables.

He must have offered to give the D.J. a break and it showed in the change of music.

Yasmin and Frank joined the dance floor crowd and quickly got down and dirty. Now, Yasmin dancing like this was unheard of. Everyone watched open mouthed, this was their boss in a never seen before new light. They were bloody good and it encouraged more people onto the dance floor, once the initial shock had worn off. I even got Luke out of his comfort zone and showed him a few moves of my own, though they were sadly inferior to Yasmin and Frank's.

The signal for a break arrived when two tables offering both hot and cold food began to be dangerously overloaded. Everyone headed towards the tables and helped themselves. Luke and I selected what was on offer then I put a bit of everything on a plate for Christine. I guarded Luke's plate of food while he took one up to our room. I had given Luke totally unneeded instructions to check on Adam to make sure he was alright.

When Luke returned it turned out that Adam was fine though it didn't stop me from worrying about him.

Luke went over to Sir Ian Clayton concerned that he had been left on his own. I took the opportunity to go and talk to Sheryl and James. It was their last night in London and they would be catching the train home in the morning after breakfast. It had been wonderful seeing them both and catching up, I would be sad to see them go. Sheryl and James were a link to my past and our short time together in London had made me realise how much I missed them. I vowed to be a better friend.

Looking over I noticed Seline had re-joined her father ... and of course Luke. I wasn't jealous of their friendship; on the contrary I welcomed it. Luke had known Sir Ian and his daughter for longer than he had known me and had been honest from the beginning about Seline wanting to have sex with him. Luke had told me that he had always resisted Seline's advances and I believed him though seeing her in the flesh and seeing how beautiful she was, the temptation to sample her wares, must have been very difficult to resist.

Chris, obviously looking for Seline came to retrieve her and hauled her off to help him spin some more discs. I didn't know if anything would come of their new found friendship, Chris had an appalling reputation with the ladies, and according to Luke, Seline had the same reputation with the men. Who knows? Perhaps they would be ideal for one-another, only time would tell.

Later my sister and David came to find me to tell me they were ready to go; Michael was standing off by the side of the dance floor obviously intending to do away with courtesy. This little shit was beginning to annoy me; I just didn't know what his problem with me was. I hugged my sister and allowed David to kiss me on the cheek then I went to find Eddie their chauffeur. On the way, I told Cheryl and James that Maureen was ready to go back to the hotel if they wanted to go now. They decided to do just that, sparing Eddie an unnecessary extra journey. I enlisted Luke's help in saying goodbye to my sister and her family, Sheryl and James. I reserved an extra special group hug for Sheryl and

James; god knows when we would see each other again. Michael sloped off without a word and, lord forgive me, I silently thought good riddance, little shit. That old saying came to me just then; you can choose your friends but not your family, and how very true that was.

As the night came to a close Luke and I danced to the last record, along with Yasmin and Frank and Antonia and Steve. Uncle Tony, Jimmy and Sir Ian lined up to shake Luke's hand and shower me with kisses before saying our goodbyes.

It had been a long, tiring, happy day, with just the one tiny fly in the ointment, but we had survived. We were finally husband and wife, we were a family. Luke actually carried me over the threshold much to the amusement of Christine our temporary babysitter. We paid her a ridiculous amount of money for looking after Adam and added another £20 for the cab fare home.

We both looked at our sleeping son, marvelling at how peacefully he slept.

Luke helped me out of my wedding dress and I climbed naked, into bed. I watched Luke undress and noticed he had the beginnings of an erection as he slipped in beside me.

It had been a long day and happily, with a helping hand it promised to be a long night.

Chapter 11

Rat Hunt, Islamabad, Pakistan

The six man group had been hastily brought together for the covert mission. They were all attired in native clothing from head to toe and sported full faced beards. They were all heavily armed with hidden, silenced weapons and the only good thing in their favour as far as they were concerned was that they had all worked together before and knew what each man was capable of.

The team was made up entirely of Americans, all except private first class Mendoza, who was only half American, the other half being Puerto-Rican. But as they frequently liked to remind him, no-one was perfect. They had been inserted into Pakistan from Afghanistan, which had been their area of operations for the last six months. During the hours of darkness the information that Lt. Brad

Overs had been given was at best sketchy. He had voiced his concerns about the relative speed of insertion, and the almost total lack of intelligence that his team had been given, to his commanding officer, Colonel Winters. The Colonel abruptly told Lt. Overs, "If you are having doubts about being able to carry out the mission you can relinquish command and another officer can easily be found to replace you, no problem."

Smarting-like hell at this uncalled for rebuke, Lt. Overs quickly assured Col. Winters that he was more than capable of carrying out the task whatever it was.

Col. Winters nodded, acknowledging Lt. Overs new found zeal for the mission.

Brad had still been prickly and smarting from, what he perceived as legitimate concerns about the lack of intelligence, when he re-joined his team. Lt. Overs was a good officer, he had put in the hard yards with his men and been accepted by them as an asset not a liability, it still rankled that his commanding officer would think so little of him just for questioning the lack of intelligence, after all, it may well effect the success or failure of the mission, and more importantly to Brad, compromise the lives of his men.

Once in Pakistan and on reaching the area near to where the command post had been set up, they decided to split up and approach the building singularly, or in pairs, to avoid attracting too much attention. This sounded easy but to the uninitiated this was Pakistan and hostile eyes were everywhere, very little happened here without someone noticing something.

In Islamabad, strict Islamic laws were enforced by the wealthy powerful elite on a restive modern population. Corruption was widespread from those in the highest echelons of power, be it government or military, secret service down to the ordinary policeman on the street; it made for a powder keg waiting for a spark. Pakistan was supposed to have friendly relations with the western powers but as had been proven many times during the country's short history, those relations had been at best strained and at worst darn right hostile.

Lt. Overs was last into the building temporarily being used as the command centre, when a young man in western clothes approached and asked him to follow down a corridor and into a side room.

His team were all seated around a long table, some smoking awaiting his arrival. A screen had been set up and a young woman was fiddling with a projector whilst he slid into an empty chair, still no-one had spoken as the projector whirred into life and the overhead lights were switched off.

Lt Overs and his team, battle hardened though they were, watched as the uncensored version of the bombing in Istanbul was shown in all its gory detail. Everyone in the room was squirming and fidgety by the end. Then the unmistakable face of Abdul Rahman came on screen laying out his demands to the Turkish government.

The projector cut leaving Rahman's flickering face on screen for all to see, and then the lights were switched back on.

A slight but steely eyed man addressed the room having entered unannounced, "Abdul Rahman, gentlemen, is responsible for the carnage you have just witnessed and a whole list of other atrocities besides, and the reason why you have been brought here in such haste."

Everyone looked at this unassuming individual waiting for more.

"We have reliable intelligence from our allies that within the last 24 hours Abdul Rahman has arrived here in

Islamabad."

Lt. Overs half raised his hand to ask a question, "Which allies sir?"

The steely eyed guy, whose name still eluded them, waited a couple of beats before answering, "The British."

Several groans were audible and one definite "Aw fuck" from the seated team.

The guy waited for the cursing and obvious disappointment to die down before calmly offering, "This time the intelligence is good, voice analysis confirms Abdul Rahman was here within the last 24 hours."

Everyone immediately shut up waiting for more information.

"Our people have been working tirelessly since the confirmation and have since managed to isolate a three storey building where it is thought Rahman may be holed up."

This brought murmurs of interest from everyone in the room and obvious nods of approval.

The guy brought them back down to earth with a bump, "I said it is where Rahman may be holed up. Our people have been monitoring the airwaves for signs that Rahman is still here but since the original intercept there have been no more communications. We simply do not know, hence the reason for you being here.

Lt. Overs decided to take the bull by the horns and in plain language so that there could be no mistake, "What exactly is our mission sir?"

Looking him straight in the eye the guy said, "Your mission Lt. is to enter the building as quickly and quietly as possible, eliminate anyone you perceive to be a threat, whilst looking for Abdul Rahman. If Rahman is there kill him and photograph his body, gather any mobile phones, laptops or anything you think would be of use to our intelligence people and then return here. Is that clear enough for you Lt.?"

"Crystal sir," replied Lt. Overs. Now that everyone in the room had heard the mission laid out plainly he felt that he was on much firmer ground. "Do we know the layout of the target building sir?" asked Overs.

"We are not sure but we think it is very similar to this one, breeze block type structure and three floors high, comprising four rooms on each floor with a central concrete staircase. If it differs from this one I would be very surprised as it seems pretty standard design for this area."

Overs seemed satisfied with the guys input then asked, "How far to the target building?"

"400 metres or so but we have a covered truck that we can use to get your team within 100 metres of the building and eyes on, so you can check it out."

This guy wasn't bad thought Overs, then finally asked, "What's the estimate of people in the building?"

"We do not know the exact number for sure, but it is definitely more than six and could be as many as twenty. Sorry we can't narrow it down for you" apologised the intelligence officer.

Lt. Overs took this on board satisfied with the answer, then gathered his team together to ask how they wanted to do this. He had his own ideas but wanted his team's input to see if it coincided with his own.

They decided on three two man teams to each floor, clearing rooms as they went, going up, they would do the same on the second and third floors until all the rooms were secured.

After a thorough weapons check, and a drink of water they were pumped up and ready to go.

The truck was parked at the back of the building and reasonably out of sight so that was an advantage thought Overs. A guy they didn't know was behind the wheel as they clambered into the back of the truck. The tarpaulin at the back was pulled closed as Overs sat up close to the driver's end. He told the driver they were ready and felt the adrenalin rush as they pulled away. Moving out through the gate and into traffic, Overs could see through the gap in the tarp how busy the streets were.

Overs thought that this covert mission could well end in the mother of all fuck ups, but decided nonchalantly, so what was new? Looking at his team he realised that he was doing his men a disservice, and needed to snap out of it. They were all good men and would do their job without question, and so long as he did his he would get them home safe.

The truck pulled passed the target building and came to a stop by the roadside. Looking through the gap the driver pointed out the target building to Overs.

Lt. Overs estimated the distance from the truck to the building at about 80 meters give or take. He allowed the team to get eyes on through the tarp and waited until they were ready.

Sgt. Briscoe broke their concentration by asking, "How do you want to do this Lt.?"

After a moment's thought Lt. Overs said, "I think we should park the truck in front of the building and act like we belong, by going in through the front door."

The grins all round confirmed that his idea met with their approval. "Alright driver, pull over to the building and leave the engine running; we may be leaving in a hurry."

The driver did a U-turn causing several drivers to stand on their brakes and hold down the horn helping them blend in perfectly.

As the truck came to a stop Lt. Overs said, "Alright let's do this."

The team barely registered with the polluted streets general population, as they entered the building via the front door. Splitting into their designated teams they worked both sides of the corridor. The first three rooms were empty but either a television or a radio was on in the fourth. Sgt. Briscoe and PFC. Mendoza bracketed the door to the fourth room and on his nod entered the room, silenced weapons levelled and ready for action. The lives of two young men were ended just like that. Exiting the room they quietly joined the others who were already heading up to the second floor. Signalling back, Lt. Overs designated PFC Mendoza to remain at the head of the stairs to guard their rear in case trouble came their way, via the stairs. Once he was in position they worked the first two rooms without incident. Coming up to the last two, several voices could be heard from the left hand rear. Lt Overs and PFC Hudson positioned themselves either side of the door with Sgt. Briscoe ready as back up. Lt. Overs signalled with his fingers 3,2,1, and they entered the room ready for action.

Clustered around a table were four men, clearly interested in the map spread out upon it. They were startled to see the intruders burst in with weapons drawn and reacted far too slowly to save their skins. Sgt. Briscoe finished off the last man who was still breathing and looking at him through hate filled eyes.

Lt. Overs thought he recognised one of the dead men but couldn't remember where from, so he photographed each of the newly dead before readying himself for the final ascent. If Abdul Rahman was still here it would be somewhere on the top floor and he took a deep breath before heading up.

Again the first two rooms were empty except for the bunk beds, obviously the top floor was where they bedded down. The last two rooms loomed large and on entering the third on the Lt.'s command, PFC Hudson shot an armed man who had positioned himself behind a bunk bed. The last room was being used as store room and a quick search revealed no hidden bolthole, no Abdul Rahman, the rat was not here.

Lt. Overs said quietly, "Fuck,"' but could still be heard by Sgt. Briscoe who reminded him to get the dead guys picture. Overs did so and ordered a quick search for mobile phones and laptops. All business now the team searched the rooms, the map in the second room was rolled up, and mobile phones were dumped in a sack alongside a much prized laptop.

Picking up PFC Mendoza, they went down to the ground floor giving it a quick search, finding two more mobile phones which went into the sack and Lt. Overs snapped pictures of the first two casualties.

PFC Mendoza opened the front door looking for hostiles. He noted that the truck they had arrived in was still on station and adding to the general pollution of the atmosphere.

Covering their weapons the team exited the building as unobtrusively as possible, and climbed into the back of the truck. It was moving away before the last of the team was seated and ten minutes later it was parked behind the command post, engine switched off and ticking as it cooled down.

Lt. Overs and his team were once again sat at the same table being de-briefed by the same guy who had sent them out. They learned that his name was Anders, a major in intelligence and they each told him the part they had played during the mission. The photographs were being developed while they were being de-briefed; the mobile phones would be gone over with infinite care but the stars of the show the laptop and the map, would be sent up the chain of command for more detailed scrutiny.

As the de-briefing came to an end an intelligence guy entered the room asking for Major Anders. "Would you follow me please sir?" They all looked at one another questionably, but said nothing allowing the adrenalin rush of combat to dissipate.

After ten minutes Major Anders came back in carrying a metal bucket filled with ice and bottles of genuine Budweiser. He handed them each a bottle of bud, taking the tops off, before doing the honours on his own. They all looked at him for the nod, then as one, they threw their heads back and drank deeply. God it tasted good.

Major Anders, bottle still grasped tightly in hand placed a photograph on the table in front of Overs. It was of one of the guys they had just killed, the one he had thought he recognised from somewhere.

Looking up at the Major, begging him for the answer, pleading with his eyes but stayed silent.

"Masood Hassan, Abdul Rahman's protege and number two in his organisation."

He let that sink in for a while before picking up the photograph and placing it in his top pocket then said, "We didn't manage to get the king rat this time gentlemen, but with your help we managed to get rid of the rat in waiting," and with that said, he toasted them with Bud, ''To you gentlemen, well done!" Overs had previously thought how good that Bud tasted, now it tasted a whole lot better.

Chapter 12

MI6 operations room, London

James Martin had been allowed into the operations room merely as a courtesy and he knew it. He kept quiet and in the background, closely following the progress of the hastily scrambled covert mission that had been set in place by the Americans. It had been his information that had been chewed over by the various departments before being given the green light as information, probably genuine.

Time was of the essence and he had been frustrated by the amount of time it had taken before his information had been acted upon. Once Abdul Rahman's voice analysis had been verified as genuine a lot of wasted time had elapsed, it was both frustrating and totally unacceptable in his view.

That the Americans had managed to mount this mission at all, at such short notice was testament to how much they wanted Abdul Rahman.

The British would have liked the opportunity to have mounted the mission themselves, it was true, but with the meagre amount of resources available to them in Afghanistan, it just wasn't feasible.

Successive governments in turn had cut the armed forces of Britain to the bone, so it was chiefly left to the Americans to mount these types of clandestine missions. Several politicians from both sides of the house had raised concerns about the continued lack of funding and the steady decline of personnel for all three services but to no avail, their warning falling on deaf ears. The heads of the armed forces said much the same, one actually daring to say, "It was no longer fit for purpose".

The politicians had been shouted down in derision, some of the top brass had been marginalized and eventually retired and some had just given up in abject frustration. All were pointless actions of course as the lack of funding and the general run-down of personnel still continued unabated.

James Martin had quietly been kicking around these thoughts whilst following the Americans' progress. He hoped with all his heart that Abdul Rahman would be found in the building and eliminated like the murderous rat that he was, but somehow he doubted it. Rahman was notorious for not staying in one place for long.

Had they acted upon his information straight away when he had handed it in to his boss they might have stood a chance at catching the fucker, but not now, far too much time had been wasted.

An hour later he had been proved right, Abdul Rahman had not been found inside the building. Once again he had disappeared; probably back to some rat hole in Afghanistan, that would be his guess anyway.

Later on there was a bit of excitement in the operations room when it was confirmed that Rahman's second in command, Masood Hassan had been killed during the mission and positively identified.

That cheered James up a little bit, they may have missed out killing 'King Rat' but killing the next rat in waiting was better than nothing. This just made James even more determined to end this evil fucker's reign.

In hindsight the Americans had had a success and he applauded them for it, the fact that they had all returned safely made the success all that much sweeter.

Chapter 13

The Almeda's Residence, London.

The old Ford turned into the Almeda's driveway and was confronted by having to manoeuvre around the Almeda's family car. Usually when Harry Spencer parked his Ford, Mr Almeda had already left for work. Harry had only seen the Almeda's car, an Audi, on two other occasions and that had only been because he had been still working when Mr Almeda had returned home from work, but as this was morning and a little after 9.00 am, by Harry's watch anyway, this was both unusual and unexpected.

Mr Almeda was known to be a bit of a workaholic and was renowned for being punctual, so yes Harry was surprised to still find him at home. Harry decided to leave plenty of room for the Audi and parked his Ford out of the way and over in the corner.

Harry calculated that it had been almost nineteen years since he had replied to the Almeda's advertisement for a part time gardener and thinking about it, he could count on one hand the number of times that he had met the man of the house. Normally Harry would arrive and begin work for an hour or so before Mrs Almeda would call him over for coffee and a chat. That had been their routine almost from the day that he had started working for them.

But today would be different, today Mr Almeda was at home.

Going through the side gate Harry looked at the house for signs of movement but saw none. He thought that was strange as normally there would be a light on or signs of movement from within the house, today there was neither.

Shrugging it off, Harry headed over to the far corner of the garden to the tool shed. He had been entrusted with his own key for the heavy duty padlock since the day he had started which Harry thought was good of them.

Unlocking the padlock and wedging open the shed door, Harry manoeuvred the petrol mower into position. Topping up the petrol tank Harry reminded himself that he needed to refill the petrol can for the next time as it was running low. Firing up the mower he allowed it to warm up a little before adjusting the choke. When satisfied that it was running alright Harry attached the grass collecting box and began to cut.

About an hour later Harry was satisfied with the lawn's finished condition. It had been lovingly tended over the years and he was pleased with the final result when he finally turned the mower's engine off. Deciding to let the mower cool off before cleaning it, he went into the tool shed for a pair of sharp edging lawn shears.

Setting to with the shears Harry worked his way around the lawn's edge glancing over at the house from time to time. Normally around about this time Mrs Almeda would be visible in the kitchen making coffee for both Harry and herself. But not today, there was still no sign of her.

By the time Harry had finished edging the lawns, cleaned the mower and deposited the last errant blade of grass in the composter he was beginning to get worried. There was still plenty of work to be done around the flower beds but it was getting on for twelve noon and there still hadn't been any sign of the Almeda's.

On a whim Harry picked up the now empty petrol can and headed over towards the side gate to see if Mr Almeda's Audi was still parked in the driveway. Once through the gate Harry could see that it was still parked in the same position and obviously hadn't been moved. Going over to his Ford, Harry dumped the empty can in the boot and on the way back carefully checked the front of the house for signs of life; still nothing.

Retracing his steps to the back of the house Harry knocked loudly as hard as he dared on the glassed top part of the door several times and framing his eyes with his hands looked through the glass for signs of movement. He could see that the door to the adjoining living room was open by about two or three inches but from this distance he couldn't make anything out. As a last resort Harry tried the door handle ... locked.

Deciding to have one more attempt he went to knock on the front door, this was solid wood and Harry knocked long and hard, hurting his knuckles in the process. After a no show at the door he decided that enough was enough. He was concerned for the Almeda's, for all he knew they could be lying ill or injured inside, it was time for someone with the powers of entry to be contacted; the police.

Harry retrieved his mobile phone from the glove compartment of his Ford and rang 999 asking for the police. Harry knew, from experience, that the moment he was put through that he would have the devil of a job convincing them that this was an emergency and that he needed police assistance.

The operator asked Harry what his emergency was and Harry patiently told her about his concerns for the Almeda's.

The female operator obviously didn't share his concerns doing her best to calm Harry by citing any number of reasons for the Almeda's not being home.

Harry being made of sterner stuff and knowing full well that this conversation was being recorded tried to remain calm and reiterated again and again that he needed a police presence at the Almeda's home to determine if they were alright.

The female operator finally gave in to Harry and told him that a police car would be sent out as soon as one was available, and he was to remain on site until it arrived. Harry knew from experience that this could entail anything from a one to a four hour wait, as the operator clearly hadn't judged Harry's call as an emergency.

Going round to the back of the house once more Harry decided to lock the tool shed, it was pointless trying to do anymore work now that he was waiting for the police to arrive. On a whim Harry knocked on the back door once again - but still no answer, so he went to sit in his car to wait the arrival of the police.

Harry was almost nodding off to sleep when a police car entering the drive startled him into wakefulness. Looking at his watch he calculated that from making the phone call to the police's arrival it had been about an hour and a half. Harry thought not too bad really, he had expected to have waited much longer. Making his way over to meet them he nodded at the policeman and woman.

The policeman asked, "Are you the gentleman who made the emergency call?"

Harry replied that he was and he explained in detail why he had done so. He followed them around, watching as they mirrored Harry's earlier actions, knocking long and hard on first the front door and then the back door, finally trying the handle on the back door. Now Harry thought it was decision time, would they have the balls to break the glass in the door to try and gain entry or not. The policeman was undecided and wanted to radio back to his station for permission. The young policewoman was gutsier, trusting Harry's instincts and was in favour of breaking the glass.

Harry watched as they argued for or against breaking the glass. Exasperated Harry finally said "I can do it."

They both turned to look at Harry in amusement. The policeman said, "It's not about breaking the glass, it's about breaking the glass only to find out the owners are away on holiday or out for the day, or next door visiting the neighbours."

Harry took umbrage at the policeman's assessment of the situation, "Look my concern is for Mr and Mrs Almeda, not who gets the blame for breaking the glass in the door, so please just break the glass and if everything is fine inside

I'll have the door repaired myself," offered Harry.

The policewoman must have trusted Harry because without another word she broke the glass nearest the handle with her baton. Reaching in through the newly made hole she breathed a sigh of relief to find the key in the lock and with a little difficulty unlocked the door and opened it inwards.

The policewoman told Harry to stay outside as she entered the Almeda's kitchen shouting out loudly, "Police, anyone here?"

Harry watched her progress from outside as she reached the living room door, shouting out, "Police, anyone here?" once again. He watched more closely as the policewoman pushed the living room door open and went inside.

A moment later, he had to jump out of the way as she came rushing back towards him gagging and retching, only just managing to make it outside before vomiting in the raised flower bed. Leaning over and trying to control her breathing she fished a hanky from her pocket and wiped her mouth.

Her companion had meanwhile retraced her steps and gone into the living room.

Harry asked the policewoman if she was alright then tentatively, "Are the Almeda's dead?"

Breathing more normally now, she replied, "Yes."

"Oh," was all Harry could say and although he had been proven right to call the police he wished with all his heart that it hadn't ended like this. After a while Harry realised that he would never see either of them again, his gardening days for the Almeda's.were over. The policeman came back outside, a handkerchief firmly held over his mouth and nose. Looking at his companion he asked, "You alright Sue?" she replied, "Yes I'm o.k. now."

He nodded saying, "I'm going to let the station know what we have found, and we are going to need a full team here."

Sue just nodded and said, "OK."

Harry's day had started out promisingly enough but never in his wildest imagination could he have foreseen it ending so badly. It was several hours later and only after he had given a statement to the police that Harry wearily drove home.

Chapter 14

Thursday May 12th, Walpole court Gardens, London

Yasmin and Frank got up late, showered together and ate a healthy breakfast. They both liked to keep fit and ever since Frank had moved in with Yasmin they had decided to exercise together. Both were serious about their fitness but not obsessively so and since they had started on a fitness regime that worked for them both, it had proved to be both enjoyable and beneficial. Their sex life, already very good, had improved as a result; neither of them smoked and only drank occasionally, in moderation.

Claire's wedding reception yesterday had been the exception to their normal intake of alcohol hence the extra quarter of an hour exercise today to try and repair the damage inflicted upon their bodies. Frank had already noticed the benefits of the regime on his own body and was almost back to the fitness level of his army days.

Yasmin almost had a six pack to rival Frank's and had an arse that was both pleasing to look at and firm to touch. Frank was very pleased with life at the moment and knew he was one lucky sod to have Yasmin as part of it.

With Claire and Luke now finally married, Yasmin reflected on their own situation. She had asked Frank to marry her a while ago and he had accepted without hesitation, but that was before the assassination attempt on both their lives by agents of her brother Ali. She would need to bring the subject of marriage up to Frank once more, in order to clarify if he still wanted to marry her, but that could wait until later, she had a telephone call to make and now seemed like the right time to make it. Scrolling through her list of numbers, Yasmin found the one for Almeda and Associates and keyed it in, it was picked up by the third tone and a voice Yasmin recognised as belonging to Beverley, Mr Almeda's personal secretary, informed her that she had reached 'Almeda and Associates', how can I help you?"

Yasmin jumped straight in, "Beverley it's Yasmin Hussein, can you put me through to Mr Almeda, it's rather important." It was a lie of course thought Yasmin, but by claiming that it was important she thought she could cut through all the red tape and find out if Mr Almeda was alright.

Worryingly when Beverley informed Yasmin that Mr Almeda was not in his office and hadn't been seen for several days, alarm bells began ringing in Yasmin's head. Deciding to level with Beverley, Yasmin told her the reason she was ringing was because she was worried about the Almedas. She told her that Mr & Mrs Almeda had not turned up to her friend's wedding yesterday and would she mind checking his appointment book, on yesterday's date, to see if he had forgotten to write it in. Yasmin knew she was asking Beverley for information that she really had no right to ask her for, but felt that the urgency of the situation warranted it.

Nevertheless Beverley complied with Yasmin's request and after a few moments read out, "According to his schedule Mr Almeda had a meeting with a client pencilled in for 10 o'clock, then had written wedding, Bloomsbury and that's all."

Yasmin nodded at Beverley's information then realized that she could not see the gesture and said in reply. "So it seems that the Almedas were definitely set on attending the wedding."

"Yes according to his appointment book anyway." Beverley reiterated.

"Well thank you Beverley you have been most helpful as usual, but it's just made me even more worried for the Almedas." Then as if to herself, "I suppose the next step is to try ringing his home telephone number."

Beverley came back with, "We have already tried ringing his home number several times but have had no response. As you can appreciate we have documents that require Mr Almeda's signature and they are beginning to mount up. Look, I'll tell you what Miss Hussein, let me try his home number again and I promise I will get back to you if I get a response, how's that?"

"Would you please Beverley? That is good of you; I will wait to hear back from you then, bye for now."

Frank had just made coffee for them both whilst trying to decipher the result of the one sided telephone conversation. Yasmin helped him out by filling in the blanks.

"Mr Almeda hasn't been into work for several days and

according to his secretary the Almedas both fully intended to attend Claire's wedding. She is ringing me back if she has any news."

Fully appraised of the situation, Frank sat with Yasmin, dark thoughts playing in his head, quietly sipping his coffee whilst waiting for the phone to ring with any news.

When it finally did ring, managing to startle them both, even though they were expecting it, the news from Beverley was the worst kind.

Once the telephone had been picked up in the Almeda's hall Beverley had to undergo a cross examination from an unknown male on the other end of the line. Finally, managing to convince whoever it was that she was who she said she was, the gentleman on the telephone had identified himself as a police officer. Beverley was then given the information that she was now giving to Yasmin. Unfortunately Mr and Mrs Almeda had been found dead at their home in suspicious circumstances and there was now an ongoing police enquiry. That was all the information they

could tell her for now. They had asked if someone could formally identify the bodies as soon as possible, said an upset Beverley. Yasmin relayed this information to Frank and he offered to go to the police station to do this. Beverley was tearfully grateful.

A shocked Beverley had just finished telling an equally shocked Yasmin what the police had told her. Yasmin thanked Beverley feeling numb and empty inside, as she ended the call.

Frank concerned for Yasmin said, "What did Beverley have to say?"

Yasmin swallowed hard, clearly upset and struggling to find the words, finally she gave voice to them, "The police are at the Almeda's house, apparently they are both dead, but the police are withholding the cause of death until they have finished their investigations."

Frank reached for Yasmin putting his arms around her to try and give comfort to his partner in her distress. Her sobs stifled slightly by his shoulder clearly showed Frank how much the death of the Almedas had affected her. Frank held onto Yasmin letting her give vent to her grief whilst quietly wondering how the Almedas had died. Until they knew for certain the cause of death they couldn't really speculate. But Frank had the uneasy feeling that Yasmin's brother Ali, was somehow involved.

When Yasmin finally extracted herself from Frank's comforting embrace she uncharacteristically wiped her eyes on the sleeve of her cardigan, dragging in a large lungful of air she began to pull herself together saying, "I need to let Claire and Luke know about the Almedas and I need to talk to them face to face. A telephone conversation isn't an option."

Frank was always amazed by how soon Yasmin could rally around. Once she had let go of her grief her brain quickly switched back on, working out what was needed and then putting the thoughts to action. She amazed him again when she said, "If the Almedas have met with foul play we cannot rule out the possibility that my brother may have had something to do with their deaths and we need to warn Claire and Luke."

Obviously Yasmin was on the same wavelength as himself, this was one very switched on lady, Frank mused.

Looking at the kitchen clock Yasmin calculated that Claire, Luke and Adam would be back home by now and grabbing her car keys said to Frank, "Come on let's go and see Claire."

Chapter 15

M.I.6. building, London 13th May

It beat Doug Simon's why his boss chose to have an office down here deep in the bowels of M. I.6. He could easily ask for and receive an office where there was actual daylight and the air was much fresher and breathable. Instead he chose to spend his time down here.

James Martin's intelligence though had never been in question; it was just a shame that the general consensus of opinion whenever Martin's name was mentioned was that he was an arsehole.

Martin, had you asked him, would have argued that the isolation allowed him to think clearer, though another explanation could have been put forward - that no one really liked working with him.

Whatever the real reason was, it was Doug's lot in life

to seek out his boss and give him the information that may just help catch the bad guys.

James Martin heard Doug's approach before actually catching sight of him, perking him up a little when Doug arrived at his door. Doug's arrival meant information and information was what Martin needed in order to be able to function properly.

Martin greeted Doug affably in anticipation of gaining useful information, right at this moment it was just what he needed.

The intelligence that Martin had recently passed on had almost resulted in the death of Abdul Rahman. Had it been acted upon immediately when he had first passed it on, Martin felt certain that Rahman would now be dead. The opportunity to kill him was wasted and lost in the endless bureaucracy that seemed to blight the service. That Rahman's number two had been killed in his stead had been merely a consolation prize and in Martin's opinion, had only been achieved through pure damn luck.

Martin mused, that once again they were playing catch up, and as far as where Rahman was concerned, he suspected that he was holed up safe somewhere in Afghanistan with a hundred foot of solid rock safely protecting his head whilst he planned his next atrocity.

Doug watched his boss, quietly waiting for him to return to planet earth and acknowledge his presence. He had seen his boss in this state many times before and didn't like to interrupt him when clearly he was lost in thought.

Then just as quickly Martin was back and said, "Yes Doug what have you got for me?"

"We have had news from our mole at the Met. sir, concerning the Almedas," answered Doug.

"Oh right!" said Martin, his mind now fully focused.

"Just run me through it will you?"

Doug complied and told his boss what he knew, "Mr and Mrs Almeda were found dead in the living room of their home yesterday, 12th May. Mrs Almeda had been tied to one of the dining table chairs; mouth taped shut and shot once in the face. Mr Almeda was found face down on the living room carpet some distance from his wife. Shot once in the back of the head. The mole goes on to say that they were killed facing one another. A thorough search of the property rules out robbery, as money and valuables were in clear sight and not touched. Apparently, they have been dead for several days."

"So ... that means the killer or killers are long gone," commented Martin.

"Looks that way sir" agreed Doug.

"Well if robbery wasn't the motive for killing the Almedas it proves that the telephone intercept was correct and that they were killed for information that they possessed," mused Martin, almost to himself.

Doug said nothing, watching as his boss searched through the haphazard piles of paper spread across his desk.

Martin seized upon the paper he was looking for and familiarized himself with the name he had written down, Claire Wilson, the address was already committed to memory. Coming to a decision Martin gave instructions to Doug.

"Doug I need you to find out everything you can on this Claire Wilson." Handing over the sheet of paper Martin continued, "We need to know why Ali Hussein is so interested in her."

Martin then impressed on Doug the importance of speed by saying, "Top priority Doug, we don't know how long it will be before one of Ali Hussein's killers, pays her a visit."

Taking the paper from his boss Doug said, “Leave it with me sir,” and left his boss still seated behind his desk but once again lost in thought.

Chapter 16

Claire's Residence, London

Claire was supporting Adam as he shakily made his way along the length of the sofa. His squeals of delight never failed to bring a smile to her face. Adam was coming along in leaps and bounds and she almost missed it as he took her by surprise by saying, "Mum", not once but twice. Claire blinked, delighted with Adam's new word, it certainly made a change from Dad, although she was annoyed that Luke was asleep upstairs and had missed it. Adam was a bundle of energy and Claire supported him whilst he retraced his steps along the sofa now on the opposite direction and growing ever more confident with each new step.

Claire knew for a fact that once Adam had mastered the technique of being able to walk unaided she would have to be extra vigilant, as the fun and games would really start then. Deciding that Adam had done enough traverses of the sofa for now, she placed a wriggling, unwilling Adam in his playpen. Looking at the hurt expression on his face as Adam stood up at the bars and looked back at his mum, Claire imagined Adam saying, "What have I done to warrant being locked up?" that's how it seemed to Claire anyway as she looked back at him with fondness and wonder.

Going to the kitchen Claire topped up the kettle and set it to boil ready for Luke getting up. Coming back into the room she sat watching Adam for a while playing with his toys. She noticed that his favourite soft toy was a small dark brown bear that Claire had bought for him herself, that pleased her no end. She had thought at the time, when purchasing it, that Adam would really take to it and had been proved right. As Claire watched Adam playing with his bear he suddenly looked up and said "Dad."

Claire herself had not heard a sound but knew with utter certainty, that Adam had either heard Luke getting up or sensed him, either way Claire waited for Luke to make an appearance knowing that Adam was never wrong.

As soon as Luke appeared, Adam held up his arms for his dad to release him from prison. Dutifully Luke lifted his son into his arms and dogging Claire's footsteps into the kitchen, planted a smacker on her waiting lips and said "Hi."

Claire responded with, "Hi yourself," and seating herself at the kitchen table, opposite Luke and Adam, placed two mugs of tea on place mats on the table's surface. Adam instinctively reached for the mug and just as instinctively Claire moved Luke's mug away from him in the daily game of Adam chess that they had invented.

Adam looked at his dad with a puzzled look on his face as if to say, "What's she playing at?"

Luke looked Adam in the eye and said, "Sorry son, mum's kitchen, mum's rules."

Claire affirmed this by declaring, "Too right!"

They drank their teas happy in their own company, but it wasn't long before their thoughts returned to yesterday's revelation concerning the Almedas.

Yasmin and Frank's sudden and unexpected arrival had taken them both by surprise, the unwelcome news that they had brought with them was both shocking and upsetting. It had seemed to hit Claire harder than Luke but that was understandable as Luke hardly knew them, whereas Claire had known Mr Almeda for years.

The cause of their deaths was still unknown so until they knew for certain how they had died they couldn't rule out the possibility that Yasmin's brother AIi, was somehow responsible. That was the consensus of opinion that Yasmin and Frank had arrived at and Claire tended to agree with their way of thinking. Luke favoured a wait and see approach, which Claire thought was unusual for him given Ali Hussein's track record, but, hey everyone had a right to their opinion so Claire could live with it. Eventually the truth would win out but until then, they had decided to be extra vigilant.

Chapter 17

The next day at Claire's residence, London

Our worst fears were confirmed the next day; the murder of the Almedas was front page news. Most of the tabloid press had run with the story, one was more forth coming than the rest, they had reported that the Almedas had been shot execution style, in their own home. Obviously, someone in the police force was leaking information to the press.

So, now we were in no doubt, even Luke was in agreement with the rest of us, Ali Hussein was the chief suspect in ordering the Almeda's murder. None of us knew why he had ordered them killed but given Ali Hussein's evil disposition, it was enough to think that somehow the Almedas had fallen out of favour with him, and that was all it needed for him to order their deaths.

We now knew that we all had to be extra vigilant and of course Chris my cousin, and by association part of our inner circle of friends, would have to be warned too. I must confess it was worrying to think that anyone even remotely viewed as being called a friend, by any one of us, could potentially be added to Ali Hussein's hit list.

Even more worrying, was the reality that literally anyone could be a threat, we simply didn't know who we had to guard against. Let's face it, all Ali had to do was remain at home in Jordan and make one phone call to order our deaths.

The solution was obvious we needed to neutralise the threat. Ali Hussein needed killing; we all agreed, including Yasmin, but how on earth were ordinarily working class people supposed to go about achieving that?

Chapter 18

M.I.6. Headquarters. London

Doug Simons looked up from his desk just as his boss James Martin entered the room. Waving his arm to attract Martin's attention Doug beckoned him over. Pulling up a chair Martin sat and without preamble asked, "What have you got for me Doug?"

"I've got the information you asked for on Claire Wilson sir," answered Doug.

James Martin cleared his mind then said, "O.k. Doug, give me what you have."

"Right sir, the short version, Claire Wilson was born in Lincoln, has an older sister Maureen, abandoned by their father when Claire was too young to remember him. His whereabouts in the country are currently unknown but he is thought to still be alive." Doug looked over momentarily to see if his boss wanted him to dig out more information on the errant father. When he said nothing Doug took that to mean no. "Miss Wilson's mother is dead" continued Doug, "she has a cousin Christopher Booth, who just happens to be the co-manager of Yasmin Hussein's club; apparently they both run the club together as joint managers."

James Martin raised his eyebrows at this information saying, "Interesting."

Doug digested that himself, then carried on reading aloud the relevant facts that he thought his boss was really after.

"It was on Chris Booth's recommendation that, after her mother's death, Miss Wilson came to live in London in order to work at the club. She began as a junior management trainee. When she had completed her training she was then put on the club books as management. You probably know sir, that Yasmin Hussein, on reaching the age of twenty eight, inherited the apartment block she currently lives in and also received a one third ownership share of the club."

Doug read the report, skipping the more mundane facts, "Miss Wilson was co-sharing a town house with Chris Booth at the time of her traineeship, but on Yasmin Hussein's insistence she moved into Apartment 4, Walpole Gardens."

That piqued Martins interest and he asked, "Lover?"

"It appears not sir, both are reported as heterosexual." Read Doug.

"All the same that's one heck of a move from relative obscurity to millionaire status in just a few short years. Miss Wilson certainly landed on her feet when she moved to London," Mused Martin. "I could do with luck like that."

"You and me both sir," smiled Doug. Reading on, the rags to riches fairy tale became even more fantastic when

Doug read out, "just a few years later Yasmin Hussein signed over the apartment in its entirety, to Claire Wilson."

James Martin, reading between the lines and in possession of information that Doug Simons wasn't aware of, could hazard a guess why Yasmin Hussein would gift the apartment to Miss Wilson, but chose to keep silent.

Doug read further down the report, "Miss Wilson gets herself pregnant and moves the boyfriend, Luke Henderson, into the apartment with her. It says here she has a son, Adam, not long afterwards. Some sort of swap with Chris Booth takes place and Claire, Luke and Adam all move into the townhouse previously occupied by Mr Booth and he moves into Apartment 4, Walpole Court Gardens."

"Sounds cosy," offered Martin, "but that could be a problem."

"How so sir?" asked Doug, failing to understand why.

"Because Doug, Ali Hussein still thinks that Miss Wilson is living in Apartment 4, Walpole Gardens, when in fact, Mr Booth is in residence."

"So if Ali Hussein sends someone after Miss Wilson he will find Mr Booth instead," finished Doug.

"In a nut shell Doug and being in possession of this vital piece of information we now need to take responsibility and forewarn them." James Martin's thoughts had just begun to piece together how to bring this about, when Doug interrupted his train of thoughts again.

"Incidentally sir, I neglected to mention that Miss Wilson is Mrs Henderson now, they were married last Wednesday, sorry sir," apologised Doug.

James Martin nodded in acceptance and quietly said, "Married eh ... I wonder what that's like."

It seemed a strange thing for his boss to say but then thinking about it, apart from seeing him here during working hours, Doug knew nothing, absolutely nothing, about James Martin's private life.

Chapter 19

Deep inside the cave systems in Afghanistan.

Ever since Abdul Rahman had learned of the death of his number two, Masood Hassan, he had been planning his next atrocity in retribution. He had received reliable information from fighters inside Pakistan that it had been the Americans who had carried out the executions whilst looking for him.

He realized that he had only escaped assassination by just a matter of hours and now he was thirsting for revenge.

At first he had wanted to hit back at the Americans, so much so, that he imagined he could taste it, but after a moment of clarity he managed to rein in his wild thoughts. With the information in the first place, the only logical answer was the British.

So it would be the British he decided who would satisfy

his need for vengeance.

He sent out his orders and his acolytes were only too eager to do his bidding.

In a few days' time, for many British holiday makers now enjoying the Spanish sun, it would be the last thing that they ever saw. Of course many other nationalities would also be caught up in Rahman's warped thirst for vengeance, but that, to his way of thinking was acceptable. Every day thousands of people lost their lives to random acts of violence worldwide; it was just part of life!

Chapter 20

The telephone call Yasmin had received yesterday was both unexpected and disturbing. Upon learning who the call was from, her immediate inclination was to end the call, the person who was calling was both known to her and despised.

However logic won out over Yasmin's revulsion when she realized that ending the call would only bring James Martin to her door. Reluctantly she decided to hear what he had to say. The last thing she wanted was this loathsome creature invading the sanctity of her home. The gist of the matter centred on the recent murder of the Almedas, which immediately focused Yasmin's attention. Martin quite rightly wouldn't discuss details over the telephone but wanted a neutral place to meet and generously allowed Yasmin to choose its whereabouts. He then asked that she be accompanied by Frank White, Christopher Booth and Claire Henderson.

He hadn't asked that Luke should also be present, but knowing Luke, he wouldn't allow James Martin to meet with Claire unless he was present. Yasmin thought carefully about where to meet with Martin, finally opting for her own club. It was a place she knew well and felt reasonably safe in.

That had been arranged yesterday and now today the invited participants, together with the uninvited, namely Luke and Adam, were sat awaiting the arrival of James Martin.

When Martin did arrive he wasn't alone, he had with him a younger man. Claire couldn't help noticing that both Frank and Luke were like two coiled springs in full threat attack mode; they were like two protective Rottweilers and it made her smile. All the same, Claire was glad they were here they made her feel safe.

Pre-empting Martin speaking first, Yasmin introduced Chris, Claire and Luke, Frank they had already met. Not for the first time Yasmin Hussein had Martin on the back foot and he felt obligated to formally introduce himself and his companion Doug Simons.

Once the introductions had been made, Yasmin again tried to orchestrate the meeting by asking Martin about the Almedas.

This time Martin took charge of the meeting by saying, "All in good time Miss Hussein, first you need to know the chain of events that have brought us here." Looking sideways at his companion Martin nodded for him to tell them what they knew.

"A while ago our intelligence people deciphered a telephone conversation made by the terrorist,known as Abdul Rahman. The gist of it concerned the gathering of certain information known by the Almedas."

Martin closely watched everyone's reactions whilst Doug gave them the facts. He expected someone, anyone, to ask what information, but was not disappointed when no one did.

Doug continued, "The telephone conversation was to Ali Hussein ......, your brother Miss Hussein!" Doug emphasised for effect.

Martin watched her reactions closely and gauged from them and that of her companions, that they had thought Ali Hussein was involved in the Almeda's deaths for themselves.

It was now that Claire decided to ask, "What information?"

Martin indicated, imperceptibly, that Doug should continue.

"Your name Mrs Henderson," answered Doug, "or should I say your name as it was at the time, Claire Wilson."

Everyone looked at each other in confusion, wondering why on earth Ali Hussein would want Claire's name.

"Not only your name Mrs Henderson but your address as well," added Doug.

"But why?" asked Claire, "I've only seen the man once and have never spoken to him."

"That we don't know Mrs Henderson, but we think you must have information he wants, that perhaps you're not aware of. If that is the case, and I think it is, then Ali Hussein will send someone after you to get this information. Once he has it of course, you will be killed. Just like the Almedas," finished Doug.

Luke who had been listening intently to the conversation so far, thought that he knew the answer. Wrestling with his conscience over whether to share his thoughts with James Martin or not, he decided that if James Martin was made aware of all the facts, he may just be able to help them.

Luke spoke up, "I think I know what this information is."

Everyone turned to face Luke, waiting for enlightenment. "Ali Hussein is looking for the men who invaded his family home to free his sister Mr Martin," answered Luke, "and that would be myself and Frank."

James Martin appreciated Luke's honesty and nodded in thanks. Now that the puzzle was complete Martin could better understand the workings of Ali Hussein's mind. His ego had been badly bruised, he had been made to look a fool in his own household and for that reason alone, people had to die. Martin realised that Ali Hussein was no more than a spoiled petulant child, a dangerous one, admittedly, but a child nevertheless.

Now that they thought they had a reason for Ali's enmity, Yasmin Hussein voiced what had been occupying her thoughts, "Am I responsible for all this? I sent the letter to Mr Almeda and now they are dead. Claire's name was on the letter and now her life is at risk. This mess is all my fault," said Yasmin in despair.

Chris had listened patiently up to now, failing to see where he fitted into the equation.

'Where do I fit in?" he asked simply.

Doug had temporarily lost his train of thought but quickly recovered,"The Almedas had given Claire's address to Ali Hussein's hired assassin, as Apartment 4, Walpole Court Gardens, Mr Booth."

Claire interrupted, "That's where I was living at the time when Mr Almeda brought over Yasmin's letter."

Now it all began to make sense thought Martin.

"So that means anyone looking for Claire will be calling on me first," retorted Chris.

"Exactly," agreed Doug, "although Mr Martin has a plan, if you will agree to his suggestions Mr Booth."

"Alright let's hear it," said Frank, when everyone else stayed silent.

"Chris temporarily moves out of his apartment so that two M.I.6 female operatives can move in, as no one knows Ali Hussein's time frame agenda." Martin continued. He envisaged a duration time of between two and ten days. He figured he could swing that with the boss, unless of course a major incident in London occurred to upset his plans.

Chris mulled over James' suggestion and reluctantly agreed. When faced with a professional killer he didn't really have a choice.

Martin asked Yasmin, "Can my team fix up a temporary surveillance camera around the back of the building, as we think that would be the assassin's favoured point of entry. The fire escape at the rear of the building could be used as a potential means of entry as well as being a necessary means of escape from fire. A partially opened rear window would provide the final embellishment."

Once Martin's suggestions had everyone's approval he was keen to set them in motion. He asked Chris, "Can you move out today?"

Looking up at Martin, Chris agreed with a nod of his head.

Yasmin told Chris, "I will reimburse you, within reason for accommodation expenses, but I will need receipts."

Yasmin may have been viewed as soft by some but she certainly wasn't daft.

The meeting broke up with Martin and Simons hurrying off to set the wheels in motion.

Claire was thinking about letting Chris have his old room back during his temporary eviction from his apartment.

It was Chris himself who saved her the bother when he announced that he intended asking Seline, Sir Ian Clayton's daughter, if she would put him up.

This was news indeed; none of them knew that they were still seeing one another. Chris had the reputation of an alleycat and if he was still seeing Seline it was almost unheard of.

Luke asked Chris pointedly if he had previously stayed at Sir lan's overnight.

When Chris replied that he had Luke felt a cold chill run down his spine. He viewed Sir Ian first and foremost as a good friend but more importantly as a vulnerable father figure. Luke loved the old man and Chris' reputation with the ladies had left a trail littered with broken hearts. Chris treated women badly; he used them and tended to move on without as much as a backward glance. Luke hoped with all his heart that Seline didn't end up like the rest. He feared that if Seline became yet another one of Chris' victims it would end up destroying her father.

Luke had been thinking all this to himself and was wondering if he should say anything to Chris. He knew that he had no right to say anything, they were both adults and just as bad as each other at disregarding lovers, so Luke chose to say nothing but felt deep down in his gut that this would end badly ..... for both of them.

Chapter 21

Ever since Luke had got up he had been sitting quietly, not talking, and that to Claire wasn't like

Luke. Adam had even picked up on it and that was a sure sign that something was troubling him. The unfinished mug of tea that Luke was holding had gone cold long ago.

Claire decided that this simply wouldn't do and removed the mug of tea from Luke's hand without protest. She came back from the kitchen to confront the zombie sitting on her sofa. "Alright Luke, what's bothering you? And don't tell me it's nothing because clearly there is something, was it the meeting yesterday?"

Luke looked sideways at Claire and Adam as they sat down beside him. "If you must know, I'm worried about Seline and Chris. I hadn't realised they were still seeing one another, I thought that it would have fizzled out by now."

"Why are you worried? They are both adults and have equal track records as far as I can see," said Claire, clearly annoyed.

Luke tried to explain his reasoning to Claire, "It's not that I'm worried about Seline and Chris so much. I'm worried that if it all ends badly, the effect it will have on Sir lan, he dotes on Seline. Chris' track record is far worse than Seline's and if, as I suspect he will, he breaks her heart Sir Ian will be left to pick up the broken pieces."

That was quite a speech thought Claire prompting her to ask," Do you love her Luke?"

"Yes ... but not in the way that you are inferring, I love Seline and her father like they are my family," said Luke with conviction.

"Good answer," said Claire planting her lips on Luke's and making Adam squirm between them.

When they surfaced for air Claire said, "So what are you going to do about it?"

"Nothing," said Luke, ''They will only tell me to mind my own business if I say anything, so I'm staying out of it."

''That would have been my advice to you had you cared to ask me," chided Claire. Her stomach rumbled on cue and she handed over Adam saying, "Here, play with your son while I go and sort out some food."

Luke knew that Claire was annoyed with him and she had every right to be. He was still new at sharing his feelings with her after having been on his own for so long. He was getting better but he still had the odd re-Iapse, like just now. Shaking off his negative thoughts Luke concentrated on Adam deciding to give his son a little education.

He had bought a book of animals a couple of days ago from a street trader. It had many coloured

pictures of animals on its pages with the names of the animals printed across their torsos. Opening to the first page Luke sat Adam comfortably so that he could see the animals, and then pointing to each one in turn, Luke said aloud what they were.

Adam, though not attempting to say the names, pointed at the animals just like his dad was doing.

He was clearly interested in the animals and by the time the last page was opened Claire looked in

and announced, "Dinner in five minutes."

Adam looked up momentarily then back down at the book. He still had a full page of animals to point to and Luke dutifully obliged. This time Adam pointed to the animals in turn and Luke read out the names, and only when the last one was pointed out and named did Adam allow his dad to close the book.

Luke knew without a shadow of a doubt that something momentous had just happened. He was sure that Adam had inherited his ability to memorize data. If this was true surely it was way too early to tell, Adam was too young, thought Luke.

Over dinner Luke broke the news to Claire, this was news that he definitely needed to share.

Chapter 22

The two female agents had been firmly ensconced in Christopher Booth's apartment for the past three days. They had been on high alert the whole time and were beginning to feel a little jaded with the assignment. Neither Sue Turner nor her assigned partner Anne Parish had stepped outside since moving in.

At first both had been amazed at the sheer size and opulence of the place, it just oozed wealth.

Marvelling at the luxuriant marble bathroom that had, incidentally, proved too much of a temptation for them both to resist. They marvelled at the Queen Anne sized bed revelling in trying it out. The walk in wardrobe made them both envious and prompted Sue to comment, "My bedsit is only slightly bigger!"

Nothing had happened for three days and being cooped up for all that time didn't help. Inaction was allowing boredom to creep in and that could prove fatal, given the nature of their assignment. They needed to sharpen up, re-focus and that was why Anne had been doing sit ups. She had managed to work up quite a sweat in an effort to keep in shape but now needed a shower. She asked Sue to keep alert whilst she showered.

Sue said, "OK," and went to keep watch.

That had more or less been their routine since arriving; exercises, watchfulness, sleep shifts and taking it in turns to cook. It turned out that Anne was a half decent cook, managing to make very tasty fayre from the little that she had found in Chris' fridge-freezer and the few tinned vegetables in his cupboards.

Both Anne and Sue made sure that everything they used was written down. Once the assignment was over the apartment would be professionally cleaned and all the food that they had used would be replaced.

Bored they may be but they were still professional agents and had kept in touch with their team leader, who was sitting cramped up with two others, in the command vehicle and checking in every two hours on the clock diligently for the past three days. It didn't help when the reply from the British Telecom van, being used as the command vehicle, always replied, "Nothing happening, sit tight."

The girls in the apartment may have been feeling a tad bored with the assignment at the moment but it could have been worse, a whole lot worse.

The three guys in the B.T. van were virtually living on top of one another and had been reduced to pissing in a bottle during the hours between 6pm and 6am. This was necessary in order to restrict the comings and goings from the van if they were to catch this killer.

All three of them were dressed in B.T. uniforms and wore hard hats when outside during the day. They had screened off a section of pavement and lifted an inspection cover in order to fool the public. Proper safety signs were in place and to all intents and purposes it looked the part.

One person monitored the screen at all times even during daylight hours. The screen gave a good view of the fire escape and driveway but the general consensus was that he would choose the hours of darkness to make his approach.

It had been another long uncomfortable day in the van. It was Allen's turn to monitor the screen whilst the others tried to get some sleep. Anne had called in at 2pm to be told, "All clear sit tight," by Allen. He could imagine how pissed off she was feeling, he could hear it in her voice. He wasn't exactly feeling overjoyed at the prospect of spending another five or six days living in the van himself.

Just the thought of breathing in his companion's farts for the next few days was enough to 'put hairs on his tongue'. Looking momentarily at his watch, it read 2:22pm when movement caught his attention. A guy dressed in dark clothing and wearing a hoodie had appeared at the target's driveway. At first it appeared like he was about to take a leak, he was certainly looking warily all around.

He appeared to be spooked by a passing car and walked away.

Allen was disappointed having felt sure this was their man. He was even more sure when hoodie returned from the opposite direction. This time Allen woke his sleeping companions and wasted no time in alerting Anne that she was about to have company, via the fire escape.

Whilst Allen monitored the screen giving Anne updates, Barry and John left the van to go to the assistance of Anne and Sue.

This needed to be done as quickly and quietly as

possible, so speed was vital. The whole team had been impressed with the importance of securing a live prisoner as opposed to a dead one by their boss.

The last update from Allen to Anne was that the intruder was at the partially opened window and help was on its way.

Anne was relieved to hear that back up was on the way but told Allen to cease with the updates as "We have this!"

Admonished, he realised they needed to concentrate without having him constantly in their ears.

Anne and Sue had pre-arranged the bed to look as if someone was asleep in it. In the near dark it would certainly fool an intruder. Anne had secreted herself in the walk-in-wardrobe with the doors partially open, whilst Sue was in deep shadow in the corner behind the door. Both Sue and Anne's eyesight had long since become attuned to the dim lighting in the room. They were ready!

The squeal of the window being raised set their teeth on edge. The tension in the room was almost palpable. Would the noise from raising the window scare the intruder off?

The wait seemed interminable but finally an almost silent footfall could be heard approaching the bedroom. The darker shape of a man's silhouette appeared in the doorway. He seemed to hesitate momentarily, probably letting his eyes adjust to the dim light and getting his bearings, before approaching the bed.

He had his back to Anne, presenting her with the perfect target, silently she approached him from behind, Taser in hand and ready for action. Now, close in she shouted, "Freeze or you will be

tasered." The intruder did not comply so she aimed and fired at the large mass of his back. It was a positive hit and she depressed the trigger, feeling the surge of the unleashed power. It should have knocked him to his knees only for some reason it didn't, instead he spun around and lashing out with

his gun caught Anne square in the face across the bridge of her nose. She felt the impact all the way to her toes as it knocked her to her knees dazed.

Sue hadn't hung about, quickly coming to Anne's aid she also shouted, "Freeze or you will be

tasered," again he did not comply so she tasered him, also aiming for the mass that was his back.

This time it had the desired effect, bringing the assailant to his knees.

Meanwhile Anne had recovered enough to regain her wits and stand unaided. Holstering the Taser, Sue with Anne's assistance, removed the intruder's gun and managed to turn him onto his stomach.

They secured his wrists with handcuffs, non-too gently, just as his strength was beginning to recover.

Anne, still feeling aggrieved, made sure that the cuffs were ratcheted up tight.

The cavalry arrived, too late in this case, through the open window by the fire escape. Sue turned on the lights making them all wince while their eyes adjusted to the glare.

Whilst the boys searched the intruder Anne went to the bathroom to inspect her injured, bloody nose. The face staring back at her confirmed Anne's worst fears, her nose was broken and she would carry a scar on the bridge of her nose for the rest of her life. Even so she was still upbeat about the take down. The girls had managed to subdue a killer and perhaps more importantly keep him alive.

Anne figured a broken nose was well worth the result.

Barry had already filled Allen in on the girls' success and had asked him to send for the snatch squad.

Within three minutes a black van and four large men

had pulled up outside the apartment block. John let them in and beckoned them up the stairs.

The intruder was immediately hooded and manhandled down the stairs none too gently; not a word was exchanged during the process.

John witnessed them throw the hooded man in the back of the van, then saw them get in after him. From van arriving to leaving and out of sight had taken less than two minutes.

Anne had managed to clean herself up and with the aid of cold water she had just about stopped her nose from bleeding.

It was just left for John and Barry to group hug the girls and to congratulate them both for a job well done.

It was a short wait for the cleaners to come and sanitise the apartment, once they had arrived Sue and Anne could be released to get Anne's injuries medically assessed.

The boys had returned to the van, this time via the front door, to clean up the surveillance sight but unfortunately before anyone could go home they would all have to make out an operations report. Red tape was a pain in the arse and the bane of their lives.

Chapter 23

Somewhere underground, London.

The black SUV holding the snatch squad and prisoner took a right turn and headed down the ramp. Several turns later and still heading down it entered a large underground car park. Which on the face of it looked just like any normal car park, except that this one was deep underground and off limits to the general public. The tyres squeaked their way across the smooth concrete floor finally coming to rest beside a steel door set into the concrete wall.

Everything about the place resembled a bunker, which in reality was what it was. There must have been CCTV cameras placed somewhere because the steel door suddenly opened inwards and four men dressed in similar black clothing emerged and came to stand at the rear of the SUV: one of them banged on the back door.

The prisoner was hauled out of the SUV and handed over to the new four man squad. He was still hooded so couldn't see. His hands were still hand cuffed behind his back, so with a guard on either side he was guided through the steel door.

He heard the boom of the door closing behind them as they walked down what he presumed was a corridor. They took a right turn and walked for about another fifty paces before he was stopped. He could hear one of the guards fiddling with what sounded like a bunch of keys. He was proved right when he heard one turn in a lock.

Again he was guided into a room and halted and left to stand. Still no one had spoken.

Suddenly the hood was removed and he had to look down away from the harsh overhead light because it was hurting his eyes. As his vision acclimatised to his new surroundings he counted four men besides himself and all larger than he was.

One of the men came to stand in front of him looking squarely into his eyes all the time. He seemed to be the one in charge.

Someone from behind undid the handcuffs allowing the blood to circulate freely. Bringing his arms forward brought a wave of instant relief and he took the opportunity to massage his wrists. But the respite was short lived. The one in his face ordered him to strip.

At first he thought that he had misheard the command and was actually thinking of refusing to comply when he was suddenly and very painfully brought to his knees by a vicious blow to his kidneys from behind. Before he had even had time to think he was hauled back to his feet by two of the guards still gasping with the pain. Quickly, realizing the futility of resisting, he slowly began to undress.

As each item of clothing was removed one of the guards placed it in a large paper sack. Eventually he was standing in just his underwear. Naively he thought he would be allowed to keep them on. He was sadly mistaken when the same guard as before said, "Underwear too."

Reluctantly he removed his underwear, ashamed to be seen naked in the presence of these men. He felt humiliated by the whole experience and very, very vulnerable. Sadly the humiliation was not over.

One of the guards had just put on a pair of sterile gloves and had a grin on his face that he dearly wanted to smash. He was ordered to spread his legs and to bend over. He complied with the order even though his mind fought against it. It was both a humiliating and degrading thing that he had just been ordered to do.

The prisoner may have thought the procedure was unnecessary but the fact remained that any number of things could have been secreted up his anus. Just ask anyone on the prison service.

The procedure having been endured, appeared to be over. He stood still, completely naked and watched as the guard with the keys unlocked the door. They left him alone in the room; the clang of the metal door still echoing in his ears long after they had left the room.

He took the opportunity to survey his surroundings and did a mental inventory of the room. It was made of smooth solid concrete, not breeze block he noted. Quite large, 10 x 10 and 9 feet in height he calculated. Almost a cube he idly thought. The door was solid metal, no spy hole or grill and no internal handle, just a key hole. A light was set into a recess in the ceiling with a protective metal grill over it. There was no visible means in the room for switching it on or off so obviously it was controlled by someone outside the room. Along one wall was a metal framed platform at the moment raised up. Pulling it down he could see that it doubled as both a chair and a sleeping platform. A very thin mattress was somehow attached to the frame. There was no pillow. Over in one corner was a stainless steel toilet; both the seat and lid had been removed. A new roll of toilet paper stood beside it on the floor. A tiny stainless steel sink complete with cold water tap only completed the room's furnishings. Oh! And a plastic beaker, must not forget that and that was it; it was very spartan and deliberately so, he realised.

Sitting on the bed he had no concept of time. He had tentatively at first taken a few sips of water with no noticeable adverse side effects so reasoned that it was probably safe to drink. He knew for a fact that he was being constantly monitored but hadn't managed to spot a camera. It was probably mounted near the light fitting he reckoned and that is why he hadn't spotted it.

A key inserted in the door announced the arrival of two guards. One entered the room and handed him a rough woollen blanket, a pair of black shorts, a white t-shirt and a pair of flip flops, the other guard waited in the corridor, they both then left; all without a word.

He quickly donned the clothing glad to be at least partially clothed again; he draped the rough blanket across his shoulders. It smelled of cat piss and he wondered if that was actually what it was. He didn't really care it provided some warmth and was certainly better than nothing.

Sometime later he was woken by the door rattling and swinging inwards, two guards told him, "On your feet."

He just had time to slip his feet into the flip flops before he was marched a short distance to another room. Inside were two guards standing and a man dressed in everyday clothes seated at a table.

He was instructed to sit in the vacant chair by one of the guards and did so.

The man opposite him gave him a cursory glance then returned to studying what appeared to be a file.

After a while James Martin closed the file, lifted his head and looked directly at the prisoner. Taking a pen from inside his jacket pocket he readied it for action by clicking it and then said, "Right let's begin shall we? Name?"

The prisoner stared defiantly back and said nothing.

Waiting a few seconds James Martin said, "One more chance, Name?"

Again the prisoner said nothing and fully expected the rough treatment to begin. When it didn't happen he was surprised and slightly baffled. Instead he was taken back to his cell and locked in.

The file in front of James Martin was just empty pages, a mere prop nothing more. It was just something with which to occupy his hands whilst he studied this unknown individual. The prisoner's clothing had revealed nothing, just some loose change. No identification on his person marked him out to be a pro. If he continued to remain silent there were other options available to him and he wouldn't hesitate to use them if need be, but he was banking on the gun recovered from the apartment for a break through. He was hoping that it had history. He had ordered the ballistics to be fast tracked and realised that by now the gun would have been test fired and be in the process of being matched with those on the police data base. If a match could be found he would have something to confront the prisoner with.

Martin yawned involuntarily it had been a long day and he was ready to go home. He was certain that the prisoner would crack eventually; after all he had all the time in the world!

Before he left the building he had given instructions to withhold food for the prisoner for another twelve hours. Hunger tended to focus the mind reasoned Martin as he drove home.

Chapter 24

Luke had just made one complete circuit of the sofa with Adam. He was supporting Adam who was gripping his fingers as they took the corner into lap two. In truth it was Adam himself who was supporting his own weight through his legs.

Luke thought to himself, another week my son and you will be doing this on your own, and then the real fun and games will begin.

Approaching the end of lap two, Adam stalled to look out onto the still bare garden.

Luke asked Adam, "Where's mum Adam?"

Adam looked up at the ceiling pointing then said, "Mum"

"That's right mum is upstairs," added Luke.

Having nothing of real interest to look at, Adam regained his second wind and was ready for lap three. Coming hot on to the long straight Adam stopped and looked over towards the telephone then clearly said, "Yasmin."

Luke knew his son, so quickly scooping him up and making him giggle in the process, they got to the telephone just as it rang. Luke picked it up and said, "Hi Yasmin."

Taken aback Yasmin on the other end of the line said, "Luke, how did you know it was me?"

Luke faked it and said, "Inspired intuition Yasmin. What's up?"

There were a couple of seconds delay whilst Yasmin mulled over Luke's vague response, then she said, "I'm ringing about Chris actually Luke."

"Chris! What about Chris? Is there a problem?" asked a concerned Luke.

"I'm not sure Luke, I hope not anyway. This morning when Frank and I arrived home from the club we found Chris passed out at the bottom of the stairs drunk. I don't know what is going on with him but he hasn't been in to work and quite frankly I'm worried about him. Look I think you should know from what little sense Frank could get out of him I think he and Seline have broken up," finished Yasmin. Now it made sense, what Luke had predicted would happen had happened and Chris had come off worst in the encounter. Meanwhile Adam could clearly hear Yasmin's voice whilst being held by his dad decided to try out his new word. Pointing at the telephone in Luke's hand he said, "Yasmin."

"Luke was that Adam?" asked a clearly excited Yasmin.

"Yes it was, his new word for the day," admitted Luke. Luke eyeballed his son and winked.

Adam looked at his dad trying and failing spectacularly to copy him, by closing both eyes.

Yasmin couldn't see this interplay between father and son of course, but decided that Adam's new word merited a visit. She asked Luke, "Is it alright if Frank and I come to visit?"

"Of course it is Yasmin," answered Luke."I'll have the kettle boiled by the time you arrive."

As Luke ended the call Adam announced the arrival of "Mum" pointing in her direction.

Claire came up for a hug saying, "What have I missed?"

Luke kissed her making Adam squeal and told Claire Adam's new word. He also told her that Yasmin and Frank were on their way over and that Seline and Chris had broken up.

"Wow, I was only kidding when I asked what I had missed," said Claire amazed.

Chapter 25

M.I.6. Building, London.

Doug Simons had the ballistics report for the prisoner's hand gun on his desk, ready for when his boss James Martin arrived. He knew that he would want it pronto.

He had also cross checked with the ballistics report on the Almeda slayings but sadly they weren't a match. The Almeda's had been killed with a .45 calibre handgun and the one recovered from the apartment was .38 calibre, a different type of weapon entirely, but the test firing of the .38 had revealed that it had been used twice before in two unsolved murders.

Doug read the report. One unsolved murder victim in Birmingham, about nineteen months ago. By all accounts Mohammed Khan was a moderate teacher from a faith school, who was shot and killed outside his school. One shot to the back of the head according to eye witness accounts. He apparently spoke out in favour of religious tolerance and closer links between all faiths. The police had had no leads and no-one had ever been charged in connection with the murder.

The second murder was more recent, eleven months ago in Leicester, Doug noted. A prominent business man Mehmet Hassan. He wrote a column in the local 'Leicester Clarion' denouncing the barbarity of so called honour killings. Someone obviously disagreed with his philosophy, thought Doug, because it earned him a bullet to the back of his head for having the guts to speak out.

Doug wrote down all the relevant facts for his boss, leaving out the more mundane parts. He attached a photograph of the two unsolved murdered men to his notes with satisfaction. If this helped his boss to nail this son-of-a-bitch, thought Doug, then this would be one less murderous fucker walking the streets.

When James Martin came into the room looking for his underlings, Doug thought that his boss looked drawn and very tired. He knew that his boss had been putting in sixteen hour days for quite some time. It was beginning to show; he didn't look healthy at all.

Straight to the point Martin asked, "Have you got the ballistics report?"

Doug handed it over and brought his boss up to speed on the .38's previous history.

Martin's eyes lit up clearly pleased with the good news. "Thanks Doug ...finally we might have the fucker."

Doug watched his boss head out of the building with the report in his hand. There was a definite spring in his step that hadn't been there when he had arrived, so perhaps this was the break through that they needed. He certainly hoped so, because so far the prisoner hadn't spoken a word, and they hadn't a clue who he was.

James Martin was already seated and studying the report when the prisoner was escorted into the room.

He lazily sat in the opposite chair waiting for Martin to look up.

When he finally did so he placed a photograph in front of him and said, "Mohammed Khan."

Martin watched the prisoner's momentary flicker of recognition before he managed to mask it.

Carefully placing a second photograph before the prisoner, Martin said, "Mehmet Hassan."

This time the prisoner didn't bother to look at the photograph feigning indifference instead.

It hadn't fooled Martin; clearly the prisoner recognised the name.

The breakthrough came surprisingly quickly when the prisoner angrily asked, "When do I get to see a lawyer?"

Martin looked at him coldly, as if he had asked him something obscene. Managing to stare him down before answering, "First you start to co-operate, then we'll think about a lawyer."

"Well what about some food? I haven't had a fucking thing since I was brought here," challenged the prisoner.

It was obvious to Martin that the prisoner's anger was mounting; he was clearly under a lot of stress, maybe if he pushed a little more, thought Martin.

Maddeningly he offered up the same mantra, "First you start to co-operate ..." was a far as Martin got before the prisoner lunged across the table to try and get to grips with his tormentor.

The guards had been waiting and were ready; in a flash they had him caught in a grip of iron and slammed him back into his chair.

Martin made a deliberate play of putting the photographs back into the folder and then in a quiet but menacing voice said, "Alright, we have asked you nicely, now it's out of my hands."

Martin gave an imperceptible nod to one of the guards who returned the slight gesture.

Martin left the room and walked a short distance away down the corridor to enter another room. It had seating arranged to look through a glassed viewing window into another larger room, from the perspective of people in the other room they saw a mirror instead of a window but most people weren't fooled by it and knew exactly what its purpose was. It was also wired for sound and Martin switched on the microphone in order to hear.

He donned a headset so that he could communicate with the head guard when they arrived with the prisoner. A short time later, the guards brought in a fully restrained prisoner. The head guard looked to the mirror and said something quietly into his head set.

Martin confirmed that he was receiving loud and clear.

Once that was confirmed and without further delay the prisoner was held down and the water boarding began.

Martin looked on dispassionately as the prisoner bucked and writhed in an effort to try and escape his torturers. It wasn't that Martin was particularly cruel or sadistic, he wasn't. He merely saw the prisoner as someone who was an enemy of his people and by that definition, his country. Trying to gain information by being humane had yielded nothing so he had had to resort to other tactics, simple as that.

The prisoner was strong, Martin had to give him that, but he knew that it was only a matter of time before he broke and that time was fast approaching. Again the prisoner's head was uncovered allowing him to force the water out of his nostrils and mouth. Taking in great mouthfuls of air he angrily shouted at his tormentors, "Go fuck yourselves."

Martin had to smile as he told the head guard to, "Go again."

The prisoner was held down again, the soaked cloth was replaced over his mouth and nose and the water was poured in a steady stream over the cloth.

It took eight attempts in total before the prisoner broke and agreed to co-operate. Each attempt had lasted a little longer than the one before. The final attempt had Martin worried that the prisoner might actually drown. He breathed a sigh of relief himself when the prisoner finally gave up.

When he was brought back into the original room, now free of restraints Martin, had a word with one of the guards to go get him a large hot coffee. It sat on the table between Martin and the prisoner, the aroma was strong in the air.

Martin pushed the coffee over towards him and nodded that it was alright for him to take it.

Using both hands he held it to his lips and tasted his first hot drink in almost ninety six hours. Martin waited until he had drained the last drop of coffee from the Styrofoam mug then began his questioning.

Once he had started to co-operate fully, Martin had someone bring him scrambled eggs on thick buttered toast.

Everyone watched fascinated as he attacked the meal with hardly a pause for breath.

Martin had enjoyed breaking the prisoner as he had proved to be a tough adversary and he had a sneaking admiration for his fortitude. Jamal ldrisi had earned James Martin's respect.

Once Idrisi had finished eating, the interrogation

continued without pause until Martin had got what he wanted.

Finally satisfied Martin had Idrisi taken back to his room where he was given clean jeans, a sweat shirt and a 'v' neck t-shirt. He was also given a thick pair of woollen socks and a new pair of size 9 trainers. The interrogation now over he was brought another hot strong coffee and left alone to drink it.

Meanwhile, Martin had despatched a team to check out Idrisi's address; a flat in Islington. Everything would be gone over with a fine tooth comb. If there was anything of importance to find Martin knew that they would find it. Idrisi also owned an old Toyota car and that too would be brought back to the workshops and taken apart.

Now that Idrisi had given up the information Martin felt ... jaded. It was always the same with him, he pushed himself for long hours and days at a stretch, until he had achieved his goal, then once he had attained his goal he felt a little deflated and at a loss as to what his next one would be.

As Martin headed back to M.I.6 he was a little more upbeat with himself, thinking one down only five million to go.

Chapter 26

I had been lying awake for what seemed like hours and I knew that was wrong because I had slept but it felt like I hadn't. Adam's new mobile status had been on, my mind, correction; Adam was always on my mind. Luke had mentioned that given another week Adam would be walking unaided, but the worrying thing was it hadn't been another week it had only been two days and now Adam was freely walking on his own. We now had safety gates fitted at the top and bottom of the stairs. They were necessary, as Adam was into everything.

Just yesterday Yasmin had called round to spend some time with us. She had seen Adam's animal book and picked it up with the intention of naming all the animals for him. Pointing out the first few animals Adam allowed her to name them without interruption but she was absolutely gob smacked, that is the only way I can describe it, when they reached E for Elephant , Adam deliberately moved Yasmin's hand away and pointing at it himself said, "Elephant."

Adam then continued through his book page by page pointing and correctly naming each animal in turn, only stopping when he had reached Z for Zebra. Then with a flourish closed the book got down off the sofa and went to look for some other stimuli.

I had looked on from the wings making occasional eye contact with a wide eyed Yasmin. I shrugged my shoulders at Yasmin's querying look both proud of Adam and genuinely concerned at the same time.

Yasmin said, "Your son is very, very clever."

What could I say except, "I know," but I did add, "I am worried about him not having other children around to play with." It seemed that Adam only had adults in his life and ... maybe that was the problem.

Ever the practical Yasmin said, "Take him to the park, maybe if he see's other children playing he will want to join in."

So that is what I proposed to do and the reason why I was awake. I heard Luke come in and make his way upstairs. He looked in on Adam as he always did before coming into our bedroom. Quickly getting undressed he slid in behind me and we spooned. We talked for a while and I was going to mention that I planned on going to the park with Adam but Luke's rhythmic breathing told me that he had drifted off. Not long afterwards I joined him in dreamless sleep.

Later I left the warmth of Luke's side and had a quick shower and got dressed, saw to Adam and dressed him for going out. After breakfast I made up a juice drink for Adam and some bread and jam sandwiches in case we needed a snack. I was reminded with fondness of my own childhood, growing up in Lincoln I practically lived on bread and jam sandwiches in those days. With sadness I thought of my mum wishing, not for the first time, that she could have been here for Adam, she would have known what to do.

Leaving a note for Luke, simply saying, gone to the park with Adam, I placed Adam in the pushchair and headed off to the park. The weather forecast had predicted warm and sunny and it proved to be right for a change.

On reaching the play area I negotiated the staggered gateway struggling with the push chair. It was sad to think that everything nowadays seemed to need protecting, in one way or another, from mindless vandals trashing the kids swings to talentless graffiti artists spray painting anything not moving.

I headed for a vacant bench seat and parked the push chair, still holding a wide eyed Adam, beside it. There was only one other young woman there, with whom I presumed was her daughter. The woman was pushing the girl, who looked about three, ever higher in the swings and she was obviously enjoying the experience from the squeals of delight that she was making.

Adam couldn't take his eyes off the girl except to look up at me, the obvious question begging in his eyes. Looking Adam in the eye I asked him, "Do you want a go?"

For his answer he got out of his push chair and grabbing me by the hand led me to the swings.

I said, "Hello," to the young woman and watched as Adam seated himself on the swings. I positioned Adam's hands on both support chains making sure he was sat correctly and told him to grip firmly. He seemed to be totally captivated by what the young girl was doing so I reminded him to hold onto the chains. Then tentatively, I started to gently push him backwards and forwards. Adam must have enjoyed the experience because he squealed out in absolute delight.

The girl, who was swinging much more freely and ever higher, kept glancing sideways at Adam. He obviously wanted to match her so reminding him to hold on tight I pushed him higher and higher. To say that it was Adam's first time on the swings it was a masterful performance but after five minutes Adam had the swings mastered much to the delight of both children.

After a few minutes of swings the young woman introduced herself as Helen Moore and her daughter was Elizabeth, Lizzie to her friends.

I introduced myself to Helen then lamely said, "This is Adam and we call him Adam."

She must have thought that I was either stupid or a little touched in the head but if she did, gratefully she failed to mention it.

With the swings mastered, Lizzie now wanted to introduce Adam to the slide. It wasn't particularly high as slides go, but to Adam it must have looked like the north face of the Eiger. Adam held tightly to my hand as he watched Lizzie eagerly climb the ladder. He couldn't help but notice that this was an entirely solo effort and if he wanted to join in with Lizzie it would have to be by his own efforts and un-aided, mum wouldn't be there to hold him. He watched Lizzie execute a perfect slide. He looked on weighing up the dangers of this daunting piece of apparatus.

Lizzie was making her second ascent of the ladder, watched closely by Adam, the delight on Lizzie's face must have finally overcome Adam's caution.

Letting go of my hand he looked at me for reassurance and I nodded saying, "Only if you are sure."

I stayed behind him as he slowly climbed the ladder while thinking christ I hope he doesn't fall. Adam was careful at the top seating himself correctly, just as he had seen Lizzie do. Making my way to the front, ready to catch him, I watched Adam launch himself down the chute squealing with delight,

thrilling at the sensations that he must be experiencing. Collecting a beaming Adam at the bottom he couldn't wait to go again. Before letting him go to join a waiting Lizzie I told him to be careful. And that was it Adam had mastered the slide and gained his first girlfriend.

Helen and I retired to a nearby bench and watched them both taking turns on the slide. It was absolutely wonderful watching Adam and Lizzie play and laugh, having fun. A great weight had suddenly been lifted from my shoulders watching Adam and Lizzie playing in the sunshine.

Helen must have assumed that Adam was close to Lizzie's age. I didn't contradict her otherwise I'm sure that she would have been truly shocked to learn that Adam wasn't even half her daughter's age.

Once they had tired of sliding I coaxed Adam over for a drink of his juice. That is when I introduced everyone to my famous jam sandwiches. Lizzie was the first to succumb. First looking and then sniffing before taking a nibble of one corner. The delight on her face proved to everyone that it was both edible and nice to eat. Everyone, including Helen had at least one.

It had been an enjoyable few hours with Helen and Lizzie but it was time for us to head off home. We said our goodbyes and going home via the long way through the park I still had one more treat for Adam. One slice of bread minus the jam was destined for the ducks. I let Adam out of the push chair once more to see the ducks up close. The ducks helped Adam out by coming closer when his pieces of bread landed short. It was an extra few minutes of frivolity and it was wonderful.

Once we had bid goodbye to the ducks but before we left the park, I did something else. Almost without thinking I removed Adam's shoes and socks; encouraging him to run through the grass so that he could feel it between his toes. His laughter ringing in my ears told me far more than words ever could.

When we arrived home Luke was already up. Once freed from his push chair and still without his shoes and socks on Adam headed straight for his dad who hoisted him up, dirty feet, and all.

"How did it go?" asked Luke eyeing Adam's dirty feet. Without hesitation Claire answered, "Absolutely wonderfully" with a smile like sunshine.

Chapter 27

Deep underground Doug Simons made his way along the dimly lit corridors of M.I.6 where the air was both warm and stale. Doug was in search of his boss, James Martin, and cursing quietly to himself and not for the first time either, questioned just why his boss would choose to have an office in such an unhealthy atmosphere. The light was bad, the air too, so why? He just couldn't fathom it out, it wasn't natural, but then again neither was his boss thought Doug.

Eventually Doug found himself outside his boss' lair. He knocked once and entered without being asked. He found his boss standing leaning over a large map spread across his desk and looking closely through a large magnifying glass at one particular highlighted area. The large scale map Doug could see was of Afghanistan. Martin was so engrossed in what he was doing he hadn't even registered Doug's presence. He was clearly startled when Doug said, "Got a minute sir?"

Recovering his composure Martin seemed to come back from wherever he had just been and said, "What's on your mind Doug?"

"Jamal ldrisi sir," answered Doug.

"Oh, what about him?" said Doug his curiosity aroused.

"Well the fact is sir I have been thinking about him," said Doug tentatively.

"Why?" said Martin, clearly at a loss as to why Doug should be thinking about Idrisi.

Doug was unsure how to frame his thoughts when met with Martin's abrupt response. Stumbling on Doug had another go, "Well all the searches carried out by the team have come back negative on him having any links or affiliation with terrorist organisations. Idrisi's parents, though both born in Pakistan, raised no flags either, in fact sir, ever since coming to this country they both appear to have been hard working law abiding citizens. Idrisi himself was born and raised here with no concerns either. Idrisi's parents, now dead, had no other living relatives, just their son Jamal," said Doug.

"I'm not sure I'm following you Doug, why the concern for Idrisi? He is a killer who we managed to flush out and capture. A good result for the team surely," said Martin.

"Yes sir, I agree, but if he is sent to prison for the next 25 to 30 years I just think that it might be a

waste," answered Doug.

"Now you have definitely grabbed my attention Doug, spell it out for me," nodded Martin intrigued.

"This is what I'm thinking sir from the team's findings on Idrisi," Doug ticked off what his ordered brain had come up with to his boss. "He is neither motivated by religion or politics, he is not a member of, or affiliated to, any terrorist organisations that we know of, his only motivation or vice if you will, seems to be money," finished Doug.

Martin looked at Doug long and hard making him feel uncomfortable before asking, "So what is it you are actually proposing Doug?"

"That we offer Idrisi a job sir. Ask him to come and work for us," said Doug.

"But Doug, that would mean letting a known killer walk away scot free, not only that, we would be complicit in allowing it to happen," added Martin. "You yourself Doug, if I'm not mistaken, wanted this fucker off the streets, isn't that so? So what has changed?" asked Martin.

Doug could see his boss was mulling over the pros and cons of what he had just delivered and didn't want to interrupt him whilst he was thinking. Clearly Martin's interest in Doug's proposals had taken root; the stare into space was a sure fire sign.

"Just supposing we manage to bring Idrisi over to our side Doug, there would be no guarantee that somewhere down the line he would try to fuck us over, what then?" queried Martin.

"Well we have his two statements admitting to the murders he committed and of course we have the gun," counted Doug.

"Those two statements could be construed as given under duress Doug," parried Martin, "what's to stop him retracting them? He only needs a good defence lawyer and a half sympathetic jury and he is home free."

"Perhaps sir, but if I were in Idrisi's position and facing 30 years in prison I think I would take the job offer. If we offered to pay his rent and put a decent wedge into his bank account monthly I think that would prove a real incentive, being as we know his motivation is money."

Martin had listened to Doug's proposals with interest, "I

see you have given this a lot of thought Doug, how come?" asked Martin.

"Well sir, given how easily Idrisi slipped underneath our radar but most importantly the police's, and given how long he was able to resist interrogation before caving in, I realised that he could be a very valuable asset that we could use sir," finished Doug.

Martin sat quietly for a while obviously thinking of all the pitfalls ahead for such a bold endeavour.

Again Doug didn't interrupt his bosses thought processes. He knew that he would come up with a solution when he had it all worked out.

"Of course we would have to give him another identity," said Martin, "and maybe a change of address to another area of London. The motor pool will have to sort him out a decent car too, that Toyota of his is fucked," added Martin, ticking off the things Idrisi would need.

Doug was secretly delighted that his boss now seemed to be totally on board with his ideas but had just one concern that he needed to voice.

"Of course we would have to keep close track of him sir. I suggest for the first six months at least just in case he decides to do a runner."

"That goes without saying Doug, that's a given, but, and I insist on this Doug, it only happens if the top floor sanction it. I refuse to put our arses on the line for Jamal Idrisi without it, agreed?" said

Martin.

"Agreed sir," parroted Doug.

"Right I'll see if I can set up a meeting with the boss," said Martin.

Chapter 28

It had been one whole week since the soft drinks box van had been stolen from the industrial estate just outside Alicante.

The perpetrator of the theft had been living and working in Alicante for the past eight years.

Abu Barzan, a Moroccan by birth, had been waiting for the call ever since his arrival in Spain. He had had help in finding both accommodation and a job. Keeping well under the radar of both the police and homeland security he made it his mission in life to fit in.

Almost eight years of being a model citizen until the call to arms had come. Admittedly his part was only a small one, but vital all the same. After all, he was only one small link in a very long chain. When the call finally came he did what was asked of him following the instructions to the letter.

His task was to steal a small box van and change the

vehicle's number plates. Once this was completed he was to drive the stolen vehicle to an address on an industrial estate two miles outside of Benidorm. The toll booths were the only place where something could have gone wrong as there was always a police presence there. The changed number plates saw him safely past the toll booths and on his way.

He had a little trouble finding the building on the industrial estate but apart from that everything had gone smoothly. Once the van had been delivered it was no longer Barzan's problem. He had been driven back to Alicante to resume getting on with his life as a model citizen once more. That had been a week ago.

Once the box van had been delivered the two men who had taken delivery looked on in dismay as they opened the van's rear doors. The interior of the van was filled to capacity with plastic crates filled with empty glass bottles. They realized they would have the un-enviable task of unloading all the crates by hand.

Once the crates had been unloaded and stacked out of the way, the bomb could be placed centrally and secured to the floor. They hadn't planned on using the crates and glass bottles as shrapnel but realised that it presented the perfect opportunity to get rid of them.

Once the bomb had been secured, the crates were tightly packed back into the van. The bomb was now completely hidden by the stacked crates. The designated driver had already been contacted and had been instructed precisely as to what his part in the operation would be. He was fully prepared for martyrdom. Just like the fake ambulance driver in Istanbul he had been prepared but it was explained to him again that martyrdom was not required of him this day. His task was to park the van where it would cause the most casualties and then remotely detonate the bomb from a safe distance.

The driver of the bomb laden truck Mahmood Yafai was sweating profusely, but it wasn't from fear,

it was just unfortunate that the van's air conditioning had ceased to function. The temperature outside the vehicle was making it an uncomfortable ride, his shirt stuck to his back. Yafai, a Syrian by birth, had lived in Spain for almost three years and he knew Benidorm quite well so that's why he had obeyed the call to arms, just another link in an endless chain.

His instructions were to drive the van through the narrow streets that made up Benidorm's old town. Once he had driven to where the tourists and locals alike liked to eat out for lunch he was to park up, blocking the narrow road and in the process snarl up any traffic. He was now two minutes from carrying out his orders.

The traffic was heavy and pedestrians stepping out in front of him made for slow progress. It didn't worry him unduly; he wasn't tied to a strict time table as such. He breathed out slowly calming himself down; he was making steady progress, just a little further. Another few minutes driving brought Mahmood Yafai to his ultimate destination. Slamming on his brakes he almost caused the driver behind to run into him. The driver gave vent to his feelings by leaning on his horn blasting

Yafai.

Yafai grinned saying to himself, blast away, soon you will be in hell. Removing the ignition key he left the van much to the annoyance and frustration of the other, now grid locked drivers.

Yafai was seeking safety and needed to get a reasonable distance from the van. He also needed to put something solid between him and the explosion. Quickly making his way through the crowds, Yafai spotted a sturdy looking building that suited his needs. Now shielded by a heavy column that was holding up a cross beam Yafai punched in the pre-programmed number.

The explosion and the concussive forces knocked Yafai to his knees even shielded as he was from the worst of the blast by the column. He was still dazed and disorientated; his ears had been damaged and were bleeding, such was the force of the explosion. Shaken and a little dizzy Yafai knew that he had to get away from here and quickly.

Looking back he saw that the van was no longer visible, nor was the angry motorist's vehicle who only a few seconds ago had blasted him with his horn. Yafai staggered unsteadily away leaving the devastation that he had caused behind him.

The massed pedestrian streets that had been so full of life only moments before had been scythed clear, the dozens upon dozens of tables and chairs occupied only moments before had been blasted together to form a scene from hell. People both whole and dismembered had been blown together to form some obscene tableau from Dante.

Tables and chairs, which a short time ago had been occupied with living people, now formed a macabre and almost impenetrable barrier across the once beautiful vista. There wasn't a window left whole, most of the buildings had suffered blast damage but had remained mainly whole and were still standing.

The blast had been funnelled along by the buildings themselves. The narrow roads and open spaces had borne the brunt of the explosion clearing them of people, but if the badly injured survivors, and there were many of them, thought that their ordeal was over they were sadly mistaken.

Help was on its way but evil was already there.

Phase one of Abdul Rahman's plans had been completed, phase two was only minutes away.

Phase two consisted of a three man sleeper cell that had been long embedded in Benidorm's bustling hotel culture. The call had come and they had answered.

They had been called upon to make the supreme sacrifice. The weapons had been delivered two days ago; machine guns with six full magazines, a hand gun each with four clips of ammunition and four hand grenades each. Their task was to wait nearby until after the explosion and then slowly make their way towards it. Their mission was to kill the emergency personnel; doctors, paramedics, firemen and police. The emphasis was to kill the police as they would be the ones bearing arms.

All three men had prepared their bodies beforehand so it just remained for them to stay out of sight until after the explosion. Instructions had been precise: wait until the emergency services had begun to arrive then co-ordinate their attack giving one anther mutual aid. The final instruction from Abdul Rahman himself was to inflict as many casualties as possible and God willing, I will see you soon in paradise.

The sirens of the emergency services could be heard all over Benidorm as they homed in on the old town.

The three man group headed for ground zero readying their machine guns as they went.

Up ahead a police car was already on scene trying to organise a way through for an ambulance.

One of the gun men shot the young policeman before he had even had time to realize that he was under attack. The female officer quickly followed him into the afterlife.

Badly injured survivors, some of them themselves

on the brink of death, looked on incredulous at this new atrocity. One of the gun men waved the ambulance forward, apparently trying to guide it through and then stepped in front of it, callously shooting the driver through the windscreen. His companion couldn't take in what he had just witnessed when the gunman casually opened the driver's door, aimed and fired. Shock was still written on his face as he bled out joining his companion in death.

A young woman in an upstairs room had just witnessed what had happened. She rang the already overloaded emergency number, miraculously someone answered.

The young woman's name was Sophia and she relayed to the operator what she had just witnessed, she wasn't sure whether the female emergency operator had believed her but pressed on, trying to sound as rational as possible.

Eventually the operator believed what Sophia was telling her and she asked, "Sophia, whereabouts are you calling from?"

"I'm in my apartment building on the 2nd floor across the street from where the explosion occurred."

The operator asked, "Sophia, are you injured at all?"

"No just a little shaken up that's all and all the windows have been blown in."

"Sophia I now have someone from the authorities with me, can you tell me once again what you have just told me please?"

"Yes of course, three men armed with guns have just shot two police personnel and the two ambulance personnel." It was obvious to Sophia that the operator, as well as recording the conversation, was also transcribing it. The operator read it back to Sophia word for word and asked her if it was correct.

"Yes that's right," she added, "they seem to be targeting

them, specifically."

The operator must have relayed what she had been told to someone else because after a short pause the operator then asked, "What are the gunmen doing now?"

"They seem to be waiting for the emergency services to get here." Sophia told her.

"Alright Sophia now listen carefully, I want you to keep the connection open but first go and barricade your door with something heavy, can you do that now?"

After what seemed a long time, but actually wasn't, Sophia came back on the line to tell the operator, "I have done it."

"That's good Sophia," the operator began....

But Sophia broke in. "Wait... .. I hear a motorcycle let me go see." Sophia looked out of the glassless window to see a police motor cycle approaching the ambulance with the two dead men inside it. She could also see one of the gunmen waiting out of sight behind the ambulance. Sophia relayed to the operator what she was seeing. The motor cyclist had just drawn level with the ambulance, as it went to go passed the gunman stepped out and shot him in the back.

The motor cycle fell heavily onto the road trapping the policeman beneath it. It was clear to Sophia that he was still alive at this point. As she kept in contact with the operator another gunman surprised Sophia when he stepped out of concealment and shot the policeman once in the chest.

The operator heard the gasp as it caught in Sophia's throat. She had also heard the two shots that

Sophia had described. It was now time for some serious muscle to be sent the operator realised.

Someone had to deal with these murderers, people were dying.

Spain's equivalent of the U.K.'s S.A.S. were now being hastily mobilized and would be on route in minutes.

Unknown to Sophia at that time she would play a pivotal role in the terrorists' downfall.

Meanwhile the police were concentrating on co-ordinating their efforts at the promenade end of the old town. They had managed to prevent any more people entering the old town from that end but the old town was a warren of narrow streets that presented a myriad means of access. It would take time and a lot of manpower to both clear the streets and block them off.

Part of the beachfront area had been cleared of people ready for the arrival of the Spanish Special Forces helicopters. The police had been advised of the two helicopters' imminent arrival.

The noisy approach of the two black military type helicopters was watched by thousands of people lined up along the promenade. Television station vans captured the images live, beaming them into people's living rooms. The press would have photographs and stories gracing the front pages of the world's leading newspapers for days to come.

The two helicopters approached from the Levante beach end going slightly out to sea, before sweeping back in to the designated area, they hovered about 80 feet whipping up a mini sandstorm before disgorging two sets of five black clad figures from the body of the machines.

Abseiling down by ropes the S.S. forces quickly made their way to the promenade. As soon as the last man's feet touched the sand the helicopters veered away in the direction they had come? Still trailing ropes.

The S.S. forces gathered on the promenade, one of them liaising with the senior policeman on site. After a quick discussion the S.S. forces men made their way down into the old town. Splitting into five man teams they took the most direct route to the site of the explosion.

The lead man of each team was in direct contact with the S.S. forces controller. They were constantly being updated on the gunmen's present whereabouts as they made their way towards them.

Sophia was the vital cog in the machine and without her they would be travelling blind. The emergency operator kept feeding information to the controller who in turn kept his men apprised of the changing situation on the ground.

The gunmen couldn't fail to hear the arrival of the two helicopters, knowing full well what the machines had brought with them. Hastily they looked for a place that they could defend. The building behind the ambulance, an office block, looked as good a place as any in which to make a last stand they decided, so embracing one another for a last time they entered the building.

Sophia had watched them from her vantage point and passed it on to the operator.

Several shots could be heard coming from the building, before Sophia saw one of the gunmen preparing a barricade at one of the windows on the second floor. This information was swiftly passed on to the operator.

The leaders of each of the S.S. forces teams had been apprised of the changing situation and now knew that they faced a foe ready to engage with them.

It didn't make any difference because they had trained day in and day out for just this type of situation. The bonus in this occasion was that they knew exactly what they faced; the information was pure gold as far as they were concerned.

As the S.S. forces teams got nearer to the blast site the badly injured and dying victims got thicker on the ground.

It was heart breaking to see these badly injured people's futile attempt at trying to raise an arm in a plea for help to these black clad figures, only for them to be ignored as they passed on by.

The S.S. forces men had to harden their hearts to the feeble cries for help as they came upon more and more dying people among the dead. Their orders had been clear; in order to help the injured, the gunmen had to be dealt with first, so that is what they were going to do. The two teams could now see the ambulance parked in front of the target building, but first they had to negotiate a six foot high barricade made up of blast blown tables, chairs and ... people they realised. The leader of one of the teams described to his commander what they were seeing. The scene was affecting the

teams; no one had ever seen anything like it. By-passing the barricade by using the shops on either end of it the two teams approached the gunmen. When they were about 100 yards away one of the gunmen opened fire on the S.S. forces. The shots were wild and widely inaccurate stopping after a short burst.

Both teams fanned out, moving steadily forward they used every scrap of cover, which fortunately there was plenty of. Both teams were now close enough to fire tear gas grenades through the buildings blast damaged windows.

On the given signal tear gas grenades were fired and as soon as the gas began to do its work two men from each team raced for the building. Shots from the upstairs windows went wildly over the

S.S. forces heads and were met with a hail of fire in return. The gun men dropped to the floor preferring something solid between them and the deadly hail. The S.S. forces men, now in the building, had managed to reach the top of the stairs unscathed. They were ready with two flash bangs, designed to disorientate, to throw into the room at the given signal. Before the explosions had had time to fully dissipate, the other two S.S. forces men were in the room, guns levelled.

The first gunman was shot twice before he had time to act. The second gunman was just bringing his weapon up ready to shoot when he was cut down by shots from two S.S. forces men.

The tear gas was just beginning to clear as the hunt for the third gunman continued. A sudden movement from behind an office desk caught the eye of one of the S.S. forces men. He just had time to recognize a grenade as it was thrown, shouting out the warning, "Incoming", before catching it with the toe of his boot and sending it back to its owner. He just managed to hit the floor as the grenade exploded. The desk was now no longer functional and only fit for firewood. Amazingly the third gunman was still alive, just. He looked like a porcupine, his body peppered with multiple shards of wood. His eyes were still shining in defiance as one of the S.S. forces team finished him off.

The dust from the explosions and the tear gas had only just cleared when the team leader confirmed that the three gunmen had been neutralised. The commander of the Spanish Special Forces teams wasted no time in getting the emergency services moving.

As the first paramedics and doctors began to arrive at the scene the Special Forces men, their job now completed, disappeared back into anonymity.

Sophia, who had played such a crucial part in ending the threat posed by the gunmen, would eventually be honoured by her country as would the anonymous emergency operator.

Abdul Rahman's evil plan had been carried out

spectacularly well, but had it not been for Sophia being in the right place at the right time, many more of the emergency services personnel would certainly have died.

Rahman's plan to kill a large number of British people was a success, as many British did die along with a large number of Spanish. In all the number of dead and injured in the Benidorm old town explosion would encompass people from twenty four countries. The final death toll would not be known for several months; the survivors would have to live on, the lost limbs and scars upon their bodies a constant reminder. Some would never recover, their minds replaying the atrocity over and over, lost in their own private hell.

All the dead and injured were innocent victims of Abdul Rahman's twisted ideology, but the frightening thing was, Rahman's evil blue print could be carried out again and again, by anyone, and not only that, it could be visited upon in any town or city anywhere in the world. Nowhere was safe it just needed evil to make it happen.

Later a D.V.D. showing Rahman's evil face would be delivered to the Spanish government in Madrid. He would claim responsibility for the atrocity but would blame the British government for having forced his hand.

The British government would also receive a D.V.D. from Rahman, this one also claiming responsibility for Benidorm and promising that Britain could look forward to a similar event, happening very soon.

It was clear that Abdul Rahman intended to carry on with his reign of terror so he had to be stopped.

The bombing of Benidorm's old town had only managed to increase the West's determination to find Abdul Rahman, find him and kill him.

Chapter 29

"Go and sit down Yasmin, I can manage the washing up," admonished Claire.

"No I want to help," offered Yasmin.

"Well alright if you insist," said Claire, handing her a tea towel, "you dry!"

After a few dishes had been dried and stacked ready for Claire to put away Yasmin offered, ''You know Claire you should get yourself a dishwasher."

"I don't need a dishwasher I find it easier to do the pots and pans immediately after eating," explained Claire, "besides in a household with only two adults and a baby I don't think a dishwasher is necessary and in my opinion they are environmentally unfriendly."

"Wow," said Yasmin, taken aback, "where did all that come from," looking at Claire sideways.

"Oh, sorry, I guess I'm just a frustrated eco warrior

at heart," answered Claire. After a few seconds of quiet reflection Claire broke the silence, "Luke tells me that Chris is back at work, how is he doing?"

"Work wise he seems to have thrown himself back into it whole heartedly, but emotionally I'm really not sure," admitted Yasmin.

"Since his break up with Seline he hasn't been round. I think he is embarrassed for some reason and is avoiding me," added Claire.

"Yes I have spoken with him on matters to do with the club and he seems to be on top of them but other than that, he seems quite withdrawn, vulnerable even," agreed Yasmin.

"Well it had to happen sooner or later," said Claire, "I just wish that it hadn't happened with Seline.

Luke blames himself for having invited her and introducing them at our wedding. It's ridiculous of course, Chris is a grown man after all, but you know Luke, he views the situation as something he himself caused!"

"Chris will get over it Claire. He just needs to, how do you say it, get back on the horse?" replied

Yasmin.

Claire laughed out loud, "I'm not sure that would fit for Chris, Yasmin, but I know what you mean." As they had finished drying and putting way the dishes, pots and pans Claire offered to make coffee.

Once this was done Yasmin took both Luke and Frank through into the living room, indicating to Claire that she was coming back and wanted to talk privately. Going back into the kitchen she pulled the door to, behind her.

Sitting opposite one another cradling mugs of steaming coffee Claire waited for her friend to voice what was on her mind.

"I'm pregnant!" blurted out Yasmin, eyes brimming full, ready to spill.

Claire immediately came around to embrace her friend whose body was wracked with emotion.

When Yasmin had managed to regain control of her emotions and mop up the overspill with tissue

Claire asked, "Does Frank know?"

Wiping her eyes and blowing her nose Yasmin nodded, affirming that he did.

"And?" asked Claire, prompting "what does he think?"

"He thinks it's wonderful," admitted Yasmin, finally regaining control of her emotions. "Better than sliced bread were his exact words when I told him." said Yasmin.

"So what is going on? I thought that you both wanted children," asked a puzzled Claire.

"Oh we do," gushed Yasmin, "it's just been so long happening that I was beginning to think that it never would and I worry that something may go wrong with the baby," admitted Yasmin.

"All mothers think that way Yasmin. Look at the mess that I was in when I found out I was pregnant with Adam," said a relieved Claire.

"You really think so?" asked Yasmin.

"Yes of course I do, you will be fine. You have Frank, Luke and me to help. What more do you need?" laughed Claire. Then on reflection, "Well, maybe a doctor and midwife on hand to pitch in as well," added Claire.

Yasmin laughed, "Yes perhaps we should include them just in case."

After they let the news settle for a few moments Yasmin admitted, "We want to be married as soon as possible before I begin to show."

"What sort of do are you planning on?" asked Claire.

"Register office, just a small affair with the minimum of fuss, I'm thinking of inviting just you, Luke and Adam, Chris and Jimmy, maybe Steve and Antonia, and that's about it really, and a meal afterwards," mused Yasmin.

She was obviously cobbling it together in her mind as she went along thought Claire. "Look, talk it through carefully with Frank, decide on what it is that you both want and when you are ready. We will be there."

"Alright Claire that is a good advice," admitted Yasmin.

"Oh I forgot to mention earlier, but I didn't think the dining table was a fit and proper place to bring it up, Adam is clean at night now and potty trained too, " beamed Claire, obviously very proud of her son.

"Claire that is wonderful news" said Yasmin obviously delighted.

"Yes it is, but he has also developed two worrying traits as well," added Claire finishing her coffee. Yasmin waited for her to finish, concern edging her features.

"Yes! He has leaned a new word ... shit!" admitted Claire with reluctance, "according to Luke he thinks I'm the culprit who taught it him. Apparently I say it half a dozen times a day without even realising."

Yasmin didn't know whether to laugh or cry on discovering Adam's new word so she kept it to herself.

"It is true of course," Claire had to admit Luke was right, "I bang my wrist on the door handle and the word just pops out. I drop a glass on the floor and say oh shit! Well you get my drift. The trouble is Yasmin, Adam's brain at the moment is like a dustbin, he hears a word, stores it up and then blurts it out, usually at the most inopportune moments. It's embarrassing."

This time Yasmin couldn't help laughing.

Claire had to join in it was infectious, laughing along

with her friend. When at last they managed to stifle the hysterics Claire chided Yasmin with the words, "You are not helping Yasmin," which set them both off again.

After a while Yasmin asked, "What is the other thing? You said traits, as in more than one?"

"Oh yes, he has become fascinated with the door keys for some reason. Every time our backs are turned he removes the keys from the front and back doors. I wouldn't mind but I couldn't get out of the house the other day," finished Claire.

Yasmin was laughing again at Claire's misfortune and she felt compelled to join in.

Frank and Luke came to the door wondering what was so funny. Seeing them both standing there with looks of bewilderment on their faces cracked them both up until they were both helpless too. God knows what they were laughing about! All Claire knew was that it was the simple things in life that made it all the more worthwhile, laughter with good friends was one of them.

Chapter 30

Maureen's house, Peterborough

"Michael! Stop playing with the computer game and start laying the table please," yelled Maureen from the kitchen.

"In a minute, I've nearly reached the next level," Michael shouted back.

"Now please!" insisted Maureen, "I know how long your minutes take," she volleyed back.

"Awwww," could be heard as Michael reluctantly switched off the computer.

Maureen, still in the kitchen, muttered, "Just once I'd like him to do something that I ask without having to repeat myself."

Michael, unwilling but compliant began setting out the dining table as requested by his mum. Placing cutlery beside the place mats Michael looked up staring through the large window that looked out over the garden. The garden's boundary was defined by a continuous three foot high privet hedge that was broken only by a centrally fitted wooden gate. Movement on the other side of it had attracted Michael's attention. He stopped what he was doing trying to see what it was. A man looking back at him prompted Michael to call out to his mum, "Mum there's a ... tramp watching us at the bottom of the garden."

Maureen came in from the kitchen wiping her hands on a tea towel, "Where?" she said.

"There look, down by the gate," pointed Michael.

Maureen looked to where Michael was pointing and caught sight of the half hidden watcher.

Michael asked her, "Should I call the police?"

Putting down the tea towel Maureen said, "No. Wait here and keep watch whilst I go and see what he wants."

"Mum no!" protested Michael, "he might be a nutter!"

"Just wait here Michael, please. It will be alright," said Maureen unconvincingly.

Michael watched as his mum walked down the path to confront the watcher at the gate. They seemed to speak at length before, horror of horrors; the man was brought through the gate by his mum.

Michael could see by his appearance, even from this distance, that the man's hair was unkempt and he badly needed a shave but most of all, he was just plain, dirty.

Maddeningly his mum had brought the man inside the house. Michael couldn't help but notice the faint but unmistakable smell of unwashed body. Keeping the dining room table between himself and this unknown person for protection, Michael looked him up and down in obvious distaste.

Maureen surprised Michael by saying, "Dad this is my

son Michael and Michael this is your grandfather."

The look that they gave each other was long and penetrating.

Surprise was etched on Michael's face as they weighed each other up.

Maureen broke their eye contact when all business like, she took charge.

"Right, first things first, dad I'm going to run you a bath."

She waited for the protestations to begin but when they didn't materialize she beckoned her father to follow her upstairs.

He meekly obeyed following in his daughter's footsteps.

Whilst Maureen began running a bath for her father, he rummaged through his back pack eventually emerging with clean underwear, socks, tee shirt and jeans.

Seeing the clean clothing coming out of his back pack Maureen gave a silent thank god. There was soap and shampoo already available for his use but he hadn't got a razor of his own so she made available for his use, David's, her husband. She just hoped that he wouldn't mind too much.

Asking him to put his dirty clothing in the laundry basket Maureen handed him a large bath towel and left him to it.

Michael was all questions on his mum's return, which under the circumstances, was perfectly natural. Dinner was slowed down so that this interloper could join them at the dining table once he had cleaned himself up.

"Mum!" Michael began, "Why is he here? I mean.... I know he's your dad and all that but why now?"

It was a reasonable question to ask thought Maureen, she was asking herself much the same thing, she could guess why of course, knowing her dad's track record, but Michael was her father's grandson so she had to be careful what she said to him.

"Well you know that I haven't seen my father since I was very young, I told you that much," answered Maureen.

Michael nodded, affirming it to be true.

"And I also mentioned that he was living with a woman up north in Durham," added Maureen.

Michael nodded again still following his mum's train of thought.

"Well your aunt Claire and I learned that he had had a son and a daughter to this other woman. Our half brother and sister, who we have never met, I might add." Maureen could see that Michael was fascinated by what she was telling him, but she was struggling with how to word it without making it sound so harsh. In the end Maureen decided that saving her father's feelings just to make him more palatable in the eyes of her son, wasn't the best way to describe him. Besides she thought, it would be doing a disservice to both her and Claire to paint her father as a paragon of virtue.

Truth won out when Maureen said, "Your grandfather, my dad, was a lazy, idle man who preferred to live with women who went out to work in order to keep him. My mum, your nan, was one such woman, so my guess is that his latest wife has had enough of his idleness and finally kicked him out, it's as simple as that."

"But what is he doing here? How did he find us?" insisted Michael.

"He's probably here for what he can get," answered Maureen truthfully.

Michael digested this information with distaste, obviously disappointed with his newly found grandfather's life qualities.

"In all truth Michael I don't really remember that much about him and your aunt Claire doesn't know him at all. And by the way if your grandfather asks you for her address you don't know it! Are we clear Michael?"

This was delivered eye to eye to enforce Maureen's directive. She enforced it once more by saying, "I mean it Michael."

"Alright I hear you" answered Michael sulkily.

Maureen had judged that enough time had elapsed for a major transformation to have occurred in the bathroom. Going upstairs she knocked on the bathroom door, "You decent dad?"

A half-dressed, half decent looking human being opened the door, "Just about."

"Well hand me your dirty clothes and I'll put them in the washer."

Handing them over to his daughter he said, "Thanks Maureen," in that vaguely familiar Geordie dialect.

Coming back downstairs she went to put them in the washing machine and turning it on she left it to work its way through the grime.

A transformation had taken place; what had once been a tramp, in Michael's eyes, now stood a half decent looking man. Michael couldn't help noticing that although his grandfather's hair was greying, it was both full and thick. He quietly hoped that he had inherited these same genes in his own make up; Michael hated the idea of going bald.

Although strangers, they sat to the table together. Maureen had made beef stew and dumplings and the meat was both lean and tender, surrounded by thick vegetables and gravy. It was good tasty fare by anyone's standards and quite filling. Maureen remembered having it at home when her mum was alive; it always seemed to make her nose run then. The one they were eating now achieved the same result.

Gradually over the meal dad coaxed Michael into words of more than one syllable. Maureen remembered when her mum, on the odd occasion spoke about him, she did so with fondness, and told her what a charmer he was. She thought wryly to herself, the bastard's still got it.

After they'd eaten Michael took him to show him his videogames. Maureen didn't mind it gave them a chance to connect and clearing the table she went to wash up, leaving them to it.

David, Maureen's husband was on the afternoon shift and wouldn't be home until after 10p.m. It would be re-heated beef stew for him but he didn't mind, always remarking that it tasted better after the second heating anyway.

She didn't know what he would make of her newly discovered father, the experience was new for them all, but one thing was for sure, after one night's kip on their sofa she had made up her mind, it was 'adios dad and fare thee well'. He wasn't going to become a permanent fixture in their home.

The washing up done, Maureen made them all a mug of tea and brought them through. Michael was showing his granddad the latest game and surprisingly he actually seemed to be able to interact with him. Then it hit Maureen. Her dad must have played video games with his own son, Maureen's half-brother. It made it all the harder to watch, just knowing that he had actually chosen to abandon both Claire and her when they were no more than babies. Then to go and father two more children and for some reason chose to stay with them, well, it made her angry and at the same time envious. She simply couldn't understand why they hadn't been enough for him to want to stay?

Still it was obvious that his latest wife had had enough of him, otherwise he wouldn't be there.

An hour or so later he came to talk with Maureen. Michael was content on his computer so it was no biggie. He explained his own reasoning as to why he was out on his arse, which of course Maureen dismissed as baloney, and took it with a generous pinch of salt. She did prick her ears up though when he told her how he had returned to their old house in Lincoln only to be told that their mum was dead and they had moved away. This was genuine news to him as no one had kept in touch. But how could they have and more importantly, why would they? He had abandoned them after all a lifetime ago, and besides they only had a vague idea of where he was living.

Eventually he had managed to track Maureen down and here he was, but she told him in no uncertain terms that Claire neither knew him nor wanted to know him and to leave her alone. She told him just the bare essentials; that she was married, living in London and had a son; they were all doing well and were happy. No amount of coaxing or cajoling could wrest Claire's address from her. Eventually he gave up trying.

David came home from work less than happy at what he perceived was a cuckoo in his nest, but for his wife's sake he swallowed his bile and was prepared to let him stay for one night. They spent an uneasy night that night in their home. Maureen wondered if when we got up the next morning all their belongings would still be there. It was awful to think of her father in that way but he was an unknown quantity and his track record was pretty dire.

Maureen was up first, her father still on the sofa asleep. Their belongings were still there not spirited way in the night and breathing a sigh of relief she headed through into the kitchen to make a brew.

Her dad must have heard her because when she brought a mug of tea in for him, the curtains had been pulled back and his blanket was neatly folded beside him on the sofa.

He thanked her for the tea and she collected his newly washed clothing from off the radiators. His tee shirt and jeans were the only items she was prepared to iron. Thinking no time like the present, Maureen got the ironing board out ready and switched on the electric iron and five minutes later the freshly ironed clothes re-joined his others in the back pack.

A while later Michael and his dad came downstairs, helped along by the smell of bacon cooking. They always had a proper fry up on a Saturday so her dad had dropped on lucky, otherwise he would have had to settle for toast and cereal, their normal fayre, but today it was bacon, sausage, fried bread, fried egg, and beans with a side plate of bread and butter, all washed down with a mug of tea. They all cleaned their plates with satisfaction, her dad going one further by smacking his lips in appreciation of a fine breakfast. David and Michael cleared the table and went to do the washing up leaving Maureen alone with her dad. Going over to the bureau where she kept her purse, she opened it and retrieved the notes from within, £70, and handed it over to her dad, all the cash she had until she could go to the bank later.

He thanked her for it and put it in his pocket. She in turn told him not to say anything to anyone as it was her secret. Maureen didn't normally keep secrets from David, but this one was hers and besides it was her money anyway, to do with as she saw fit, that's how she chose to rationalize it anyhow.

They all had another mug of tea before finally saying goodbye.

David said his farewells in the living room so Michael and Maureen walked him to the gate to say theirs. He must have made a hit with Michael in the short time that he had been with them because he gave him a final silent hug.

Maureen had asked him earlier what his plans were and he had said, "I'm sorry but I'm going to London to try and find Claire. I have to see her."

Maureen thought, oh fuck, she would have to ring her and give her warning.

Chapter 31

Luke

We were sat on the sofa watching a repeat of the Excellent Yellowstone Park wildlife series. Adam was sitting propped between Claire and me fascinated by it. He watched anything that had wildlife in it and we encouraged him to do so.

A pack of wolves were trying to get a herd of bison running in order to separate them from their calves but the bison were presenting a formidable united front, thwarting the wolves tactics. One of the bison must have had enough because she charged one of the wolves, head down and almost hooked it with her horns. After a period of stale mate the wolves loped off, probably in search of easier prey.

Adam turned his head and pointed towards the telephone. Claire got up, reaching it just as it rang.

I could just about tell that the caller was Maureen, Claire's sister.

After a bit of muted questions and answers conversation Claire exclaimed loudly, "Oh shit!"

Adam joined in by saying, "Mum said shit."

"Yes Adam mum did!"

Claire turning temporarily put her hand over her mouth then smiling said, "Oops." It was too late by then of course the word had already escaped Claire's mouth and been picked up by an ever vigilant Adam.

After a few minutes Claire returned to the comfort of the sofa to give me the glad tidings.

"My father turned up at Maureen's yesterday, completely out of the blue," hence the use of the 's' word by means of an explanation.

"Oh, did she say what he wanted?" I asked.

"No, other than to say that he was on his way to London," replied Claire, "to find me, but he needn't bother because I don't wish to see him." Then as an afterthought, "I don't want him in my house Luke, if he calls here, father or no father."

"Well alright, if that's what you want," I replied.

Claire nodded in response then said, "Yes that is definitely what I want."

Chapter 32

As soon as Doug Simons entered the building Tony Parsons made a bee-line for him.

"Boss wants to see you Doug."

"Oh, where is he, down below?"

"No, not that boss Doug, the boss," indicated Tony pointing upwards.

Doug tried not to show surprise at Tony's upwardly pointed finger but failed miserably to mask it.

Inside, Doug's guts were doing somersaults. A summons upstairs usually meant one of two things, either a promotion or an arse kicking. He favoured that he was in line for the latter as he certainly wasn't due a promotion for at least a couple of years. Christ thought Doug with sudden clarity, I hope the Jamal ldrisi scenario hasn't come back to bite me on the arse already.

As Doug nervously waited for the lift doors to open he realized with a horrible sinking feeling that this could well be the only possible explanation as to why he was being summoned.

Arriving at the top floor Doug took his time walking to the office of the head of M.I.6 choosing instead to prolong the agony.

Mary Wallace had been appointed head of M.I.6 purely on merit. She had been in the position for the last three months and had already gained a fearsome reputation among some of her male colleagues. There had been two resignations from two senior members of M.I.6 who had felt that the position should have rightly gone to them.

Mary Wallace had accepted both their resignations with immediate effect, secretly glad to be rid of them. She had her own ideas on running M.I.6 and the old boy network was not one of them.

Her family name Wallace could be traced back centuries. Indeed many of her family's ancestors had filled the rank and file of some of the finest regiments in the British army. In short, Mary Wallace had an impeccable pedigree, as well as a first class mind.

Doug stood outside Mary Wallace's door composing himself, ready for his arse kicking. He knocked loudly and waited, "Come," came from within.

Doug entered saying, "You sent for me ma'am, Doug Simons," by way of introduction.

Mary Wallace put down the paper she was reading appraising the young man standing before her.

After a pause she said, "How long have you been understudy for James Martin?"

"Three years ma'am," answered Doug.

"And how long has your work with Mr Martin been to do with finding Abdul Rahman?" asked

Wallace.

"For about twelve months, ma'am."

She seemed to weigh up Doug's response before asking, "How long would it take you to get up to speed if I gave the task of finding Abdul Rahman to you Mr Simons?"

Doug was genuinely surprised by the question but unfazed answered, "Three days ma'am."

Mary Wallace had secretly liked the speed at which this young man had responded to her questions.

"Very well Mr Simons, I'm going to take a chance on you. I've assigned you an office on the second floor." Mary looked around for the piece of paper authorizing Doug to take over the room. Handing it to Doug she said, "Room 2C."

Doug took the paper slightly bewildered but said, "Thank you ma'am."

"Now I realize that you will need to bring all of Mr Martin's files and reports upstairs to your new office so I have assigned two uniformed officers to assist you in the task. They are already downstairs waiting for your instructions. Now, unless you have any questions Mr Simons, time is of the essence, I suggest you get to it," finished Wallace.

Doug nodded said, "Ma'am,' and got half way to the door before stopping and turning.

Mary Wallace, already back to reading her correspondence, looked up and said, sharply, "What is it Mr Simons?"

"What happened to Mr Martin?" asked Doug, mystified.

"Hasn't anyone told you?" asked Mary.

When Doug didn't answer Mary quietly said, "Obviously not, James Martin is on sick leave Mr

Simons, how long he will be off I have no idea but until he returns I want you to make it your priority to find Abdul Rahman's whereabouts. If you can do that Mr Simons then the sooner we can lock the murdering fucker away for good and throw away the key. Is that clear enough for you Mr Simons?" asked Mary.

"Yes ma'am," answered Doug with new purpose in his stride.

Doug descended to the claustrophobic bowels of M.I.6 heading towards James Martin's office and the two officers awaiting his arrival.

They had with them a portable trolley and a large number of strong cardboard boxes. Doug nodded to the two men in greeting who in turn nodded back awaiting his instructions. Looking around the cluttered room Doug set the men to work, first to emptying and boxing the contents of the two filing cabinets. Once they had done that they were to box everything from the shelves.

Doug decided that everything on James Martin's desk was the most important place for him to concentrate his own efforts. Giving specific instructions to the two officers to leave it untouched he carefully removed the weights from the map of Afghanistan spread across Martin's desk, rolled it up to take with him. The contents of both the 'in' and 'out' trays were rubber banded and boxed.

The drawers were emptied and searched for any personal items belonging to Martin.

The boxing up and transportation of James Martin's office took three trips altogether and most of the morning. Now surrounded by stacks of cardboard boxes in his new office Doug looked at them in dismay. He realized that his rash prediction of getting up to speed in three days may have been a tad optimistic.

Before he let his temporary work force go however, Doug asked if they could find him a wall board large enough to mount Martin's map of Afghanistan on.

"We will try," they answered and left Doug to his boxes.

The room was quite spacious. It boasted a large window that let in a lot of light and even had a view, though Doug knew he wouldn't have much spare time for idle gazing. There was a large desk that had been pulled near the window to take advantage of the light. On it were in and out tray's that thankfully were both empty and an imitation ceramic beer barrel filled with an assortment of pens, pencils and different coloured marker pens. The drawers either side of the leg well were empty of everything but dust. The chair was adequate.

Filing cabinets lined one wall, more than capable of storing Martin's files. The computer was old but at least in working order. There was no water dispenser in the room but plenty of electrical sockets. Tomorrow, thought Doug, he would bring in his own electric kettle, mug, tea bags, a jar of coffee, sugar and a jar of powdered milk. If he was destined to be spending a lot of time in this room he wanted to make sure that he had a ready supply of liquid stimulation.

The box containing the contents of Martin's 'in' and 'out' trays seemed the most logical place to start. They would have the most recent papers and communications in what Martin had had to deal with.

Opening up the box, Doug knew with a certainty that this was only the start of what would prove to be, a very long day.

Chapter 33

In the cave system, North-West of Kabul. Afghanistan.

Deep within the mountains Abdul Rahman was putting his body through a regime of punishing exercises, for a man of Rahman's age it was pretty impressive. The fact that he could still do it was even more impressive. He believed in rigorous daily exercise just as he believed in the one true God.

His philosophy was a healthy body in order to serve God. The men under his command revered their leader, often trying to emulate him when exercising themselves. They strived to achieve physical perfection as well as proficiency in the use of arms. The constant training had resulted in a formidable fighting force. Every man here was a volunteer and totally committed to laying down their life if necessary, in order to protect Abdul Rahman.

The cave system in which they lived and trained no longer resembled the idea of a cave. For the last five years the extensive cave systems in the mountains had been both extended and enlarged. An army of workmen, no longer employed in the production of opium, had been recruited to work in the caves, secretly strengthening them with both concrete and steel.

One cave housed six four ton trucks and eight armoured jeeps, all mounted with twin 50 calibre machine guns. The men themselves slept in purpose built dormitories, protected from air strikes by concrete and steel. There was a kitchen adequately stocked with enough food and water to withstand a siege of three months. It even boasted a fully functional hospital looked after by two volunteer doctors.

The arsenal was extensively stocked with weapons of many types and calibres. Boxes of ammunition were kept dry on pallets of wood, too numerous to count. There were crates of hand grenades, mortar rounds, and shoulder launched R.P.G.'s. There was enough to repel an invading force and that was the general idea.

The latest addition to the cave system was a bath house fed by its own water system. The running water had been discovered whilst enlarging another cave. It had been piped to the bath house and the men had seen it as a sign from God. It now proved to be one of the most frequently visited rooms within the cave system.

All of the work had been undertaken and achieved under the so called 'eyes in the sky' a euphemism for both the American and British satellites in orbit. Controlled drones were a more recent invention that also had to be avoided.

The British, under much public scrutiny, pulled out its combat troops from Afghanistan, the so called advisors who remained had been left to train the Afghan army still loyal to the government in Kabul.

Rahman knew that the British S.A.S. were still active in Afghanistan along with American Special

Forces and that is why, his men trained day in and day out so that they would be ready for combat when his lair was finally discovered. Oh, he was under no illusion that that day would come. It was only a matter of time before he was discovered. But, God willing, his men would be ready and inflict many casualties among his enemies.

The cave system boasted one final surprise that was yet to see completion. Besides Rahman, only the work men labouring on its construction knew about it. An escape tunnel was slowly being

hacked through the mountain. It was hard physical work for those employed in the task. The spoil alone was a nightmare to dispose of but the work continued day and night without ceasing.

The latest estimate of distance before a breakthrough was 400 yards, still a long way to go.

Rahman hoped that his whereabouts would remain undiscovered until the tunnel was completed.

Chapter 34

"Adam, please come here and let me get you dressed," said Claire, exasperated.

She had been trying, unsuccessfully, for the last five minutes to get Adam dressed. No sooner had she got him into socks and pants than Adam shucked them off like a snake shedding its skin.

He preferred to be naked; that much was clear as once again he laughingly evaded his mum's clutching hands.

Claire sat on the bed watching her son's antics with a feigned look of displeasure on her face. Inside she was trying not to laugh at her son's mischief knowing full well that if she did, it would only encourage her son to do it all the more.

Trying a different tack Claire threatened Adam with the words, "No clothes - No park." She wanted to see what he would do so she remained sitting on the bed. Lo and behold, miracle of miracles,

Adam came to Claire to be clothed. Claire thought mmm, the perceived threat of not going to the park had obviously born fruit. Adam let Claire dress him, this time keeping his clothes on. She could hear someone knocking on the front door.

Luke shouted upstairs, "I've got it."

Opening the door Luke was confronted by a medium built, older man. Luke waited for the man to speak.

"Oh hello, I was wondering if ... erm Claire Wilson lives here"

"You have the right address." Luke finished for him, "but Claire does not want anything to do with you, sorry, her words not mine."

The man stood there on the door step apparently lost for words. Then seeming to come to a decision, he tried again, "Are you sure she won't see me? Only I have come a long way."

"Yes I'm sure," reiterated Luke.

The man seemed crest fallen at Luke's firm stance. Slowly he turned and walked away, shoulders slightly slumped.

Luke watched him walk away and couldn't help feeling a little bit sorry for him. Closing the front door he came back in just as Claire and Adam arrived downstairs.

"Who was at the door?" asked Claire.

"Your father," replied Luke.

Claire looked at Luke searchingly, "Has he gone?"

"Yes," said Luke.

Claire knew what was bothering Luke and gave voice to it, "Don't feel sorry for him Luke, it's what he does, he's a manipulator."

"I know," agreed Luke, "but perhaps you could at least listen to what he has to say."

"No! Luke," said Claire angrily. Then after a few moments she realised that she was aiming her anger at the wrong person. "Sorry, I'm not angry with you; I just don't know how that man has the nerve to show up on my door step. I've lived my entire life until now without knowing him and now all of a sudden he wants to play happy families!! ... No! Luke I cannot forgive him just like that," declared Claire.

Luke didn't say anything letting Claire give vent to her feelings whilst getting Adam's buggy ready in the hall. He waited whilst Claire made a few sandwiches and a juice drink for Adam. Securing him in the buggy Luke decided that a visit to the park was just what they all needed.

Claire loaded up the supplies and they left the house en route for the park. Adam was only too happy for his dad to tag along; he wanted to show him what he could do.

Luke pushed the buggy purposely towards the park unaware that Claire's father was following their every move. Helen and Lizzie were already at the park along with some other mums and their children taking full advantage of the fine weather. Helen was seated on one of the benches watching out for Lizzie, who was taking a turn on one of the swings alongside other children.

Adam could see that the swings were fully occupied so when his dad released him from the buggy he grabbed one of his hands and led him towards the slide.

Luke watched as his son confidently climbed the ladder then executed a perfect slide. The grin on both their faces said it all and for the next five minutes Luke watched his son complete slide after slide in a dizzying display of exuberance. After the last one Luke scooped up his son and noticed Claire's father watching from the other side of the railings.

Anyone else seeing this older man, who in turn was watching Adam, would have assumed that he was up to no good. People read about it every day in the newspapers; there was something on the

T.V. about paedophiles almost daily, so it only needed one frightened mother to shout out the word and Claire's father would be carted away in handcuffs. Luke hoisted Adam up letting him dangle his legs whilst seating him on his shoulders. Supporting Adam's arms with his own he walked over to the railings. Confronting Claire's father Luke said, "Come into the park man, before one of the other mums notices you and gets the wrong idea."

Mortified at the realization of what it must look like to other people, Claire's father did what Luke suggested. Luke let Claire know that her father was here but Claire stiffened with anger. When she confronted this stranger she said, "Luke told you I didn't want to see you. Why have you ignored my request?"

Helen asked Claire if everything was alright.

Claire not wanting to air her dirty linen in front of strangers said, "Yes, fine." Then she ushered her father away out of earshot.

Luke watched for a while just to make sure that things weren't about to get physical. After a while he thought that it was reasonably safe to leave them to it, so he let Adam down onto terra firma and he headed towards a vacant swing.

Adam, now proficient on swings, joined Lizzie. Luke smiled at her and said, "Hello," Adam was soon urging his dad to push him ever higher so that he could keep abreast of Lizzie.

Luke, marvelling at his son's nerve, managed to keep one eye on what he was doing with Adam and the other on

Claire and her father. Both were using their arms to help enforce whatever it was they were saying to one another. Eventually Claire's father turned and left the park through the gate.

Claire came back to sit with Helen.

Luke watched them both, heads close together in quiet communication. Probably discussing her father thought Luke. Later, after sandwiches and frenzied duck feeding, Luke dared to ask Claire about her father.

"He is coming around later," said Claire, "he says he wants to talk so let's see what he has to say."

Luke decided to keep his own council; the fact that Claire was prepared to at least listen to what her father has to say, was a shift of seismic proportions.

Chapter 35

M. I.6 headquarters, London.

Doug Simons had told Mary Wallace, the new head of M.I.6, that he would be up to speed in three days' time. He had sadly underestimated his own ability. It had taken him four days of back breaking arse numbing research.

James Martin's idea of a filing system didn't come anywhere near that of Doug Simons'. It was haphazard, and in many instances incomplete. Old case files had gotten mixed in with new and it made for long frustrating hours to sort it all out. It didn't help that notes made out in Martin's own illegible handwriting, also had to be gone through, for both relevance and importance; he just dare not miss anything. Doug also had the ever increasing notion that perhaps the most important pieces of information hadn't even been written down but were locked inside James

Martin's head.

Whilst Doug was trying to make sense of his old boss's paraphernalia, fresh information on Abdul

Rahman was piling up in his in tray. He hadn't even got around to making a start on it yet, but he knew that he would have to soon, missed information could be vital in M.I.6's war on terrorism.

As well as being tasked with finding Abdul Rahman's whereabouts, Doug had heard a disturbing rumour concerning his old boss, the rumour doing the rounds was that he was in a private medical facility having suffered a complete breakdown.

Doug had tried, so far unsuccessfully, to find out where Martin was being treated, but the answers he received were always a bit vague. No one seemed to know for sure and more worryingly still no one seemed to care. He decided that he would go direct to the top if necessary in order to find out where James Martin was being treated.

The large map of Afghanistan was now secure on a wall board. Two areas of interest had been highlighted by James himself.

Doug had concurred with Martin's reasoning that all the relative information concerning Rahman's possible whereabouts, pointed to two specific areas of interest. The only trouble was it wasn't specific enough; Doug needed to narrow down the search areas to just one. Perhaps something in the in tray would help. He hoped so anyway.

Chapter 36

Claire

My father had been living with us for a few days, everything I had promised myself wouldn't happen, had happened. Allowing him inside my home, something I had vowed not to do had been my biggest mistake. As promised he wanted to talk and boy could he talk. He had the gift of the gab and was a real charmer. Within a couple of hours he had Adam hanging all over him. The old fucker even had Luke fooled and I was still in the minority, unwilling to succumb to his earnest entreaties of wanting to get to know us.

He had a meal with us that first night, all rather civilized, even going to the extreme of offering to wash up the dinner plates; that was going too far for me. He wasn't going to get under my guard that way.

He slept on the sofa the first night easing his way in. The next morning his blanket was neatly folded and he was dressed ready for when Adam and I got up. The kettle had been filled and had already boiled when I entered the kitchen. The charm offensive was continuing unchecked.

Seeing to Adam's breakfast first, I busied myself in the kitchen determined not to let my father spoil our routine.

Luke arrived to join us, freshly shaved and showered. Luke was civil to my father saying "Morning," before sitting to the table with Adam on his lap. It was usual for Adam to do so, it was what we normally did and I'm glad that it was continuing, even though I thought we had a stranger in our midst.

I couldn't bring myself to call this stranger dad, likewise father; he was still very much an unknown quantity. A few hours spent under my roof wasn't going to change a lifetime's anger anytime soon. If he felt a little hurt by my obvious anger and mistrust towards him he didn't show it and I wasn't really bothered if he did anyway.

Later Luke and I talked about my father's sleeping arrangement on our sofa. I didn't like the idea and said so. We had a small box room filled with odds and ends. It was big enough for a single bed, just, but we didn't have the luxury of a bed. So now the choice was, did we want to go to the expense of buying a single bed and mattress or not?

I certainly didn't want him permanently sleeping on our sofa, that was for sure.

Luke was amenable to my father staying a while longer so that meant us having to buy a new bed.

There was a furniture shop on the high street. Luke offered to go with me but I didn't want to trail

Adam out with us so I said, "No that's okay I'll go; you stay here and look after Adam." I still wasn't willing to trust my father with looking after Adam. That sort of trust had to be earned.

Leaving Luke to entertain Adam, and my father too I suppose, I headed to the high street in search of a bed.

The door to the store had an old fashioned bell that dinged when you opened it. It reminded me of

Dawson's sweet shop back home when I was a kid. The guy who materialized was definitely of Indian origin. He had a full set of face whiskers and a smile that showed off his perfect teeth. He also wore a turban which I thought marked him out to be a Sikh though I could have been wrong in that assumption. His accent completely threw me; he spoke with a heavy London twang that made me smile.

I told him I was looking for a single bed and mattress but stressed that I needed it delivering today.

The expected, "Very sorry but the delivery van is already out making deliveries," didn't wash with me.

In reply to this I said, "So pick up the phone and tell the driver to call back to the shop so that he can pick up my order and make another," took the shopkeeper completely by surprise.

He certainly wasn't used to being confronted like this, especially by a woman.

He looked me squarely in the eyes and I smiled sweetly back at him. I think that he could see that I was well used to the guile of shop keepers; so set about showing me his stock utterly defeated.

I chose a bed that took to pieces and a decent mattress, heavily wrapped in protective polythene. I even got him to throw in a pillow for free on the proviso that it would all be delivered within the next four hours. Paying a deposit we settled for the rest in cash upon delivery.

He must have liked me because he was still smiling

when I left his store.

Arriving back home Luke and I emptied the box room whilst my father kept Adam entertained. When the delivery driver and his mate arrived, they carried the bed and mattress upstairs for us, even going to the trouble of bolting the bed together. I paid the balance in cash and got a receipt.

That was four days ago and dad was well and truly here, snug as a bug in a rug.

That night I let Maureen know that my father had arrived and was living, all be it temporarily, with us. She was shocked to learn that I had taken him in knowing the way that I felt about him, but she was quick to point out that she hadn't given him my address.

I quickly alleviated her worries by telling her that our father had got my address from Michael, her own son. I didn't say anything offensive about Michael's betrayal of both mine and my sister's trust, but let her know, that the blame lay squarely at his door.

Michael was Maureen's son; let her deal with him, I thought afterwards. I would have liked to be a fly on their wall tonight when Michael got home.

As the days wore on and I gradually learned a little more about my father, I slowly came to realise that this wasn't the first time that he had been kicked out. Apparently it had happened on several occasions, usually not long after he had either been made redundant or far more likely, simply packed his job in. This gave me hope that maybe a reconciliation was not beyond the realms of possibility so I fanned the embers hoping to re kindle the flames of hope, when I discovered that he was missing his kids, especially his son.

Putting that seed of thought in his mind I gave it time

to grow. Eventually the temptation to telephone his wife became too much for him and I silently shouted for joy when he asked if he could call his wife.

Luke and I listened as discreetly as we could to try to gauge from his tone whether the omens were favourable or not. After quite a while the omens proved to be very favourable indeed. His wife and kids were missing him too and wanted him home.

Annoyingly dad wanted to stick around until the weekend; we weren't shot of him yet.

When we finally bade him farewell it cost us full train fare to Newcastle. Luke also gave him £500, of his own money, to help sweeten the journey. Looking back on it we may have got off pretty lightly.

The sad thing that really got to me though, was once he had gone, I was sure that if he had stuck around for Maureen and I when we were growing up, l knew that we would have loved him.

You hear of some people being affectionately called a loveable rogue, well, I don't know if my father quite fit that bill, but if he had taken the time to get to know us, I would have liked to have found out.

Chapter 37

From the intercepted telephone calls and communications coming out of Afghanistan, Doug was almost ready to put his job on the line. He had been tasked with finding Abdul Rahman's hiding place. His former boss James Martin had done the lion's share of the work in pinpointing two areas of special interest where Rahman was most likely to be.

The latest intelligence that Doug had painstakingly analysed seemed to confirm Martin's conclusion that the area north west of Kabul, that Martin himself had highlighted, seemed the more likely place for Rahman to be holed up. The other area highlighted on the map was now looking less likely, because the terrain was too open and far less mountainous. Rahman liked to have the safety of rock above his head. Also there had been far less communication of late coming from that particular area.

Doug was almost ready to rubber stamp his more favoured search area but couldn't quite commit to doing so.

What he really needed, was to see his former boss. He may just hold that vital extra piece of information in his head that Doug needed before giving the go ahead for a search of the area.

Knowing he couldn't put it off any longer, he needed to see Mary Wallace to get her o.k. to go and visit Martin.

As Doug walked down the corridor leading to Mary Wallace's office his stride this time was more confident. Reaching her door he knocked and waited.

"Come," came from within.

Doug opened the door and made his way towards Mary Wallace.

"What can I do for you Mr Simons?" asked Mary.

"I need to see James Martin ma'am." Doug answered.

"Oh! Why?" asked Mary, puzzled.

"He may hold information in his head I'm unaware of ma'am. It's to do with an area in Afghanistan where Rahman may be holed up," explained Doug.

"I see. Well of course that changes things," agreed Mary. "You are aware that Martin is being treated in a military medical wing in Colchester?"

"Yes ma'am that is why I'm here really. The military don't always look kindly upon members of

M.I.6, they like to keep us waiting, ma'am," explained Doug.

"And you want me to smooth the way for you is that it?" finished Mary.

"Yes ma'am, I believe that the information may well be important, so if you can cut through the unnecessary bull shit for me it would save time and in the long run possibly save lives. Excuse the profanity ma'am," finished Doug.

"No not at all Mr Simons," said Mary, "you have put your case to me very well. When are you thinking of going?"

"Now ma'am if that is possible," replied Doug.

"Alright Mr Simons, I will put through the call for you," agreed Mary, smiling.

"Thank you ma'am," beamed Doug, just before he left.

Mary Wallace was still smiling after Doug Simons had left the room. She was beginning to think that she had made the right choice in appointing Doug Simons to James Martin's job.

Then remembering why Doug had just been to see her she picked up the telephone and asked her secretary, "Get me a direct line to the C.O. of Colchester Barracks please."

It was after 2pm when Doug arrived at Colchester Barracks. He stopped at the main gate checkpoint showing his I.D.to the guard on duty.

After a thorough check of Doug's I.D. he was instructed where to park once the barrier was lifted.

Driving to where he had been directed, Doug had no sooner turned off the ignition when an army Land Rover pulled into the space beside him obviously the guard had telephoned through his arrival.

An army Lieutenant got out of the vehicle and approached Doug. After introducing himself as

Lieutenant Stevens he asked Doug to "Please get in my vehicle, I have been instructed to drive you over to the medical unit."

Doug did as he was asked and got in the Land Rover. Nothing else was said during the short drive.

Lt. Stevens delivered Doug to the medical wing, pointing out where he was to go. Then said, "I will be waiting just over here," indicating a few marked out spaces to their left, "for when you are ready to leave."

Doug entered the building through the double doors. He showed his I.D. at the desk to the female corporal on duty. She asked, “Who are you here to see?” she seemed very surprised when he asked for James Martin.

Picking up a telephone, the corporal uttered a few hurried words and an orderly, dressed in a long white coat, appeared by Doug’s side. The orderly’s name was Frank and he had been instructed to take Doug to James Martin’s room. Unlike the lieutenant and the corporal Frank was both friendly and talkative.

Doug asked Frank, “How is James doing?” expecting the usual, as well as can be expected line.

When Frank stopped mid corridor with a worried look upon his face, Doug felt a little anxiety running down his spine.

“Hasn’t anyone told you?” questioned Frank.

When Doug shook his head perplexed Frank replied, “I think it’s best if you see for yourself.”

Stopping at the door marked J. Martin, Frank opened it fully allowing Doug to slide passed him.

Light was streaming into the room showing how spartan it was. There was a small wheeled cabinet on one side of the bed and on it were a plastic jug and a beaker with a straw in it. A single wardrobe, army issue, stood along the wall opposite the window. There was just the one chair. Doug could see by the shape of the blankets that someone occupied the bed but as yet no one had either spoken or moved.

Coming round to the side of the bed nearest the window, Doug visibly flinched and audibly gasped at seeing the ghastly apparition lying in the bed.

Frank the orderly, watched Doug’s reactions as he slowly began to process what it was that his eyes were seeing. The face staring unblinking towards the window was the face of one belonging to that of a 90 year old man.

At first Doug thought that Frank had brought him to the wrong room. He was about to say so, when looking again more closely something familiar about the apparition's eyes stayed his words. The eyes had sunken deeper into their sockets, that much was true, but nevertheless the eyes still belonged to James Martin. The hair on his head, once mostly coloured and tinged with grey, was now a shock of pure white.

Doug was physically shocked by James Martin's appearance. Looking at Frank, Doug's mouth had gone dry. He was having trouble swallowing in an effort to loosen his tongue. Eventually Doug managed to say, "How long has he been like this?"

"Since he was brought here," answered Frank truthfully.

"Does he ... does he speak at all?" asked Doug with obvious difficulty.

"Nothing since he arrived," said Frank, then seeing that Doug was struggling and sensing his reluctance to ask, offered, "He just stares out of the window, we have to keep turning him regularly otherwise he would get pressure sores, unfortunately he will probably get them anyway. He is able to take in food and water with help but the other end, well; he now wears a padded nappy as he is unable to go to the toilet by himself. The physio is coming in every day just to keep his limbs moving otherwise his muscles will waste away. I'm sorry, was he a friend of yours?"

The wording, by Frank, was just about right, was he a friend? He spoke as if he was already dead!

Not answering Frank's question Doug thought Christ, he's breathing on his own but otherwise he was realistically dead.

"You know," said Frank, trying to be tactful, "you are the only person who has asked to see him since he has been here. Do you know if he had any family or relatives? We may need to contact them, you know just in case."

"No ..... he has no one," replied Doug.

Frank nodded at Doug's answer, quietly confirming what he had thought himself.

With the state that James Martin was in, there was no further reason for Doug to remain here, but seeing him in this state had visibly shaken Doug to his core. Truth is, he couldn't wait to get out of there.

Walking back down the corridor Frank clasped Doug on one of his shoulders in a friendly fashion.

"Don't worry about your friend, I'll make sure that he is well looked after on my watch," promised

Frank.

Doug stopped and said, "Thanks Frank."

Going back outside Doug met back up with Lieutenant Stevens and was once again whisked back to his car. Now sitting in the driver's seat Doug needed a few minutes to both pull himself together and gather his thoughts. James Martin known by all and sundry at M.I.6 as 'the arsehole' had given everything to the job and in return the job had taken everything from him, including his dignity.

Seeing James reduced to what he had now become angered Doug. As far as he was concerned

Martin had been used by both the government and M.I.6. Once his usefulness had come to an end, he had been discarded and conveniently forgotten about.

Doug made a solemn vow to himself before setting off back to London, that he wouldn't allow the job to reduce him to the same condition as that now afflicting James Martin, so help me god.

Chapter 38

Luke and Eric were working the big room which encompassed the dance floor. Ever since Chris had taken over the decks from the resident D.J. whilst he was on a break, the dance floor was heaving.

Luke had to give Chris his due he certainly knew how to fill a dance floor.

The club was almost full to capacity, business was certainly good. So far Luke and Eric had only had to remind guests heading onto the dance floor to leave their glasses or bottles at their tables. It was club policy that drinks were not permitted on the dance floor. So far everyone had good naturedly complied with the request.

But Luke knew from experience that when alcohol was consumed it only needed one inebriated guest to take exception to being asked to return their drink to the table for compliance to swiftly turn to aggression. Alcohol was a fickle friend; some people could handle it, most couldn't. Normally the most mild mannered individual, when partaking of alcohol, could suddenly turn into a different person. Luke had a phrase for it, 'Jekyll and Hyde syndrome'. Whilst the next morning Jekyll may be contrite, apologetic even, after some altercation the night before, Hyde was always ready to reappear.

That's how Luke rationalised it anyway.

Luke did another slow circuit of the dance floor then went to check with Jimmy the Bar Manager.

"Hi Jimmy, is everyone behaving themselves?"

"So far Luke, the bloody place is heaving. We haven't had a chance to catch our breath. Fuck, the lagers just gone! I'll have to go and change the barrel. See you later Luke."

"Yeah okay Jimmy," said Luke feeling sorry for him. Just then Luke had Frank, who was managing the front entrance with Pete and Linda, alert him through his ear piece.

"You there Luke?" crackled in Luke's ear.

"Yes Frank, what's up?"

"Just giving you a heads up, your friend Seline and a party of five have just rocked up. Where is

Chris?" asked Frank.

"He has taken the D.J.'s spot," answered Luke.

"Well Seline's party are on their way through, keep an eye on them Luke, Chris too," finished Frank.

"Will do," replied Luke, heading over to the double doors. Luke just managed to arrive in time to greet them.

"Hello Seline," Luke said, smiling.

"Hello Luke! How's married life?" replied Seline slurring the words a little.

"Wonderful thank you," replied Luke.

Seline digested this answer for a beat then asked, "Are there any spare tables?" indicating her party with a wave of her hands.

"I'm sure I can find you one," said Luke quietly to Seline, and then more loudly, "please follow me."

Arriving at a table meant for six there was only one single occupant seated at the comfortable fixed backrest. Luke leaned in conspiratorially and politely asked if he would mind sliding over a touch to make room for Seline's party of six. The guy good naturedly complied.

Once everyone was seated, Seline set about introducing Luke to her guests. Luke shook hands with everyone as Seline introduced them. First up were Freddie and Charlie Bartholomew, twins, and whose 25th birthday was being celebrated today.

Luke shook hands with them both and wished them happy birthday. Next was Seline's female friend Gabrielle Lister. Luke gallantly kissed her hand and said, "Hello." He had seen Gabrielle here before on several occasions and from what he understood she was very high up in the fashion industry and had graced the covers of some of the more well-known fashion magazines.

Seated next to Gabrielle was George Calvert. Luke shook his hand and said, "Hello" but couldn't shake the feeling that they had met before, strangely for Luke he couldn't remember where.

The final member making up Seline's party was Edward Hartshorn. He had a firm grip and looked Luke steadily in the eye as he said, "Hello."

Luke said, "Hello" back, then, "I will send over a waitress straight away."

Luke headed over to the station reserved for the waitresses and asked Pamela if she wouldn't mind going over to Seline's table, number 32, to take their order.

Pamela looked over to where Luke was pointing and

said, "Yes of course."

The next order of priority for Luke was Chris. The break up between Seline and Chris had hit him hard and to Luke and Frank's knowledge Chris had not dated anyone since.

As he made his way over towards Chris, Luke good naturedly, fended off several would be groping females trying to get him to dance. Finally arriving on the raised platform beside Chris, Luke looked out over the sea of bobbing heads and gyrating bodies.

Chris knew it was unusual for Luke to seek him out when he was working so obviously something must be up.

"What's up Luke?" asked Chris.

"Seline is here with a party of five." Luke leaned in close to tell him, "She is here with the Bartholomew twins, Charlie and Freddie. It's their 25th birthday." Luke looked for any adverse signs from Chris and the news he had just delivered.

Chris seemed to mull over what Luke had just told him. Then shrugging it off leaned towards Luke and said, "Send over a bottle of Krug to her table with my compliments and put it on my tab."

"Are you sure?" asked Luke. Chris nodded, "Yeah that bird has well and truly flown."

Luke breathed out a sigh of relief; the last thing he wanted to be involved in was bad blood between Chris and Seline. He liked them both too much.

Luke delivered the Krug personally, properly chilled in ice, and six glasses, saying to Freddie and Charlie, "With the compliments of Chris the D.J. Happy Birthday!"

Everyone looked over towards the turntables suitably impressed.

Later, as Chris handed over the turn tables to the D.J., I watched Seline make a beeline for him. I tensed trying to read the body language to determine whether the encounter would prove to be friendly or otherwise. After a while I relaxed Seline had just given Chris a hug before returning to her table, it looked like they had made their peace.

As the club gradually closed down and people started to drift off, either to another club or home I noticed Chris sat at a table with a very attractive leggy blonde.

When he finally left with her, Frank and I looked at each other in that knowing way.

Yasmin, who we were waiting for, asked, "What are you two grinning at?"

Frank put her out of her misery by telling her, "It looks like the drought had finally ended for Chris!" looking none the wiser at Frank's vague answer it took a while for the penny to finally drop, but when it did, Yasmin smiled too.

Chapter 39

In the Penthouse Suite, of the Palms Hotel, Amman, one of two hotels owned by the Hussein family in Jordan, Ali Hussein was incandescent with rage, stamping his feet and waving his arms about like a demented spoilt brat.

Mehmet Yafai, Ali's head of security, looked on at his employer's childish antics, only just able to control his true feelings at witnessing such an unmanly display. Not for the first time Mehmet wondered how he had come to be working for such a man.

Also present was Omar Hassan, sent as Emissary of Abdul Rahman, to report to Ali Hussein in person. The information Hassan had just delivered to Ali had proved to be most vexing, hence the childish display they were both now witnessing.

Yafai had to avert his eyes from Hassan's lest he betray his true thoughts. Not for the first time had

Yafai witnessed this type of behaviour from his boss. In

his eyes it was not seemly but most of all it showed a total lack of control.

Yafai prided himself on being efficient at his job, but most of all by carrying himself with dignity in all things.

When Ali's tantrum finally began to run out of steam he flopped helplessly into a palatial chair thoroughly miserable and disheartened.

Hassan had been tasked with delivering what amounted to be another failed attempt to gain information. Abdul Rahman had ordered a known asset, already based in London, to gain certain information from a woman named Claire Wilson. This same woman lived in an apartment owned by Ali's sister Yasmin. Once the asset had extracted the information required Miss Wilson was of no further use and was to be eliminated.

Ali had learned from Hassan that none of these things had happened. Instead on further enquiries made by using underhand methods, it was discovered that Claire Wilson had not lived at the apartment for some time, worse still, her whereabouts were unknown, but more worryingly, nothing had been heard from their asset either and his whereabouts were also unknown.

It was frustrating news for Ali and he was at a loss as to what to do next. He had freely given millions of pounds to further Rahman's cause. In return Rahman had given Ali access to his endless supply of assets. If this access suddenly ceased, Ali was up the proverbial creek without a paddle. When it came to organising a hit, Ali was a complete novice. He simply didn't know what to do or even how to go about it.

Abdul Rahman was unavailable because he was a hunted fugitive these days with a ten million dollar bounty on his head. Ali wondered how he had remained free for as long as he had. The bounty said dead or alive, but everyone knew how that would end.

Ali realized that time was fast running out for Rahman, he was trapped in his stronghold fortress in

Afghanistan. Once his enemies discovered his whereabouts it was over and once Rahman was dead his usefulness to Ali would also be at an end, as his endless supply of assets would be closed to him.

Thinking more clearly now that he had calmed down Ali asked Hassan, "Can I help you in any way?"

"No sir, but thank you for asking," replied Hassan respectfully.

Ali had expected this answer from Hassan but felt obliged to ask it anyway. He breathed a sigh of relief then asked, on a whim, "Is your room satisfactory?"

"It is most satisfactory, thank you."

Ali nodded at Hassan's answer, "Please avail yourself freely of my hospitality whilst you are here," offered Ali, arms open wide.

Realizing that he had just been dismissed, Hassan thanked Ali and nodded once to Mehmet before leaving the room.

Once Hassan had left Ali turned to his chief of security, "You know Mehmet I don't think Abdul

Rahman has much longer for this world."

"No sir!" agreed Mehmet. "He may have created a stronghold in that shithole of a country, but really, it's just a place in which to die, there is nowhere else for him to go."

Ali nodded in agreement, "A pity though, I could have done with a list of his assets before he goes."

Mehmet thought for a while before breaching the subject with his boss. "You know sir, you could always recruit and train a small team of your own. That way you wouldn't be dependent on

Rahman's assets."

Ali looked at Mehmet with different eyes. Realisation of the truth of his words lifted the black cloud of depression from his countenance. Why hadn't he thought of this for himself? Ali sat up straighter in his chair, Mehmet's suggestion breathing fresh life into his previously demoralized body. The more Ali thought about it, the more he came to realize that it made perfect sense; a small team of men working exclusively for him. The very idea of it lifted his spirits, as a plan began to take shape in his mind.

"Do you know of any likely candidates Mehmet who would fit this role?" asked Ali.

"I believe I do sir," answered Mehmet.

Ali nodded in appreciation then asked, "How many do you suggest we recruit?"

"I was thinking no more than five or six to start sir; we are only building a team not creating an army after all." Mehmet suggested.

"Alright Mehmet, I'll leave the arrangement's in your capable hands," said Ali, agreeing to Mehmet's suggestion.

After Mehmet had left the room, Ali's black cloud of depression had completely evaporated. He even allowed himself the luxury of a smile as he quietly voiced the words, "A team of my own!"

Chapter 40

"Hello Luke, what are you doing on front of house?"

"Hello Sasha. I should ask, what are you doing back here? I thought we had revoked your membership after your last visit." Luke questioned.

"Ahh just a slight misunderstanding, it's all good now," parried Sasha. He held up his new membership card for Luke to inspect.

Luke examined the card and saw it was good and handed it back to Sasha with a nod. Transferring his attention to Sergei, Sasha's brother Luke said, "Hello Sergei, how are you?"

"I'm good Luke, it's been a while." Then conspiratorially leaning in towards Luke said, "Don't worry I will keep an eye on Sasha, I promise."

"Alright Sergei, have a good time, "offered Luke. Sergei clapped Luke on the shoulder good naturedly as he passed him.

The two female companions accompanying Sasha and Sergei had said nothing to Luke preferring to leave the talking to their men. Both women were tall and cat walk thin; they had high cheek bones inherited from their parent's which spoke of mother Russia. The women looked at Luke like he was dinner, as they passed by.

Luke gave a heads up to Frank in the big room that Sasha and Sergei were on their way through.

Sasha and Sergei Abromovich were old acquaintances of Luke's, but only by default, it was actually their father Mikael who Luke knew best. Years ago a third party had contacted Luke on Mikael's behalf asking if he could secure for him some Russian icons that had come onto the market. Luke had managed to secure the icons despite the competition and had then been asked to deliver them to Mikael Abromovich's home, in person.

The house that Luke rolled up to that day was one more befitting a prince. It spoke of money and unimagined wealth. When Luke rang the front door bell he was greeted by a young Sergei. He was quite chatty and obviously revelled in showing Luke the various works of art and sculptures on display. The young man was quite knowledgeable on the subject matter that surrounded them and was delighted that Luke was suitably impressed. Reluctantly the tour came to an end and Sergei took Luke to meet his father.

Mikael Abromovich was a bear of a man, there was simply no other way of describing him. He was also very affable, greeting Luke with a strong two handed hand shake over his own. He spoke good English but couldn't quite mask its Russian origins. Once introductions were over Luke unlocked his carry case and opened it allowing Mikael to remove the icons himself.

The look on Mikael's face spoke volumes to Luke,

obviously these particular icons meant a great deal to him. The reverence that he had for them couldn't be faked. Recovering, as if from a trance with glassy eyes, Mikael said, "Where are my manners? Sergei, ask Maria to bring us coffee." Sergei left them alone to go in search of Maria.

"Please Luke sit," said Mikael pointing to an enormous settee. Whilst Sergei was out of the room

Mikael paid Luke his fee. It was a hefty one but he didn't bat an eye lid as he handed it over.

Luke's terms were strictly cash. The tax man wasn't having his money.

Mikael was only too willing to oblige Luke; he didn't agree with governments stealing their money either.

Previously, Luke had done some digging of his own on Mikael Abromovich, before agreeing to secure him the icons. He was born in Russia and had made himself a billionaire mainly through oil and natural gas. There was some sort of falling out with the then government of the time but Mikael had seen the way the wind was blowing and had managed to remove most of his fortune out of Russia before the Russian government could relieve him of it.

Leaving almost all their private and personal possessions behind in Russia, Mikael had got his wife and both of his sons out before the axe could fall. He made his new home in London and here they were. Unlike some Russian exiles, supposedly pining for mother Russia, Mikael had embraced his new home whole heartedly, in fact since moving to London he had invested his money wisely doubling his already considerable wealth.

There were rumours of course that perhaps some of this wealth was built on both the drug trade and prostitution. That may well have been true, although Luke didn't really know. What he did know was that Mikael treated him well and with consideration and that is what he chose to remember.

Sergei, the oldest son, had a business head on his shoulders and it fell to him to learn from his father. Sasha was the youngest and a bit of a hot head. It was no secret that he had a temper and it had got him into trouble on more than one occasion. The last time he had been at the club, his then girlfriend had been enjoying herself on the dance floor, perhaps a little too much for Sasha's liking.

The young man, who had been dancing with Sasha's girlfriend, obviously had visions of spending the night with her. The sexy way she had let him feel her shapely arse certainly didn't dissuade him from thinking otherwise.

What sent Sasha over the edge was the way his girlfriend didn't seem to mind the attention being lavished over her. But Sasha thought otherwise and took exception, promptly flooring the guy. He then dragged his girlfriend off the dance floor by her hair.

Yasmin and Frank duly intervened on the girl's behalf and perhaps a little unfairly kicked them both out of the club. That was just over three months ago so obviously Sasha now had a new card he must be at the end of his three month exclusion.

Luke just hoped that Sergei could keep a tight rein on his brother. Luke liked Sergei but it hardly seemed fair that he had to police his brother's actions.

Chapter 41

Claire was in a deep sleep. She had been restless and irritable most of the evening before going to bed. Adam had been unusually quiet before being bathed and put to bed, which too was strange; usually he was full of questions he wanted to know the answers to.

Somewhere in Claire's subconscious a child was sobbing, not a hurt or angry wail, a genuine sorrowful sobbing.

Something tugged at Claire's memory. Her eyes opened quickly, gradually coming into focus as the fog of sleep began to dissipate.

Through the room's gloom Claire's eyes took in the sight of her anguished, sobbing son standing by her bed, "What is it sweetie?" Claire asked throwing back the bed covers so inviting her son to get in beside her. Snuggling him down against her warm body she covered them both up. Carefully wiping her son's tears away with the corner of the bed sheet she tried to soothe his still sobbing little body.

Whatever had frightened or upset her son, Claire knew that it must have been something truly monumental, as Adam rarely cried at all and certainly not for no reason. As Adam's closeness to his mum began to calm him down his sobbing slowly ebbed away. Claire dabbed away the last remnants of Adam's tears using the bed sheet once more.

Now that he was calmer and safely cocooned by his mother's body and surrounded by her love she felt that time was right to ask him what had upset him.

"Why were you upset sweetie? Can you say?"

Claire knew that Adam would tell her in his own time; it was no good trying to rush him. So she waited.

Eventually he answered, his voice a little croaky and subdued, "The animals."

"The animals," Claire repeated, trying to coax it out of Adam but afraid to rush him. Letting him think about it Claire asked, "What about the animals Adam? Did they frighten you?" again Claire waited for Adam to answer.

"They were in cages and couldn't get out, fire, burning .... The animals were screaming." Adam's body was once more wracked with uncontrollable sobbing.

Claire pulled him in tight to her body shushing him, trying to comfort him. She held him for a long time before his sobbing finally stopped. She was still cradling him long after he had fallen asleep when Luke came in from work.

Slipping into bed beside her Luke saw that Claire was cradling Adam, "Is he alright?" Luke whispered concerned.

Adam stirred in Claire's arms, "Dad."

"Shush go back to sleep, it's not time to get up yet." Claire soothed, "It's early."

Patting Luke's leg with her free hand she turned to him and whispered, "I'll tell you later."

Later that morning while Claire was getting hers and Adam's breakfast ready she was listening to the radio when the nine o'clock news, interrupted what passed for music these days. The main feature reported a fire at a small private zoo in Kent. Apparently bales of straw stacked beside the Tapir hut had caught fire; the mother and her new born calf had burned to death. Cages adjoining the Tapir hut and containing other small animals had also perished. The blaze was being investigated by fire officers at the scene. At this time foul play could not be ruled out.

Claire looked at the radio as if she had been struck with it and then at Adam. He was eating his toast with gusto, his sobbing in the early hours seemingly forgotten. Claire knew that this couldn't possibly be a coincidence but who would believe her...Luke..? Certainly, but no one else, not even Yasmin.

Somehow or other Adam had known about the fire, not only that he had heard the animals' screams and had felt the terror of the animals caught up in it.

Claire sat down at the table physically drained. If Adam had somehow seen the fire, experienced it, what sort of a future did that hold for her son?

Nightmare, sprang immediately to Claire's mind. Christ, he was only a baby, this wasn't right!

Burying her face in her hands Claire tried to shut out these troublesome thoughts.

When she took her hands away and looked at Adam he said, "Boo!" and laughed. This made Claire's despondency evaporate making her laugh too.

Chapter 42

It was squeaky bum time. Doug Simons had had various agents and technicians at M.I.6 working flat out. He had the tech people blow up the highlighted area on the map of Afghanistan that James Martin had favoured to be Abdul Rahman's stronghold. It now showed much greater detail; Doug had painstakingly followed the trail of breadcrumbs left by his predecessor.

The work had been both solid and meticulous; Doug could not fault his former boss's logic, everything gathered from the information pointed to this area as being Rahman's stronghold.

Doug had made his decision from solid intelligence. It was now time to put his reputation, and future career prospects, on the line. He had the technicians draw up ten dossiers based on the latest intelligence gathered on Abdul Rahman then had the blown up area of interest added to them.

What came back to Doug, and for M.I.6 in such a relatively short time, was a very professionally executed set of dossiers. He hoped to Christ that it would be enough. He had been asked to present his findings in person by Mary Wallace, head of M.I.6, but she hadn't done him the favour of telling him how many people would be present.

Doug knew that several chiefs of staff, of the various armed forces, would be there as well as an

American full colonel, but he couldn't rule out the possibility of some big wigs from government muscling their way in, they seemed to pop up out of the wood work whenever brownie points were likely to be won.

Doug had put the dossiers in a brief case that he had recently bought for himself. He couldn't very well arrive with them tucked under his arm. This was make or break for Doug; he needed to look professional, even if he didn't feel professional.

He knocked loudly on Mary Wallace's door. The shouted, "Come," from within was that of a woman.

Doug entered the smoke layered room. Obviously the no smoking policy didn't apply here thought Doug.

Finding an empty chair, Doug, put his brief case on it, opening it up he took out some of the dossiers and started handing them out. Coming back for more Doug silently breathed a sigh of relief, eight persons present including himself.

Earlier Doug had consulted with Miss Wallace to have the original highlighted map of Afghanistan brought up to her room and put on prominent display on an easel. Now that everyone had a dossier in front of them Doug nodded to Mary Wallace that he was ready.

She took his lead and introduced Doug to everyone in the room then said, "The floor is yours Doug."

Doug was flustered for a beat, but managed to recover admirably. His boss had just thrown him in the deep end. Everyone's eyes now focussed on Doug waiting to see what he had to say. Doug knew that he needed to seize the initiative here and quickly. Crossing over to the large map of Afghanistan, Doug stood to one side of it pointing at the highlighted area, "This area here gentlemen I believe to be the strong hold of Abdul Rahman. If you look inside your dossiers you will find a blown up map of this area."

Everyone in the room opened their dossiers and looked at the map in question. No one said anything at first.

The American colonel was the first to speak, "This area, it is still a pretty big area to cover."

Doug answered truthfully, "Yes it is sir, but all the intelligence points to Rahman's stronghold being within this area."

"But how can you be sure?" insisted the colonel, putting Doug once more in the spotlight.

Doug was ready for the colonel's trap. "I can't be sure sir, but with the thousands of man hours of sifted information both going in and coming out of Afghanistan our people have managed to narrow it down to this one area. It has taken months to pin point, but the only sure way of knowing if Rahman is actually there, is to put boots on the ground.

A furore erupted, mainly amongst the British top brass when met with Doug's suggestion. When it finally began to subside a little, the American colonel asked Doug, "What exactly do you have in mind son?"

"Well, four teams of special forces inserted into the area, two British and two American, the troops required are already in the country so it would not take too much disruption to deploy them to this area. If the search is carried out on a grid system I estimated the area could be covered in ten days," finished Doug.

The colonel seemed to chew on this for a while before coming to a decision, "Goddam! That could work. As Doug said, we already have the troops in the country so it would just mean deploying them to the area."

The British top brass had listened to the American colonel's acquiescence of Doug's proposal. Now that they realized that it didn't involve putting more large numbers of boots back on the ground, they were more amenable to his suggestion.

Mary Wallace thanked Doug for his presentation, before dismissing him.

Doug closed the door on the smoky room still unsure if they would act on his information. Well, thought Doug, he and his colleagues had done the best that they could, now it was up to the brass.

Once Doug had left, the colonel addressed Mary Wallace, "You know Mary, that young man performed rather well under the circumstances, you kind of threw him under the bus."

Smiling Mary said, "Yes I kind of did didn't I colonel? I think that young man's proposal is a sound one. Should we give it a go?"

"I believe we should,"' answered the Colonel, "it certainly beats sitting on our arses but I suggest we do it soon." The consensus around the room was one of agreement. Doug's proposals were about to come to fruition.

Chapter 43

Jamal Ahmed stood waiting at a respectable distance whilst Abdul Rahman and a number of his soldiers were at prayer. He had important news to deliver but it could wait; he would not interrupt his mentor whilst at prayer.

When Abdul's devotions were finished he and his soldiers reverently rolled up their prayer mats. He could see his number two in command waiting discretely over in the corner. Taking his time Rahman let his soldiers go to their assigned tasks before making his way over to Jamal.

Smiling Rahman greeted Ahmed in a friendly manner, "What is it Jamal?"

Quietly, so that no one else could hear he replied, "We have a breakthrough in the tunnel sir!".

Excited by the news, but controlling his emotions admirably, Rahman took in the appearance of his number two. He was covered from head to foot in a fine film of orange-brown dust; it was in his hair and beard and stuck to every visible part of his skin and his clothing was thoroughly permeated with it.

Allowing a smile to finally crease his face Rahman gripped Jamal's shoulder in a brotherly fashion then went passed his own private cell to return his prayer mat to the cedar box made especially for that purpose. Once that was done he allowed his excitement to finally show, "Let's go see Jamal!"

The tunnel that his work force had been working on was 750 meters long and it had been a massive undertaking made all the more miraculous because it had all been done by hand. Rahman likened it to the building of the pyramids. No explosives had been used in its construction, just skilled manpower wielding picks, hammers and chisels, had managed to carve out a tunnel tall enough for a man to comfortably walk its length. It was wide enough for a man to stand central with both arms outstretched enabling him to just touch the sides.

Both tunnel walls gradually sloped inwards meeting at a point just above head height. The way it had been constructed negated the need for roof support as it was self-supporting. The only real problem had been the excavated rock and soil; there was just so damn much of it and it needed to be got rid of as soon as possible for work to progress. Many of the lesser side tunnels in the natural cave systems had been packed tightly with the waste but once these had been filled it became necessary to transport the soil further afield. This was essential because of the American's eyes in the sky. A soil heap suddenly materializing in the area would alert them to signs of tunnelling activity.

It had been a close run thing but if Jamal's news of a breakthrough was correct it was welcome news indeed.

Rahman finally arrived at the breakthrough point. His mouth was dry and felt gritty. His work force pressed themselves flat against the sides, their teeth gleaming white against their dirty encrusted faces, allowing their boss passage. Rahman headed towards the hole. On inspection it was large enough for someone to look out of but the trouble was although the tunnel was both straight and relatively level it had broken through the side of the mountain about 20 feet above the canyon floor.

At first Rahman was a little dismayed that this was so but on reflection he began to see it as a positive sign, being 20 feet up from the canyon floor made it harder for enemies to infiltrate the tunnel from there.

Bringing Jamal to the site of the breakthrough he explained to him what he wished him and his team to do.

"Keep the hole small; just make it large enough for our men to comfortably negotiate. Get rid of any soil from here; do not allow it to remain around this area, move it somewhere else. It is important that it is not noticeable from outside or from above." Jamal listened carefully to his boss' instructions, "Then camouflage the entrance. Take your time with this," Rahman emphasised to Jamal, "our safety depends upon it. Once this is done, fasten two anchor points either side of the tunnel, strong enough to support two climbing ropes. Have the ropes coiled ready for use. You understand?" Rahman asked.

"Yes sir!" answered Jamal.

Rahman clapped Jamal on the shoulder, "I know you do, I'm just being over cautious, forgive me."

Jamal felt immense pride in that moment, being singled out by his boss; he would have done anything for him, anything!

Walking a short way back along the tunnel Rahman

addressed his work force. "Brothers, what you have achieved here is something truly magnificent! The world outside will never know the true extent of what has been done here, but I know brothers, and you know. That is enough and I thank you for it."

The brothers looked at Rahman through pride filled eyes basking in his praise. Everyone here was a willing volunteer. He had asked them to leave their poppy fields to come and work for him and the cause. In return their families had been well looked after whilst they were away; they had the best food, water, good clothing and money.

For every six weeks of construction work, each man was rotated home for ten days leave, but also received two gold sovereigns. In Afghanistan that was a fortune!

Now that their tasks were coming to an end it would mean going back to the uncertainty of cultivating the poppy. Those of them who had wisely hoarded their sovereigns would be able to live out their lives in quiet luxury and provided that they didn't bring unwelcome attention to themselves by a careless slip of the tongue; they could enjoy a good life. They could even supplement their income by returning to opium production; most of them probably would!

Some would come to the attention of the Taliban and would inevitably forfeit their lives. They were under no illusions, for almost five years the living both for them and their families had been good. Now it was coming to an end, that was all. It was life. It was who they were, it was Afghanistan.

Rahman had one final message for them, "When your task here is completed, go wash away the sweat of your toil and the dust from your bodies. Change into clean clothing and when that is done, I will provide you with a feast to remember!"

Rahman's words were good in their eyes and as one they cheered. The echoes were still reverberating in the rock as Rahman walked away.

Chapter 44

Claire

I had accompanied Yasmin to doctor Cooyman's private clinic at her behest. Frank was with her as well of course but I think Yasmin wanted the support and company of a woman, someone who had actually gone through the whole experience of child birth.

We sat waiting for Dr Cooyman to summon Yasmin and we didn't have long too wait.

Yasmin greeted the doctor with a brisk handshake, just like a bank manager would greet a prospective client, I thought. Frank followed Yasmin in and I brought up the rear.

Dr Cooyman was just as pleasant as ever, surprising me by remembering not only my name but Adam as well. Greeting me warmly she asked, "How is Adam doing?"

I was genuinely pleased that she had remembered us and told her, "He is doing exceptionally well thank you."

Passing by Dr Cooyman at the door I sat in the seat furthest away from her desk. This allowed Yasmin and Frank to sit together and afforded them the illusion of privacy so Dr Cooyman could ask questions that only Yasmin and Frank could answer.

My mind drifted back to earlier at home and Adam's early morning distress began to replay in my mind and my heart went out to him once more. He had been so upset and affected by his nightmare, if that was what it was, I still wasn't sure. Adam's fear had partly transferred to me; his little body had been literally shaken by the whole horrible experience.

I did what I suppose a million other mothers do in the circumstances and gave him comfort and tried my best to soothe his fears. It must have helped because at breakfast he had been his normal happy self.

Later when Luke got up I told him what had happened and what Adam has said, then I told him about the news report on the radio confirming that there had been a fire at a zoo.

Luke seemed to take a long time digesting this information but I didn't want to rush him. Since Adam's birth we didn't have secrets anymore, we told each other everything. We knew that Adam had inherited some of Luke's skills; in fact in some areas, Adam's skills already exceeded those of his father, and yet Adam was still only a baby. God just thinking about it made me sick with worry! Adam's true potential was ... well limitless, we just didn't know what it was.

Luke finally seemed to have a handle on it. He explained it as simply as he could. "Imagine hundreds, even thousands of things happening all over the world simultaneously. Now imagine that sound carries on the air, which it does," I nodded encouragingly, so far so good. "Now imagine Adam as some type of receiver." I gave Luke a worried look, unsure of where his reasoning was heading, "I know, I know," said Luke, "it seems too fantastic to be true, but bear with me. We already know that he knows when the telephone is about to ring and who is on the other end of the line. He is definitely linked to me by his thoughts and I believe, to you too."

My eyes grow wider at this revelation.

Luke just nodded in confirmation, "I believe that Adam is experiencing things that are happening in reality as thoughts similar to how sound is carried. His young mind when he is asleep, is unable to switch them off, he simply hasn't learnt how to do it yet."

"Can you do it?" I asked. Luke hesitated but only for a beat, "Yes, but only for limited distances, and I can turn it off or on. Adam is much better at it than me though," admitted Luke.

"Should we be worried? For Adam I mean," I clarified.

"I don't think so. Once Adam learns how to control it he should become more settled."

"Do you think it will take long for him to be able to do this?"

"With the speed that Adam's mind is developing, no I don't think it will take long at all," said Luke.

"I just worry that others will notice the differences in him Luke. He's so damn smart you just can't ignore it; and his growth, he's still only a baby yet he is like a three year old, and we are going to have to think about his schooling soon and that is bound to get him noticed, what are we going to do Luke? I'm worried for him."

Luke fetched me to come and sit on his lap doing what he could to allay my fears. Adam grabbed Luke's leg wanting to join in the fun. "Sorry partner only room for mum."

Adam looked at both of us unimpressed and went to play with his toys.

"It's still early days yet," said Luke, "but I don't think ordinary school is the way to go as Adam would stand out. Boarding school, as an option, is unthinkable to both of us, so that leaves us with either private day school or home tutoring. I don't see we have any other choice."

I listened to Luke's reasoning with interest, as far as Adam's welfare was concerned their interests coincided. I kissed Luke full on the mouth and it was returned with fervour. I would have liked it to continue on in the bedroom but knew that Adam was well aware of them and their intentions so that was out of the question, at least for the moment. Later perhaps!

I realized I was squirming uncomfortably in my chair, and focusing on the conversation in the room once more, realized that I had become sexually aroused. Hoping that Dr Cooyman hadn't noticed anything untoward , I tried to retake control of my wayward thoughts.

A further appointment had been made by Yasmin to see Dr Cooyman and an ultra-scan was scheduled at the same time with Natalie.

This was confirmation enough that life was growing within Yasmin. I was happy for Yasmin, and Frank too, it meant that their clan was growing, the more the merrier.

Chapter 45

"You okay to look after Adam for an hour or so Luke?" shouted Claire from the kitchen.

"Of course," answered Luke, "why?"

"I need to go clothes shopping and it's easier if Adam is not with me," Claire replied.

"Do you want me to come with you?" offered Luke.

"No, it's okay. I'll be quicker if I go alone. Besides, I may need to try them on and it's just easier if I go alone," offered Claire by way of explanation.

"Alright," agreed Luke, "I may take Adam to the park for an hour or so if you don't mind?"

Claire came into the doorway that separated the kitchen from the dining room, wiping her hands on a towel, "No of course I don't mind, it will do you both good."

Adam, who was busy playing with his toys on the living room carpet near the patio windows immediately got up and came to stand beside his dad looking up at him with unspoken questions on his lips.

"Yes mate, nothing wrong with your hearing is there, but first please put your toys back in the toy box and then we can get ready," said Luke.

With the offer of an outing to the park with dad riding on his compliance, Adam immediately set about clearing away his toys. Claire looked on with annoyance. Normally when she asked, it would take Adam several times of being asked before he would put his toys away, and even then Claire would often end up helping him.

Moments later when they were all ready for leaving Luke asked Claire, "Have you got your key?"

Claire patted her pockets just to be sure, feeling it she said, "Yes."

They parted at the front gate with Claire giving Luke a peck on the cheek and saying, "Bye Adam, see you both later," and with a wave she was off.

Adam gave a half-hearted sort of wave back, clearly eager to be off to the park.

The day was fine but cloudy, the sun only managing to break through the heavy clouds in glimpses, but nevertheless it was warm and dry; the wind of the day before having finally blown itself out.

The familiar gates of the park soon stood before them. Luke negotiated the metal barred gates like a pro. Once inside he noticed that two of the bench seats were occupied by mothers or nannies. So he headed Adam's buggy towards the one furthest away from the swings. Parking beside the only unoccupied seat, Luke put the brake on allowing Adam his freedom.

"Where to first?" Luke asked.

Without a word Adam headed towards the last remaining swing and got on board, Luke trailing behind.

"Good choice," said Luke, under his breath.

Adam looked to the swing on his right, it was occupied by Lizzie.

Of course it was occupied by Lizzie, that's why Adam chose it thought Luke. After a few cursory attempts at pushing Adam's swing he soon let Luke know that he had mastered the art of propelling the swing by himself and that Luke was surplus to requirements. Luke soon got the message and went to sit on the bench seat, but not before telling his son to be careful; Luke's way of retaining his pride.

Watching them swinging and chatting together, without a care in the world, Luke thought this was how it should be, after all they were only kids.

Luke kept a careful eye on the swings but gradually he began to take in his immediate surroundings. A couple of slightly older kids were playing on the slide, a boy and a girl. No one seemed to want to go on the see-saw. Perhaps it was no longer in fashion mused Luke, Adam certainly wasn't interested in it and neither was Lizzie.

Just then a cool breeze ruffled Luke's neck hairs raising goose bumps for an instant. The immensely tall man who had sat down beside Luke was the cause of it. He had taken Luke by surprise, something almost unheard of.

The stranger spoke first, "Hello Luke."

Luke looked sideways at this unwelcome stranger, "Michael! Why are you here?"

Not replying at first but looking directly into Luke's eyes Michael replied, "Relax Luke, I'm not looking for you."

A long pause elapsed before curiosity got the better of Luke and he said, "Who are you here for then?" Knowing full well that Michael probably wouldn't answer, Luke was surprised, when he said "Ezekiel."

"Whoa, there's a name I haven't heard in a long time." Luke waited a while before asking, "Anything serious?"

Michael smiled like a predator savouring the kill, drawing out Luke's discomfort, and curiosity, in equal measure.

Luke was so predictable thought Michael, even after all these years. When he thought that he had drawn out Luke's agony long enough he broke the tension, "No, just a warning ....this time."

Luke breathed out audibly, relief clearly visible on his face, "I didn't know Ezekiel was here in London," admitted Luke.

Still smiling Michael said, "Well London is a pretty big place Luke."

"Yes but apparently not big enough to hide from you," quipped Luke.

"Yes, well l do have divine help," admitted Michael, "and with that sort of help no one can truly hide."

"Of course," agreed Luke, acknowledging the truth of his statement.

"Any way I understand you are married now," said Michael.

"Yes I am," admitted Luke.

"Congratulations." Michael nodded at Luke's admission, trying to understand. "But why put yourself through all this unnecessary suffering? She will eventually get ill and/or grow old and die, so why do you do this to yourself. Haven't you learned anything from the past?"

"I don't expect you to understand Michael, but Claire is special. We have been through so much together that it physically hurts to be away from her. Now I savour every moment when I am with her."

“Does she know what you are?” asked Michael

“Yes, including the fact that I will go on living long after her death,” admitted Luke.

“And will you be able to? .....go on living I mean,” asks Michael.

Luke hesitated just a fraction of a second too long, for Michael’s liking.

“Yes, I will have to; we have a son, Adam.”

“Ah yes of course. Is that him?” asked Michael looking towards the swings.

“Yes,” said Luke, with obvious pride.

“A fine looking boy,” admits Michael, “what is he like?” This takes Luke by surprise.

“Wonderful” begins Luke, wondering how best to describe his son, “he is very intelligent, always asking questions and so full of energy. His mum has her hands full with him that’s for sure.”

As he listened to Luke talking about his son, it was clear how much he loved him. The love he had for Claire was another thing entirely; when it came time for her passing he doubted that Luke would be able to survive the pain.

Luke, to Michael, was an enigma. He simply couldn’t understand why he would choose to live like this, knowing with certainty, the tragic outcome of such a liaison. It had only been a small detour out of his way for Michael to find Luke as he had been tasked to meet him and see the boy in person. He would give his report later, but for now Ezekiel was in need of a reprimand.

Michael left Luke sitting on the bench seat as quietly as he had arrived.

Luke watched Adam’s face with delight as he took yet another slide down the chute. Lizzie followed him down a close second, as Adam raced to climb the steps once more.

After a while Luke heard Lizzie's mum shout to her that it was time to go. Adam waved to Lizzie and her mum, watching them all the way until they left the park, then in a final hurrah, slid down the chute one last time before arriving back at Luke's bench seat.

"Who was that man you were talking to dad?" asked Adam.

Luke looked steadily into Adam's face before answering him, "That was Michael, an old friend."

Adam casually asked, "Like us you mean, dad?"

Luke shouldn't have been surprised by Adam's question, but he was, "Yes Adam, just like us, but Michael is much more powerful."

That seemed to satisfy Adam's curiosity, at least for now, as they left the park. Luke would tell Claire all about Michael and his questions when he got home. The time for secrets and subterfuge were over; he had had a life time of those. Now it was truth or nothing, however painful it was to hear.

Chapter 46

The Wedding - Claire

The marriage ceremony had been performed in an almost perfunctory manner. Our small band, consisting of Luke, myself, Adam, Chris, Jimmy, Steve and Antonia, had gathered together at the registry office as requested, to witness Frank and Yasmin's matrimony. It was admittedly only a small gathering but it represented Frank and Yasmin's closest friends.

It was a brief ceremony and in my opinion, unworthy of people as lovely as Yasmin and Frank, who didn't mind where they were married. He still couldn't believe that someone with Yasmin's beauty and brains would even contemplate marriage to him. He still considered himself totally unworthy of her.

Frank was selling himself short as usual. He wasn't

handsome in the conventional way, like a film star but he wasn't ugly either. I suppose you could describe him as rugged. He was also intelligent, knowledgeable in a variety of subjects, brave, immensely loyal to his friends; but he was also deadly when it came to dealing with his enemies. Perhaps it's best we not speak of that now; today was a day for celebration.

There was no official photographer to record the proceedings. Whether this was by accident or design we did not know, so everyone snapped away willy-nilly, capturing disjointed pairings and haphazard groupings of our small gathering. A group photograph had not been captured on film simply because everyone wanted to be in the photographs and there was no one else free to take any. Yasmin was wearing a pale yellow silk trouser suit, the jacket was styled in the oriental fashion with a mandarin collar and her long raven hair fell straight to below her shoulders; she looked stunning and I, in comparison felt quite shabby. Frank wore a very well fitted silver grey three piece suit, white shirt and dark grey tie. They made a very handsome couple.

A table had been booked at a small but fashionable restaurant nearby, within walking distance.

It was just then as the impromptu photo session had ended that the dark, heavy rain laden clouds decided to dump their load upon us.

We rushed to find shelter under the registry offices portico. The thought of walking to the restaurant now abandoned in favour of a short cab ride instead. Once we had secured cabs the short ride was accompanied by the pounding rain.

As soon as everyone was inside out of the rain, the women headed for the ladies to repair any damage caused by the down pour. It was left to the men, Frank really, to secure our table reservation. Luke had a highchair brought for Adam. An ordinary dining chair with a cushion on it would still have left him shy of being able to reach his dinner plate, though the high chair was proving to be a little tight to fit his frame comfortably. If he kept on growing at his present rate, high chairs would soon become redundant anyway. It was a tight fit but as usual Adam didn't make a fuss and simply made the best of it.

When the women folk came back I remarked on the tight fit of Adam's chair to Luke, unfortunately there wasn't much that either of us could do about it so we had to let it go.

Everyone ordered from the menu, except Adam of course, I did the ordering in his case. It was good we were all together once more, happy in each other's company. The conversation was both friendly and lively, our inhibitions consigned to the past. Whilst we waited for our orders, glasses had been brought to the table and an ice bucket complete with a decent bottle of champagne soon followed.

Yasmin allowed the waiter to pop the cork and charge our glasses. Adam unfortunately had to settle for juice, though I saw Luke slyly let Adam take a sip from his glass. Adam's face screwed up at the first sip; obviously champagne wasn't to his taste.

We toasted the bride and groom's health and happiness whilst standing, much to Yasmin and Frank's embarrassment. Both of them mightily disliked any kind of fuss or attention being lavished upon them, even at their own wedding. It got them noticed, made them feel uncomfortable and literally made them squirm and that is why we did it, wicked I know, but we were close friends and that's what friends do.

Our meals duly arrived, everyone tucking in once they had been served. Luke helped Adam when he needed it but mostly he coped pretty well on his own. He still needed his meat and veg cutting up pretty small of course, but he was a dab hand with a spoon.

The meal and conversation went down exceptionally well; so much so that everyone was loathe to leave each other's company. We settle on a compromise; and headed to the bar lounge instead. Adam was glad to be out of the restrictive high-chair and settled in cosily beside Yasmin on the plush seating. Yasmin put a protective arm around him, pulling him in close.

I looked on with approval thinking; she still acts like a surrogate mother, and then remembered that Yasmin would be a mother herself before long. I just hope that when Yasmin's baby arrived the dynamics of our friendship wouldn't alter too much. I valued her friendship too much and vowed to not let that happen.

Luke had gone to the bar with the men to buy everyone a drink. Chris and Jimmy had each claimed a stool preferring that and the sturdiness of the bar to lean on, plus the fact that everyone else had a female partner and they didn't, might have had some baring on the seating arrangements; but no one mentioned this fact. Luke, Frank and Steve returned from the bar carrying drinks.

Adam had been presented with a bottle of diet coke with a straw already inserted; it was his first, so Luke very seriously, said to Adam, "Please don't get any of it on Yasmin's clothing."

Adam moved a few inches away from Yasmin before he took hold of the proffered bottle. Now holding it, he knew the dynamics of what he was supposed to do, but the bubbles still made him cough, forcing some of the liquid out through his nose. Luke was ready with his handkerchief before any damage was done, but it was a close call.

Mopping up, Luke asked him, "Are you okay?"

Adam who was feeling embarrassed in front of Yasmin just nodded. Seeing his discomfort Yasmin said smiling, "Its okay everyone does that the first time, and I'll let you into a secret- I still do sometimes,"

Adam turned to look at her with big wide eyes, "Really?"

"Yes, even your dad does it," said Yasmin, conspiratorially.

Adam looked at his dad with big eyes.

Luke nodded to confirm that it was true and left them alone to let Adam be soothed by Yasmin.

Once Luke had left, Yasmin encouraged Adam to try again, "But this time try taking a smaller suck on the straw," she advised "just till you get used to it."

Adam tried again this time with much better results. His taste buds now working overtime brought a ray of sunshine back to his face.

"There, that's much better isn't it?" said Yasmin pulling Adam back beside her.

I had been watching Yasmin work her magic on Adam and I couldn't help thinking, god, she is a natural. She is going to make a great mum.

Luke broke into my thoughts by saying, "Perhaps I shouldn't have bought him fizzy pop."

"Naw he's got to try it one day. Today is good," I said.

"I think he was a little embarrassed to have snorted in front of Yasmin," admitted Luke.

"Yes, he was but he's fine now, Yasmin has worked her magic on him once again," I agreed.

As everything settled down into easy conversations I looked around at this special gathering of friends and couldn't help thinking, Luke and I were the first to get married, now Frank and Yasmin had gone and done it, who next? Looking at Jimmy first I thought, what do I know about Jimmy? Not much, but from the snippets of conversation between myself and Jimmy and others, I understood that Jimmy had once had a wife. She had tragically died from breast cancer and as a result Jimmy had remained single ever since.

Chris on the other hand had had ample opportunities to find a suitable partner. Only to turn them all down in the end, but then again Seline had managed to get under his skin in a big way before finally dumping him for someone else. So I suppose we couldn't write him off just yet.

My money was on Steve and Antonia. Against all the odds they had managed to hit it off and stay the distance so far.

Steve had met Antonia whilst doing some work for her father on the family home. Antonia's father had surprisingly got on well with Steve. He actually gave Steve his blessing when he asked Antonia out on their first date. Several more dates soon followed the first and Steve had become a regular visitor at her family's home. It had stood the test of time and was still going strong.

Once Antonia had been introduced to us she had fitted in just fine. So my money was on Steve and Antonia.

Luke interrupted my thoughts once again, "Where are you?" he asked.

"Scheming," I answered, nonchalantly.

"Am I involved in your scheming?" Luke asked warily.

''You'll find out when I get you home" I said smiling mischievously.

"That's sounds good to me," answered Luke gruffly.

The small gathering of friends broke up with a myriad amount of hugs and kisses. It had been another good day and we could mark it off on the calendar as such.

Chapter 47

Mehmet Yafai, Ali's New Head of Security

Mehmet Yafai was the youngest son of Omar and Fatima Yafai. Mehmet's parents ran a small electrical goods store in the centre of Amman. It had been their main source of income for over forty years. It also provided them with a home. Above the premises were three quite spacious rooms which provided the Yafai's with living accommodation. I suppose they could be classified in the low to middle class wealthy elite category. They weren't what you would call rich but they weren't poor either. They had made a reasonably good living working side by side in the store throughout their mostly happy marriage.

Their first son, Masud, had been a planned pregnancy and unlike most Jordanian newlyweds they hadn't rushed into starting a family. Instead they chose to wait, working hard in the electrical goods store to make sure that they could provide a steady, stable income before starting a family. Three years after Masud was born, Mehmet entered the world bloodied and screaming for attention. It had been a traumatic birth for Fatima and for several days after the difficult birth, her life had hovered between living and dying, but on the fifth day after Mehmet's birth she rallied and came back to live with her family. Life in her particular case proved to be too strong to be extinguished, but the doctors advised against having any more children. The Yafai's heeded the advice and decided that being blessed with two healthy sons was enough.

As the years passed and the boys grew, Omar dreamed that his sons would follow him, firstly helping him to run the store and then, daring to think of the future, hopefully to buy another store to begin a chain.

Sadly Omar's hopes for the future were not shared by his sons; Masud had his heart set on joining the police force.

He had not been particularly gifted as a student whilst in school, but his grades had been good enough for him to pass the police entrance exam. After a nerve wracking few weeks Masud had been accepted into the police force.

Mehmet had been entirely different, his grades in all his subjects had singled him out for something better, and so it had proved. Realizing that Mehmet wouldn't be following him into the family business either, Omar accepted that his wife's dreams and his own would not be fulfilled, it was bitter and disappointing. Their dreams of founding a dynasty were over!

Mehmet did however work in the store to provide him with enough money to see him through university; he came out with a degree in civil engineering. The Yafai's were ecstatic. Their son had achieved something that no one else in their family had thought possible.

Imagine their dismay when Mehmet told them that he had joined the Jordanian army as a commissioned officer with the rank of Second Lieutenant.

The Yafai's simply could not understand why Mehmet would choose a career in the army over a lucrative career as a civil engineer. Mehmet, if asked, couldn't properly explain it either, it just worked out that his path through life began in the army. He worked hard at being a professional soldier for the first two years, after which he was rewarded by being promoted to Lieutenant. It was a year later that Mehmet was offered the opportunity to join army intelligence. This work suited Mehmet admirably. It was while he was in army intelligence that he got the chance to travel abroad.

First he did six months as an exchange officer at Sandhurst Military College in England and whilst there he not only improved his English but managed to rub shoulders with other military personnel from all around the world. That was Mehmet's first overseas assignment, but not his last.

Two years later he was accepted for a six months placement to West Point Military Academy in the U.S.A. Whilst he was there he was treated warily, but alright. As an Arab he was viewed with suspicion. He couldn't really blame them as most acts of terrorism committed against the states or its citizens had been carried out by Arabs. I suppose it was the old cliche, one Arab to them looked just like another! Mehmet was glad when his six months posting came to an end.

A few months after returning to his post in Jordan Mehmet's promotion to Captain came through. It had taken Mehmet twelve years to achieve this lofty position.

He knew that promotion from this point onwards would probably take him the rest of his army life and he was becoming disillusioned with where his life was heading and was looking for a way out.

Meanwhile Mehmet's brother Masud had done hard time on the streets of Amman and in turn the streets of Amman had hardened Masud. Based at Amman Central Police Station it was both the largest, and as such the most important, station in Amman.

The Chief of Police at Amman Central was Mohammed Ahmed. He had recognised the potential in Masud Yafai. At the chief's insistence he persuaded Masud to sit the sergeant's exam, and with his chief's help and coaching Masud had passed the exam at the first attempt.

That was history now and years later Masud Yafai sat behind a desk as senior police sergeant at Amman Police Central.

Most of the paperwork destined for his boss Mohammed Ahmed, now had to pass across Masud's desk for inspection, before being forwarded on to him. It was a no brainer to Masud that the chief disliked this mundane part of police work, so it became Masud's task to cut through all the bullshit and only deliver what his boss really needed to deal with.

It also became apparent to Masud that his boss was on the take. Once a month a plain brown envelope addressed simply to the Chief of Police crossed Masud's desk. Just once the brown envelope had not been sealed properly and Masud had carefully looked inside to see what the envelope contained, five crisp one hundred dollar U.S bills winked back at him. He had hastily resealed the envelope properly.

After a little time had passed and with very careful police work Masud found out whose pocket the Chief of

Police was in. It was non-other than Ali Hussein! This sort of information was gold dust Masud knew, but it was also very dangerous and In order to remain healthy he knew that he had to keep it to himself.

Mehmet and Masud had kept in regular contact with each other when their careers permitted. They also visited their parents whenever possible, often bringing them a little offering in the form of money to sweeten the visit.

Masud had a wife and two children, both girls, who he spoilt rotten. As a senior Sergeant, Masud was eligible to live in subsidized police accommodation and he took full advantage of this perk of the job, as the houses were more modern and spacious. Mehmet was still unmarried but always enjoyed his visits with his brother. The two girls were both pretty and well behaved and Masud's wife was also quite pretty but painfully shy and reserved, whenever Mehmet visited.

It was on one of Mehmet's visits with Masud that he betrayed his true feelings about the army to his brother, he told him that he was thinking of resigning his commission in the army to return to civilian life. Masud managed to persuade him to hold off for a while and in return he would keep his eyes and ears open to see if a suitable position became available for him.

It wasn't long after Mehmet's visit with Masud that the position of 'Head of Security' for the Hussein family came to Masud's notice. He left a message at the army barracks where Mehmet was billeted to urgently get in touch with him.

When Mehmet finally did get in touch with Masud he was at first a little annoyed with his brother. The urgency of the call made Mehmet think that something had happened to his parents so when at last Masud assured his bother that all was well with them Mehmet managed to reign in his annoyance and listened to what his brother had to say.

Mehmet had to admit the proposition on offer certainly sounded interesting, and the money being offered for the position of head of security was currently twice that he was already receiving as captain. The brothers arranged to meet at the weekend.

Meanwhile Masud would find out everything he needed to know about the Hussein's to enable his brother to secure the position.

Masud's first mistake, was finding out about Ali Hussein father's so called road traffic incident. The file, reported by the road traffic police at the time, was kept locked away at the police station, and once it had been secured and read it was obvious that it was no accident. Ali Hussein's father had been deliberately run off the road.

George Hussein's car, a silver Audi, had been hit from behind several times by a black painted vehicle. When the road traffic police arrived at the crash site the driver of the vehicle had already been pronounced dead at the scene. After the body had been removed from the vehicle, measurements and evidence on the road were taken, as well as from the Audi by a police investigator and although no other vehicle was at the crash site, officers concluded that the Audi had been deliberately run off the road by a person or person's unknown, driving a black vehicle, thought to be a Mercedes. This was all in the incident report seen by Masud.

It had been written up as a road traffic accident and not as a deliberate attempt at murder. The signature was almost illegible but he could just about make out the surname, Bakri. The name didn't ring any bells with Masud but he would keep it in mind.

Masud's second mistake was to take his findings, along with the file, to his chief of police, who was not pleased by Masud's discovery; in fact he was so incensed by it that he suggested in the strongest possible terms that if he wished to remain on the police force it would be best if he forgot about the file.

Masud left the chief's office smarting at his own stupid naivety. How could he have possibly forgotten that his own chief of police was being bankrolled by the very man who had probably ordered his own father's murder?

A couple of days later Masud risked checking to see if the file was still in the filing cabinet - it was missing along with any evidence linking Ali Hussein with his father's death.

Mehmet needed to know what type of man he would possibly be working for. When they met, Masud filled his brother in, sparing no detail!

Mehmet thanked his brother for sticking his neck out for him; however it panned out he would be the one to make the final decision. The choice was simple really; what it boiled down to was, could he work for someone capable of murdering members of his own family. After thinking long and hard about it Mehmet decided that he could, he had been forewarned by his brother and was therefore forearmed. This could be seen as a positive advantage, provided that he carried out his work well and efficiently. He decided that he would make himself indispensable to Ali Hussein.

Mehmet's application and C V also had something that the other two applicants didn't - a signed letter of recommendation by the Amman Chief of Police. Masud had typed out the letter of recommendation for his brother personally. All it needed was a signature from his boss. This was achieved by subterfuge and was done amazingly simply. Masud waited until he had amassed a dozen or so papers that his boss needed to sign and then he simply slipped the fake recommendation midway in the pile and got his boss to sign the lot all at once. Job done!

Now it was just a matter of waiting for the formal interview, which came a week later. Mehmet had been instructed to present himself to the front desk of The Palms Hotel Amman, between 10 and 11 am. Use the lift and go up to the penthouse suite. Coming out of the lift Mehmet was confronted by a security guard who asked his business.

Mehmet stated his name and that he had been sent up from the front desk for an interview. The security man checked on his phone system and seemed satisfied, then knocked briskly on the penthouse suite door, opening it for him as he ushered Mehmet inside.

The opulence of the room struck Mehmet as over the top, wealth for wealth's sake, in Mehmet's opinion but he kept it to himself, his face an inscrutable mask.

The gentleman seated behind the large ornate desk was dressed in full Arab clothing; Mehmet wasn't sure if this was Ali Hussein or not as he did not introduce himself. Mehmet surmised that if indeed it was Ali Hussein he was painfully thin, quite possibly taller than Mehmet but he couldn't be sure as he was seated.

Not a word was spoken whilst he went through Mehmet's application form, so he waited to be addressed. "I see that you are currently serving in the military, is that a problem for how soon you can start?"

"No sir, I can resign my commission with immediate effect," answered Mehmet.

Shuffling the papers the interviewer came to the chief of police's recommendation. Mehmet's heart leapt into his mouth at the sight of it.

"You have here a letter of recommendation from Amman's chief of police, how is it that you know him?" he asked.

It was quick thinking on Mehmet's part when he said, "I only know him vaguely sir, it is actually my brother, Sergeant Masud , who got the chief of police to sign the letter of recommendation for me. Sergeant Masud works directly for him."

It was part truth and part lie, but a quick telephone call to the chief of police could easily reveal him to be a fraud.

When the interviewer just shrugged and accepted Mehmet's testimony as truth he allowed his body to relax slightly.

Mehmet realized that his body had been wound up like a coiled spring throughout the whole interview. Mehmet now expected to have to wait a few days before being told whether he had the job or not.

Instead the interviewer told him there and then that he had been successful in his application and he was to present himself at the front gate of the Hussein residence Monday morning, 9 am sharp, at which time he would be formally inducted into the Hussein residence as the new head of security.

Mehmet, still standing, realized that the interview was now concluded. The interviewer stood also and leaning forward he limply shook Mehmet's hand with the words, "Welcome aboard."

Realizing that this must be Ali Hussein, Mehmet said, "Thank you sir!"

Then, remembering, Ali produced a pass in a leather holder from his desk drawer. Handing it to Mehmet he said, "Show this to the man on the gate when you arrive on Monday morning."

Afterwards Mehmet thought, as of Monday morning I will be working for someone most likely guilty of patricide. He still wasn't quite sure yet how he felt about that.

The world turned and Monday morning arrived and saw Mehmet's V.W. Golf pull up in front of the Hussein's security gate. He showed his pass to the security man and waited whilst the electronically operated gate slowly slid open to allow him access to the grounds. He had been instructed by the gate guard to park his car in the vehicle compound, so he followed the road in the general direction indicated by the guard.

Mehmet hadn't quite realised just how huge an area the Hussein's household covered. The vehicle compound grounds had been properly marked out just like a large car park. He slid easily into a space carefully making sure that he was between the lines and not straddling them. First impressions said a lot about a person, thought Mehmet.

He had only just stepped out of his vehicle when another security man approached him. Mehmet flashed his card at him but it wasn't needed. "Please follow me sir," said the guard.

Mehmet did as he was asked and eventually arrived outside Ali Hussein's private office in the main building. The guard knocked on the door and waited for admittance.

"Yes come," was the response from within.

The guard ushered Mehmet inside but didn't follow him in.

"Ah! Mr Yafai, welcome, you are very punctual, good," was all Ali said. This time he made a point of stepping forward and shaking Mehmet's hand.

A totally different welcome from our previous meeting thought Mehmet, as he warmly shook Ali by the hand.

Ali went back to his desk to retrieve a hand tooled brown

leather pocket sized wallet which he then handed over to Mehmet. "This is your security badge and identification. Please carry it on your person at all times."

Mehmet flipped the wallet open to reveal, on one side a metal star shaped badge, it took all of Mehmet's self control to stop himself from laughing as it looked for all the world like a sheriff's badge depicted in Westerns, but with security stamped across it, and on the other side a tough plastic card clearly stamped with Head of Security. At least that looked alright.

"I have arranged for you to meet the household staff Mehmet but first let me show you to your own office and living quarters, this way please," gushed Ali.

It didn't take him long to start using my first name thought Mehmet casually. Clearly something agreed with him this morning which was totally different from their first meeting.

Mehmet's office was just down the corridor from his bosses. The only difference was that carrying on through Mehmet's office brought you to a small but comfortable lounge area with a compact kitchen-diner. Further back was a small bedroom with its own en-suite bathroom. His office and living quarters were combined. Mehmet realized, of course, that it made sense really, as head of security he needed to be based as close to his boss's office as possible.

However the Hussein's private living quarters were situated in another part of the living complex and from what Mehmet could understand, were off limits to the hired help. That suited him fine.

Next Mehmet was quickly introduced to the security personnel who would be under his command. From the little he had seen of them, Mehmet wasn't impressed. Once he had found his feet he intended to have his own little interview session. Next was a quick introduction to the staff in general. There were simply too many of them for Mehmet's liking It was going to take him quite a while before he would get a proper handle on who was who.

In fact it took two full days just to familiarise himself with the general lay out of the Hussein's residence before Mehmet felt confident enough not to get lost. It was also revealed to him during this time the real purpose for having been selected. The Hussein's had suffered a home invasion by person or person's unknown. The previous head of security had lost his job because of it, but even as Mehmet began to discover the facts about the home invasion he was still only being told half-truths. It was like pulling teeth, without anaesthetic, both painful and frustrating as hell. If only Ali Hussein had been straight with him from the beginning a lot of wasted time and needless effort could have been avoided.

The story that gradually unfolded before Mehmet's eyes and ears differed greatly to the one Ali Hussein had fabricated. Mehmet had been tasked with the questioning of all the household staff and security personnel. The reason was to find out if they had somehow been complicit in the home invasion. It didn't help that Mehmet had to learn second hand from them that Yasmin Hussein, Ali's sister, had been the root cause for the home invasion.

To hear Ali's version of events Yasmln had come to Jordan specifically to attend her father's funeral. Once this was done Yasmin was taken back to the Hussein's residence, together with her mother and brother, for a period of mourning.

In actual fact from what Mehmet had pieced together and learned from other sources, Yasmin had become a virtual prisoner. Admittedly the Hussein residence was a luxurious prison but it was a prison nevertheless. Her passport had been confiscated by Ali himself. Armed guards prevented Yasmin from leaving the compound and she had been denied both telephone and internet access. No one was allowed to carry either a message or letter for her outside of the compound walls. To do so would result in immediate dismissal or death.

Mehmet learned, by fits and starts, what happened when the home invasion occurred.

Ali, suspected that the young guard tasked with guarding his sister's corridor, had somehow been involved or coerced into aiding and abetting her escape.

The previous head of security, now smarting under the shame of having been absent from the residence at the time of the invasion, now set too with a vengeance at Ali's insistence, to extract a confession from the young guard. To his credit the young man managed to withstand a savage beating from the head of security and two guards, maintaining his innocence throughout and doggedly stuck to his story, which was that he had been surprised and tasored on Miss

Hussein's landing by one man, a westerner. He had then been tied up and left in Miss Hussein's bathroom where members of his own security team later found him. He did mention that Miss Hussein knew the man, calling him by name, but unfortunately the guard understandably couldn't remember what she had called him having just been tasored. Mehmet had thought at the time that to succeed in freeing Miss Hussein by using just one man was very audacious but once again Mehmet had only been told part of the story. It was only later that he learned of the so called part collapse of the compound wall in the vehicle park from other members of the staff.

Mehmet concluded from this new information that it had to be a distraction and therefore meant that at least two people had to have been involved. Mehmet was slowly getting there but it was so frustrating.

In the short time that Mehmet had been in charge he had neither met nor been introduced to Ali's mother. Had he known then, what type of woman she was he wouldn't have minded if he never had to meet her.

When Ali's mother first arrived at the Hussein household as a young bride there was already another strong woman in place. Mrs Bashir was head of the household staff and she ran a tight ship but was scrupulously fair, especially when dealing with matters pertaining to the household.

The young Mrs Hussein had expected to take up the duties normally carried out by Mrs Bashir but when that didn't happen, the new bride foolishly complained to her husband. She fully expected him to side with her but when that didn't happen, she was bitterly disappointed to learn that the running of the household was the domain of Mrs Bashir and it was to be left in her capable hands. From that moment on, Mrs Bashir had become a target for the new Mrs Hussein. She would not rest until she found some pretext to get rid of her.

A steady drip, drip was directed first at her husband and later at her son Ali in an effort to try and remove Mrs Bashir from the household. Mrs Bashir had endured an endless amount of criticism and complaints from her nemesis, all without foundation, but finally with the house invasion Ali's mother seized her chance. She accused Mrs Bashir of secretly carrying and posting a letter for Yasmin.

The accusation was completely false of course and was vehemently denied by Mrs Bashir but this time Ali listened to his mother's lies. He had Mrs Bashir questioned by his then head of security. She denied any wrong doing and maintained her innocence during the interrogation.

The then head of security at that time reported to Ali that he believed Mrs Bashir was telling the truth but Mrs Hussein's steady drip, drip of poison continued unabated and it fell to Mehmet as the new head of security to question her again; this time at the behest of Ali's mother.

Mrs Bashir answered all of Mehmet's questions promptly and with dignity and just like the previous head of security he announced that he believed Mrs Bashir was telling the truth and was therefore innocent of any wrong doing.

So in conclusion, Mehmet delivered his findings to Ali, that he believed the young guard who had been tasered on Yasmin's corridor to be innocent of any wrong doing other than failing to foil the intruder.

Ali thanked Mehmet for his diligence but as head of the household he reserved the right to pass judgement.

When, later on Mehmet thought on the matter, he didn't think anything was amiss with Ali's ruling, he was after all their employer so it was only right that the final judgement should rest with him, but the security issue was still a problem that hadn't been solved and it became an itch to Mehmet that was just out of reach.

A few days later Ali asked Mehmet to come and see him in his office. He had made a decision about the young guard - he would be dismissed! Regrettably Mrs Bashir was also to be dismissed. Ali looked in Mehmet's direction for his reaction. Mehmet took both statements with calm detachment as there was nothing he could do about the situation, Ali was their employer.

If he expected Mehmet to protest in some way or plead their case then he was sadly disappointed. Mehmet's own position as head of security was just as tenuous as theirs.

Ali had made his judgment and that was the end of the matter as far as Mehmet was concerned, but he did have concerns of his own to do with the security of the Hussein residence and the perimeter wall. One of the guards who had been on duty when Ali's sister had been here was morbidly obese, as a security guard he was totally useless and as such Mehmet wanted him dismissed.

Ali blinked at this suggestion staring at Mehmet as though he had just slapped him across the face. Mehmet wondered if he had overstepped the mark at this point but now committed had to continue as there was more; "With the loss of these two guards the security team is now under strength so we need to recruit three more guards to be able to monitor the grounds properly on a 24 hour basis. Also, I have walked round the perimeter wall marking out the most vulnerable places and it would be beneficial if we could have extra C.C.T.V. cameras installed in these areas."

Mehmet handed Ali an overview of the buildings and perimeter wall marked with six 'X's.

Ali took the overview from Mehmet looking with interest at where he had marked. Mehmet didn't think Ali was used to his head of security taking his job quite so seriously. It was obviously a new concept for him.

Surprisingly Ali came on board with the suggestions. Home invasion tended to focus the mind more clearly when it happened to you.

He asked if Mehmet would be prepared to conduct interviews for new security staff, "Yes sir. I think that would be best, thank you," he said.

"You don't have to thank me Mehmet, I feel like I have a proper head of security working for me now unlike the last one," added Ali

Mehmet felt that with Ali's help he was beginning to finally get somewhere. As he was about to leave Mehmet noticed a thick leather zipped folder on Ali's desk, the writing on the front was the wrong way round but he could clearly see that it said London.

Ali noticed him looking at it and asked, "What is it?"

Something about the folder had aroused Mehmet's curiosity, "Excuse me sir but that folder,I couldn't help noticing that it's marked for London."

Ali found nothing unusual in Mehmet's observation.

"Yes it's the monthly run on documents and letters to my family's lawyer in London. What of it?" he asked.

"If it's not too impertinent of me to ask sir, how is it delivered?"

"I have It flown there direct. Many documents for correspondence needing my attention are flown back the next day, why?" asked Ali.

He didn't answer straight away and Mehmet thought that they both came to the same answer at the same time, but he said it out loud just for his benefit, so there was no room for doubt, "That's how your sister got a message out. She must have slipped a note or letter inside somehow."

Ali couldn't very well dispute the fact it was so blindingly obvious.

Had Mehmet known about it beforehand, Mrs Bashir's position there would have been safe. But Ali had made his decision and however unfair it was, Ali would not go back on it.

Ali's mother would now have her dearest wish fulfilled; Mrs Bashir banished from the kingdom and herself installed as head of the household. It had taken a lifetime of hate and spite to achieve her objective but at last it was done.

So Mehmet, completely by accident, had solved the

final mystery of how Yasmin had got a message to London. It must have infuriated Ali like hell to realize that he had provided the means himself.

Later when he was resting in bed and his mind wouldn't shut off; Mehmet couldn't help smiling at the irony of it. He reflected on the probable fact that he was now working for a murderer, and of course there was the small matter of Ali and his mother conspiring to keep his sister prisoner. Mehmet added to his mental list that Ali was a known liar and fabricator of the truth so what was there not to like.

Then, there was of course, that evil viper of a woman, Ali's mother to contend with. Mehmet decided that he would do well to stay out of her way; she could make life very difficult for him. Thinking seriously about her it wouldn't surprise him at all if she wasn't just as complicit in her husband's murder as Ali.

So began Mehmet's role as head of security for the Hussein's. One thing was certain, interesting times lay ahead for Mehmet.

Chapter 48

The summons upstairs to see Mary Wallace no longer held any terror for Doug Simons. He wasn't being complacent about it, far from it, but the idea of being summoned upstairs no longer had his guts squirming in knots.

Exiting the lift on his boss' floor Doug marvelled at how relaxed he felt. Knocking firmly on Mary Wallace's door Doug waited for the command to enter.

"Come," could be heard plainly from within.

Doug entered her domain and walking purposely to within a few feet of her desk he said, "You sent for me ma'am?"

Looking up from her paper work Mary Wallace secretly appraised Doug Simons' apparel with approval; smart but functional, clean shaven and well-groomed at all times. Mary Wallace thought that Doug Simons was a credit to both himself and his chosen profession. Realizing that she had left him unanswered for long enough Mary put him out of his misery, "Yes Doug, it's about our last meeting and your plan to find Abdul Rahman's strong hold. It has been approved."

Doug said nothing waiting instead for Mary to give him more details.

Mary noted with pleasure that Doug had appeared to grow within himself. He stood up straighter for one thing, seeming more confident. Mary had hoped that Doug would grow to fill his new role and it certainly appeared to be working. She could tell for instance that he was no longer intimidated by her. The transformation in him was a definite improvement.

"As of last night special forces teams from the United States and the United Kingdom in a joint operation have put your plan into action. They are searching the proposed area of interest on the grid system that you yourself suggested," finished Mary

"I see, thank you ma'am," said Doug. "Now it's just a matter of wait and see," he muttered to himself.

"Yes precisely. Now we wait and see. As it was your plan to begin with, I thought it only right and proper that you be Informed of it being put into action, by me personally," explained Mary.

"I appreciate that ma'am, thank you," replied Doug.

Mary dismissed him with a simple nod of her head, her mind already back to dealing with her paperwork.

Going back down the few flights in the lift, Doug didn't feel elated by the news as such, instead he felt a little tense as things could get worse from now on. If Abdul Rahman's strong hold wasn't discovered within the next ten days it meant that Doug's whole hypothesis was wrong. If that proved to be the case where did that leave Doug? Probably up shit creek without a paddle. His whole credibility as an information analyst would be brought into question. As such, he would be deemed unreliable. Christ thought Doug, life used to be so much simpler.

A mental image came unbidden into his mind of the white haired cadaverous like body of his former boss, James Martin, now lying helpless in a military hospital bed having to depend on the good will of strangers, unable to even wipe his own arse. Poor fucker, thought Doug. God! I don't want that to be me.

Chapter 49

A trip to the seaside - Claire, Luke and Adam

We were at home waiting to be picked up by Frank and Yasmin. A couple of days ago we were all having dinner at our place having invited Frank and Yasmin round. As was normal nothing special, just a friendly get together with dinner thrown in, though I must admit I took great pains with the joint of beef, to make sure it was cooked just right; it was, it was done to perfection.

The television had been left on in the living room,'with the sound turned down low, but we still managed to hear the weather forecast for the next few days. It promised good weather until the weekend and then a band of rain was to follow. On a whim Yasmin suggested that we all go to Brighton on Wednesday whilst the forecast was good. Everyone was caught up in the suggestion and agreed it would make a nice day out.

I was especially pleased for Adam as he had never been

to the sea side before and besides, he needed his horizons broadening. The only time that Adam had seen the sea was on television. He, like millions of other viewers, had been captivated by David Attenborough's, The Blue Planet, so it would be an experience for Adam to see the real thing, though admittedly, it would only be a small part of it. I only hoped that it would live up to his expectations.

Frank was bringing the club's mini-van as opposed to their own car. It meant swapping Adam's car seat to the van but we could then all travel together and we would have more room. Adam's pushchair along with his other bits and bobs needed for the day could be easily accommodated in the van.

A cheerful Frank arrived with Yasmin beside him. I noticed that Adam's seat had been fixed central. Good that meant one of us would be seated either side of him to keep him occupied during the journey.

We loaded the van up with Adam and his necessities. Yasmin gave up her seat beside Frank so that Luke could sit up front. She preferred to have Adam beside her and myself on the other side so that we could talk. There was no fuss or discussion about the seating arrangements it was just who we were, comfortable in one another's company – like family.

As Frank set off Luke didn't bother him with unnecessary small talk - Frank didn't need the distraction. Instead he needed full concentration to navigate London's busy roads.

Yasmin and I by comparison talked incessantly. It was only yesterday that Adam and I had gone with Yasmin and Frank for her ultrasound at Dr Cooymans' clinic, which had been at Yasmin's insistence, yet still we always found more to talk about.

Adam had sat beside me only yesterday quiet and serious. He now knew that Aunty Yasmin was pregnant and would be having a baby of her own. He had been as good as gold throughout Yasmin's examination but I could tell that something was troubling him.

It would be fair to say that Adam looked on Yasmin as his second mother; after all she had always been there for him. So it had come as a shock at first to learn that Yasmin's priorities would now lean first to her own child and not to Adam.

I had to explain to him as tactfully as I could so as to not hurt his feelings, that even when Yasmin had her own baby she wouldn't stop loving him, as she had more than enough love to go around, it just meant that because the baby was new and small it would need her help more, but once he or she was a little bit older and less dependent on her she would be able to spread her love more evenly.

I was making a hash of it I know, but I finally managed to convince Adam that Yasmin would never stop loving him. Christ! He was only a child, a baby really, and here I was trying to convince my son that Yasmin wouldn't stop loving him.

Yasmin had asked Natalie to please not reveal the baby's sex, content just to know that the baby was healthy.

That night whilst bathing Adam he had revealed to me the sex of Yasmin's baby - a girl!

Unconvinced at first I asked, "How do you know?"

Playing with his boat he was quiet at first then said, "I just know."Then, thinking about his answer for a few seconds, a flash thought popped into my head, "Does your dad know too?"

Adam answered, "If I know, dad knows too -'Out of the mouth of babes'!" I asked him not to tell Yasmin that he knew the sex of her unborn baby.

He solemnly promised me he wouldn't but then asked me, "Why not?"

I then had to explain that Yasmin wanted it to be a surprise.

He did what most kids do and asked, "Why?"

I realised that this could go on for quite a while so looking for a short cut instead I said, "Because some women like to know what sex their baby is before it is born but not all women do. I wanted to know what sex you were purely for practical reasons. Yasmin is different. She views motherhood as something akin to mystical; it is enough for her to know that the baby is healthy. If she found out the baby's sex before it was born it would upset her, so rather than upset her we have to respect Yasmin's wishes and keep the baby's sex a secret until he or she is born, understand?"

Adam nodded that he did.

Whilst I put Adam to bed I didn't know whether to be annoyed with Luke or not but then thinking about it rationally, was it after all such a big deal? It only stood to reason that if Adam knew the sex of Yasmin's baby then Luke would also know. He was damned if he did and damned if he didn't. I decided to give the poor guy a break and revealed to him what Adam had just told me.

Luke looked crestfallen then nodded and said, "Sorry, I didn't know what to do."

I could sympathise with him it was an awkward position to be in, but that was yesterday and now we were leaving London's crowded streets behind us in the rear view mirror.

Adam was stuck between us both and going nowhere, had been chatty and perhaps a little over excited but that was to be expected. This excursion was something new and a whole heap different from his normal routine.

As we finally arrived on the outskirts of Brighton, Frank slowed down marginally,looking to follow directions to a multi-storey car park off West Street, he found it in Russell Road. Taking a ticket lifted the barrier and Frank headed up. He kept going until an empty space presented itself.

Next stop for everyone,was the toilet. Again!

Following the signs we found one open near the top of West Street. Suitably refreshed we re- traced our steps back towards Kings Road and for Adam his first view of the sea. I'm not sure if it lived up to Adam's expectations of the Blue Planet, I'm not sure anything could, but all the same it was the ocean, even if only a tiny fraction of it.

The weather had remained sunny as promised but the breeze coming on land from the sea was a little cool. We went into a huddle deciding where to go next. Yasmin suggested the Sea Life Aquarium and that seemed to meet with everyone's approval.

Walking down Kings Road towards the aquarium we took in the architecture of the fine old buildings along the front, most of which seemed to be hotels. Just passed the Palace Pier it was just a short distance to the aquarium.

Once we had paid our entrance fees and were inside, Adam's eyes widened and suddenly his world was transformed. For the next two hours, what he had only previously seen on television, was now only separated from him by a sheet of glass.

Adam loved every minute of it and was reluctant to leave, long after the adults had lost interest. Nevertheless all good things eventually come to an end and so it was with the Sea Life Aquarium.

Yasmin mentioned wanting to see the Royal Pavilion so that is where we headed next. The streets around the Pavilion area were very busy with buses, all types of vehicles and pedestrians in abundance. We walked part way around the Pavilion wondering about the incongruous placing of such a structure. We even pondered joining the queue to look inside then changed our minds, deciding instead that as we were hungry we would find either a cafe or a restaurant that wasn't full to capacity; this proved to be nigh on impossible. We walked for a while searching for that elusive cafe /restaurant until we came to The Lanes.

These narrow old streets held numerous antique shops, jewellers and boutiques. It was here that we found a diamond in the rough, the elusive tea shop. We left Adam's push chair outside as it would have caused a problem bringing it inside. I just hoped that someone didn't take a fancy to it!

Seating ourselves around the only available table Adam had to make do on his dad's lap. We ordered two pots of tea, a juice for Adam and buttered scones all round. It all arrived in and on proper china ware, complete with knives and a pot of strawberry jam, and very nice it was too! Adam had trouble finishing all his scone so I was forced to help him finish it off - perks of being his mum. A quick wipe with a paper towel restored Adam to cleanliness and we were good to go.

It had been a lovely day out but sadly it was time to head off home.

Following Frank's lead we headed in what we thought was the general direction of the multi-storey car park onto North Street. We kept pace with Frank until we arrived at the junction with West Street. Here we were on familiar territory and relaxed. It wasn't long before we were all safely back in the mini-van. We had just left Brighton proper when Adam finally gave in and fell asleep; it had been a long, tiring day for him, but a good one all the same. Adam would probably talk about it incessantly for days to come but that was alright, new experiences were good for him.

When we got home Luke managed to remove Adam from his seat without waking him up. Frank helped carry Adam's push chair for me and I brought the rest. Yasmin hugged and kissed us both saying goodbye. I kissed Frank on the cheek thanking him for a lovely day.

He just said, "You are very welcome darling," in his typical rugged way.

We waited by the front door waving them off. Finally tired but happy I closed our front door to the world. Then, I don't know why, but I suddenly thought, treasure these days because they help to make a happy life.

Chapter 50

Saturday night at the club proved to be hectic. Members and their guests had been piling in ever since official opening time. The fact that we had a prominent disc jockey advertised might have had something to do with it. Either way the club was almost full to capacity. There was every real chance that a 'Club Full' sign might have to be displayed out front.

So far the D.J. was proving to be well worth his eye watering fee. The dance floor was full and shaking. Sweat was freely flowing from the energetic dancers; perhaps memories of Ibiza's hectic nightlife were still fresh in many of the club clientele's minds. Whatever the reason the club was heaving and doing great business.

They had been ordering bottles of Krug and Crystal like it was going out of fashion. Chris had gone the extra mile in securing the D.J.'s services for just the one night. Usually he could only be found D.J. ing for huge party crowds whether in the south of France, Ibiza, Japan or Rio de Janeiro. So we were talking mega crowds, generating mega money.

Frank had rotated the security detail letting Sue, Eddie and Mark police the front of house and Pete and Bridget were tasked with the quieter areas and toilets. That left Luke and Frank to police the main room and dance floor. We were all in contact via internal communications, so help, should it be needed, was only seconds away.

It had been a while since Luke and Frank had worked a room together, I say together but really they were not together, not in a holding hands type of together, they each had their own specific area to police. Tonight Frank had the bar area, toilets and rear corridor leading to the emergency exits and Yasmin's private office and Luke had the dance floor, surrounding tables and private cubicles to keep an eye on. It seemed unfair that he had the largest area to police but Luke didn't mind. Next time it would be someone else's turn and of course if they needed help they had the internal communications.

The job itself required common sense and tact. You were there to be seen and to instil a sense of security, whilst at the same time trying not to appear too obstructive. Luke had quickly found out that you got far more co-operation from the clientele if you asked them politely not to take their drinks onto the dance floor rather than telling them. Mostly it was just enthusiastic club goers who, upon hearing a favourite song they like just automatically got up to join the dancers, whilst holding a glass or bottle in their hand. It merely required a polite request to achieve the desired result, nine times out of ten.

When it didn't work, well that's when things got interesting, but so far everyone had been well behaved and good natured, enjoying the lively atmosphere. Luke held his ear piece whilst Frank gave him an update.

"Just going into the gents' toilets Luke."

"Okay Frank."

When Frank entered the swanky men's room, he was confronted by two men, one standing wiping his nose with his fingers and the other one bending over a line of white powder, hoovering it up his nose off the marble sink top.

Frank had been shocked at first by what he was witnessing. It made his reactions that much slower. He was just about to call for Luke's assistance when the man who was standing produced something from his jacket pocket. Frank registered what it was a split second before he was hit over the head with it. Instinct now took over and Frank delivered a telling blow to his attacker's face rocking him sideways, but the damage had been done, Frank fell heavily to the floor with small geysers of bright red blood spurting from his head wound.

The two men could have inflicted a lot more damage on Frank whilst he was down but chose to run instead. Luckily Luke who had been waiting for an update from Frank had decided to go and check on him.

Frank was trying vainly to haul himself upright off the floor when Luke found him. Frank's head was a mess of bright red blood. Luke wadded up a bunch of paper towels and held them to the wound whilst helping him to his feet. He was unsteady and had to lean heavily against the marble top to prevent himself from falling to the floor again. Luke could see the head wound would require stitches; it was also possible that Frank had a concussion. Whatever Frank's feelings about Luke's diagnosis he would require hospital treatment. Luke got onto the front desk to send for an ambulance.

Frank protested that he didn't need an ambulance in

the foulest of obscenities that Luke had ever heard strung together in one sentence, but when he tried to walk unaided he almost fell on his arse, Luke only just managing to catch him.

Luke watched as Frank was helped into the ambulance closely followed by Yasmin. Satisfied that

Frank was in good hands he then made sure that everything was running smoothly and that the security team was refocused on their jobs. Luke moved Pete and Bridget up into the main room and brought Eddie into the quiet area from the front of house. It was the best he could do before heading up to the control room. Arthur had been brought up to speed on what had happened to

Frank. He had replayed the discs to within five minutes of Frank entering the men's toilets.

Arthur and Luke watched the replay in slow motion. Frank had mentioned two men, mid twenties, white, both unknown to him, doing drugs.

They both watched the screens avidly searching for the two men, eventually isolating two men fitting the description and time frame. They continued to watch as the two men, laughing, snorted the white powder, then Frank entered the men's room and the same two men hurriedly rushed out.

They replayed the same bit of tape over and over until they could freeze frame it at the best possible angle for identification. The police would have to be notified as it was a drugs related crime by a member of the public carrying a concealed weapon, who had physically assaulted a member of staff.

First Luke asked each member of the security team to come up to the control room one at a time.

Everyone was eager to eyeball Frank's attackers but sadly no one recognised the men. The discs were removed from the machines because they were now evidence and fresh discs were inserted and set to record.

The night was still relatively young and the club was still packed and making money. Frank spending the night in hospital wouldn't alter things, life would go on.

As it turned out later Frank needed eight stitches in his head wound. He as suspected, had a mild concussion and was kept in hospital for two days observation.

The police came to take swabs of the substance found on the marble top in the men's room. It was confirmed to be cocaine. The club gave them one of the discs with the time frame identifying Frank's attackers on it but kept the other one back for their own identification purposes, just in case the one given to the police, mysteriously got lost.

Frank stayed off work for the rest of the week returning before opening up time on Thursday night.

Everyone was glad to see him back as he gathered together the security team.

Confirming what he had previously only told Luke, whilst in a concussed state, that one of his attackers had used what looked like a telescopic police baton.

Everyone looked around at each other. If what Frank had just told them was true, and Frank's head injury was living proof that it was, then they needed to be extra vigilant.

Frank decided that in future two team members would be required when checking the wash rooms. He wanted to make sure that no one else was going to be caught out like that again.

Chapter 51

Afghanistan, in country.

Red One and Red Two had been in the country for the past five days. Daylight would be lost soon but they were coming to the end of their designated grid search pattern for another day. It would soon be time to dig in and settle for the night.

Red One and Two were the code names for the two American special forces search teams deployed in the hunt to find Abdul Rahman's so called stronghold. No one really knew for certain if it actually existed.

Each team was comprised of a first lieutenant, a top sergeant and two privates, first class.

Lieutenant Schaefer, leader of Red One, would have to send another short satellite burst transmission declaring his status. It was coming upon time to bounce it off the satellite and it would

be yet another negative on finding Rahman's stronghold.

His counterparts Green One and Green Two were searching the two grid references to his right. Green One and Two were British contingents made up of members from the S.A.S. and they too were coming to the end of their designated search area for the day. The terrain, as was expected, had proved to be difficult to traverse but it couldn't be denied; it was ideal country in which to build a strong hold. It would soon be time to send his report in before digging in for the night. Five hard days of searching had resulted in absolutely nothing. Sergeant Neame wondered if, and not for the first time, they were on a wild goose chase.

The whole command of the operation had fallen under the leadership of the Americans. Portrayed on national television and to some extent in the popular press, much was made of the so called special relationship that existed between the United States and Great Britain. In reality, it was an uneasy alliance at best, with snide remarks aimed at one another's ineptitudes. The soldiers on the ground were no exception. The Americans thought that the qualities of the S.A.S. were big on reputation whilst sadly lacking in substance. The British for their part thought that the Americans weren't team players and were generally pussies. It didn't bode well for the success of the operation. Admittedly the Americans were footing the bill for the whole operation. The $10,000,000 bounty on Abdul Rahman's head told of how seriously they wanted this fucker dead, but with the recent atrocity committed in Spain they now wanted the whole thing, body included.

This was necessary for propaganda purposes. The world was watching, waiting to see if the

Americans could pull it off. Careers could be made and

elevated if Rahman could only be found and eliminated.

Politicians would be salivating at the thought, hoping to hitch a ride on the coat tails of any success but would be ready to distance themselves at the first hint of failure. Someone once described politicians as the lowest form of pond life. I myself think, that that was a fair assessment.

As the Red and Green teams bedded down for the night one man on guard duty, they all secretly wondered if tomorrow would be the day.

Chapter 52

And on the 6th day....

When day light broke it was chilly, the sun only just beginning to break surface. It was amazing how cold the nights were here whilst the days were constant searing heat.

Lt. Schaefer roused his men from sleep ordering them to get some chow, it could well prove to be another long day of fruitless searching but his men needed to be on their mettle, so food first in order to carry out their grid search pattern reconnaissance. Water was also a worry and they each had to carry two litre water bottles on their belts as well as a gallon of water each in their backpacks because if today proved to be another hot one he may have to arrange for a re-supply rendezvous.

On a grid reference over to Schaefer's right, Sergeant Neame's team were in pretty much the same situation. He was thinking along much the same lines at Lt. Schaefer; at least they had that much in common, as well as the English language, of course. Whatever their differences both men were professional soldiers and would carry out their assigned duties to the letter, neither man wanted to fail in their respective missions.

Four hours later the sun had climbed much higher in the sky and it beat down relentlessly on the searching men. Lt Schaefer blinked the sweat from his eyes for the umpteenth time pausing for a moment to wipe it away properly. He looked over to where Sergeant Vasquez was searching close to a ravine.

All of a sudden Sgt. Vasquez held his carbine over his head, attracting the attention of Lt. Shaefer.

Seeing the sergeant's signal he did the same with his own weapon attracting the attention of the man to his right, noting that he in turn did the same thing, thus attracting the last man in line. It was the signal meaning contact had been made and as such was a call to come together as a group.

Lt. Schaefer joined up with Sgt. Vasquesz closely followed by the rest of Red One team.

When they were finally all together Lt Schaefer asked, "What have we got sergeant?"

"A cave system in the ravine ahead, heavily camouflaged," said Vasquez.

Excitement began to build as they hurriedly dropped their backpacks to the floor.

Lt. Schaefer lifted out his field binoculars before heading towards the edge of the ravine. Now crawling on their bellies to reach the edge unseen it was immediately clear without the aid of binoculars, that the cave system was intensive. The camouflage netting had been expertly placed rendering the cave system almost invisible from above. No wonder the eyes in the sky had failed to find it! Checking, with the aid of his binoculars, Lt Schaefer began to sketch out on a small drawing pad what he could make out through the camouflage netting.

Several large entrances could be made out fairly easily. There also appeared to be extensive concrete and steel modifications added to the interiors of the caves but the angle of sight was wrong to be able to see inside to any depth. Handing the binoculars over to Sgt. Vasquez for his opinion, Schaefer waited while he assessed the cave system. After careful examination Vasquez concurred with Lt. Schaefer that it appeared to have prepared bunkers, within the caves themselves.

One cave in particular looked quite a lot bigger than the others but they couldn't see inside it far enough to ascertain its use. Then five minutes later a truck was slowly backed out as if on cue, closely followed by two men dressed in work overalls.

Lt. Schaefer now had his answer, it was a vehicle garage. He now urgently needed to pass on the intel to headquarters. Looking at his watch he realised that he had eighteen minutes before the next overhead pass of the satellite. He needed to keep it short but to the point. Settling on: Red One, grid ref number, extensive cave/bunker system found in ravine, heavily camouflaged, garage situated in cave system, vehicle numbers unknown, number of enemy combatants unknown but possibly in excess of 200 due to size of cave system, awaiting instructions, out.

Lt Schaefer sent the satellite burst transmission at the earliest opportunity relaxing visibly amongst his men once it was done. They backtracked a little way form the ravine to avoid detection, finding concealment amongst some large boulders.

The Red One team couldn't see it from where they were hunkered down, but they had stirred up a hornet's nest, back at headquarters.

Most of the headquarters team had been sceptical about the bunker/cave system actually existing from the beginning. After all, wasn't it based on intelligence gleaned from the British and they all knew how unreliable intelligence was from that quarter, so when Red One team actually hit pay dirt it sent them running around like headless chickens.

It needed a steady hand to take control of the situation and evaluate the information. They found it in newly promoted Lt Colonel Anders of Military Intelligence. Anders had only just recently been promoted from Major for his exploits in Islamabad, Pakistan. Now he had been brought here to both steady the reins and give direction.

First he had a message of, 'Well-Done', sent to Lt. Schaefer and his team before instructing both Red and Green teams to march south away from the ravine and make for grid ref.1 by 18:00 hours for ex filtration by chopper.

Lt. Schaefer said after receiving his orders, "Get your asses in gear boys we have a chopper to catch."

Red Two team were cocker hoop that their fellow countrymen had found Rahman's rat hole and disappointed only by the fact that it hadn't been them.

The Brits of Green One and Two teams were spitting feathers that the yanks had beaten them to the prize. But only because they had bet that the losing team would have to buy the booze for the next week, guess the Brits were going to be a bit out of pocket, that really hurt.

Now that Abdul Rahman's stronghold had been found, it needed swift military action asap. Any delay now, could well see Rahman slip through the west's fingers once again.

Lt. Colonel Anders bucked the chain of command at

his disposal by going over his immediate superiors head. It could well have disastrous consequences for his future career prospects, but he thought, fuck it. If a little insubordination resulted in Abdul Rahman's death, it would be well worth the risk. His immediate superior was Colonel Monahan.

A notoriously slow witted, chair bound, warrior, if it was left to him, then the element of surprise would be lost.

Anders bit the bullet and asked his adjutant to arrange an urgent meeting with General Mayweather. The die was now cast and it was too late to turn back, Abdul Rahman's fate and possibly his own, were now in the hands of General 'mad dog' Mayweather.

Chapter 53

Luke was surprised when just Frank arrived to pick him up. Opening the front passenger door Luke eased his frame onto the seat and snapping his seat belt into place he said, "No Yasmin?"

"No, she wasn't feeling too good so she decided to give it a miss," replied Frank.

Luke didn't comment deciding instead to keep his mouth shut. Yasmin rarely ever had time off so taking one night off now that she was pregnant seemed totally justified to Luke anyway. Besides if the boss couldn't take a night off now and then who the hell could?

Arriving at the club Frank parked the car in the designated parking space reserved for management at the rear. Frank and Luke got out, giving Chris's Subaru a cursory once over, thinking more or less the same thing, young men and their toys!

It seemed ironic to Luke that the parking spaces were situated close to the row of dumpsters! I mean was that a conscious decision when the car park was marked out or an afterthought, just saying!

Early bird Chris was talking to Jimmy Small, the club's bar manager, who had vast experience in the London pub trade, when Frank and Luke caught up with them, so they listened in on their conversation. Jimmy was having a serious altercation with Chris about a new draught beer he had ordered in from a new brewery, without Jimmy's knowledge. The club's clientele, despite the beer being heavily promoted and reduced in price, had tried it once then left it alone.

Luke caught Jimmy's last comment about what he thought of it. "Its shite Chris, the public who have already tasted it don't come back for more. Besides I've said it before if there is nothing wrong with the beer we have been flogging for years why try and replace it? Stick to the beer that the public like. That's all I'm saying."

"Alright Jimmy I hear you," said Chris, "but what are we going to do about the barrels that are left?"

"I'll stick them on special offer until we have got rid of it, then ring the new brewery and tell them thanks but no thanks," said Jimmy firmly. "Honestly Chris stick to what you do best, running the club and leave the bar management to me. It's what you pay me for."

Chris raised his hands in final capitulation bowing to Jimmy's wisdom and then went to check on the music selection for tonight's entertainment before the club opened properly for business.

Frank sidled up to Jimmy, Luke in tow, ''Trouble in paradise Jimmy?" he said conspiratorially.

"Naah, Chris just got carried away with a new brewery that have set up shop, without asking me first, have you tried this beer?" asked Jimmy.

"No," Frank answered.

"Well don't fucking bother! It's like paint stripper," offered Jimmy, "anyway where's your good looking other half?"

"oh she is feeling a bit tired so she's taking the night off."

"Well give her my best," said Jimmy then wondered off, muttering to himself about shite beer.

Frank and Luke just looked at one another smiling at Jimmy's retreating back. Then they decided to have a safety check walk through, checking the toilets and removing the security chains from the fire exit doors before first the staff, and then the punters, begin to arrive.

It had become almost second nature for Frank and Luke to do this before the club opened its doors.

One never knew what would be facing them unless one checked. Once not long ago a water pipe in one of the ladies toilets had sprung a leak, which could have been disastrous, but the walk through an hour before opening time meant the stop cock valve could be turned off preventing further flooding. The floors were mopped and out of order signs placed before the paying public arrived.

When running a business it paid to be careful. Friday night usually heralded the start of a very busy weekend. It was the prelude to the weekend entertainment, a promise of things to come. This Friday night would be no exception to the rule.

The warm weather had brought the ladies out in force. As they arrived they were all attired in various modes of dress or in various modes of undress. As the night wore on the security staff was certainly kept on their toes, more than one amorous couple had to be reminded that they were in a public night club and not a hotel room, but other than that it was a reasonably good natured crowd who were hell bent of enjoying themselves.

The hours raced by, seemingly in a blur to Luke and towards the end of the night the club goers began to thin out, some to go on elsewhere perhaps another club or party, others tiredly, happy home to their own beds, or someone else's! Either way as the crowds began to leave, everyone on staff helped the beleaguered bar staff collect glasses or bottles etc., the tables and chairs had to be put back in reasonable order ready for the cleaning staff's arrival later in the morning. In essence everyone pitched in to help so that they could go home.

Eventually only the trio of Frank, Luke and Chris remained in the club, had Yasmin been on duty last night it would have been four.

A quick walk through in reverse looking for hidden revellers as well as to secure the building revealed no bodies. Frank told Luke he would wait for him in the car park. Luke waited with Chris whilst he set the alarm system before locking the double doors.

Then heading off around the back of the club Chris and Luke just had time to see someone moving swiftly towards Frank from behind the dumpsters, his arm upraised.

Luke immediately made a beeline for Frank's attacker moving at a phenomenal speed for someone his size.

Frank half turned realizing that someone was moving up swiftly from behind and fractionally to the side, just in time to avoid the oncoming blow. However Frank's attacker would not entirely be denied and the blow connected with finger numbing force on to Frank's shoulder. The pain radiated straight down to his fingertips with immediate effect.

Before Frank's attacker could land another blow,

this time aimed to his head, Luke arrived, kicking out and dislocating his attackers kneecap. Chris watched in disbelief. The first scream of pain was swiftly followed by another as Luke broke the wrist of his opponent, the one holding the baton.

Luke now had hold of the telescopic baton just in time to meet two further assailant's newly arriving for combat. They must have been hidden by the dumpsters and had almost taken Luke by surprise; but almost wasn't good enough, especially when facing someone like Luke.

Luke's philosophy when faced with two similarly armed opponents was simple - attack first and with deadly force. Striking out to his right Luke connected with his baton smashing the first attacker square across the face, breaking his nose and splitting it wide open. Then, ducking low Luke spun towards his second attacker striking him across the knee cap, there was a loud crack as the kneecap shattered eliciting a scream of pain from his attacker forcing him to edge away, but Luke hadn't quite finished yet, and he hadn't even broken into a sweat. Turning his attention back to the first attacker he struck him hard across the temple, watching as he fell heavily to the car park floor.

It wouldn't have ended there if Frank hadn't timely intervened. He had slowly regained feeling in his shoulder and arm whilst impotently watching as Luke systematically took the three men apart. It was only when there was a very real likelihood of death that Frank stepped in to prevent it. As Luke was about to deliver a killing blow to his kneecapped adversary, Frank managed to persuade Luke that they had had enough. It was all over in a matter of seconds.

Chris had taken pictures of all three adversaries on his phone and was almost certain that the one who had originally struck Frank with the baton was the same one captured on C.C.T.V. from a couple of weeks before.

Frank and Luke warily watched as two of the attackers helped their dazed comrade to his feet, then half carried, half dragged him away, amazed they were all still alive, whilst eyeing Luke with genuine fear.

Luke, still holding the baton, checked it out. He felt sure that it would have a serial number on it somewhere. That proved to be correct when he located it on the largest segment of tubing.

"Chris can you take a picture of this serial number. If those three are actually in the police force we can positively tie them to this incident," said Luke.

Chris took the photo then mentioned that Frank's attacker looked very much like the one on the club's C.C.T.V.

"Well if that's the case we can identify him from this serial number and if he is in the police it will be on his records," added Luke. "Right go home and get some sleep, we'll see you later."

"Or, they may have got them on the internet," joined in Frank.

That burst all their bubbles realising that it may well be true.

"Are you okay to drive Frank?" asked Luke.

"Yeah, feelings just about come back now," said Frank, gingerly working his arm and shoulder.

The car rocked slightly as they both got in. They didn't move for a while quietly reliving what had just happened. It was obvious to Luke that something was on Frank's mind, so he waited for him to give voice to it.

"Thanks Luke," said Frank.

Luke said nothing in reply knowing that there was more to come. "You know Luke, I have seen some shit in my time but that was fucking unbelievable. You were just a blur; where the fuck did you learn how to fight?"

Luke again said nothing. Frank probed a little further trying to coax his friend to finally open up, "I know that you weren't in the regiment," mused Frank, "so you my friend are a dark horse. Have you undergone some serious military training somewhere?" When again no answer looked to be forth coming Frank said as a wild guess, "I know you, were in the French Foreign Legion!"

It gave Luke a life line to his dilemma, how to stop Frank's interminable questions about his past. Deciding to run with it Luke gave a long searching look into Frank's eyes. It spoke volumes to Frank. "Fuck me. You were weren't you?" Frank digested Luke's unspoken words as affirmation that his wild guess had been correct. Frank sat quietly for a while trying to piece together the latest information about his friend. "Now it all makes sense," said Frank, as much to himself as to Luke.

"Alright mate now I begin to understand. Your past life is your own business, I can understand that; Christ, I've got one of my own so I should know, but some of those Foreign Legion types are really bad asses Luke and though it really pains me to say this, so are you. But, if it hadn't been for you tonight ... well l could have been lying on a slab in the mortuary, so once again, l owe you mate."

They shook hands solemnly the already strong bond between them now unbreakable.

Luke hated to deceive his friend but what alterative did he have? Only two people in this world knew what Luke really was and if it gave Frank comfort and a little piece of mind to think that he knew Luke's secret then so be it, but in truth it would take Frank several lifetimes to learn the full capabilities of what Luke could do.

It was easier this way. Frank would keep his secret safe and hopefully stay his questions, for now at least.

Chapter 54

At the Hussein residence on the outskirts of Amman, Jordan.

Mehmet Yafai, Ali Hussein's head of security, had just completed a snap inspection of his security team. He was known to make these inspections without warning and at any time of the day or night.

So far he had only had to give one lax member of his security team a humiliating dressing down to impress upon him the seriousness of his chosen profession. It seemed to have done the trick but he wouldn't stop the snap inspections, Mehmet took his position very seriously. Calling into the control room Mehmet asked bored security man if all was well.

Kamil Ahmed sat up straighter as his boss addressed him, "Yes sir, nothing to report."

" Alright Kamil, give it another hour and I'll have Syed come and relieve you."

Mehmet well knew that watching the T.V. monitors was a boring, eye straining job that required intense concentration but it was necessary, though it was very unlikely anyone would choose daylight hours to penetrate the walls of the Hussein residence. The last time that had happened was at night and before Mehmet had arrived, but Mehmet wouldn't relax the surveillance. He didn't intend that it should happen again not on his watch! Arriving back at his office Mehmet checked for any messages. Seeing that there weren't any he went into his small kitchen/diner, filled the kettle and set it to boil.

Hearing footfalls at his open office door he was surprised to see his boss, Ali Hussein, framed in the door way.

"Mehmet I thought I heard you come back. Can I have a quick word?" said Ali.

Mehmet followed his boss down the corridor to his office, "Close the door Mehmet," he said.

Mehmet did as he was asked wondering what was wrong. Ali was now seated in the chair behind his desk and indicated for Mehmet to sit in the opposite one. Getting straight to the point, which was unusual for Ali, he said, "On our last trip to Dubai, Mehmet, you mentioned that you could possibly recruit me a small private army of my own. I know I said that I would leave it with you but it has been a while now and I am rather anxious to learn what progress, if any, you have made."

Mehmet visibly relaxed in the chair, "So far sir I have managed to recruit two reliable men, both are known to me from my days in the military. I expect to recruit two more in about three weeks' time, when their military service comes to an end. I prefer to recruit men I know and trust as it saves time in the long run sir."

Ali Hussein almost jumped for joy. He hadn't realised that Mehmet had already started recruiting his own private army. Then thinking back to Dubai Ali said, "But that will only bring us up to four men Mehmet, didn't I advocate recruiting five or six?"

"Yes sir you did but after thinking about it logically, four well trained men with me at their helm would make it five and five men would be more than adequate to complete the job," replied Mehmet.

Ali blinked in surprise, "You would do this for me Mehmet?"

"Of course sir, it would be the only way to ensure that the job was carried out properly," concluded

Mehmet.

"Then you have my thanks. I have seriously underestimated your loyalty Mehmet, but you will not go unrewarded, you have my promise."

"Thank you sir," replied Mehmet.

"How soon do you think before your men will be ready?" asked Ali.

"It is three weeks before the other two men arrive so I think we can be ready in three months sir," calculated Mehmet. Ali beamed openly with obvious delight. "That could well coincide with my planned trip to Dubai Mehmet, with you at the helm of my army you could use the Learjet to travel on to London and finish the job."

A strange look of euphoria swept across his boss' features, Mehmet thought, obviously he was envisaging the murder of his sister and enjoying the thought of it, not content with murdering his own father Ali wanted his sister dead too.

Mehmet, not for the first time, felt ashamed to be

employed by such a man. Managing to mask his true feelings was becoming increasingly difficult for Mehmet but to bring his plans to fruition this charade needed to continue at least for a little while longer, at any rate.

Ali's glazed eyes returned to normal as he self-consciously managed to pull himself together, realizing that Mehmet was still present, "Thank you Mehmet, you have put my mind at rest."

"Thank you sir," said Mehmet, secretly sick to his stomach at being complicit in Ali Hussein's murderous machinations.

Chapter 55

The General

Lt. Colonel Anders had been sitting on his arse outside General Mayweather's office for the past forty minutes while the adjutant had been ceaselessly shuffling papers, and manning the telephones, since his arrival. The overhead fan had an irritating squeak that was seriously beginning to get on Anders' nerves. He could have tolerated the squeak if the fan was actually doing anything to alleviate the heat, but sweat was still managing to make itself felt along his spine annoying him still further. Anders was taken by surprise when General Mayweather himself opened his door beckoning him, with a wave, to come in.

General Mayweather was a bear of a man, 6' 6" in his stockinged feet, though the general's body was slowly beginning to turn to fat, you wouldn't want to bet against him in an arm wrestling contest. Following the general into his office Andres respectfully closed the door behind him. Now standing at attention two paces from the general's desk, Anders waited on the general to sit down.

General Mayweather was an imposing figure, his steel blue eyes seemed to penetrate Anders' body.

His skin began to crawl and it felt like he was being studied under a microscope.

General Mayweather's voice boomed loud and clear, "You have five seconds to try and convince me why I shouldn't have you busted back down to Major!"

"Abdul Rahman sir," Anders answered in a firm steady voice.

At the mention of Rahman's name, the general stiffened noticeably, "Go on, I'm listening."

"Our special forces teams have located his stronghold sir," answered Anders.

"You are certain of this?" asked the general.

Without having 100% bone-fide evidence that Abdul Rahman was actually in the cave/bunker complex, Anders stuck out his already precariously extended neck, "Yes sir!" he said now fully committed.

The general weighed up the man still standing to attention before him. He already knew about the

Special Forces teams missions to find Rahman's stronghold, he had signed the orders authorizing them. He had also been amongst the first people to be appraised of what Red One team had found, but then of course he should have been, as it was he who set the plan in motion in the first place. He also knew a little about Lt. Colonel Anders. He knew he was instrumental in finding and killing Rahman's number two in Pakistan.

It had taken guts Mayweather acknowledged for Anders

to go over his commanding officer's head and come to him with the information directly. He had done the same thing himself once at the beginning of his own career. Luckily he had been awarded with a silver star for his efforts instead of spending time in the stockade.

Anders' C.O. was notoriously inept as a combat soldier he was more suited to wrestling with administration rather than the enemy.

So General Mayweather completely understood why Colonel Anders would choose to jeopardize his career by going over his head, but it was still insubordination so he would have to be seen to chew him out if only for the benefit of his adjutant and the men in the next room. The general knew for a fact that the chewing out would get back to Anders' C.O. and thus, hopefully help save his career.

The general's tirade boomed loud and long before finally mercifully running out of steam. Once it was over, the general told Anders to stand at ease, then winked at him and conspiratorially confided in him that the tirade had been for his own benefit.

Lt. Colonel Anders wasn't stupid; he had realized that the general was merely going through the motions. Then he listened respectfully whilst General Mayweather outlined his plan of attack.

"As we are not supposed to be here in a combat role, but merely in an advisory capacity, the Afghan government forces will have to do the actual fighting. We can give them all the technical information and help that we can, without putting our own men at risk. We, together with the Brits have been training the afghan army for months; so far they haven't exactly distinguished themselves. How they will fare going up against fortified positions doesn't bear thinking about. I just hope that the $10,000,000 bounty placed on Rahman's head will prove the spur needed to get the Afghan general's in fighting mood.

"It would be suicide going into those caves without the protection of armour sir," said Anders.

"Please don't have the temerity to try and tell me my job colonel. I'm well aware that the Afghans need the support of armour," flared General Mayweather.

"No sir, sorry sir," apologised Anders.

The general waited a beat before continuing, "I will advise my opposite numbers that the use of armour would help save the lives of many of their men, whether or not they take my advice we shall have to wait and see, but rest assured Colonel I will give it nevertheless."

As an afterthought general Mayweather added, "I'm also going to lend the Afghans a half a dozen of our sniper teams, placed in various positions of advantage, purely in an advisory capacity of course."

Lt. Colonel Anders smiled, "that would be most helpful sir."

"Yes I thought so too. I managed to think of that all by myself," said General Mayweather. "Now I think we are done here Colonel, but if you would take a piece of friendly advice, make this the last time you buck the chain of command, it's not healthy!" Then loudly enough to be heard outside the door, "Now get out!"

"Yes sir, noted," Lt. Colonel Anders came once again to attention and saluted the general before about facing and marching out of his office.

All eyes in the outer room were studiously averted rendering Lt. Colonel Anders invisible to their scrutiny.

The chewing out by the general was purely for show he knew, and hopefully word would travel swiftly thus helping to save his career, but really it didn't matter to Anders if going over his C.O.'s head resulted in Abdul Rahman's death, then it would have been well worth the gamble.

Now everything would depend of whether the Afghan army would be willing to fight.

Chapter 56

The shots were evenly spaced and loud in the low ceilinged room, if it wasn't for the fact that they were all wearing ear defenders the occupants would be suffering significant hearing loss.

Mehmet Yafai still standing in the classic preferred shooters stance had just finished discharging his weapon. Bringing in the distant target to better assess his score he grunted with satisfaction. His skill with the hand gun had improved markedly over the last few weeks.

Mehmet was one of four shooters using the police shooting range which was two floors below street level. The other shooters were Masud Yafai, Mehmet's older brother and a senior sergeant in Amman's central police station. Others present were Kamil Ahmed and his brother Syed, recently discharged from military service in the Jordanian army.

Mehmet had known the Ahmed brothers from his own

time in the army. He had sought them out and actively recruited them for Ali Hussein's fledgling army and two more ex-soldiers would be joining their ranks within the next three weeks.

Of the four shooters, Masud was by far the better shot. His groupings were always spaced within a hands span. Kamil was a close second just going wild with one shot in almost every clip. Mehmet had improved to the point where he was a close third but Syed was still a work in progress, only managing to score 50% of the time. Still hopefully when the time came, the actual target would be a lot closer.

Adding fresh targets to the four separate lanes they sent them off into the distance, reloading their weapons for one last practice session. The room above the shooting range housed the police cells, though no one had ever considered whether any prisoner in the cells could actually hear the firing coming from below, why would they?

The Ahmed brothers before their discharge from the army had been approached by Mehmet to see what their plans were for civilian life. As Mehmet had correctly thought, they didn't have any real plans so he gave them a brief summary of what was required of them if they decided to join up. At first when they found out who their actual employer would be they were not too keen to commit. However when Mehmet told them, that in actual fact, they would be dealing and working with him and not Ali Hussein direct, it made a considerable difference. That and the fact that they would be receiving pay 1.5 times more than they had been receiving whilst serving in the army.

When it came to recruitment of Ali's private army, Mehmet had been given carte blanche, so a small house close to the central police station had been rented for their sole use. A telephone had been installed so that Mehmet could keep in constant touch should he need them. They would be armed and fully equipped, all at Ali Hussein's expense.

Twice a week, on Tuesday's and Thursday's between 8 p.m. and 9 p.m. Mehmet would collect them from the rented house so that they could practice on the police shooting range. This had all been arranged by Masud on the understanding that all the expended ammunition would be replaced, again all at Ali Hussein's expense. So far this arrangement had been honoured.

It had to be on those given days because Mohammed Ahmed, Amman's chief of police, chose to leave work early in order to visit his mistress of several years. It was supposed to be a well-kept secret known only to a select few, but of course it was common knowledge at Amman Central, even the cleaners knew about it.

One thing was for certain if ever the chief's wife found out about the affair, there would be a vacancy at Amman Central!

In a few weeks' time Ali Hussein's private army would number five in total, if all went to plan. The training will have been completed, the team fully equipped and ready for action by the time Ali's planned trip to Dubai was ready. Now it was just a matter of waiting.

Chapter 57

Aftermath

Claire was lying in bed awake when she heard Luke open the door. The light mornings meant that she was only half asleep whilst waiting for Luke to come home from work. Usually he came upstairs straight away to slide in beside her, but this morning was different, so she got out of bed padding naked over towards the door where her silk dressing gown was hanging up and slipped it on. Moving soundlessly so as not to wake Adam in the next room, she headed down stairs where she found Luke sitting on the settee nursing a mug of tea.

Sitting next to him she said, "Hey big guy, why are you sitting down here all on your own when you could be upstairs with your sexy wife?"

"Just winding down and thinking," replied Luke.

"Mmm that sounds ominous, what's up?"

"Frank got jumped in the club car park tonight," answered Luke.

"Oh no," exclaimed Claire, clearly concerned, "is he alright? Are you alright?" Claire looked at his face closely.

"Just a bruised shoulder I think and I'm fine," replied Luke, "just need to wind down a bit.

Now Claire knew that there was definitely more to this. "Alright Luke spill, what happened?" She said in a no nonsense tone.

Luke relived the scene as he saw it in his mind, "We were coming out of the club. Frank went to get the car whilst I waited for Chris to set the alarm and lock up. As we walked across the car park we saw someone coming from behind the dumpsters and attack Frank. He appeared to be holding a club in his hand."

"Oh no. Not again," said Claire interrupting Luke.

"I went to help Frank but before I could get to him he had already been struck once with what turned out to be a police baton. Luckily it struck him on his shoulder and not his head. Before he could strike again I arrived and took the assailant out."

Claire knew that there was more to it than that, Luke was just being modest.

"It was then that two more bodies came from behind the dumpsters to attack Frank and me, both of them were wielding police batons ...... so going into full attack mode, the red mist descended, and I quickly took them both out," finished Luke.

Claire knew Luke and also that that wasn't the full story, "What are you not telling me Luke?"

Luke took a deep breath before answering, "If Frank hadn't stopped me when he did, I could well be locked up now in a police cell and facing murder charges," admitted Luke.

"Oh Luke, how bad are they?" Claire wanted to know.

"A few broken bones, cuts and bruises, and probably .... No definitely, one hell of a headache," finished Luke.

Claire sat quietly digesting what Luke had just told her. Thenshe asked, "Should I be worried?"

"I honestly don't know Claire. I've always been so in control when faced with situations like this, but this time I really wanted to kill them for hurting my friend. I know that it's no excuse but that is how I felt. Also it turns out that the guy who attacked Frank was the same guy who brained him in the club's toilets two weeks ago."

"You are sure?" asked Claire.

'Yes, Chris took mug shots of all three men and he recognised the one who attacked Frank from the C.C.T.V. footage in the club," confirmed Luke.

Claire knew deep inside that it was wrong, but she felt immediate vindication towards Luke's actions once she knew that it was the same guy from before and that he had come for Frank again. It made her feel a little bit better for Luke to have admitted wanting to kill the three men. It can't have been easy, but what did that make Luke? A potential murderer! Claire could not believe that for a second, she certainly didn't want to.

"What did Frank say about it, afterwards I mean?" asked Claire.

"He had always thought me a real dark horse, but to quote his actual words he thinks I'm a bad ass ...oh, and he also thinks I've spent time in the French Foreign legion!"

Claire's eyes widened with total disbelief.

"Purely his own assumption I can assure you," said Luke, clearly exasperated by the whole experience.

"So, let me get this right, I'm now expected to field questions from Yasmin about you having served in the French Foreign legion, something neither of us knows anything about?" gasped Claire.

"I don't think so; Frank seemed content to learn something from my past, even though it's not true. I don't think he will say anything to Yasmin but if he does and she mentions it to you; just say that I'm not allowed to talk about it and leave it at that," offered Luke.

"I don't like lying to Yasmin," said Claire, "I just hope the subject never comes up in conversation."

Luke, remembering the baton fished in his pocket bringing it out to show Claire, "I took this off Frank's attacker."

Claire held the baton feeling the weight of it. "I wonder why Frank's attacker, not content with one attack, would come back mob handed for a second go?" she hoped with all of her heart that Luke's beating would dissuade them from making any further attacks, for their sakes really because she was sure of one thing, if Luke was involved it wouldn't end well for them.

So now that Luke had laid it out for her she felt strangely calmer, then feeling mischievous she asked, "Have you finished your tea Beau?"

"What did you call me? Beau?" smiled Luke, playing along. "I did. I think it's time you carried me off to bed, we have just about got time before Adam wakes up," said Claire huskily, winking.

Luke didn't need telling twice, hefting her across his shoulder he smacked her behind, making his way upstairs with his damsel, like she weighed nothing.

Soon twining bodies removed all previous tensions and thought from their minds. Peace had been restored.

Chapter 58

A few home truths

Mehmet had been sitting outside the women's fitting room shining the seat of his pants for almost an hour. Ali's mother had an army of female attendants ferrying various items of clothing to her for her to try on. This was the third high end store that they had visited so far this morning. Now it was almost noon and not for the first time Mehmet wondered if this woman ever tired of endlessly trying on clothing.

Only yesterday he had had to sit whilst this loathsome excuse of a woman had tried on, and rejected, literally hundreds of pairs of fashionable shoes, until finally settling for a mere dozen pairs, at an exorbitantly eye watering total price, that she would probably never wear anyway.

It was laughable really how Mehmet had been singled

out for this onerous task. When Ali Hussein had first broached the subject with him he had wanted to decline on the grounds that his first loyalty was to Ali, citing that any of the home security team were more than capable of providing security for a proposed shopping trip by his mother.

Ali had actually agreed with Mehmet, albeit silently, preferring that his head of security should remain here but sadly his mother had asked for Mehmet specifically, so with reluctance he had acquiesced to her demands. Why she had asked for him personally still eluded Mehmet's reasoning. In all the time that he had been in the Hussein's employ Mehmet had only spoken to Ali's mother on perhaps half a dozen occasions. It would be fair to say that Mehmet went out of his way to avoid contact with her whenever possible. He found her to be rude, arrogant and totally lacking in basic good manners. She viewed the hired help as an inconvenient necessity; something to be tolerated.

How she would be able to function in a world devoid of this army of underlings consistently at her beck and call he truly would like to see, but for now Mehmet's arse was getting decidedly numb from sitting on the chair. He lifted his cheeks again to try and get some circulation going. This assignment was making him increasingly miserable!

They also had staying with them at the Palms Hotel, Ahmed, the Hussein's personal driver. Mehmet wished that he could swap places with him. A spot of driving would certainly alleviate the tedium of this interminable shopping spree. At least Ahmed only had to follow her instructions whilst driving the car, Mehmet had to deal with the woman directly; a far more prickly encounter.

The Palms Hotel was one of two hotels in Amman belonging to the Hussein portfolio. It was where

Ali and his mother stayed when away from the family home. The hotel was modern, clean and extremely well run. It was also a favourite of international travellers. The Penthouse Suite, situated on the top floor, was for exclusive use by the Hussein family only.

Mehmet's room was on the same floor at the end of the corridor, far too close to Mrs Hussein's room for his liking. She viewed his appointment detail as a 24 hour a day duty. Quite seriously she didn't think that, like her, Mehmet needed to sleep, amongst other things. She perceived the head of security as someone permanently on duty and therefore constantly on call.

At last! Things were looking up, a flurry of activity from the fitting room announced Mrs Hussein's arrival surrounded by half a dozen female helpers.

Mehmet got in touch with Ahmed on his mobile alerting him to have the car out front ready to meet

them and breathed a sigh of relief when he realised Mrs Hussein's many purchases would be hand delivered to the Pent house Suite courtesy of the fashion house.

Mehmet didn't like Mrs Hussein, that was a given, but he tried not to let it show as he held the back door of the Mercedes open for her, waiting whilst she was properly seated before closing it. He was solicitous of his charge realising that he needed to remain professional at all times and put his personal feelings to one side.

Mehmet got into the front passenger seat beside Ahmed, breathing out a sigh of relief as Mrs

Hussein directed him to drive back to the hotel.

Once back at the hotel Mehmet rode the lift up to the penthouse with his charge, it was his job to check the rooms and it would have been unprofessional of him had he not done so.

Mrs Hussein had the good sense to realise that it was for her own benefit to allow Mehmet to do his job without interference. Once Mehmet had proclaimed the rooms to be free of assassins he asked her, "Will that be all ma'am?"

"Yes and I don't think I will be requiring your services again until tomorrow," she replied.

This was very welcome news to Mehmet as he left her room quietly closing the door. He was hungry, hot and tired and needed to shower and change first.

Mrs Hussein had all her meals brought to her room but Mehmet preferred to take his in the hotel restaurant. The food was good and varied, providing western as well as Middle Eastern cuisine. It made a change from having to prepare and cook his own meals so it was nice to take advantage of what was on offer in the restaurant.

Looking around he found a table for two in the far corner. He had lentil soup to start, followed by a delicious spicy goat meat stew that reminded him of his mother's own cooking. Eating the last of it he noticed a man, a westerner, looking over in his direction. He was with a mixed party of five men and three women. They were quite noisy and their accents betrayed them as either American or Canadian. This particular man continued to look over from time to time attracting Mehmet's own curiosity. Something about him did seem familiar but his memory couldn't place why.

Eventually the man got up, leaving his party to approach Mehmet. Smiling as he got closer he said, "My god, it is you isn't it Mehmet?"

Mehmet smiled back with a little uncertainty realizing that they must had met somewhere before, but who and where still eluded him.

"Brad Dillman," the man said, offering his hand in friendship, "West Point."

The veil of recognition was now lifted from Mehmet's eyes as he shook the preferred hand.

Memories now came flooding back at the mention of Brad Dillman's name. The last time they had seen each other was at West Point Military Academy. They had both been in uniform at the time,

Mehmet as an army exchange officer serving in the Jordanian army and Brad as an officer in the U.S. marine corps, seconded to West Point M.A.

Brad had been one of the only two serving officers whilst at West Point to offer him the hand of friendship. It was completely understandable of course, Mehmet was Jordanian, and as such had been kept at arm's length by the majority, 9/11 and the Twin Towers crashing to the ground were still too fresh in people's memories to overcome prejudice.

Brad shook Mehmet's hand warmly then apologised almost immediately as he explained, "Look I'm officially still on the clock," indicating with his hand the table he had just left, "but if you would like to catch up I can meet you in the bar at about 7 p.m.," offered Brad.

"Yes I would like that," said Mehmet, genuinely pleased to accept as he watched Brad return to his table. It would certainly beat sitting in his room waiting for Mrs Hussein's next summons.

Later when Mehmet made his way to the bar he was relieved to see Brad already there nursing a beer. As predicted just as he was about to leave his room to go meet Brad his nemesis rang his room to discuss tomorrow's shopping itinerary.

His mood lifted lightly as he slid onto the bar stool beside Brad, who asked, "What are you drinking?"

"A large coke with ice and lemon please," answered

Mehmet.

"Still not drinking hey," said Brad after ordering the drink.

"No, still not drinking Brad," smiled Mehmet. As he remembered back, thinking of West Point, Brad had tried unsuccessfully to get Mehmet to have a beer with him but his faith forbade it. He had never once given in to temptation, though it didn't stop Brad from trying. He had bet him $10 that he would get him to have a beer with him before he left West Point.

Mehmet, realising that Brad still owed him said, "You still owe me $10."

Brad, looking sideways at Mehmet smiled, "You still remember that eh?"

"Yes I do," smiled Mehmet.

Fishing in his inside coat pocket Brad brought out his wallet.

Embarrassed now by the memory Mehmet tried to stop Brad from paying the debt but of course he wouldn't hear of it and plucked a crisp $10 bill from his wallet and gave it to Mehmet saying, "A bet is a bet. I welched on it and you were right to remind me."

Mehmet looked at it carefully savouring the feel of it then said, "I think I'll have it framed!"

Brad reacted in horror, "Hell no, money is for spending not framing!"

Mehmet slid the note into his pocket and said, "Thanks."

Brad took a pull on his beer then said, "So what are you doing here?" indicating the hotel, "You still in the army?"

"No!" Mehmet answered, sipping his coke, "I'm in a new job, Head of Security."

"No kidding ... what here in this hotel you mean?" asked Brad.

"No as head of security for the family that own the hotel."

Brad stiffened visibly then relaxed trying to maintain the easy banter of before, but it was too late

Mehmet had noticed the subtle change in Brad the moment the Hussein connection had been mentioned. He tried to lighten the mood, "So what about you, are you still in the military?" asked

Mehmet.

"No, the military and I have gone our separate ways. I have my own security firm now, in fact I'm heading up security for the American Trade Delegation, they were who you saw me with earlier," said Brad.

Clearly the atmosphere between the two had changed dramatically since Hussein's name had been brought up. Something was bothering Brad. Mehmet risked spoiling the atmosphere further by asking him outright, "Ever since I mentioned my employer by name you have become guarded, what is wrong?"

Brad again looked sideways at Mehmet saying, "You noticed that huh! ...Alright I'm going out on a limb here, so let's lay our cards on the table. How much do you know about your employer? And don't give me any bull shit; you are his head of security for christ sake."

Mehmet needed desperately to confide in someone, in fact he had needed to for some time, but

Brad Dillman was a foreigner, worse still he was an American, both despised and hated by millions of Arabs throughout the Middle East. The tension stretched on until finally Mehmet came to a life changing decision, he went with his gut deciding to trust Brad.

The barman was too close for Mehmet's liking so he suggested that they move to a table far enough away so as not to be overheard. Once they were re-seated Mehmet recounted to Brad what he had found out about the Hussein's.

Brad listened intently to Mehmet's testimony only interrupting to query a point. He now knew from

Mehmet's own mouth that Ali Hussein, possibly with the collusion of his own mother, had orchestrated his own father's murder. Also that he, with the connivance of his mother, had kept his sister captive whilst trying to marry her off, unsuccessfully, in order to steal her birth right from her, but that had failed and she had been freed by persons unknown. He told Brad how Ali had hired assassins to follow her to London where another attempt was made on her life. Fortunately that attempt had also failed but it hadn't dissuaded him from trying again; he was most determined to see his sister dead. Finally, and this was the most difficult part Mehmet had to admit to knowing, was that Ali Hussein was openly funding and collaborating with known terrorists.

Brad sat back appalled when Mehmet finished relating his story. It was a lot worse than he had previously thought, but he believed every word of it to be true. As Brad digested every unpalatable thing he had just learned about the Hussein's he realised how difficult it must have been for Mehmet to divulge these secrets, to him, a virtual stranger. He figured he owed him!

Leaning over conspiratorially to Mehmet, Brad thanked him for being so candid, and then said, "Now, here's something that you don't know about the Hussein's, there's a million dollar bounty on Ali Hussein's head."

Mehmet looked at Brad in total disbelief until he confirmed, "It's true my friend." Nodding to hammer it home, "and that's why you need to get away from this arsehole asap, before someone comes looking to collect on that bounty and anyone getting caught in the crossfire will wind up just as dead, whether innocent or not."

Mehmet thought hard about what Brad had just told him. He had planned on leaving Ali Hussein's employment when he and his fledgling army accompanied him to Dubai in three months' time but that was before he had learned there was a million dollar price tag on his head. Now another plan was beginning to take shape.

Brad gave Mehmet his card stressing that he was available, any time, night or day.

Mehmet pocketed it and then warmly shook hands with Brad. No more was said as they headed off but there were plenty of ideas sparking in his head as he made his way towards the lift. Brad had given him much to think about; he just hoped that his brain wouldn't betray him during the next three months.

One thing was for sure, for the germ of his plan to succeed, meticulous planning was needed.

Chapter 59

The long room was divided by a heavily constructed wooden table. Arranged along one side of it were members of various units of the Afghan armed forces and at least one of them was of a high rank. Ministers from the Afghan government and interpreters were freely spaced among the military personnel.

Opposite them sat General Mayweather and several of his military aides. Further along down the table sat the British contingent Brigadier Anthony Villiers and his aide Colonel Chesterton. It was well known by all persons present that Villiers was only there as a military courtesy, by dint of being an ally, and not in any official capacity.

Above the heads of the assembled personnel sat a thick blanket of dirty grey smoke, interspersed with threads of silvery blue. The air conditioning wasn't working so it couldn't disperse the toxic cloud. It was making the eyes of non-smokers smart and greatly adding to their discomfort.

The temperature in the room was slowly rising making it even more uncomfortable and people were beginning to sweat freely making the room smell like a zoo. To make matters worse they were all overdressed for the occasion adding to their misery.

They had been sitting here for almost two hours without a break. The general and his aides had presented the Afghan delegation with photographic proof as well as the co-ordinates of Abdul

Rahman's stronghold. The General wanted a strong attack to be mounted on Rahman by the Afghan government troops, but the sticking point kept coming back to the fact that Rahman's presence in the location couldn't be verified and the Afghans wouldn't commit their troops unless

Rahman's physical presence within the bastian could be confirmed.

So here we were, going round and round in circles and getting nowhere.

The General's famous temper, when faced with ineptitude and crass stupidity of this nature, was the stuff of legends. It had threatened to explode on a number of occasions and had only been kept in check by the cool diplomacy of one of his aides. A mass walkout by the Afghan contingent had been narrowly averted, when at one point, the General's temper did surface as his patience was not inexhaustible and he was fast approaching the point where he would seize the initiative for himself.

The stalemate concerning an attack on Rahman's stronghold had finally been taken out of their hands and passed on to the Afghan president and his senior ministers to either approve or veto.

Whilst the Afghan presence in the room chain smoked their way into lethargy whilst awaiting news from their government, Mayweather was formulating a plan of his own; a contingency plan in case the decision for a strike should be unfavourable. He knew deep down in his gut that the Afghans were unwilling to fight. It still beat the hell out of him why his own government would still want a

U.S. involvement in this shit hole of a country at all, but he had been a soldier for a long time and he didn't intend to foul up at this stage in his career.

The telephone rang, breaking the deadlock and eliciting curious glances from all around the room.

The Afghan minister picked up the receiver and listened carefully to what was said for several seconds before placing it back down. Wasting no more time he addressed General Mayweather

respectfully. "I'm sorry sir, my government refuse to sanction a strike on the stronghold without positive identification of Abdul Rahman!" was all that he said.

And that was enough to bring the meeting to a close. The Afghan government had refused to commit Afghan troops.

Mayweather was done here.

It was time to wield the big stick if the Afghans were unwilling to fight he would freeze them out and do what was needed to be done.

He knew that under the terms of his remit that he was expressly forbidden by his own government to commit U.S. ground troops in a combat role but he still had enough authority to issue orders for the U.S.A.A.F. to bomb the crap out of Rahman's so called stronghold.

One thing was for sure, he didn't intend to sit around with his thumb up his arse and do nothing!

Chapter 60

Luke and Claire's place

I got Adam up earlier than usual and we dressed and had breakfast in record time ready for the day. I must confess that I felt more nervous than Adam who was exhibiting signs of just ordinary good natured normality.

I had taken the step of enrolling him into a pre-school creche three mornings a week; it was called Little Bees. The only stipulation from the creche was that Adam should be toilet trained, so we were good then, as Adam had that particular skill mastered.

Little Bees was only a twenty minute stroll with the pushchair, so it was no hardship to get to and from it, also it had the added bonus of allowing me to be able to sit in and help with the children's activities, after the usual checks had been completed, which I very much enjoyed. It would give me the added opportunity to both monitor Adam's interaction with the other children whilst enabling me to step in if things became awkward.

Leaving Luke fast asleep in dreamland, Adam and I set off on our new adventure. Looking upwards I thought, at least it isn't raining yet, though the sky was steel grey tinged with ominous black clouds in places. The air felt humid as though it was building up for something more, but thankfully we arrived at the Little Bees gated entrance dry and unharmed by the elements.

Parking Adam's pushchair inside the creche's entrance I helped him off with his coat and hung it next to mine on the row of pegs.

Going into the large open room I noticed Adam's eyes grow big, like saucers. Jo Paine saw us and immediately came over to say hello.

"Hello," I said as Jo made a big fuss of Adam, before leading him away to a group of children sat in a circle on the floor. They were building things with various coloured bricks and shapes that had been upended from a large plastic box.

I saw her with the other children, obviously introducing them to one another, as she made them spread out so as to include Adam amongst them. God, she was a natural. She had just succeeded in kidnapping my son without the slightest hint of a protest from him. He was already happily joining in with the other children as Jo came back to me.

She smiled at me, seeing how lost I was, "Don't worry, I've been in your shoes, trust me after eighteen years of doing this sort of thing I find it's easiest if you just put the children together and they decide, in a very short while, who they get on with and who they don't. They are the ones who are really in charge, not us," she laughed.

Josephine Paine was her official name but everyone called her Jo. Little Bees was Jo's place but she had two other helpers, Ann Whiley and Susan Tully.

Jo introduced me first to Ann who seemed pleasant enough but was grossly overweight. She had a group of five children sat around a small table set out with paints, brushes, crayons, coloured pencils and blank sheets of paper. She was showing the children how to mix together the primary colours in order to make different colours. She was sitting on a small child's seat which I couldn't help thinking was in imminent danger of collapse. How it was defying the basic laws of physics I'll never know.

Next we went over to another table where a group of children were making things out of plastercine. Red elephants and green people seemed most popular. Jo introduced me to Sue who seemed genuinely friendly and we hit it off straight away and as it was Adam's first day in the crèche it allowed me free access for the morning session; so I joined Sue's group.

I couldn't help stealing glances over in Adam's direction but they were all chatting to one another amiably, playing nicely together, so I slowly began to relax. It was hard for me trying to let go, knowing that Adam's capabilities far surpassed those of his playmates, but it was essential for his development to mingle with other children so that he wouldn't be singled out as something different.

Luke and I still hadn't decided how best to deal with the thorny subject of compulsory education but being in the fortunate position of having wealth we were seriously coming around to the idea of private day schooling. One we looked at we particularly liked was Monaghan's Private Academy but it was a three quarters of an hour commute for Adam which meant one and a half hours a day travel to school for both of us. The place was set in its own grounds and very exclusive. If we did decide to send Adam there, they had their own mini coach and driver; which would solve the daily commute. But of course it meant a longer day for Adam. We had spoken at length to the principal, Mr Frederick Goulding, and were leaning more and more to sending Adam here. Mr Goulding was most interested in Adam who answered all his questions with alarming speed and very concisely. To say that he was intrigued by Adam's intelligence, would be putting it mildly.

The academy took pupils from both sexes from age 5 to 18. So if Adam could fit in here he may well have his school sorted in one go. That it would prove to be expensive for us was not a problem.

The other advantage in choosing Monaghan's was that it would give Adam stability. So the more I thought about it the more convinced I became, that Monaghan's Private Academy would provide for Adam's education, but as of now he was happily playing with his new class mates building things.

Later on the children were rotated; Adam's group now had to don the protective apron's left behind by Ann's group. When we were all suitably attired Sue and I squeezed around the low table so Sue could show the children the wonder of making new colours. Adam seemed completely engrossed by the new concept of making and changing colours.

Once they had had time to familiarize themselves with the general rules governing making different colours they were allowed to try out their own ideas on paper. There were the rudimentary shapes of both mums and dads, balloon topped trees and even an aeroplane from one little boy. Adam however painted a dog, which I found strange because we didn't have a dog. But as I watched the dog take shape, it became clear to me what type of dog it was; a black labrador, plain and simple no mistaking it for anything else. Just one look at it identified the breed.

Sue looked at Adam's first attempt at painting with a critical eye, "Is that your labrador Adam?" she asked tentatively. Adam straight away said, "No its Mr Paley's dog, Ralph."

I listened attentively to Adam's reply trying to wrack my brains as to who Mr Paley was. Then I remembered, about a month ago, when Adam and I were in the park a man with a black Labrador had let Adam pet his dog. The dog had loved the attention and when Adam had stopped, nuzzled him for more of the same, much to Adam's delight.

I had completely forgotten about the encounter but of course it was safely stored in Adam's brain and instantly accessible. This was truly Adam's first attempt at painting, yet he had already achieved something that I couldn't do, execute a very passable likeness of a common breed of dog. Adam's first day at the creche had gone by in a blur. We said our goodbye's to everyone, Adam holding tightly to his rolled up painting. He was taking it home to show his dad. I had already decided that I would get him some paints and a sketch pad; if he had a talent for it I intended to give him free rein.

It was difficult to know how far to go with Adam. I wanted him to grow up in the company of other children yet I didn't want him to attract too much attention to himself. The labrador that Adam had painted had been good enough to single him out and I could almost hear the gears in Sue's head whirring as she quietly asked the question, "What have we here?"

Well it was no use worrying about it, Adam was Adam and no matter what he did in life people were going to ask questions about him, I just had to get used to it and not to be so sensitive about it.

So, as far as first days in a creche go, it had been a most enjoyable experience, one I couldn't wait to share with Luke.

Chapter 61

Firestorm

General Mayweather had wasted no time in gathering together the necessary forces at his disposal. He had even managed to enlist the aid of the British R.A.F. which helped somewhat to smooth their previously ruffled feathers. It was to be a joint operation between the two allied forces.

The British had sent over from Cyprus four F35's. They were now being refuelled and loaded up with American ordnance whilst the crews were being briefed about the mission, alongside their American counterparts. A three dimensional map of the target was on display before them, proving to everyone present how difficult a target the stronghold would be to hit. Also, being in a narrow ravine there would be no margin for error.

Everyone in the briefing room knew how important this

mission was. Abdul Rahman had been allowed to live for far too long. Hopefully in another hour or so his life would be ended.

The American 'fly boys' had suggested a strike just as dawn was breaking using Napalm, a highly inflammable jellied petroleum, followed closely by staggered waves of British and American fighter bombers, who would bomb the cliff face to try and bring down tons of rock and earth, effectively sealing the terrorists inside the cave system. That was the plan such as it was.

Mayweather had deliberately withheld news of the air strike from the Afghan military. It was no secret that he didn't trust them to try and foreworn Rahman of the planned attack. He would bring them up to speed once it was over.

By the time the first of the American fighters arrived on target it was light enough to clearly make out the ravine. The first aircraft, the lead, went straight into attack, dropping his two cylindrical containers between the cliff faces, he pulled out and banked to his right. At first nothing happened then a tremendous whoosh of fire and smoke erupted in his wake. The other three aircraft watched from a safe distance judging the effectiveness of their leader's strike.

Once the fire ball and smoke had diminished sufficiently enough to allow a second strike the number two in the formation peeled off to deliver his payload. He delayed the release of his ordnance to spread it further down the ravine but in doing so he almost misjudged the pull out, but thankfully he managed to lift clear with feet to spare. The resulting whoosh of fire and smoke was quickly followed by muffled detonations within the cave system.

The pilot of the second aircraft said over his throat mike, "Any closer leader and I think I would have been toast."

The leader replied drily, "I had noticed. Good strike anyway."

The group leader didn't want to risk bringing home the remaining tanks of this lethal cocktail of ordnance, so he ordered his remaining pilots to unleash their loads on the target at safe intervals.

Their part was now complete, the Napalm leader informed command, "Mission accomplished, heading back to base, over."

Now it was the turn of the other pilots. Their mission was to bring down the cliff face by laser guided bombs, two sticks of four F35's arrived over the target area, oily black smoke was still visible two miles away from the ravine.

The Americans, whose show it was, claimed the right of first strike.

The British stick of four watched from a safe altitude whilst the American's plastered the ravine. The shock of the explosion on the cliff face must have been tremendous to the combatants hiding within the cave system.

Part of the cliff face had been brought down covering one of the caves, but it needed more ordnance dumping on it, testimony to how difficult it was to effectively judge the correct placement of the bombs.

The British now taking their turn tried to place their bombs where they would do the most damage. At the end of their runs the cliff face had been brought down and tons of rock and earth now covered the entrances to the cave system.

Grudgingly the American leader radioed, "Well done," to his British counterparts before ordering the pilots back to base.

Deep underground, within the bunker system.

The early risers were at first prayer when the air was

suddenly filled with the deafening roar of aircraft. It was so sudden and so unexpected that many were still in the attitude of prayer when the first cylinder of Napalm struck. They had been taken completely by surprise.

The toxic lethal mixture engulfed the earnest worshippers nearest to the cave's entrance.

Their bodies were swiftly immersed in the fiery nightmare that was death. A dozen or so, perhaps the lucky ones, were fused together still in the attitude of prayer, like in some obscenely arranged tableau. Those less lucky, the ones still capable of breathing, were less fortunate, their blackened smoking heads, skin cracked open and revealing under lying bone in places were going into shock.

Some had had their hands fused together in the fire storm and when they tried to pull them apart the skin came away revealing the bones.

The pain for some was indescribable. It was beyond pain of another dimension. Those mostly unaffected by the first strike barely had time to come to the aid of their stricken comrades before the second strike had hit. Thankfully it was further down the ravine and away from the first explosion but it still caused casualties in the next cave, which were further exacerbated by the exploding ammunition that was stacked by the entrance.

Further strikes made the able bodied wary of venturing too near the cave entrances. It was just too gruesome a death to contemplate, even to these battle hardened fighters and to many of them there was something just too ungodly in this manner of death, so they sought refuge from this rain of fire deep within the cave system.

Many of them thought that a ground offensive would swiftly follow this onslaught by fire so they bravely rushed back to repel the invaders. What they received instead was the concussive forces of further air attacks.

The cave/bunker system had been well constructed and reinforced over the years but it wasn't designed to withstand repeated attacks by laser guided bombs. One section of cave collapsed killing two and injuring a third person.

When the cliff face finally came down burying the entrances to the cave system the power failed and plummeted the interior into total darkness. The survivors, shocked, covered in dust and disorientated, still had to deal with the smoky, dust laden atmosphere. Some were fearful of moving lest a further attack by air materialised.

It was minutes later that Abdul Rahman himself and a few survivors wielding battery powered torches came to check on the injured. Sweeping the torch around he assessed what needed to be done first.

He sent a man off with a torch to get the emergency generator started. Once they had restored power and light they could organise help for the injured.

Playing his torch over the sealed cave entrance he saw how futile it was to try and clear it, just then the emergency generator restored power to the interior flooding it with light.

Switching off his torch he surveyed the scene of carnage in the harsh glare of the neon lights. It was a sickening sight, even to Rahman, this maestro of unnatural death, but mostly he was saddened by the way his men had died. He had promised them a glorious death worthy of martyrdom. Instead they had been struck down from the sky before being able to fire a shot. They had trained so hard over the last five years and were truly a match, he believed, for any conventional ground troops pitted against them. Now reduced by at least one third he calculated as he totted up the bodies that he could immediately see.

Remembering that there were still the injured to attend to he set about giving orders to his shell shocked men. The slightly injured could be cleaned up and seen to by their comrades.

The more seriously injured were ferried to the medical room for the badly harassed doctor to try and patch up. Most of the badly burned survivors were beyond even his medical skills. Luckily there was no shortage of morphine.

He shot them up with enough to dull the pain but even then it wasn't enough for some. The injured with simple breakages thankfully he could help but the others, the ones that were beyond his help all he could do was make them as comfortable as possible.

The strike had come so suddenly and with such devastating force they had been caught well and truly napping by the hated Americans. Had his moles in the Afghan army forewarned him of the air strike he could have pulled his men deeper into the cave system thus preventing any casualties at all but for some reason they had remained unusually silent. Perhaps, mused Rahman, the Americans had finally learned that the Afghans were not to be trusted and had ordered the strike without their knowledge.

Later the formal death toll arrived at by the doctor numbered 74. Most of the badly burned had simply lost the will to live and given up the fight, as for the rest, there were four walking wounded capable of helping themselves and eight in sick bay waiting to die.

The dead were buried within the cave system by their brothers in a sombre affair. The morale of the men was as low as it could get; rock bottom. It was now up to Rahman to try and restore confidence to his demoralised men. They needed leadership now more than at any time before, but most of all he had to give them some form of hope. Realising that this position was no longer tenable he addressed the survivors.

"Brothers we have been dealt a cruel blow, our hope of bringing the hated Americans to battle had failed. This position is no longer defensible and if we stay here it will only become our tomb."

Murmurs of assent reached Rahman's ears.

"I plan on fighting my way to the Pakistan border and once there to disappear into the hinterland and from there carry on the fight. I can do no less for the memory of our fallen brothers."

This hit a cord with the majority.

"I would be honoured if my brothers would accompany me," said Rahman. Arms outstretched to indicate the gathered men.

It wasn't a particularly rousing speech as speeches go but it met with the survivor's approval, one and all.

The doctor bravely chose to stay behind, as he still had men under his care and refused to leave them, but now that Rahman had given his men a purpose, a goal to aim for, he needed them to focus their attentions on to what they were; a fighting unit. So he issued orders that everyman should strip his weapons and thoroughly clean them ready for battle.

This gave them a physical purpose as well as serving a practical one. It gave them something to do with their hands as well as distracting their thoughts from the horrors of before.

Next he ordered that everyman should clean himself before joining him in prayer.

This met with everyone's approval.

After prayers a vast meal was prepared. For men could not travel far on empty stomachs.

Rahman walked around his seated men whilst they ate offering encouragement here, a friendly word of advice there, to try and bolster their confidence. It was a pity, in some ways, that Rahman had chosen a dark path to travel because he was a born leader of men. Who knows what he could have accomplished had he chosen a different path, but that was mere conjecture, perhaps Rahman's path was always headed for darkness.

After the meal everyman loaded up with as much ammunition, food and water as they could safely carry in their back packs. Then they filed off in orderly fashion heading for the escape tunnel.

Rahman and his number two went down the ropes first, then as the men began to come down he had them assemble into ordered ranks, until all who were coming with them had arrived. Two walking wounded came down the ropes last, wincing in pain. They would have to keep up with the main party as best they could. There was to be no exception to that rule, not for anyone, including Rahman himself. Those were his orders and he expected them to be obeyed.

Once they were all assembled Rahman and his number two strode off at the head of the column. There was a long way to go and the odds were stacked heavily against them, but at least they resembled a fighting unit once more.

Chapter 62

True to my word I brought Adam a paint set, though it was only a water colour set, I must admit. I had added a blank sketch pad and a couple of different sized brushes for good measure. He already had a good selection of different coloured pencils as well as a number of wax crayons and a couple of colouring books had been added at the last minute for variety. I had shown him the basic skills needed in order to effect a good water colour sketch, making sure that he understood to thoroughly wash his brush before attempting another colour. I was no expert you understand but Adam seemed to master the basics in no time at all.

I had long since tired of trying to paint a countryside scene, and to be honest I lacked the skill for it, but Adam still persevered. I on the other hand had taken up a colouring book, filling in the basic shapes to the truest approximation of the colour that it ought to be. I had to accept that my particular talents as an artist were woefully inadequate.

At least Adam had a legitimate excuse; he was a child and had had no formal training, but at least we were trying and companionably so.

Adam had just cleaned his brush for the umpteenth time and was taking a few moments before choosing the next colour. Pointing towards the telephone he looked at me to see if I had noticed. I got half way towards it when it began to ring. Picking up the receiver I automatically said, "Claire Henderson speaking, how can I help?"

The woman's voice on the other end of the line made the fine hairs on my neck and arms stand up, it was Seline, "Oh, hello Claire I was hoping to catch Luke, is he in?"

"He is still in bed, but I can take a message for him," I said in irritation.

"Yes of course .... err.....sorry I'm a bit of a mess, its daddy, he's in hospital," Seline said. Upon hearing that Seline's father, Sir Ian Clayton, was in hospital my prickliness quickly evaporated. "Oh Seline, I'm so sorry to hear that, what is wrong with him?"

"He tripped on the stairs and he has broken his hip," Seline said, obviously frustrated. "Look he's having surgery sometime today to see what they can do, only I didn't know who else to ring and I didn't have Luke's number, so I got in touch with Chris and he gave it to me. I hope you don't mind," Seline gasped out in a rush, almost out of breath.

I most certainly did mind but managed to just about stop myself from saying so and lied. "No, of course not. Look what hospital is your father in? I'll tell Luke as soon as he wakes up as he will want to see him."

I wrote down the name of the hospital for Luke. I had no intention of keeping this from him. Sir Ian was the closest thing to a father figure he was ever likely to have. Thanking

Seline before ending the call I returned to Adam.

To say that there was no love lost between either myself or Seline would be an understatement but Sir Ian was a different matter, it was just a pity his daughter was such a bitch.

Even though Luke had made it perfectly clear to Seline that he was unavailable she openly continued to pursue him in an effort to get Luke's notch firmly on her bedpost. Apparently being married and a father was no obstacle to Seline, where Luke was concerned anyway.

Claire felt proud that Luke had chosen her and not Seline. After all she was good looking in her own right and she was the mother of their son, but she just couldn't understand how she allowed Seline to constantly get under her skin. Where Seline was concerned Claire always felt so dammed inadequate.

Adam had picked up on the conflict raging inside his mum and stopped painting. Looking at her he said, "You alright mum?"

Realising that she had been staring at the colouring book ever since the telephone call had ended Claire's focus returned, "Yes just a bit of bad news that's all. A friend of your dad's and mine has had to go into hospital."

"Seline's dad?" asked Adam.

"Yes Seline's dad," said Claire, "Do you remember them Adam?" asked Claire, not quite sure why she was asking.

"Yes they were at your wedding," answered Adam.

"Are you sure you remember them Adam, you were only very young," asked Claire.

"Yes I'm quite sure, Seline was talking to Uncle Chris."

"Yes she was but I thought you would be too young to remember," replied Claire, astonished.

"No I remember it quite well, though sometimes I get things jumbled up just a little," laughed Adam.

Believe me kid, you have got a full head start on most of the human race, and you are only a child, thought Claire to herself.

Chapter 63

Abdul Rahman - War of Attrition

By the end of the first day when they made camp they had seen no hostile enemy forces. The only other human contact had been a goat herder: and his flock. They paid him no heed as he wearily watched them march on by. Thankfully the hated American air force stayed away. After about an hour the group's spirits were lifted when the two walking wounded stumbled wearily into camp.

Despite Rahman's orders they had helped each other this far and everyone was glad to see them. It did much for morale and they were given hot tea and food, welcoming them back, the company whole again.

As they bedded down for the night Rahman looked up at the night sky. It was brilliantly laid out above them and seemed to go on forever. Against such a mighty back drop he felt the group must have seemed like ants, insignificant in the vast scheme of things. It sounded philosophical even to Rahman's own ears, but he was no philosopher, merely a man, as his tired eyes closed and rendered him up to sleep.

The next morning they rose with the dawn's early light pointing their way of travel. They were not used to sleeping on the rough ground; even Rahman had to work the aches and pains out of his joints before he felt able to travel. Once Rahman and his men had eaten they moved off once again as a unit, the movement doing much to loosen their joints, as they eased into the rhythm of the rocky terrain.

They had been going steadily for about two hours when they cameacross the entrance to a rock strewn ravine. Rahman halted the men telling them to rest while he and half a dozen of his best men would take a look around. They hadn't gone very far into the ravine when a line of boulders, obviously put there by the hand of man, confronted them. A man dressed in tribal clothing stepped out in front of them, a Russian made Kalashnikov automatic rifle hanging from a sling across his chest. He came forward a few paces, hand raised, palm outstretched and asked, "Who are you?"

Rahman stepped forward, having handed his rifle to his number two, his hand raised in the same manner. "I'm Abdul Rahman and these are my brothers," indicating with his free hand to the men behind him.

The tribe's man seemed to ponder Rahman's answer his curiosity clearly aroused, "You are not Afghani," he said pointing to Rahman's chest.

"No I am Egyptian, but my brothers are Afghani," he said again indicating his men with a sweep of his hand.

A huge smile creased the tribesman's face when he asked, "Where are you leading your brothers?" delivered with obvious sarcasm.

The tone in the tribesman's question could not be mistaken, but it required an answer.

Rahman told him truthfully, "Pakistan."

Hah! Light of understanding now flooded the tribesman's eyes. "This land belongs to my Lord Omar Al Shamahi. If you wish to cross it unharmed you must pay him tribute."

Rahman looked back at his number two as if to question if he had heard him correctly.

To offer his support he came up to Rahman's side then whispered so as not be overheard, "I have heard of this Shamahi, he is a feudal war lord and a tribal leader commanding at least 500 warriors. They live by tribute. Even the Afghan army fear him and leave him alone," he said.

Rahman, clearly annoyed at this set back, asked him, "Why was I not warned of this before we set off."

"I do not know where Shamahi's land begins or ends." He answered honestly by way of apology.

Rahman accepted that, it wasn't the fault of his number two, the plan had after all been hastily put together, though this new setback had to be settled and quickly.

Speaking louder to the tribesman he said, "What tribute does your master require?"

"15 rifles or 15,000 U.S. dollars," the man answered still smiling at this exorbitant sum.

Rahman was now in a dilemma, he couldn't afford to lose the rifles, though the money was no great loss, even though he had planned on using it to bribe the border guards to allow them free passage into Pakistan.

Just at that moment the problem was taken out of his hands as movement from behind the rocks was met with a single shot from one of Rahman's men. Another tribesman had appeared, his Kalashnikov rifle pointed threateningly in their direction. The situation had now changed dangerously, as rifles were levelled at one another.

Another tribesman had joined his stricken brother, rifle pointed at Rahman's men.

Rahman bravely held his hands up shouting, "No more shooting," to his men, then asked the tribesman, "how is your comrade?"

Warily checking him over the nearest tribesman indicated to his leader that it was just a flesh wound nothing more.

That was lucky thought Rahman. A dead tribesman here in this harsh terrain could go badly for them. Enough was enough he thought and decided to pay the $15,000. The money was quickly recovered from their backpacks and handed over to the tribesman.

Upon hearing the shot Rahman's men had come up at once to give added assistance.

Thankfully it wasn't needed as they were allowed to go on their way.

The wounded tribesman was calmly smoking a very fat home rolled cigarette whilst his shoulder was expertly bandaged by his companion. They had mysteriously disappeared from sight by the time the two walking wounded of Rahman's party negotiated the road block.

They tried to put as much distance as they could between them and the road block before nightfall and they managed to find enough kindling to get fires going to both cook on and to provide guidance to the back markers but it was close run thing.

Still on edge from the shooting incident, Rahman had ordered a night watch rota, set to be changed every two hours. By morning light, the two walking wounded had failed to arrive at the camp. The men kept anxiously looking back over the trail hoping to catch sight of them whilst they ate their morning meal. It was with heavy hearts that they moved off, wondering what had happened to them.

Around the next bend in the trail they found out, their companion's heads had been cut off and placed on spikes, hammered into the ground, but that wasn't all, before their death their eyes had been plucked out. A quick search of the surrounding area couldn't reveal the whereabouts of the unfortunate men's bodies.

Clearly something else was in play here. The tribute had been paid yet two of his men were now dead. Rahman gathered his men about him. They had the right to decide whether to go on or to turn back and try and find an alternative route. When the vote was taken only three men voted to go back, the others voted to carry on. Faced with the horror of what had befallen their comrades they decided to stick it out with the rest. Now Rahman and his men were faced with an unseen enemy; an expert in ambush and guerrilla warfare. Mostly they saw nothing at all. A shot would be heard and a man would fall, his unseen killer safely hidden amongst the rocks.

Two or three men were lost an hour, often without sighting a single enemy. It was a relentless nerve shredding slaughter. That was the only way to describe it, they shot people at random; there was no discernible pattern to it.

Rahman's men now fearful, began shooting at shadows hitting nothing but rock. One of the unit lost his mind completely firing his rifle at nothing until it was empty, then a single shot rang out from the rocks, the bullet placed neatly between his eyes, dropped him neatly onto his back. They were playing with them; it was obvious even to the dimmest amongst the group.

Rahman and his men lit no fires now when they made camp, to do so would invite death, but even that didn't seem to make much difference, death still came in the night. They lost the outlaying guards first. Often, the merest scrape on a rock was all that could be heard before a knife ended their lives, and in the morning their heads could be seen mounted on spikes.

By the morning of the fourth day the group numbered 29...... 29 out of 113 and were still no nearer to the Pakistan border. They slept at night now in a defensive circle but that couldn't stop the dawn from breaking or the slaughter from continuing. Rahman decided to risk making a fire, it was light now anyway and there wasn't much point in not doing so, the men needed proper food and a hot drink inside them. They ate their meagre food and drank hot tea still glassy eyed from lack of proper sleep, thinking that this was probably their last day, although no one said as much.

After eating, Rahman decided to pray, his men following his example joined him in prayer.

A lump came into Rahman's throat as he realised, that even now, they saw hope in him and he realised, that he wasn't worthy of them. If Shamahi's followers had decided to attack at that point, then it would have been all over for them. They must have been watching whilst Rahman and his men prayed but for some reason, stayed their hand.

It didn't much matter anyway because the slaughter began anew half a mile from where they had just made camp. The rifle fire increased in intensity from that point on and by noon there were only seven left alive. The water was nearly all gone but what they had they shared out. As far as Rahman and his men were concerned this was it. Concealing themselves in a little group hidden among the rocks and deciding that it would end there, they would go no further, it was pointless to offer themselves up as a target by moving on.

After a while the strategy began to bear fruit. One of Rahman's men spotted movement amongst the rocks and watching carefully he trained his sights on a tribesman trying to work his way closer. Firing he watched with satisfaction as the tribesman's head exploded in a shower of blood and brains. He had shown the others by his example that they were still capable of fighting; all that was needed was something to aim at.

Now, adopting an all-round defence the men repositioned rocks to try and protect themselves better. Half an hour later Rahman's number two claimed his first tribesman hitting him squarely in the chest. Rahman clapped him on the back; this was much better than being picked off like rats in a barrel, much, much better.

The one thing they did have plenty of was ammunition but it would be the lack of water that would do for them in the end he was sure. They lost another man to a tribesman who had patiently worked his way down, unseen, suffering a shot through the throat his blood sprayed out widely in an arc, only stopping when death finally took him.

Rahman himself ended the life of the tribesman a split second afterwards with a clean shot to the chest. Now there were only six of them still alive, with just a mouthful of water apiece, it wouldn't be long now Rahman thought.

Rahman would be ashamed to admit it, but himself and his men were all asleep when Shamahi's tribesmen overwhelmed them, just as dawn was breaking. One member of the group, Hassan, tried to fight back as he was startled into wakefulness. The tribesmen simply bashed his brains in for his trouble.

The last surviving five were forced at gunpoint to hand

over their rifles, side arms and ammunition, and then to remove footwear and clothing. Now, totally naked with their hands bound behind their backs, a noose was placed around each neck and connected together via a tether. Rahman and his men were all given a mouthful of water flavoured with grit from a goatskin water bottle. The water was warm but it helped ease very parched swollen tongues. The men were then forced to march across the rocky terrain with infrequent stops, where just enough water was given to keep them alive but no food was offered.

Many hours later they arrived at Shamahi's camp, a valley sprawling with tents. At this point their feet were no longer recognisable as human feet they resembled chopped liver. Rahman was separated from his men immediately upon arrival and was forced into a tall cage, just about wide enough to fit him in, though he could neither fully stand up nor sit down, no comfort was intended. It was something like you would put a parrot in, and perhaps in truth that is what it was.

The worst was yet to come; he was made to watch whilst his men were forced, at gunpoint, to dig holes in the hard ground. The remaining army of Abdul Rahman were fully resigned to the fact that they were digging their own graves and praying whilst they dug. Had they known the manner of their deaths, they would have attacked their captors to help hasten it.

The holes themselves were dug down into the earth, not horizontally but vertically, this should have alerted them that something evil was planned for them. At last the holes were deemed deep enough by the tribesmen and the prisoner's hands were again bound behind their backs before they were dropped into the holes, one by one, with their necks at ground level, compounding the horror of their captor's intent. As the earth was gleefully put back into the holes, around the men and packed down hard, Rahman, who had been forced to watch and listen to his men's screams for mercy, wished with all his heart that he could help them, but alas he could not. One man had tried to run and was gunned down before he got two feet away, but at least his suffering was cut short. He prayed for Allah to have mercy on their souls. It would be many hours before thirst and the sun finally killed the last of his army.

Rahman himself was not to get away with only the torment of watching his men die in agony. There were lots of children running around camp in feral groups; it seemed to Rahman that they were allowed to do pretty much whatever they wanted. One particular group sidled over to him. He was a curiosity to them hunched naked in his cage. One of the boys suggested to his companions that he was much like a circus bear and should be performing tricks for them. So he sharpened a stick and prodded Rahman in his side drawing blood. This seemed to delight his followers and taking up sticks of their own they sharpened them and joined in the game.

They prodded and stabbed with their sticks, shrieking with delight every time they succeeded in drawing blood and within minutes Rahman's side was a mass of vicious puncture wounds, oozing blood. His torment was only stopped by Shamahi's intervention.

Chasing the children away from his cage, not because of what they were doing, but because their shrieking had got on his nerves.

Rahman was clearly hated for his cruel actions throughout the so called civilised world, but he realised, he had much to learn from these nomad people.

Shamahi had known of the bounty that had been placed

on Rahman's head by the Americans. So that was why he had had his second in command take pictures of Rahman, on his mobile phone, before sending him on horseback with two companions to make contact with the Americans.

When the two American guards, in the tower overlooking the gate, saw the three horsemen approaching they looked at one another in amusement.

One said, "What the fuck is this all about?" watching them warily.

One of the horsemen handed his rifle to a companion, then holding up both hands to show he wasn't armed he rode a little way forward shouting, "I need to talk with an officer, now!"

"What do you want?" shouted one of the guards.

"I need to speak with an officer," he repeated then added, "We have captured Abdul

Rahman!"

That was enough for them to ring through to the officer's mess. The word was passed from one person to another in typical army fashion until someone senior enough came back on the line who was willing to listen. He repeated what the tribesman claimed again and thankfully, it was Lt. Colonel Anders, who was last in the relay of command, who took the call.

Intrigued, Anders had a corporal drive him over to the main gate telling the guards to keep their rifles trained on the man. Upon his arrival he said, "Open the gates." Anders knew that it was a very foolish thing to do but he did it anyway. If this man was wearing a suicide vest it was better that just one man died rather than several. That was how he rationalized it. As he approached the tribesman he looked for any tell-tale signs of nervousness on the man's face.

The tribesman in turn, appraised Anders as he

approached him.

When they were within speaking distance Anders said, "My guards tell me you have Abdul Rahman. Do you have proof?"

The tribesman nodded and said, "A mobile phone in my saddle bag. Tell your guards not to shoot."

Turning back to the tower Anders shouted, "Put your weapons up. He's going to get a mobile phone from the saddle bags."

As the guards complied he turned back to the tribesman and said, "Get it out, slowly, find the photo and then pass the phone to me."

The tribesman did as he was asked passing the phone to Anders. The dishevelled creature that was hunched within the cage was dirty, bloodied and most certainly Abdul Rahman.

Anders told the tribesman he was satisfied with the evidence.

"My master asks is the $10,000,000 still payable for Rahman's head?"

"Yes", answered Anders, "Where can the exchange take place?"

"Bring the money to Ghowband in two days' time."

"Whoa that's a lot of money and at short notice," gasped Anders.

The tribesman just hunched his shoulders at Anders protestation, "If you want Rahman,

Ghowband in two days' time," he repeated. Then he rode off with his two companions.

"Fuck!" said Anders to himself as he watched the tribesmen ride away. His commanding officer along with all the other senior top brass had been called away to Kabul. The Afghan President and his minions had furiously asked for a meeting after learning of the allied air strike on Rahman's stronghold. That the Afghans had been purposely kept in the dark about it until after the event might have had something to do with wanting the meeting.

Anders needed to get in touch with someone much higher than his pay grade. He had in his hands positive proof that Rahman was alive and in captivity. Once he was back in the admin block he had everyone ringing round to try and reach General Mayweather.

Eventually they hit pay dirt when they reached General Mayweather himself. Anders silently gave thanks to god as he hurriedly reached for the phone. Anders cut straight to the chase giving the general the short version.

Mayweather a soldier's soldier, knew when to listen and when to speak, allowing Anders the go ahead to talk.

"And you have positive proof that Rahman is the prisoner of this so called war lord?" he said, when Anders had finished.

"Yes Sir, I have the phone with me which came straight from Omar Ali-Shamahi's men,"

repeated Anders.

"And he is insisting on cash you say," reiterated Mayweather.

"Yes sir," repeated Anders.

"That is going to take some doing," said Mayweather. "Perhaps we should just let this

... Shamahi kill the fucker and save ourselves the money," he said, more to himself. "I'm going to have to get in touch with the Pentagon to see what they want to do, but they will need proof before any money changes hands. I'll arrange for a chopper to be sent over for the mobile phone. Don't let it out of your sight, not even for a second, even if you go to the john colonel."

"Yes sir, very good sir, of course not sir." Said Anders before the line went dead.

Two days later the small convoy of armoured personnel carriers inched their way forwards towards Ghowband. The money had been approved by Washington and flown out to Afghanistan on a military C-130 under armed guard. It had fallen to Lt. Colonel Anders to deliver the money in exchange for Abdul Rahman. The money had been packed into wooden crates, one to each A.P.C.

Anders looked out through the grill of the A.P.C. that he was riding in, warily watching the mounted tribesmen that had been following them along the ridgeline for the last two miles.

It seemed to Anders as though they were being herded towards Ghowband.

Eventually they came to a fork in the road. At least twelve mounted tribesmen were straddled across it. Anders recognised one of them as the man he had met a couple of days ago.

Slowly coming to a halt, the leading A.P.C. with Anders aboard surveyed the mounted horsemen. "Easy on the triggers boys," he said as he exited the vehicle. The only weapon he had with him was his sidearm.

The rider Anders had met with came forward. Just as he did so, hundreds of tribesmen bearing weapons of all types stood up from their places of concealment looking down on the little convoy.

Anders looked around noticing that many of the tribesmen were shouldering rocket propelled grenade launchers as well as AK-47's. If it was meant to intimidate; it was working. He swallowed nervously as he held his hands up in greeting, "We have brought the money, where is Rahman?"

The tribesman smiled wolfishly at Anders, obvious nervousness seeing the number of tribesmen arrayed against his small force, "I want to see the money first American," he said.

"Very well, step down and take a look," invited Anders.

Going to the lead A.P.C. Anders ordered the crate to be unloaded.

The tribesman watched as the crate was unloaded, looking at it carefully he said, "Does not look like $10,000,000 to me."

Anders said, "It's not, there are three more crates, one in each vehicle."

When the tribesman asked to see them, Anders said, "Not before I see Rahman."

Gambling on things not turning ugly Anders was almost shitting his pants at his own audacity.

The tribesman secretly liked the way this American did business. He was obviously afraid but still displayed courage. Putting two fingers in his mouth he whistled shrilly back to the waiting horsemen. One spurred his horse forward holding a small sack in his hand. Giving the sack over to his leader he left to re-join the other men.

"Here is Rahman, American." He said, handing Anders the sack.

Anders' stomach lurched as he looked at the contents of the sack. Rahman's head clearly recognisable stared back at him, eyes still open. He must have been killed a short while ago thought Anders as the rot hadn't even started to set in yet. Anders looked at the tribesman's smiling face as if he had expected him to ask why. Anders denied him the pleasure saying nothing.

Frustrated by Anders the tribesman said, "The bounty was for Rahman's head was it not? If so, you have it."

Anders couldn't argue with his logic especially when surrounded by hundreds of hostile warriors armed with R.P.G.'s.

Shouting to the drivers of the A.P.C.'s., "Alright unload the crates." It galled Anders that he wouldn't be bringing back a live Abdul Rahman but being the professional that he was, a dead one would have to do.

With the tribesmen now in possession of the money and Anders in receipt of Rahman's head the A.P.C.'s were allowed to turn around and leave the area unharmed.

So this ended Abdul Rahman's bloody reign of terror, not at the hands of his hated enemies the Americans, but at the hands of a feudal war lord still living in the Middle Ages.

With Rahman's death, acts of terrorism wouldn't end, the world was merely waiting for someone else to fill his shoes.

Chapter 64

Winners and losers

By the time news of Abdul Rahman's death had hit the world's press and the leading television networks, it was already old news in the United States. They had deliberately kept a tight lid on the release of Rahman's death until they could do what they did best; re-write history. It was trumpeted from the East Coast to the West Coast, from North to South, that it had been an American victory in the battle for democracy over the evil designs of an Islamist terrorist. They had helped rid the world of yet another religious fanatic.

Once the world had realised that Rahman was truly dead, hastily made effigies of his likeness were openly burned in the streets, from Tunisia to Egypt, from Istanbul to Spain, all places most affected by Rahman's evil, now, joyously celebrating his death.

It was a good thing that Rahman was dead, most right minded people agreed, but not everyone. He was mourned in some quarters and his secret army still remained hidden but was for all intent and purposes virtually intact. Rahman's death had merely created a vacuum into which any number of his acolytes could now step. The world waited patiently to see who would take his place.

When Ali Hussein saw the news for himself broadcast briefly on Jordanian T.V., he was saddened by it but not surprised; sooner or later it was inevitable that the American's would eventually find him and kill him. Rahman's network of informants and assassins were now most definitely closed off to Hussein, but no matter, he now had his own army at his disposal thanks to Mehmet, admittedly it was many times smaller but it would be just as effective, providing that it was used properly.

Soon it would be ready; he just needed to remain patient for a little while longer.

Meanwhile in London, Doug Simons had been avidly watching the news networks and reading the newspapers, from both home and abroad with his colleagues at M.I.6, in order to cut through the fog of misinformation circulated by the United States. It was obvious to Doug that they had a different agenda to the rest of the world. He just had to cut through the bull shit in order to find it.

Inevitably the death of Abdul Rahman was perceived as a great coup and as in every victory a slew of awards were presented to the winners, mostly of the American armed forces.

General Mayweather was awarded another star to go alongside the ones he already wore and this made him a very happy man as he was not far off of retirement.

The general in turn pushed for Lt. Colonel Anders to be made up to full colonel. This was almost unheard of except in times of war, as it would mean that Anders had climbed two steps in promotion in the space of a year. There were murmurs of dissent, mainly from Anders' C.O.

When Mayweather had got wind of the dissent he had a quiet word with his commander-in-chief, the President, who approved Anders' promotion in record time, personally.

The commanders of the American Special Forces teams, code named Red One and Red Two were awarded silver stars and bronze stars were given to their men.

The American air element, which played such a significant part in Rahman's demise, were awarded a mix of air force medals; one notable pilot receiving a distinguished flying medal for pressing home his attack and in his own words, almost ending up as toast.

Other shameless arseholes, namely politicians; tried to lay claim for the credit of Rahman's demise. But when these claims were vigorously pursued they were found to have no basis in fact and these same arseholes were hurriedly called to Washington to explain themselves to the president. It never ceased to amaze how low these pond scum would stoop in order to rise an inch above the weed.

As for the British involvement in Afghanistan, both Special Forces teams got a well done and they also had to buy the 'Yanks' their beer for a week, which didn't go down too well.

The air element upon returning to their base on Cyprus were told 'good job, well done.'

Doug Simons at M.I.6 was made head of section instead of acting head, which everyone agreed was well deserved.

By the time the books are written about the search for and demise of Abdul Rahman, notorious terrorist leader and the Hollywood movie version is released, the British involvement will be lucky to make it onto the credits list at the end of the film.

But that was always the way mused Doug, there had to be winners and losers in any struggle, but none had paid more dearly Doug realized than James Martin, the man who had set the whole chain of events in motion.

Doug silently raised his mug of tea in salute, 'to winners and losers'.

Chapter 65

Luke was making his way up on to the ward where Sir Ian Clayton was recovering from surgery to mend his broken hip. He, Claire and Adam had visited him only yesterday but he hadn't really been up to receiving visitors, plus Claire had clashed with Seline. Thankfully it had ended without them coming to physical blows, but harsh words were hurled at one another from both parties.

Luke wisely felt that it would be best, if only for Sir Ian's sake, that they were kept apart, so here he was on his way to see him without his family. Entering the ward Luke looked to the bed that Sir Ian occupied only yesterday; it now had a stranger in residence. Turning around to check the other beds he couldn't see him so he went to the nurses' station to make enquiries.

The head nurse told Luke that Sir Ian was now in a private room of his own in an annexe just off the main ward. Leading the way she showed Luke to room number seven.

Thanking the nurse Luke waited a couple of seconds for her to leave before knocking and entering the room. There was already a man seated beside Sir Ian's bed dressed in a Saville Row suit.

Luke apologised profusely for the intrusion making to leave.

"No, come in Luke, we have just about finished here haven't we Henry?" said Sir Ian, clearly now up for visitors.

Luke almost did a pirouette as he did an about turn to remain in the room. He watched, waiting patiently whilst Sir Ian's visitor made a great show of putting away various papers and accoutrements into an expensive looking leather briefcase. Then taking his time he screwed the cap onto his equally expensive fountain pen before putting it inside his suit jacket pocket. Luke watched the display with amusement; this guy was certainly milking it for all his worth. Hitching his chair back in one fluid movement the man stood and formally shook hands with Sir Ian saying, "Leave it with me Sir Ian," nodding to Luke as he left the room.

"This is Seline's doing. I was quite happy to remain on the ward but she wouldn't hear of it.

Insisted I have a room of my own the minx," said Sir Ian.

Luke felt embarrassed about the clash between Claire and Seline yesterday but felt that he needed to bring it up again, "I'm sorry about Claire and Seline yesterday sir, it shouldn't have happened, I apologise."

"Nonsense, there's nothing to apologise for, besides I quite enjoyed it, reminded me of

Margot, my ex, when we were younger; she was fiery too! Anyway Claire was only doing what comes naturally, staking her claim on you old boy. Seline was behaving like an alley cat and needed putting in her place."

"Well, if you are sure sir," said Luke, happy for it to be forgotten.

"Of course I'm sure, I'm old, not senile," said Sir Ian.

That brought a smile to Luke's face, that's better he thought more like the Sir Ian he knew and admired.

"Please don't tell me Claire had stayed away because of Seline, Luke?"

"Partly I think," admitted Luke.

"Bugger, "he swore, "I like Claire's company, she speaks her mind, not everyone does these days. You tell her to come with you next time and bring your boy as well. He's smart as a whip that one," said Sir Ian.

"Speaking of Seline, where is she?" asked Luke.

"I've sent her home to get some rest. In spite of appearances Luke, she does love me. When she found me at the bottom of the stairs it frightened the life out of her. Apart from her flighty mother, I'm all she has got. It was sheer desperation on her part that made her get in touch with you. There was simply no one else she could turn to," admitted Sir Ian. "We have no other living relatives, she is the last of our line Luke ....I had hoped once that she would marry you." Putting up his hands to ward off Luke's protest he continued, "Oh I know that it's too late now and clearly you made the right choice by marrying Claire, but it was the hope of an old man and not his daughter's.

Anyway that is in the past and what's done is done, which brings me to the gentleman who has just left. I have been in touch with my lawyers about amending my will. Henry has been going over a few things with me." Looking towards the cabinet beside the bed Sir Ian picked up a piece of paper and handed it to Luke.

Luke looked at it carefully. Written across the top in

very neat penmanship was the sum £50,000. Below was a list of books, by Luke's quick calculation, about ten, in chronological order. A cursory look at the list confirmed that they had been purchased by Luke for Sir Ian over the last ten years. Luke looked at Sir Ian for an explanation, "That sum of money and those books listed are for you upon my death Luke."

Luke was about to protest that it wasn't necessary as Sir Ian wasn't going anywhere.

"Please Luke hear me out. Breaking my bloody hip has made me realise my own mortality.

The money I have set aside for you is in return for helping Seline get a good price for my book collection. She hasn't got a clue what it's true worth is and some 'spiv' masquerading as a book seller will only give her a fraction of its true value, so look upon the money as your fee if you like in helping Seline sell my library. The other books on the list I want you to have. Keep them or sell them, do what you bloody like with them. You alone know their true worth," finished Sir Ian.

For once Luke was almost lost for words, "I don't know what to say Sir Ian, except thank you, from the bottom of my heart. Does Seline know of your plans?"

"She will tonight when I tell her."

Luke looked dubious that Sir Ian had done this without consulting with his daughter.

Sir Ian must have read the look because he said, "Don't worry Luke, my daughter trusts you just as much as I do, so ... do we have a deal?"

"We do Sir! And once again thank you, it is truly a privilege to have earned your trust."

"Likewise my boy, likewise," beamed Sir Ian, he was happy that Luke had accepted.

Chapter 66

Mehmet was feeling nervous. The two recent additions to his team had fitted in seamlessly, just like he knew they would, so what was making him jumpy was the fact that Ali Hussein, their boss, wanted to meet the team in person. Mehmet, for reasons of his own, had purposely delayed this meeting for as long as he could, but now the time was long overdue and Mehmet had run out of plausible excuses to delay any longer.

Ali Hussein, their paymaster, for the last few months had angrily insisted on this meeting to see how well his money was being spent.

The firing range at Amman's Police Headquarters had been echoing to the sound of shots for the last half hour. Several different calibre weapons had been discharged by all persons present, including Mehmet's elder brother Senior Police Sergeant Masud Yafai. The smell of gun smoke was heavy in the air, almost heavy enough to taste.

Mehmet had arranged to meet Ali in the police firing range so that he could observe them in action at close quarters. When he finally arrived everyone put up their weapons and stepped away from their firing positions so that they could be introduced to their mystery employer.

Mehmet dutifully did the introductions one by one but Ali did not shake the hands of the men, as was customary in any normal employer employee type of relationship, instead he looked most carefully into each man's eyes before inclining his head slightly in a sort of nod or dismissive type of gesture before moving on to the next person.

When the team had been thus introduced, Mehmet handed Ali a set of ear defenders to put on so that he could observe each man shoot in turn.

Using a variety of weapons Ali watched as each man fired at his target. Mehmet was the last to fire. His accuracy with a handgun had been steadily improving with practice week by week. It certainly impressed Ali when the target was brought in for his inspection. He nodded in appreciation, congratulating Mehmet on his marksmanship.

Mehmet surprised Ali when he had the target replaced and handed him a freshly loaded hand gun. He advised Ali to use the classic two handed grip then sent the new target away.

Making sure that his boss' ear defenders were on properly he nodded to fire when ready.

The first shot as expected hit the outer edge of the target but as Ali got used to the weapon his spacings crept closer and closer to the centre mass and by the time the clip was emptied, the target, had it been a living man, would now be dead.

Even Mehmet was beaming widely at Ali's unexpected success and with an unfamiliar weapon at that. Re-loading the hand gun for him for a second time with a fresh clip he asked his boss to shoot again, by mime action.

This time there were no wild shots, the grouping on the target when it came back was tightly bunched. A definite kill! Looking at it Mehmet said, grudgingly, "That is very impressive shooting sir!" Then half joking, "Have you been practicing?"

Basking in Mehmet's warm praise Ali admitted that he hadn't fired a weapon since he had been a boy until just now, adding, "I had been in the desert with my grandfather and an old fashioned Lee- Enfield rifle that fired a .303 cartridge. He taught me first how to look after it and when he thought that I was ready, allowed me to load and fire it. I still remember thinking at the time that the rifle felt quite heavy. But you have to remember, that I was just a boy then. I got quite proficient with it and in the right hands it can be a very accurate weapon, but up until now that is the last time I had fired a weapon," answered Ali.

Mehmet was amazed by his boss' admission. He himself had been practicing for months and only just managing to achieve a decent score. His boss comes along, fires off two clips and puts his own score in the shade. Still Ali had finally met his miniscule army and left the police station a much happier man.

Mehmet had much to think about over the next few days, for in less than four weeks' time Ali and his mini strike force would be heading for Dubai. Thereafter, Mehmet and his men would be heading to London to assassinate Ali's sister. A woman Mehmet thought who probably didn't deserve to die at the hands of an unknown assassin.

Life was fragile at the best of times but did it have to end so abruptly, so cruelly. Mehmet wasn't sure but a decision would have to be made ... and soon.

Chapter 67

Frank watched his wife's face in the half light of morning. Her body was shining with perspiration; it was as if she had been coated in a thin film of oil. Her own efforts had brought about this happy state. He knew that she was on the verge of orgasm but was trying to delay the pleasure for a few moments longer. The thickness of her breath in the back of her throat betrayed her. The orgasm, when it finally arrived, was preceded by an almost animal grunt. Unashamedly she gave way to it and surrendered her body to the powerful quivers of delight. Her legs shook with the force of it; her sex was pulsing strongly in waves gripping tightly to Frank's rigid member.

Frank, for his part, remained quite still beneath Yasmin, gripping tightly to his wife's peach of a bum as he watched her face. Her eyes were still tightly closed in concentration as she squeezed every last ounce of pleasure from their coupling.

Finally she opened her eyes to look at him, mouth open; smiling; inviting. This was the second time that they had made love since Frank had come in from work. The first time had been a hurried, urgent coupling for both of them. The need for sexual release paramount and frenzied, but her second time was purely about love. Both times tonight had been instigated by Yasmin herself. Since she had become pregnant and the morning sickness had stopped, she had quickly realized that her sexual libido had sky rocketed. Thankfully, Frank could more than accommodate her sexual appetites.

Frank was still very noticeably hard inside Yasmin as she lifted herself slightly up gripping his shaft experimentally with her sex. She saw Frank's eyebrows rise up in question, "Yes,

I think once more before we sleep," she said, saucily, "it would be a crime to waste such a rigid member."

Managing to persuade herself it was for Frank's gratification, and not her own, she began to rock once more to the dance of love.

Later, allowing Frank to get some much needed sleep she left him a note saying that she had gone to visit Claire.

Now curled up on Claire's settee and balancing a mug of herbal tea in her hands, Yasmin was curious to know if Claire had needed sex more, when she had been pregnant with

Adam.

Without missing a beat Claire said, "Yes definitely, actually now thinking back we were at it like rabbits."

Surprised by Claire's admission, but greatly relieved by it as well Yasmin said, "Oh, I was beginning to think that I had morphed into someone else."

"No it's all good, normal," said Claire smiling at her

friend. "Of course all women are different, it looks like you and I, are two of the lucky ones who actually enjoy sex."

Yasmin couldn't help smiling at Claire's down to earth logic. Thank god for Claire she thought. What on earth would she do without her good friend and confidant?

Mischievously Claire asked, "It's not proving too much for Frank is it Yasmin?"

Never quite knowing when Claire was being serious or not, Yasmin worriedly said, "No I don't think so."

Claire couldn't help it, gales of laughter burst forth, almost forcing her to spill her coffee in the process.

Yasmin, realising that Claire had been having her on, joined in with the laughter. Good company, good coffee (or herbal tea) and a dash of laughter; what better tonic could you wish for!

Adam, who had been quietly playing by the patio windows, came to see what they were laughing about.

"It's alright Adam, it's only Aunty Yasmin and mum being silly that's all," said Claire.

"Are we getting a rabbit?" Adam asked. "I heard you say rabbits, so I wondered if we were getting one."

At the mention of rabbits Claire and Yasmin dissolved into gales of infectious laughter again. Managing to control herself enough to answer Adam's question, Claire said, "No we are not getting a rabbit!"

Adam just stood there watching first his Aunty Yasmin and then his mum helpless with laughter. Leaving them to it he went back to playing. He had only wanted to know if they were getting a rabbit. He thought, I don't really want a rabbit; I would rather have a dog.

When Claire and Yasmin finally got control of themselves Claire announced quietly,

"Little pigs have very large ears."

Yasmin nodded in agreement cuffing the tear of merriment away from her eyes. Wait until Luke and Frank heard this one!

Chapter 68

The glorious sunshine continued to greet them each morning accompanied by above average temperatures which was starting to make life a little uncomfortable. Already there were rumours of enforcing a hose pipe ban if it continued.

God, thought Claire what is it with this country and the bloody weather. In winter if it snowed an inch it brought roads and airports almost to a standstill, yet in Canada and most Scandinavian countries they were almost buried in the bloody stuff and operated efficiently enough.

Trains in the U.K. were either delayed or cancelled at the merest hint of a leaf being blown on the line, for fucks sake, leaves on the line! Really! She shook her head in disbelief.

She had been out of sorts ever since she had got Adam up for breakfast this morning. Not with Adam or Luke just off it for some inexplicable reason. She could have blamed the hot weather. Brits loved to bitch about the weather; it was a favourite past time, too hot, too cold, too wet, too dry and too windy. It was hard wired into their D.N.A. it's what Brits did, but Claire still couldn't explain why she felt so out of sorts!

Adam as usual was his cheerful happy self. That in itself should have gone some way to lightening her mood. When Luke came in from work he had been both loving and attentive until finally succumbing to sleep so she couldn't blame her mood on that; whatever the reason it was usually cured by exercise.

So after breakfast she made Adam a supply of fruit juice and took a diet coke from the fridge for herself. A short while later Claire was quietly sweating pushing Adam along in his buggy.

Adam was quite capable of walking himself, but Claire needed to stride out and feel the burn in her legs and that could only be achieved by walking quickly, so Adam had to put up with the indignity of being confined to his buggy.

Claire only had on a thin summer skirt with a short top but the sun's rays combined with the exercise was forcing her to sweat. Claire had no clear destination in mind, just walking for walking's sake, nothing more. But it still came as a surprise when she found herself crossing the street marking the approach to St. Paul's Cathedral.

On a whim Claire changed her mind and direction pushing Adam's buggy uphill towards the domed master piece. She was breathing heavier than normal and slightly out of breath by the time she came to the top. Thankfully she was now in shadow, the sun was mainly hidden behind the hallowed structure. Looking for a vacant bench seat to sit on met with disappointment; all were occupied so instead she got Adam out of the buggy and they sat on the stone steps of St. Paul's.

Fishing in the buggy she gave Adam his juice before cracking open the seal on the can of coke. The first hit of fizz and coke always delighted her. She remembered reading somewhere that the simplest of pleasures in life were always the best; in this case they were right.

The walk had been good for Claire but St. Paul's, wow! She hadn't realised she had walked so far, still she was young and in relatively good shape so the return journey under her own steam shouldn't be a problem. Adam only drank part of his juice, handing it back to his mum to put away for him.

Now safely secreted back in the buggy for later, Adam craned his neck back so he could better see the building. He asked questions about the historic building which Claire tried to answer as best she could but at the end of the question and answer session, it became patently obvious to Adam that his mum didn't really know much about the building at all.

She had realized for herself that she was going to have to up her game; it just wasn't fair on Adam not to. Feeling a little bit better for the rest and with Adam back in the buggy ready to set off home, standing up perhaps a little too quickly, she suddenly felt light headed and decidedly dizzy.

An old gentleman standing a little too close for comfort saw her predicament and came timely to her rescue. He helped Claire sit back down on the steps once more. The old man was obviously worried about Claire having asked her several times, without a response,

"Are you alright? Shall I call an ambulance?"

Realising that someone was standing very close to her, holding her arm and asking questions Claire's mind and vision suddenly swam back into sync.

Again the old man asked "Are you alright? Shall I call an ambulance?"

"No thank you," said Claire, "I just felt dizzy for a moment that's all, I'll be okay." But despite her protestations she still had not managed to convince him that she had recovered her senses. Seeing that she needed to be a little more convincing she stood up, thankfully this time the world remained on an even keel.

Claire knew that he had probably meant well, but she still felt somehow relieved when she had finally managed to break his hold on her arm. Thanking him for his kindness she sought to put distance between them.

The old man reluctantly let go of Claire's arm and watched her walk away until she was almost lost from view.

Ten minutes later with St. Paul's diminishing in the back ground, Claire spotted a rare empty bench in a courtyard in the shade of a beautiful broad leafed tree.

Parking Adam's buggy at one end of the bench she eased herself shakily on to it.

Adam worried for his mum, quickly un-tangled himself from the buggy and climbed up beside her. Reaching for her hand he slipped his own reassuringly into hers. It was only then, at Adam's contact that Claire realised that she was out of breath. Looking down at Adam's frightened face she gave his hand a squeeze trying to reassure him; it wasn't enough.

Adam asked, "Mum! Are you alright?"

Claire didn't answer right away as she was still trying to control her breathing and calm herself down. She had been trying desperately to remember something during her flight from St. Paul's because no matter how Claire tried to rationalise it, she had been panicked and that had caused her to flee.

Hearing Adam's concern she said, "Yes sweetie I'm feeling much better now."

Claire had been thinking back to the last time she had felt like this. She had had that episode way back in her teens when she had voluntarily been a patient at Woodhaven Psychiatric Hospital, but though this feeling was similar she felt confident enough, that it wasn't like that.

The only other time she had felt something akin to this feeling was when she had been pregnant with Adam. A feeling of dread suddenly came over her ....no...no, surely not....I cannot be pregnant again thought Claire. She was in denial but the awful truth was, she was probably pregnant. Surely one miracle was enough Claire quietly argued with herself. The symptoms were just similar that's all.

After Adam's birth neither Claire nor Luke had bothered to practice birth control, believing that one miracle was a blessing, two an impossibility.

If in fact she was pregnant again Claire wondered if he or she would be like Adam. Oh my god! Thought Claire how would they possibly cope! Surely it would be too much.

Just then Adam broke into her thoughts.

"Mum you're hurting my hand!"

"Oh, I'm sorry sweetie. Are you okay?"

Adam just nodded that he was.

Of course Claire could put an end to this uncertainty right away - she could ask Adam if she was pregnant and he would tell her, but no, upon reflection she decided not to put the burden onto her son, deciding instead that she would hold on to the knowledge for a little while longer. Just until she had gotten her own head around it and then perhaps a visit to Dr. Cooymans clinic would be in order.

Feeling better now Claire asked Adam if he was ready

to go home.

Adam said, "Yes mum," and then in typical fashion remarked, "I'm hungry." Claire smiled good naturedly.

"Of course you are."

Chapter 69

The mood in the apartment block was sombre, the atmosphere brittle and subdued. It had come as a complete shock to the men, when Mehmet told them what was required of them from their employer,Ali Hussein. Once Mehmet had enlightened them, he allowed them to choose for themselves, even at this late stage, whether to continue with the operation or withdraw from it completely and escape back into anonymity, no harm done. That had been a week ago.

Ever since Mehmet had told the team of the true purpose behind their formation, each of the men including Mehmet himself, had raised concerns, questions and objections to try to justify the implementing of the proposed action.

Mehmet was solicitous of his men's feelings just as a good commander should be. He had known each man personally from their shared time in the Jordanian army, he knew their strengths and more importantly their weaknesses and over time he trusted them implicitly.

They in tum found Mehmet to be a fair minded and capable officer whose men's welfare seemed to rate highly on his list. So, now they were all still here quietly waiting for Ali Hussein's driver to take them to Amman airport. Each man was wearing western styled clothing, had his own small travelling case, along with 1,000 euro's and his own passport.

The time for discussion was over; the decision, though hard for each man, had now been made.

The journey to the airport was a blur to Mehmet; his thoughts were heavy and troubled.

The car was met at a private side gated entrance put in place especially for high status dignitaries and owners of privately owned aircraft.

After a cursory check of all their passports at a small security truck the Hussein driver was told to follow the security vehicle to the private hanger housing the Hussein jet.

Upon arrival the small team retrieved their own bags then watched as the limousine drove away, following the security vehicle once more.

The air craft was already opened up waiting for them to board. The pilot could be clearly seen going through the final pre-flight check list. Mehmet realised that Ali Hussein must already be on board awaiting their arrival. Once aboard the aircraft there were no second chances, no turning back. Tight lipped Mehmet led the way; climbing the few short steps he entered the sleek aircraft's fuselage.

As Mehmet had thought, Ali Hussein was already on board sitting comfortably at the front in palatial splendour as befitting his status. As he greeted them, Ali seemed genuinely relieved to see Mehmet and his companions.

"Welcome aboard gentlemen, please take your seats," indicating the vacant seats behind him with an expansive hand gesture.

The men couldn't help but marvel at the sheer luxury of the aircraft's fittings. Everything was designed with comfort in mind. They chose their own seats, stowing away their small cases.

A very pretty stewardess dressed in an expensively tailored uniform bearing the Hussein logo brought up the boarding steps, and then expertly sealed the fuselage door.

A truck with an orange flashing light appeared outside the hanger door. The aircraft's engines built slightly in volume as they slowly began to follow it to the designated runway take off point. Once they were airborne everyman was alone with his own thoughts.

It seemed incongruous to Mehmet, as the aircraft levelled out and became fully pressurised, that here they were gathered together for a specific purpose. That purpose being to murder

Ali Hussein's sister!

Yet as he looked on the monitor screen he realised they were travelling in the wrong direction for Yasmin and London, but were flying away from her towards Dubai. Mehmet thought wryly to himself, obviously his boss was not worried about the so called carbon footprint that they were creating. Admitted it had been at Ali's own suggestion that they spend three days relaxing in his hotel before going on to complete their mission.

The pilot had been instructed to relax and avail himself of the hotel's amenities for the same time they would be there. Then he was to transport Mehmet and his men to London, via refuelling stops along the way. He was then to wait in London until he was contacted by Mehmet for the return journey. He didn't ask why, he was being handsomely paid to fly the aircraft that was his job, and that was what he would do.

The stewardess was meeting up with her parents in Dubai, so she had a whole week to do exactly what she liked, and she fully intended to make the most of it.

So Mehmet and his men, once they arrived in Dubai, still had three days of wrestling with their consciences. The turmoil within them would continue to rage for a while longer.

Chapter 70

In order to try and distract my brain from thoughts that I might be pregnant once more, I started to methodically spring clean the house. At first Luke was fine with it, shrugging off my need for cleanliness as just a phase I was going through, but when it continued unabated even he lost patience with me. Luke was no dummy and he certainly knew when something wasn't right. I kept telling him that I was fine, almost convincing myself as well at one point, but a moment of clarity forced me to admit that things weren't fine.

Ringing Dr Cooymans clinic for an appointment with her brought me to this point. I told Luke a half-truth to try and explain my abnormal behaviour, admitting to him that I had been feeling unwell. He now knew that I was going for a check-up with the doctor, which was in fact true but I was going for a pregnancy test. I hadn't told Luke the real reason for my visit in case I was wrong, but deep in my heart, I knew that I wasn't.

The truth was all the last weeks' anxiety had been brought about by the fact I might be pregnant. It wasn't the thought of being pregnant that was causing it you understand, but the thought of how we were going to cope if the new baby was equally as smart as Adam. Christ! Just the mere thought of it was beginning to make my head spin.

Luke had offered to come with me for support but I thanked him and said no. Looking after

Adam for me would be a big help and besides, it was another lie of course and it always amazed me how one lie often led to another, but I didn't want him to find out I was pregnant just yet, at least not until I had had a chance to get my own head around it.

Leaving the house I managed to hail a cab at the second attempt. The cab ride to Dr Cooymans clinic hadn't managed to calm the turmoil raging within me. After seeing the receptionist to confirm my arrival I sat on the plush seating waiting for Dr Cooymans to call me in.

It had only been two weeks ago that I had seen her when I came with Yasmin for her monthly check up. The fact that I was here alone and worse still, without my friend Yasmin, felt like a betrayal on my part, as we tended to do most everything together and tell each other our inner most secrets, but for some reason I couldn't explain, I wanted to be sure for myself before letting other people in on it. If in fact it turned out that I was pregnant I would tell Luke and Yasmin myself when I was ready and at a time of my own choosing.

Dr Cooymans broke through my thoughts indicating for me to come through. Telling the doctor what I suspected saved time. She gave me a thorough top to toe examination followed by the taking of blood and a urine sample for analysis. This should prove conclusively one way or another if I was pregnant. Either way I should know within the next 48 hours.

Arriving home I caught Luke on all fours giving our son Adam a ride around the living room floor. Adam was squealing with delight at his dad's antics.

A smile from both of them brought one to my own face. The anxiety of moments before had been temporarily banished. It was wonderful that something so simple had the power to do that.

Luke asked warily, "Is everything okay?" meaning had the doctor found anything to explain my abnormal behaviour of late.

I lied again saying that she thought I was a little run down and had taken samples to see if there was an underlying reason for it. Lying was becoming easier; I hoped it wasn't habit forming. "I should have a proper diagnosis within the next few days," I said, escaping further interrogation by going into the kitchen to boil the kettle.

Now I only had to get through the next couple of days then I would know for sure.

Chapter 71

The two men entered the corridor from the stair well; the need for speed uppermost in their minds. A particular room was the focus of their attention, the one housing the C.C.T.V. monitors.

Both men were armed with pistols fitted with silencers and dressed from head to toe in matching black clothing. They could have been mistaken for members of the famous S.A.S. but there the resemblance ended, for neither of them could claim allegiance to that illustrious regiment.

One of the men had an electronic pass key in his hand. Quickly he accessed entry to the room startling the occupant within. The eyes on the surprised guard vaguely took in the two men's black garb, but he was more worried by the pistol pressed against his head. Frightened though he was, he falteringly managed to ask, in Arabic, "What do you want?"

The man holding the gun against his head answered in

English, "Face down on the floor, now, slowly."

The guard meekly obeyed followed all the way down with the gun.

"Now, hands behind your back and no stupid heroics please. I don't want to have to kill you unless you force me to, you understand?"

Replying in English the guard clearly frightened gulped, "Yes."

The other man, who hadn't spoken yet plasticuffed the guard's hands securely, testing them to make sure he had them tight enough. He then doubly secured his legs saying, "All done Moshe."

The other man soundly berated his companion for using his name, "Quiet fool!"

The guard fearfully tried to convey that he had heard nothing untoward, straining his neck in an effort to gain eye contact with the angry gunman. His life now definitely seemed to hang in the balance; it rested entirely with the gunman. After a few moments he was visibly relieved to still be alive when he was gagged.

Both men now placed their weapons in their belts and helped drag the guard over towards a secure stanchion supporting the bank of T.V. monitors. Again the guard was plasticuffed to the stanchion and doubly checked to make sure that he wasn't going anywhere in a hurry.

Now, satisfied that the guard was no longer a threat they removed the discs from the recorders and switched off the C. C. T. V. cameras.

The guard watched as the one who seemed to be the leader pocketed both discs and with an imperceptible nod of his head he made for the door. A quick look to both left and right showed the corridor to be clear of people. Once again, moving at speed they returned to the stair-well, now secure in the knowledge that the cameras were not functioning and their movements were no longer being recorded. The upward draught in the stairwell was uncomfortably warm. The clothing they were wearing didn't help to cool them down and the balaclavas covering their heads were itchy and made them sweat. The very air they were breathing was warm and moist. They followed the draught upwards watching and listening as they went.

After ascending three more flights of stairs they were at the top where they met three more similarly clad men, waiting on the landing.

The leader asked, "All set." Nothing more.

The three nodded in unison that they were.

Looking out onto the corridor he held the fire door open whilst his men joined him, then quietly they made their way to the one door ,marked Penthouse Suite. Fishing in his pocket once more he produced an electronic master pass key card. Inserting it and then smoothly removing it, gave them access to the dimly lit room. Just one corner table lamp had been left lit in the otherwise darkened room. A quick scan of it revealed it to be empty.

The bedroom door wasn't quite fully closed and three inches of darkness framed the edge of it. Now moving towards it, the men, silenced handguns pointed upwards, moved Indian file, hearts pumping loudly in their ears. With an almost noiseless fluidity the leader pushed the door open wider. The light switch was on one side of the door, flicking it down flooded the room with artificial light.

The men fanned out in a semi-circle at the foot of the bed, their guns were now trained upon the figure still laid upon his side occupying the bed.

Slowly imperceptibly the sleeping figure came to realise that the overhead lights for some inexplicable reason, that his sleep fogged brain hadn't quite worked out yet, were on. Worse still, armed men were in the room and pointing their weapons at him. Tentatively Ali croaked, "Who are you? What do you want?"

The leader of the men removed his balaclava.

Ali's eyes widened like saucers when he saw who was before him, "Mehmet! Why?"

One shot from Mehmet's gun, hit his boss squarely in the chest. The look of surprise and hurt on Ali's face was genuine. He had come to trust Mehmet implicitly and sadly he realised too late that trust had just cost him his life.

One by one each of the men stepped forward and fired one shot into Ali Hussein's chest. It was the second shot that actually killed him, but by all firing just the one shot it made them all complicit in Ali Hussein's murder. It was no good trying to dress up their actions in any other way, it was murder, plain and simple.

The job was done but Mehmet still had one small task to do. Retrieving the mobile phone from his pocket that Brad Dillman had earlier given to him, he carefully took several close-up pictures of Ali Hussein's now lifeless body. He then pressed send and waited for acknowledgement; which came forty five long seconds later.

A message came back, Hussein confirmed, money being transferred now as agreed, destroy phone A.S.A.P. out.

They covered Ali's body with his bed sheet then turned off the bedroom light and closed the door. They all had their masks off now as they were able to reconcile with one another what they had just done.

Mehmet with the ordered mind of a military man had gone through the plan of action beforehand with his men. It did not sit well with any of them to murder an innocent woman, Yasmin Hussein. So, Mehmet first contacted Brad

Dillman, and then brought his men into the loop, to suggest an alternative plan of action.

Once Mehmet had convinced them that Ali Hussein was both complicit in his own father's murder as well as being a known terrorist with a price on his head, they had needed no further convincing.

The manoeuvre was run like a well-rehearsed military operation. All the spent shell casings were retrieved and in Mehmet's pocket. They left a 'Do Not Disturb' sign hanging on Ali's door as they left the Penthouse: taking charge, Mehmet told the men to return to their rooms. Once there they were to get the laundry sack from the wardrobe and put everything they were wearing, including boots, into the sack, then wipe the guns and silencers down and lastly put them in the sack. Then shower and change into their western clothes. Once this was done they were to bring everything to Mehmet's room, leaving a 'Do Not Disturb' sign on their doors.

Forty five minutes later the team were assembled once more, this time in Mehmet's room and each man had followed his instructions to the letter. He thought praise god!

There was an incinerator in the basement and he planned to use it.

Using the lift down to the second floor, he and two of his men carried the sacks of clothing the rest of the way down to the basement, via the stairway. The sacks were tossed well into the inferno. Mehmet watched with satisfaction as the items quickly succumbed to the flames. The surveillance discs and Brad Dillman's phone were thrown in as well. Clapping his men on their backs they returned to his room.

Phase two of Mehmet's plan was for his men to get out of Dubai. For it to succeed they had to bring their own passports so that there would be no problem at the airport. They each had 1,000 euro's plus whatever else they had brought with them. He had stressed the importance to them, several times, just like a mother hen, not to travel as a group. A group would attract attention whereas travelling alone or in pairs would avoid unwanted scrutiny. He told them to leave the hotel by the back entrance singularly or in pairs and then walk a couple of blocks before hailing a cab for the airport. Again he drilled into them the importance of getting out of Dubai safely. It didn't matter if there were no flights available to Jordan, just get a flight to somewhere then a connecting flight could be arranged from the new destination. He had done what he could; the rest was up to them.

Once they were back in Jordan they were to wait in the rented apartment block until he contacted them. They would still continue to get their pay as was agreed for this clandestine agreement between Ali and Mehmet, so they wouldn't lack for funds.

Mehmet embraced them as they left his room one by one. Once he was alone he still had the weapons and shell casing to dispose of. Time was marching on for this one last task. Gathering up the weapons into a sack he made his way out into Dubai's humid night air.

Moving quickly but so as to not attract attention on the busy street Mehmet covered a distance of about three blocks before he found what he was looking for; a row of industrial sized dumpsters lined up ready for emptying. Taking a moment to make sure he was not being observed, even at this time of the morning, he seized his chance and dumped his sack into one of the containers.

Moving off a short distance he waited a while to see if anyone approached the container. Satisfied that it was safe to leave, Mehmet retraced his steps back to the hotel. Once back inside his room, nervous exhaustion was beginning to take its toll. Mehmet undressed and took another cold shower; he was actually shivering when he stepped out of the water. Drying off he slipped between the sheets. The air conditioning was slightly noisy but doing a good job as he finally drifted off into a troubled sleep.

If everything went to Mehmet's plan the guard in the C.C.T.V. room wouldn't be discovered until shift change over at 10 a.m. The horrific discovery of Ali Hussein's body should be some time after that.

Mehmet had by far the hardest job of all; he would have to weather the storm of suspicion, maybe even interrogation by the Dubai secret police. He was fully prepared for it, after all, he was Ali

Hussein's head of security, but he was hoping that the so called Freudian slip in the control room would be remembered and repeated often by the guard when questioned.

"The man spoke in heavily accented English. One of them was definitely called Moshe."

That had been a deliberate red herring inserted by Mehmet. If the feared Dubai secret police could be duped into thinking that they were looking for a 'Mossad' hit squad they would soon tire of squeezing Mehmet's balls and turn their attentions elsewhere. That's what he was hoping anyway, but whatever happened he would have to ride out the shit storm by himself.

He knew that he would have to find inner strength from somewhere for whatever was coming.

One thing that was troubling Mehmet as he fitfully tried to sleep, was the look on Ali Hussein's face and especially the look in his eyes - surprise and fear were both there, but genuine hurt and disappointment were visible too. That look would haunt Mehmet's dreams for the rest of his life.

Chapter 72

The next few days laboriously dragged by. The doctor had insisted on seeing me personally which gave me a horrible feeling of foreboding.

I had been sitting patiently waiting for Dr Cooymans with my gut churning in turmoil anxiously waiting to be summoned by her. It wasn't a very pleasant feeling and dire thoughts were going through my mind.

When she came to collect me personally it seemed to confirm my own worst fears.

Now, in her room we sat down opposite one another; Dr Cooymans all business. As she read through my notes she confirmed without any preamble that I was pregnant but that the iron levels in my blood were low; I was anaemic, which could possibly account for my tiredness and dizziness. She explained that the most common form of anaemia was iron deficiency caused by a lack of iron in the body which is necessary for the production of haemoglobin.

She mentioned that the condition could be aggravated by pregnancy so she prescribed a course of iron tablets to be taken and regular monitoring of my blood cell count, to be done when I came to see her at my future monthly check ups.

She stressed the importance of taking the tablets, then wrote me an appointment for four weeks' time.

I left the clinic clutching my tablets and now certain in the knowledge that I was definitely pregnant.

The cab ride home left me in a better frame of mind and I would tell Luke my news as soon as possible; this couldn't be put off any longer.

As I walked into the room Luke had Adam close beside him on the settee going through one of his ABC books that we had only just bought for him. Both of them looked up from the book, eyes searching mine questioningly for answers. Luke had seen the bag in my hand containing the iron tablets but he had the patience of a man, who in anyone else, would be infuriating, especially a curious person like me, but I kept my cool going into the kitchen to organised a brew.

Luke soon padded in after me and asked the question on the tip of his tongue, "So what did the doctor say Claire?"

Looking carefully at him I replied, "She said I'm anaemic and has prescribed a course of iron tablets for me to take, but says that it is quite normal for someone in my condition."

I let that sink in, but when it became obvious that it still hadn't registered with Luke what I was trying to tell him I thought, god, men. I'm going to have to spell it out, "I'm pregnant!"

Pouring the boiled water into the teapot, and then returning the kettle to its original place, I deftly fitted the teapot lid with a smile like that of Alice's Cheshire cat appearing on my face.

Meanwhile Luke's face by comparison appeared slack jawed like a simpletons. As his mind finally processed my words, the importance of their meaning began to shine through.

I had had to deal with this unexpected problem alone for over two weeks. It was only fair that

Luke should now shoulder some of the burden and share in the disbelief, joy, responsibility, uncertainty and worry; it was too much for one person to carry.

He came up behind me and enfolded me in his arms. He could have said, "Are you sure?" just like the majority of men in the world would have done, but instead, he wisely chose to say nothing, waiting for me to speak first.

"Are you happy with this Luke?" I asked, half turning to look at him.

"Surprised," said Luke, "I thought that Adam was that one in a million type of miracle, that only happens once in a thousand years, but to have two, will certainly take some getting used to," admitted Luke.

"You think?" I laughed, happy that I now had someone with which to share whatever trials the future held.

"Have you told Yasmin yet?" asked Luke.

"No but I'm going to have to now. I feel like I've somehow betrayed her for not doing so, but you're my husband and I needed to tell you first."

"Thank you for that."

Knowing how much Yasmin meant to me he was grateful I had told him first.

Pouring two large mugs of tea from the pot and automatically going over to the refrigerator to get Adam a juice, I realised that someone else was not too far away playing in the living room who would also have to be told. Thinking about it I asked Luke "Do you think Adam already knows I'm pregnant?"

Straight away Luke answered truthfully, "If Adam does know he has successfully managed to hide it from me, so I honestly don't know Claire."

I took Adam's juice in for him and placed it on the coffee table reminding him not to spill it. I returned to the kitchen to enlist Luke's help bringing in our teas and we placed them on the table mats away from Adam's reach.

He was still looking at his ABC book trying to make sense of what was on the pages, when he was flanked on both sides by his mum and dad.

Looking up first at his dad and then at me he asked her, "Will you pass me my juice please, mum?"

So polite I thought, at least we are teaching him good manners. A picture of my mum suddenly leaped into my mind, making me think, yes mum you taught me good manners too and now I'm teaching my son the same.

Luke was just about to tell Adam that he was going to have a brother or sister when Adam piped up, "I know dad."

"You know what? I haven't asked a question yet," queried Luke looking at me.

"I know mum is going to have a baby," said Adam, matter-of-factly.

Upon hearing Adam's words I was incredulous at first and not willing to believe my own ears....

"How do you know?" I asked, rather bluntly.

Adam hunched his tiny shoulders, "I don't know how I know, I just do!"

Then on a whim I asked Adam, "How long have you known?"

Again he hunched his shoulders this time taking his

time before answering, "A while now. I'm not sure how long." Then quietly he asked me, "I'm not in any trouble am I?"

Concerned now, I quickly hugged Adam and said, "Sweetie of course you're not in any trouble, you've done nothing wrong."

Slightly mollified by that, Adam returned to studying his book, well aware that his mum and dad were searching each other's eyes above his own head.

I had wanted to ask Adam if he knew the baby's sex but decided to leave that question for another day. Adam's welfare came first and he didn't need any unnecessary burdens placed upon it.

Later on I rang Yasmin to see if it was alright to visit. I couldn't put this off any longer I needed to share my news with our friends.

Chapter 73

Mehmet sank back into the thickly padded seat of the Hussein family jet. It had been a difficult few days for him, fraught with tension and a sprinkling of danger. Apart from the pilot and the stewardess Mehmet was the only other passenger on board - living that is, for they were bringing home the body of their former employer Ali Hussein, for burial in Jordan. As they quickly left U.A.E. airspace Mehmet closed his tired eyes in silent thanks.

The stewardess woke him almost immediately by being an annoyingly attentive hostess asking, "Do you require anything?"

Mehmet wearily thanked her politely answering, "No thank you."

As she left him to go talk to the pilot, Mehmet's thoughts returned to the last few days, it had been an anxious time for him, a time when he realised he would need to keep his wits about him. By staying at his post in the Hussein hotel in Dubai,he was offering himself up as the chief suspect. Ali Hussein was an important man in Dubai. His family had done much to kick start the prosperity that it now enjoyed.

Mehmet's eyelids closed once more sleep finally bringing temporary peace.

The morning following the assassination of Ali Hussein, he had taken a long cold shower and wearily climbed into bed; much as he needed to sleep, he woke up bathed in sweat.

Mehmet could not rid himself of the look in Ali Hussein's eyes as he fired the first shot and Ali's hurt expression as he asked, "Why?" He could still see it now as Ali breathed his last, his question left unanswered, it haunted him and try as he might he could not return to sleep, so he showered once more and dressed simply in light trousers and t-shirt. It was full day light now so he opened the door to the veranda and sat on a tacky plastic chair that stuck to your arse. He needed to remember what Ali had wanted Mehmet to do - kill his own sister - so he could carry on!

People were going about their daily lives as normal. The world still turned, it hadn't suddenly stopped because of the death of one evil man. He saw this as inspiration.

He must think and act normally. He was on holiday, so act like it. Go to the restaurant as usual, maybe a swim in the hotel pool. Everything must appear as normal, that is, until the time of the changeover in the C.C.T.V. room and the immobilised guard was found, then the hue and cry would truly begin.

A chain of events would then occur, although due protocol would have to be followed, before the actual discovery of Ali Hussein's body.

First the head of hotel security would have to be informed about the guard. He would then have to assess the situation for himself before informing the hotel manager. Once the manager became involved he was duty bound to inform the owner of the hotel, who unfortunately for him was here in residence in the Penthouse Suite. When the manager couldn't raise the owner by telephone he would have to go to the suite personally. He would see the do not disturb sign on Ali's door and then have to make the decision whether to disturb his lord and master, or not. Either way, Ali's body would be discovered sooner or later, it was just a matter of time. Then the shit would truly hit the fan!

The sequence of events that Mehmet had planned for, happened more or less as he had expected, it just took a little longer that's all.

The hotel was suddenly flooded with local police but no one really knew why. At one point there was a real danger that they would outnumber the paying guests, there were so many of them.

Mehmet, who had missed most of the action, was actually in the hotel restaurant half way through lunch when three police officers were directed towards his table. Now, towering over him they asked him to accompany them to the police station.

He wasn't given any explanation as to why he should do so, but noticing that their hands rested closely to their side arms he thought it best to comply with their wishes.

He was taken to a secure room where everything was bolted down and left alone to sit. Mehmet was familiar with the technique; he had used it himself many times. He also knew that he was now under observation and tried to remain calm. That was sound advice he thought to himself, but his heart rate beat a healthy tattoo of its own, proving otherwise.

Mehmet could hear other doors along the corridor

outside opening and slamming shut with a metallic boom, like the entrance to a tomb he idly thought. The room could actually serve as one, it was secure enough.

Suddenly three police men entered the room; one senior to the others. It was he who sat down opposite Mehmet, the other two positioned themselves either side of the door, impassive. He was read his rights.

If it was designed to intimidate, it was working. The senior policeman was looking at a sheaf of notes, whether they were fake or real Mehmet couldn't quite see.

No one had spoken to him yet, apart from to read him his rights, not even on the journey down to the station. Mehmet's mind had begun to wander, his thoughts dangerously loose.

They were suddenly jolted into the present when the senior constable suddenly asked him, "Do you know why you are here?"

Mehmet temporarily wrong footed simply replied, "No."

He continued in an almost conversational way, "Yet here you are." When Mehmet remained silent he continued, "Do you know what I find strange about that?"

When Mehmet again failed to respond he continued, by explaining, "You didn't protest about being brought here Mr Yafai. Not once."

Alarm bells began to ring in Mehmet's imagination but catching himself just in time he managed to keep calm and answer, "Would it have done any good?" Holding both palms upwards to emphasise the fact.

The police man smiled in an almost friendly way, "No Mr Yafai, it would not have done you any good."

Feeling a little bolder Mehmet decided it was time to go on the attack, so he asked, "Why am I here?"

The smile instantly disappeared from the policeman's

face. He was no longer Mr Nice Guy, "Do not take us for fools Mr Yafai, you are here to answer questions in regard to a murder investigation."

Mehmet knew that it was a bluff by the policeman. He had used the very same method himself to try to trap the unwary. Sometimes by withholding key information a gullible subject would furnish the element himself bringing about his or her own downfall. Now, Mehmet knew for certain that they had nothing, he just needed to remain vigilant.

"Whose murder?" Mehmet asked in denial.

That seemed to be the signal for the three policemen to leave the room. The echo of the door slamming shut reverberated around the room for a while, leaving Mehmet with his thoughts. He knew that he was once again under observation but tried to gauge the passage of time from the frequency of the questioning, as he had been relieved of his wrist watch, wallet and belt when he had been brought here and searched.

The police of course would have rounded up and brought in anyone they suspected of being involved with, or who knew or worked for Ali Hussein, including the security guard who had been monitoring the cameras in the hotel's C.C.T.V. room. He was the key to Mehmet's plan, but it would take time before someone finally took notice of the 'red herring' planted in the guards head by Mehmet.

Mehmet now felt confident that Ali's secret army was safely out of the country. Previously, upon their arrival in Dubai, Mehmet had made sure that their passports hadn't been scanned by hotel security. Ali Hussein himself had authorised the deception in the belief that after their short vacation the so called 'secret army' would be travelling onwards to London to carry out the murder of his sister, so he simply didn't want to risk leaving tracks back to him.

It had been a clever ruse by Mehmet to get Ali himself to override Dubai's strict laws governing

visitors' arrivals and departures, but it had worked like a charm. Ali's secret army didn't exist, so they should be home free as nobody would know any of their actual locations.

Eventually the guard's insistence that his attackers were Israeli would strike a chord with someone, so Mehmet would just have to ride out the storm until that happened.

After twelve hours of intermittent questioning he was taken from the room and put into a normal police cell. He was given a plastic bottle of water but offered no food. The following morning he was escorted back to the interrogation room where it began all over again, this time a more senior policeman, his face pitted horribly with acne, took up the questioning. Like the policeman before, he also had with him a sheaf of papers that he constantly referred to.

No longer attempting to keep Ali Hussein's murder a secret, the senior policeman asked Mehmet about his movements from 10 p.m. the previous night until the time he was brought to the station.

Mehmet accounted for his movement as best he could hoping and praying that no one could

remember seeing him out and about in Dubai disposing of the weapons. Instead he claimed to have retired to his room a little after 10p.m. where he stayed until breakfast the next morning.

The policeman looked steadily at Mehmet as he gave an account of his movements and whereabouts.

Then he said, "As head of Ali Hussein's security, surely you had to have had contact with your employer."

Mehmet stressed that his duty as head of security had

been temporarily relieved as he was officially on vacation, therefore it fell into the jurisdiction of the hotel's own head of security.

This had obviously been overlooked by the police. But, it seemed to clear up any further doubt in this policeman's mind at any rate.

Mehmet was taken back to his cell, probably whilst his story was being verified. His water bottle was almost empty so he asked his gaoler for another one, which was duly brought to his cell. But once again, no food. Mehmet's stomach growled just thinking about it.

By his estimation it was about three hours before he was taken back to the interrogation room again.

This time he was left alone for what seemed like half an hour. Someone must have wanted to watch him pretty badly. When the door finally opened, two policemen and a tall man in civilian clothes entered the room.

This was different, it spoke of state security. Mehmet had to be very careful from now on. The thought of electrodes attached to intimate places, made his anal gland pucker up.

He was quietly spoken but audible. He too had a sheaf of papers to which he was referring. He asked Mehmet more or less everything that the local police had asked, but in a different order.

Mehmet answered his questions, neither adding to, or taking anything away. He knew that this man was a pro and a predator. He had no illusions about that.

They went over and over the same questions without a break; this type of questioning was designed to wear him down, but somehow, he managed to stay focused. After what seemed like several hours of the same monotonous questioning, a knock at the door was closely followed by a policeman holding a piece of paper, entering the room.

The look of annoyance on the state security man's face at the intrusion could probably have turned Medusa to stone. Watching him read the note; Mehmet saw what looked like a wave of disbelief cross the man's face. To say he was more annoyed by what it said was putting it mildly. He barked at the two policemen to take Mehmet back to his holding cell, as he angrily left the room.

Mehmet spent another night in the police cell without further interrogation. He wondered to himself what had changed. Perhaps the guard's story about a 'mossad' hit squad had finally born fruit. Mehmet selfishly hoped so, for his sake.

At about 8 a.m. what few belongings he had on him when detained, were returned to Mehmet and he was released. You can say 'detained for questioning' a phrase they liked to trot out, because he had not actually been formally arrested, but he was now hungry as hell.

Hailing a cab from the nearby taxi rank Mehmet returned to the hotel. He got some quizzical looks at his dishevelled appearance by members of staff in the foyer who recognised him, he also got several more shocked looks at his appearance from both guests and staff in the restaurant. However, no one challenged him or said anything to his face. It was a good job, because as well as being hungry he was also angry.

Selecting a solitary table he placed a full glass of orange juice on it to claim ownership, then again going over to the ice cold juice dispensers, he filled and drank two glasses of orange juice in quick succession. That took care of his thirst, now it was time for some food. Looking at what was on offer, he took his time, piling what he wanted onto his plate.

After demolishing what was for Mehmet a gargantuan breakfast he went to get his room key from the reception. The girl behind the desk knew perfectly well who he was but she had never seen him in such a dishevelled state. Now clutching his room key Mehmet roguishly winked at her and said, "Been out partying!"

Later, shaved, showered and in clean clothing he sought a meeting with the hotel manager and his head of security. Mehmet needed to learn the lay of the land so as to better protect himself.

First he liaised with the hotel manager. Mehmet had been out of the loop for the last two or three days so he needed to know specifically whether the Hussein family had been informed of Ali's death. If not it would fall to him to inform them. Next order of business - had they found out anything from the police about who was behind Ali's murder.

The news from the hotel manager when Mehmet finally tracked him down came as a relief. The manager had had the onerous task of delivering the devastating news of Ali's death to his mother personally.

Mehmet could well imagine the shrieking tirade that the poor man must have endured from that homicidal bitch of a woman, on the other end of the line. He was glad that it hadn't been him who had had to endure it.

His next question was met with the manager pulling him conspiratorially over to one side out of earshot of both guests and staff alike. Whispering, he informed Mehmet that the police suspected the Israeli's of carrying out the atrocity.

Mehmet feigned anger at the assumption, but his heart leapt for joy upon hearing it voiced. If the manager of the hotel was saying it, then it was certain to be common knowledge out on the streets. His red herring had surely helped to secure his release.

A brief word with the head of hotel security more or less confirmed what the hotel manager had told him. Mehmet thanked the man for confirming to the police that he was here on vacation as a guest of Ali Hussein.

Mehmet wasn't quite home free yet, but the odds of him being hauled back in for further questioning were diminishing by the hour. Next he needed to liaise with the pilot. Together they would have the difficult task of bringing Ali Hussein's body home for burial. Being an important man, all the correct procedures in preparing Ali's body for burial needed to be observed. Mehmet would need to contact the authorities to find out about all the bureaucracy that he would have to wade through; it would be a mine field. It was also frustrating and time consuming but it was necessary however, in order to have a burial they needed Ali's body back.

The next morning, news of Ali Hussein's assassination had been leaked to the press. The authorities in Dubai had so far managed to suppress the fact that it might be murder from the media, but now it was front page news. No one in particular had so far been singled out for the atrocity but there was widespread speculation out on the streets that the Israeli's were behind it. The following day, several neighbouring Arab countries ran with the headlines that an Israeli hit squad was loose somewhere in their midst.

Whenever Israeli involvement in Arab deaths was trumpeted in the Middle East it always seemed to fan the flames of war, but without actually managing to capture anyone even remotely involved in Ali's murder, it would eventually die down. Mehmet hoped so anyway, he didn't much like the idea of being responsible for yet another Arab

-Israeli war.

Eventually the authorities released Ali's body to Mehmet, properly prepared for burial, as was the Arab custom. He was delivered in an aluminium casket, with great pomp and circumstance, as befits a head of state, directly to the hotel. The casket was placed in the middle of the hotel foyer with the top part of the casket open, allowing Ali's face to be seen for one hour. All the hotel staff were allowed to stream passed to say goodbye and pay their respects.

Had Mehmet not realised Ali's importance to the people of Dubai before, he did now. Ali was being given funeral rites normally reserved for heads of state or royalty.

Once the casket was closed it was returned to the huge cortege of vehicles and slowly driven past crowds of people lining the streets wishing to pay their last respects also. A police motorcycle escort led the way. They had finally been given clearance to return Ali's body home to Jordan.

Arriving at the airport, the Hussein jet was refuelled and ready to receive Ali's casket. The pilot and stewardess from the flight in were also there ready to go. It took a bit of awkward manoeuvring by eight burly men to get the casket on board and safely secured. Once that was done they were given clearance to board the aircraft and then told to wait and follow the control tower's instructions for take-off.

As the stewardess finished securing the door, they strapped themselves in and waited for instructions. Mehmet could see through the window and watched the police motor cyclists and vehicles rapidly heading away from the airplane.

Shortly afterwards, the pilot was given his take off instructions by the tower and they followed the security vehicle to the runway take off point.

Clearance was given and as the aircraft lifted off from the runway Mehmet gave a huge sigh of relief.

That brings us up to this point.

They had finally left the U.A.E.'s airspace for which Mehmet gave thanks, but what lay ahead was equally daunting. He would have to deliver Ali's body personally back to the Hussein family, he could do no less. He would also have to attend the funeral as an employee, it was his duty.

Once these obligations had been fulfilled Mehmet intended to hand in his resignation, with immediate effect. He had no intention of being at the beck and call of that viper of a woman, Ali's mother.

As the streamlined aircraft cut effortlessly through the sky Mehmet's eyes, already leaden, closed. He surrendered to sleep, hopefully one without dreams.

Chapter 74

Claire, London

Arriving at Yasmin's, Claire helped Adam off with his coat. He was impatient to get to Frank who was already busy sorting out drinks for them in the kitchen. Seeing Adam making a beeline for him Frank said, "Hey kiddo, what's up?"

"Uncle Frank will you help me get my toy box please?" asked Adam politely.

"Sure but first let me make a drink for your mum and dad, eh."

Adam nodded.

When the drinks had been made and handed out Frank let Adam lead him by the hand to where the toy box stood in the corner of the living room.

They all sat quietly smiling and amused by how Adam

effortlessly got Frank to do his bidding. It had been this way more or less since Adam's birth. Adam saw Frank and Yasmin as an extension of his mum and dad. No ifs, no buts, that's how it was. His toy box was evidence that Adam regarded their apartment as part of his own home and Yasmin and Frank didn't do anything to discourage the idea, in fact they openly encouraged it.

Watching whilst Frank did the heavy lifting Adam guided him to where he wanted the contents of the box tipping. No messing with this kid, straightforward, just dump the lot. Frank moved the box out of Adam's way then attempted to join in with his game.

Adam soon made it very clear that Frank was now surplus to requirements. He had fulfilled his task and was now no longer needed.

Returning to the kitchen, Frank mildly disgruntled, made himself a coffee and then re-joined the grown-ups. Sitting beside Claire they watched Adam for a while engrossed in what he was doing.

Claire interrupted Frank's thoughts, "Not be long now Frank," she said.

"What! ...oh, no I still can't believe it. A kid of our own," he said, looking across at Yasmin and smiling.

"You'll make great parents you're naturals," said Claire.

Then bracing herself and looking across at Luke for encouragement she blurted out, "I'm pregnant!"

At first nothing happened then Frank got up and enveloped her in a semi bear hug, "Congratulations darling," he said, now holding her tight.

Yasmin was speechless, one hand still across her mouth in total shock. Then struggling out of her chair she reached for Luke, planting a kiss on his cheek and congratulating him at the same time.

Then going over to Claire she joined her husband in a type of group hug; the baby bulge obvious in their midst.

Adam looked over at the grown up tableau and thought quickly to himself, shall I go and join in, then immediately dismissed the thought and carried on playing.

Frank shook Luke's hand in a manly display before congratulating him properly, "So, another one on the way, eh!" Luke nodded then quietly admitted to Frank, "It wasn't planned. This has taken us both by surprise!"

Frank kept his voice low but serious, "But you both want another one don't you?"

"Oh, yes," admitted Luke, "but we hadn't planned on another one quite so soon."

"You and Claire will be fine mate," said Frank looking him in the eyes, "in fact if Adam is anything to go by you'll be more than fine. Do you know what it will be?"

"No, early days yet," explained Luke.

Frank nodded in understanding. "You know I grew up in a house full of them. Three brothers and two sisters, but the sad thing is, I never see them now," said Frank, wistfully.

"Well that won't be the case with us mate," said Luke, trying to lighten the mood, "we will be coming round here until you get sick of us."

"No chance of that mate cos we'll be round at yours just as much," replied Frank, they both laughed at that, good friends at last.

Yasmin was now sitting with Claire, perched awkwardly on the edge of the settee. Claire had already told her that she had only found out for certain yesterday that she was pregnant. Yasmin, like Frank, then asked if she knew the baby's sex, "It's too early to say yet," replied Claire.

But Claire would know soon and she wouldn't need the aid of an ultra-scan machine. She would simply ask Adam.

Chapter 75

Doug Simons was patiently going through the latest intelligence folders gathered by his team on suspected home grown Jihadi's considered a threat to the U.K. It was painstakingly dull work but absolutely necessary in order to try and keep one step ahead of the game.

The game? Could he dare to call it that? Perhaps not, especially when one mistake, either by him or members of his team, could lead to other possible attacks on the British mainland, leading to more bloodshed on its crowded streets.

Ever since the euphoria of learning of Abdul Rahman's death had subsided, Doug and his team had returned to the hum drum task of wheedling out potential terrorists. The growing pile in front of Doug was testimony to how seriously they were treating the threat.

Doug now had his own room; his name plate was fastened to the door in proof of ownership. Ever since his team's gathered intelligence had proved pivotal in Rahman's demise, he in the capacity of acting head of section, had had his promotion rubber stamped. Doug's section was comprised of five members; two men and three women. It was now that one member of his section knocked on his door and entered unasked.

Helen Daniels pre-empted any unnecessary small talk by presenting Doug with a folder from the American section. She piled the impressive amount of documents she was still holding stealthily on one side of his desk, these being of secondary importance. Obviously Helen in her diligent opinion rated the American intelligence as a priority.

She sat uninvited opposite Doug, whilst he read through the contents of the folder. Helen, a diminutive five feet four inches tall, when wearing three inch heels, watched as her boss quietly evaluated the intelligence gathered within the folder. She was of slim build but not painfully so. Her height and build could be dismissed by many as non-threatening. But that would be a mistake on their part should they for any reason wish her harm. Helen held a black belt in karate, which she practised diligently three times a week. She was also a crack shot with both rifle and pistol, but it was her mind that had first impressed Doug.

She had an uncanny knack for sifting through reams of mind numbing intelligence, ninety nine percent of which could be described in street slang as shit, and come up with the one percent gold that made up useful intelligence.

Doug had recognised Helen's intelligence, which afforded her some leeway in her relaxed attitude towards her new boss. Her old one, James Martin, had undervalued the contributions made by the team, and not utilised them perhaps as effectively as he could have done.

Doug Simons on the other hand had fully immersed himself in the team's daily tasks. Indeed he had been one of them. No one begrudged Doug his promotion from acting head of section, to permanent head. It had been thoroughly deserved. He was also well liked and respected which went a long way to smooth the transition.

As Doug digested the information from the folders he blew out an exasperated breath in irritation then announced, "Ali Hussein is dead."

"What! ... How long ago did this happen?" Helen asked astounded.

"'A week apparently," said Doug, obviously annoyed.

"And the Americans have only just decided to let us in on the fact now!" said Helen, equally pissed off.

"Looks that way," said Doug. "Says here, he was found in his penthouse suite in his own hotel in Dubai, shot to death numerous times by person or person's unknown."

"Do you think the American's are behind it?" asked Helen.

"Possibly, though the report says that the Dubai secret police are searching for a Mossad hit squad," replied Doug.

Looking at Doug for confirmation Helen read his features.

"What ... you don't think so?"

"I'm not sure," admitted Doug, "it's audacious enough and where the Israeli's are concerned, nothing is beyond them."

"But you don't think so?" probed Helen.

"Honestly, I don't know. I'm more concerned that the American's have sat on this for a whole week before deigning to let us know," finished Doug.

Helen picked up on Doug's mood, "I thought we were supposed to be on the same side. Where is this special relationship that we are supposed to have?" She finished clearly just as annoyed as Doug.

"Helen, there's only a special relationship between the U.K. and the U.S. when uncle Sam wants something, otherwise it's America comes first and fuck the special relationship. Don't be fooled by the Americans Helen, they put their country and its citizens first and always will. Perhaps we should adopt a similar attitude, it seems to work for them," said Doug, cynically.

It was refreshing for Helen to talk so freely with her boss. She was beginning to get to know what made Doug tick and she liked it.

Doug idly wondered if his boss Mary Wallace, and current head of M.I.6, had also been kept out of the loop by the Americans. It seemed monstrous to Doug if she had, but the more he thought about it the more likely it became.

"Helen, do you know if the boss had any meetings penned in for this morning?" asked Doug coming to a decision.

"Yes she had meetings with her French and German counterparts in the conference room scheduled to finish at 11 a.m." answered Helen.

"Would you see if you can set up a meeting for me for some time after that meeting breaks up?" Then as an afterthought Doug said, "What is the meeting about, do you know?" Of course Helen knew, she worked in intelligence for Christ sake.

Feeling a little contrite at her uncharitable thoughts Helen decided to share her knowledge with Doug, "Brexit has got the French and German intelligence agencies in a flap as to what will happen to the flow of intelligence once the U.K. leaves the E. U. so they have asked for a meeting to try and clarify the situation," Helen said.

"Understandable," said Doug, "though I doubt Mary Wallace knows any more than we do. The P.M. is not exactly known for sharing her thoughts with the minions."

Standing up to leave Helen didn't comment on Doug's remarks, her mind was already focussed on setting up the requested meeting. Without any preamble Helen left Doug to work through the newly arrived stack of folders.

Lunch break, whatever that was, had come and gone by the time Helen had secured a meeting for Doug with Mary Wallace.

No longer afraid of his boss Doug stood before her giving a brief synopsis of what the American file contained.

Mary Wallace listened to Doug's shortened report with steadily mounting anger.

He himself had witnessed the red flush of anger slowly rising from her neck line and onto her cheeks.

Clearly her Scottish ancestry was only just being held in check. His thinking that she had been deliberately kept from knowing of Ali Hussein's assassination by American intelligence, was proved to be correct.

Nevertheless Mary thanked Doug for his report before allowing him to get back to work.

Doug vaguely thought he saw his boss from out of the corner of his eye reaching for the telephone, the one used for transatlantic calls just as he closed her door.

Someone on the other side of the pond was in for a good old fashioned Scottish hello! Doug was glad he wasn't the one about to experience it, but then on reflection he thought no. Fuck em! It's what they deserve.

Later that day Doug had managed to wade through the stack of files and singling eight out he put them to one side. These files represented persons of particular interest and they would be closely monitored at some stage, but by who was anyone's guess. The resources at M.I.6's disposal were not infinite.

The folders went into Doug's filing system, though the subjects weren't considered a threat just now something had warranted their name being put on file, and it paid to be cautious, in Doug's line of work anything was possible.

Something else had been bothering Doug. His mind seemed to have a will of its own wandering back to it over and over. If he had only just learned of Ali Hussein's death there was a good chance that Yasmin Hussein, was also unaware of it.

Doug argued with himself that he owed her nothing. Yet he couldn't escape the fact that at least two attempts on her life had been orchestrated by her brother. His old boss, James Martin, had once suspected that she may have been in collusion with her brother's terrorist activities. That had eventually been proved to be a false hypothesis, so on that basis he reached a decision. On the spur of the moment Doug looked through his filing system for Yasmin Hussain's home number. He rang from his office, not caring that it would most likely be monitored. Doug wasn't particularly worried as he had nothing to hide; in fact he figured M.I.6 owed Miss Hussein the courtesy of knowing that her brother was dead and most likely that there was no longer a threat to her.

The telephone was answered on the fifth ring by a man. Doug swallowed his surprise by giving him his name.

The man on the other end of the line retaliated by saying, "Frank White speaking, Yasmin's husband."

Fuck thought Doug, of course Frank from the club. Recovering smoothly Doug asked if it was possible for him to call on them at home this evening, regarding a matter of immediate importance to them both.

The line went quiet for a few seconds as he was asked to hold on. Doug thought he heard a man and woman's voice talking mutedly in the background.

Coming back on Frank said, “Yes that is fine, about 7 p.m. okay?”

Doug said it was and the line immediately went dead from Frank’s end. Replacing his own hand set carefully, Doug had to smile to himself; obviously Frank hadn’t mellowed in his opinion of M.I.6. No matter he thought, this time Doug had good news for Frank and Yasmin.

A taxi ride close to the appointed hour brought Doug to the front door of the luxurious apartment block. Pressing the intercom to Apartment Two Doug announced his arrival. A faint buzz could be heard unlocking the door and allowing him entry. As Doug had thought the interior was marble; even the central staircase. Making his way up Doug saw Frank waiting for him beside an open door. Before he had got half way up Frank said, “Not brought your side kick with you?”

Realising that Frank meant his old boss James Martin, he said, “No Mr Martin is no longer with us I’m afraid.”

Taken aback Frank thought that he meant he had died. He didn’t feel it even remotely but felt obligated to say, “Oh, I’m sorry to hear that.”

Doug understood Frank’s confusion quickly saying, “No not dead; retired.”

“Oh well, Yasmin is inside, please come in,” said Frank, allowing Doug to pass.

Yasmin was sitting in a comfortably upholstered armchair and he couldn’t help but notice that she was heavily pregnant, but declined to comment.

He was surprised she remembered his name when she asked, “What can we do for you Mr Simons?” indicating graciously for him to take a seat.

Doing her bidding he sat, and waited for Frank to join

them. He had gone over it in his mind how to break the news of her brother's death, and deciding on the band aid theory he opted for that, "I've come to inform you of your brother, Ali Hussein's death."

Delivered in this manner Doug waited for some sort of response. He saw the silent look exchanged between husband and wife but couldn't decipher its meaning.

Then Frank asked him, "You are absolutely sure Yasmin's brother is dead? There is no doubt?"

"Yes, absolutely sure, no doubt whatsoever," answered Doug. Realizing that the couple were desperate to believe him, yet still hesitant, Doug wondered how far he could safely go without putting his career on the line.

"Look I'm here of my own volition. The ministry is unaware of my meeting with you, as I am bound by the official secrets act. I may in fact already be in breach of it just by being here, but what I can tell you, is that a report landed on my desk today confirming that Ali Hussein is dead. I'm afraid that I cannot go into any specific details but believe me, that report comes from a very reliable source. I just felt obliged to come here personally to let you know of his death because of the threat he posed to both of you, and your friends. I thought you could use a little peace of mind. You will be notified officially in due course," explained Doug.

Yasmin didn't seem even remotely saddened by her brother's demise, observed Doug. The animosity between them must have run very deep. Frank on the other hand just seemed to be relieved that the threat had been eliminated. Doug, unbidden, made to get up, his message had been delivered and it was time for him to go.

Yasmin asked Doug, "Will you get into trouble for letting us know?"

Doug pondered the question for a beat, "Probably," he admitted, "but don't worry it should only be a carpeting. I've had a lot worse believe me. At any rate I will survive."

Yasmin struggled to push herself out of the armchair before a protest could come from Doug to stop her.

Reaching out with her own hand to shake Doug's she said, "Thank you."

This contact meant a lot to Doug. He had stuck his neck out when he hadn't needed to but the hand shake alone made it worth the risk and he felt vindicated by it. Frank walked him to the door and gripping Doug's hand in a genuine handshake he said, "Thank you for coming Mr Simons."

Doug replied, "You are most welcome," and meant it. Leaving them to it he left the building in search of a cab. His stomach growled loudly in protest at the lack of food, letting him know he was neglecting his body. Christ he thought I'm turning into James Martin!

Seeing that ghastly apparition in his mind's eye made Doug follow his nose in search of a kebab shop.

Once more Doug quietly repeated his chosen mantra,

"I'm not going to end up like James Martin," over and over until he almost believed it.

Chapter 76

After the Hussein family jet had touched down at Amman International Airport the pilot was instructed, by the control tower, to follow the orange flashing lights of the security vehicle to the hanger, leased by the Hussein family. Arrangements had already been furiously made by Ali Hussein's mother whilst the aircraft had been en route to Jordan, for her son's casket to be picked up directly from the airport and then to be conveyed for immediate burial.

It had been a long time since Ali Hussein's death, almost a week, and normally burial would take place as soon as possible within 24 hours. The authorities in the United Arab Emirates had been mostly to blame for the delay. Understandably they had wanted to be seen to be doing all within their power to bring Ali's murderers to justice. Sadly for them they had failed.

As the jet slowly drew up beside the hanger, the noise of the engines diminished considerably and then finally came to a complete stop. The stewardess unsealed the aircraft's door and unfolded the steps.

Mehmet, hefting his own case, stepped down from the plane to the concrete first, closely followed by the stewardess and then the pilot. A fleet of shiny black vehicles drew up close to the hanger, the largest of which came to rest beside the aircraft itself. This was the one that would convey Ali's remains to his final resting place in the land of his birth; Jordan.

There were people inside the vehicles but Mehmet couldn't quite make anyone out. All the glass windows in all the vehicles were heavily smoked, almost black. He knew that Mrs Hussein would probably be riding in the vehicle directly behind the one carrying Ali's coffin but didn't know who was in the other vehicles.

The pilot, stewardess and Mehmet stood to one side, at a respectable distance away, whilst the casket was manhandled from the aircraft. It wasn't easy but eventually it was transferred to the vehicle that would take him on his final journey.

Mehmet was expected to attend the burial, but as yet no one had spoken to him or acknowledged his presence, worse still he wasn't sure which vehicle he was meant to travel in.

The pilot and stewardess by contrast were not expected at the burial as they still had their duties to attend to. The aircraft had to be safely stowed inside the hanger and secured before their duty was done, then they would have to hitch a ride with security through the airport terminal before having to find their own way home. It didn't seem fair to Mehmet, but then who said anything about life being fair, besides he had the burial to get through.

It was the last vehicle in line that stopped beside him,

but he didn't move until the driver's window slid down without as much as a sound. The driver indicated to Mehmet that he was to get in, so throwing his case onto the back seat Mehmet slid in beside it. The other vehicle's driver had got a little way in front whilst picking him up, but they soon caught up with the entourage and then kept a respectable two cars distance behind the last one.

The driver had not spoken to Mehmet, even though they knew each other, and it slowly dawned on him that he had been ostracized by everyone on the Hussein payroll. Probably on the direct orders of Ali's mother, no one else had the authority. No matter he didn't intend to remain on the Hussein payroll himself for much longer.

The funeral cortege sped on its way to the Hussein family burial plot. Nothing in the Middle East was conducted sedately; everything was done in a hurry, even funerals. Mehmet had in his inside jacket pocket his notice of resignation. He had written it on note paper bearing the Hussein logo found amongst the stationery on board the aircraft. He intended to hand it directly to Ali's mother, after the funeral was over.

Ali's last journey finally came to a close as all the vehicles gradually stopped, disgorging their previously unseen passengers. Mehmet took his time getting out of the vehicle. There would be no friendly faces here, so why bother pretending otherwise.

It came as no surprise to Mehmet when he recognised one of the lead mourners, Mohammed Ahmed, Amman central's own chief of police. Masud, Mehmet's older brother, had found out by accident that the chief was on the Hussein's payroll; he was just one of many, some of them would be here amongst the mourners perhaps, but Mehmet didn't recognise them if they were.

Mehmet hung back; preferring to remain anonymous if that was at all possible. He could see well enough from where he was standing. Members of his own security team from the Hussein residence watched over Ali's mother. That, Mehmet supposed would be their primary mission in life from now on. He pitied them they were welcome to the task.

Eventually the burial was completed. Ali now rested beside his father and grandfather. Ali's mother still surrounded by security was the last to leave the graveside. Mehmet tentatively approached, he was watched closely by former comrades of his own security team. He had in his hand his resignation. The words almost choking him, as he handed over the note, he said, "Please accept my condolences and my resignation."

She looked at it, without really seeing what was written on it, and then her eyes, black as night, slowly came up to rest on Mehmet's. It was like gazing into a pit.

With the speed of a cobra she smacked Mehmet across his face. It sounded like the crack of a whip and stung almost as much. He watched her shuffle away, still flanked by security, to the bank of waiting vehicles until she got on board. This was the signal for the drivers to pull away.

Mehmet went to find his own vehicle, only to find his suitcase, alone on the tarmac. As the dust settled Mehmet ruefully had to smile to himself. A smack across the face and a short walk back to the main road was a small price to pay for murdering her son. Had she known that Mehmet was responsible, he was in no doubt that she would have gladly clawed his eyes out.

Mehmet managed to hitch a ride from a very talkative man, delivering baskets full of live chickens. The smell alone was enough to make him gag, but he needed the ride, so he had to suffer in silence. He hopped off the vehicle still a half mile shy of his destination which was a rented building where he hoped to find members of his hit squad, waiting for him.

He had had neither contact with nor tried to contact any of the members since the night of Ali's murder. If they had done as he asked, he would find them waiting for him inside. Mehmet breathed a sigh of relief when he heard the television on as he opened the front door, and from the sounds emitting from the living room they were watching a game of football. As he pushed open the living room door to reveal himself the room suddenly seemed to explode in a wave of friendly delighted hugs and back slapping. Everyone wanted to talk at once, drowning out each other's words.

Mehmet just stood there smiling, bathing in the warmth of their welcome. They were the first friendly faces he had seen in almost a week; it was good to be finally home. Once the initial excitement had died down, Mehmet recounted in detail what had happened to him from the moment he had bade them goodbye in Dubai, but saving his disgraceful treatment by the Hussein matriarch for last.

Each of his men told Mehmet of their own experiences in fleeing Dubai, but they soon realised that their tales paled into insignificance when compared to what Mehmet had endured.

After a wash and hearty meal, taken together, Mehmet discussed in detail what he proposed to do next. The money was in a Swiss bank account in Berne accessible only by Mehmet. He would need to fly there and get a banker's cheque, as trying to bring in cash would be virtually impossible. This was usually the point at which fallouts amongst co-conspirators happened; when the money was to be shared out.

He asked the men point blank, "Do you trust me?"

As one man they all said, "Yes sir." They were no longer in the army but old habits were hard to break. Besides they all knew Mehmet and reckoned him a pretty honourable man.

Mehmet thanked them all for giving him their trust. He would try and book himself on a flight to

Berne in the next couple of days and with luck he should be back with the money by Friday.

For now he was badly in need of sleep, nervous exhaustion had taken its toll, plus any sleep he managed to grab had often been interrupted by dreams of Ali's shocked eyes, accusing him still.

Mehmet now knew for certain that a career as an assassin was out of the question. His conscience would not allow it, and also, he now realised that he was unemployed. Perhaps, he thought, he could go back and try his luck as a civil engineer, it was certainly more preferable to shooting people.

Mehmet,slowly fell asleep in the chair, the fIrst sleep in a while, without dreams.

His friends turned off the television set so as to not disturb him then quietly left him to go to their own rooms, glad that he had returned home safe.

All being well in a few more days they would all be reasonably wealthy men and it was all possible, because of Mehmet.

So they let him sleep, he had earned it.

Chapter 77

When Yasmin rang Claire mid morning to see if it was alright to come around. Claire didn't read too much into it, except that normally she usually waited for Frank to get up and then arrange to visit as a couple.

Claire left Adam in his favourite spot close to the patio windows on the living room carpet, when she went to prepare two mugs ready for Yasmin's arrival. She set the kettle to boil then returned to Adam and kneeled down beside him. She had been helping him to learn his ABC's. Normally he absorbed information like a sponge but for some reason he was finding this particular lesson difficult.

Claire wasn't worried by this, the books they had bought for Adam were for 4 to 5 year olds, way too old for him, but nevertheless, he didn't throw a tantrum like some children, when he failed to grasp the meaning of some of the letters. Instead it made him more determined to master them. Claire had discovered that he had a stubborn streak in him when faced with things that he couldn't readily master.

She heard the front door open and Yasmin call to say, "It's only me Claire."

Both Claire and Adam looked over at Yasmin as she waddled into the living room. Claire, not for the first time, wondered if Natalie had misread the ultrasound and Yasmin was indeed having twins, she was certainly a lot bigger at this stage of the pregnancy than Claire had been.

Yasmin came over to see what we were doing. "Hi Adam, what are you looking at?"

"I'm trying to learn my ABC's aunt Yasmin but I'm not very good at it," said a slightly crestfallen

Adam.

Claire immediately came to Adam's rescue by saying, "It's not as bad as that Yasmin, he is just having difficulty with a few of the letters that's all."

Yasmin told Adam, "Don't worry Adam, we all find it difficult at first, keep trying and you will get there."

That seemed to mollify Adam slightly as he looked up at Yasmin.

"Phew, I'll have to sit down Claire, it feels like I'm carrying an elephant around," panted Yasmin.

Quick as a flash Adam corrected her, "No aunt Yasmin, you're having a baby."

We both laughed and Yasmin said, "Well I stand corrected Adam I am indeed having a baby, thank you for reminding me!"

Adam went back to his ABC book whilst Claire went to make the tea. Yasmin had changed her drink from coffee to tea the moment she had discovered she was pregnant.

Claire brought in the teas putting them on place mats on the coffee table. Yasmin sat in the armchair as it was more comfortable and easier to get up from. Claire asked Adam if he would like some juice.

"Yes please," he replied. Claire went to get it and when she returned handed it to him, reminding him not to spill it.

He took it in both hands then resumed trying to master his letters.

Finally Claire sat down and reached for her own tea and taking a tentative sip, found it to still to be too hot, so she put it back down and waited for Yasmin to speak. Claire had already twigged that something was not quite right so she waited patiently until Yasmin was ready to spill the beans.

"My brother is dead!"

Claire waited for more information but when it wasn't forthcoming she asked, "Are you sure?"

Yasmin nodded, and then added, "Yes I'm sure. We had a visit last night from Doug Simons."

When Claire couldn't place who he was, Yasmin said, "From M.I.6 remember?"

Claire nodded but only vaguely remembered the name.

Reaching for her tea Yasmin continued, "Well anyway he came to let us know. He said it was unofficial and M.I.6 hadn't authorised the visit but he thought we had a right to know. He said he would most likely get a reprimand for it but didn't care," finished Yasmin in between sips of tea.

"Wow" said Claire, "good for Mr Simons." Then after a pause, "How long ago is it since his death?"

"About a week, though no one seems to know for sure. I really don't care just so long as it's true. If anyone deserved to die-it was him!" "Are you alright? You're not upset at all?" asked Claire.

Yasmin picked up Claire's meaning, "Me, yeah couldn't have happened soon enough for me. The guy was evil Claire."

Then after a quiet few moments said, "Wow, must have

got that from my mother. Dad was a saint compared to those two."

Claire nodded then asked, "So who else knows besides Frank, you and me?"

"That's it, just us three. You let Luke know when he gets up and I'll tell Chris this afternoon if that's alright?" offered Yasmin.

"Yes that's fine. You tell Chris and I'll tell Luke. Now that Ali is no longer a threat, perhaps we can start to get on with our lives," ventured Claire.

Normally a death in any family is greeted with great sorrow, but in this particular instance, it was greeted with a great sigh of relief, as it promised hope for the future.

Chapter 78

New beginnings

The telephone call Yasmin had received earlier was troubling in its urgency. Rachel Hardy had called personally asking for a face to face meeting as soon as possible. It had something to do with her late brother's murder just over four weeks ago, but Rachel did not want to discuss the matter over the telephone.

Yasmin had been wearing out her living room carpet waiting for her to arrive. Suddenly Yasmin's intercom announced that Rachel was at the front door, awaiting entry. She buzzed her in and waited for her to climb the stairs to her apartment.

They shook hands cordially at Yasmin's open door. This was a totally unexpected call but nevertheless Yasmin invited Rachel over the threshold clearly intrigued, but managing to hold onto her curiosity, choosing to wait until Rachel revealed the purpose for her visit.

Rachel couldn't help but notice Yasmin's condition and quietly hoped that she wasn't about to give birth anytime soon. However she did comment, "I didn't know you were expecting, when is the baby due?"

Yasmin hadn't exactly broadcast to the world in general about her condition, favouring instead to keep her private life private, although the question was asked out of friendly curiosity, so Yasmin replied, "Two months."

That seemed to satisfy Rachel, for the time being anyway, but she decided to keep the fact that Frank and herself had married, private. She felt it was exclusive knowledge just for her, Frank and a few privileged friends.

Rachel Hardy had worked for her old lawyer and good friend Mr Almeda,but after the Almeda's still unsolved brutal murder, it was thought that the law firm would fold. This thankfully, had not been the case, when the terms of the Almeda's will had been revealed to his former colleagues and co-workers at the law practice.

No one could have been more surprised than they, when it was revealed that Mr Almeda had stipulated in his will that they all be made full partners and they were to continue running it, just as if he was still alive. This, they had successfully done, managing to retain most of their clients in the process.

Yasmin was still one of these clients; hence the urgent need to meet at such short notice.

Yasmin, being a good host had let Rachel get seated before asking her, "Would you like a cup of tea or a coffee?"

Rachel politely declined and instead opened her briefcase to retrieve a thick brown folder.

Mysterious thought Yasmin but wouldn't allow herself

to spoil Rachel's moment.

So taking an old official looking document from the folder Rachel discarded it onto the coffee table and composed herself before actually speaking.

A bit theatrical thought Yasmin to herself, she looks quite excited by what is in it.

"I have here the last will and testament of your late father," began Rachel. Yasmin was about to interrupt at this point but Rachel held up her hand to stay her words, "Patience please, I will explain everything but there is a lot to get through." Yasmin nodded to continue, annoyed with herself for her impatience.

"This will was kept in the strong room of the Royal Bank of Jordan, in the Hashemite kingdom of

Jordan, since your father first dictated it," continued Rachel, "we also have a copy of it in our own strong room here in London. It tallies with the original will word for word, and remains unchanged."

The importance of what Rachel was saying was now just starting to sink in, raising goose bumps on Yasmin's skin.

Rachel looked at Yasmin to make sure that she had grasped the significance of what she had just said before continuing, reading the will document,

"The will states that following the death of Mohammed George Hussein, father of Ali and Yasmin

Hussein, the running of the family business, the properties, holdings, stocks and shares etc, pass through the male lineage, in other words to your brother, Ali Hussein. However, in the event of Ali's death the said properties, holdings, etc, would then pass to Ali's eldest living son. As Ali was unmarried and had no known living issue the terms of the will change, and now for the big one," said

Rachel for effect. "If there is no male issue living at the time of my son's death, then all properties, holdings, stocks and shares, and monetary wealth held in the royal Bank of Jordan, in the Hashemite kingdom of Jordan, shall pass to my daughter, Yasmin Hussein, in its entirety."

Yasmin couldn't hold back any longer, "But surely, Ali made a will of his own."

"Not according to the bank officials in Jordan. It was they who actually contacted us about the fact that the inheritance should rightly pass to you," answered Rachel.

"Well, my mother then, surely she will still have claim by virtue of being married to dad," argued

Yasmin.

"I'm afraid not, for reasons of his own, your father deliberately left your mother out of the will. However, he does stipulate that she is allowed to remain living in the Hussein family home for as long as she wishes to do so, until death, or until such time as she remarries, in which case that would negate her right to remain living in the Hussein household. A sum of $1,000,000 U.S. dollars is to be set aside annually to allow her to maintain the property, for living expenses, pay bills, etc, etc. payable from the Royal Bank of Jordan," read Rachel.

"Wow!!" Was all Yasmin could think of to say, "I knew their marriage was in trouble but hadn't realised how bad things truly were."

"Now we come to the nuts and bolts of the will," said Rachel with apparent relish. "Two hotels in

Amman, the capital of Jordan, the Hussein family home on the outskirts of Amman also belong to you. Your mother is only allowed to live there on your sufferance," clarified Rachel. "There are numerous stocks and shares, mostly to do with Saudi oil and natural gas companies, the contracts are held in the Bank of Jordan. There are two commercial warehouses at Aqaba near the Gulf of

Aqaba, it doesn't say for what purpose," said Rachel looking up quizzically at Yasmin for clarification.

Yasmin shook her head to indicate that she had no idea of their purpose either so Rachel carried on. "There is a Lear jet, bearing the Hussein family logo, permanently stored and maintained in a hangar at Amman International Airport, with pilot and stewardess, ready for use." Rachel's eyebrows lifted slightly when she read that bit. "Now we come to the hotel in Dubai, United Arab Emirates."

Just in case Yasmin didn't know where that was, but Yasmin did know where it was, she had been to the hotel years ago when she was younger, whilst accompanying her father. She wondered briefly if it had changed much and planned on enjoying finding out. Frank and Yasmin had still not had a honeymoon yet, so perhaps when the baby was born they could finally have one.

"And finally, a 60 foot yacht moored at its own birth at the marina in Dubai called the Falcon."

At last Rachel finished reading the will, closed it, and returned it to the brown folder.

"Congratulations Miss Hussein you are now no longer a millionaire, instead, you have become a billionaire."

Standing, Rachel formally shook Yasmin's hand, "I hope we can continue to do business together Miss Hussein. If you have any questions please do not hesitate to contact me, there is a lot to think about and decisions to make."

"Assuredly, I will be in touch," answered Yasmin seeing Rachel out.

Once Rachel had gone and faced with the enormity of her new found wealth Yasmin decided to set the kettle boiling, this called for a calming drink of tea.

Finally, perched awkwardly on the kitchen stool her enormous belly getting in the way,Yasmin thought out loud, "How does one manage to spend billions of pounds?" No one answered her.

Finishing her tea she answered her own question, "I don't know, but I'm sure as hell going to enjoy finding out!"

Storm Clouds

Part 2: Good Guys

Chapter 79

"Hi Yasmin sorry I'm late, there was a right bloody queue at the barbers."

When she didn't respond to what he was saying, he looked at her a little closer. "Everything alright love?" he asked, obviously concerned.

"Come and sit beside me, I have something rather important to tell you," she said, patting the empty seat beside her.

Frank said, "Sounds ominous" as he slid onto the settee.

"Not ominous, but certainly life changing" Yasmin mysteriously replied.

"Okay! I'm sitting, what's up?" Frank wanted to know.

"While you were out I had a telephone call, from Rachel Hardy."

Of course Frank had no idea who Rachel Hardy was, but wisely remained silent.

"Rachel has taken over my business portfolio, since

Mr Almeda's death. She wanted to see me as a matter of urgency, so I asked her to come here instead of me having to trail to her office. It's not long since she left," said Yasmin.

So far so good thought Frank.

"To cut a long story short," continued Yasmin, "I am now the sole owner of the Hussein business franchise."

Frank's eyes widened, as he realised the enormity of what his wife was telling him, he had questions of course. "What about your mother? I thought that she would inherit it all, now that your brother is out of the picture," queried Frank.

"So did I," agreed Yasmin. "But apparently because my brother failed to enact a will of his own, and had no living heirs, my father's will came back into force. Father for whatever reason, had stipulated in his will that on no account was my mother to be left in charge of the business or finances.

"Wow!" was all that Frank said, truly shocked by what Yasmin had just told him. "So your mother gets nothing at all," probed Frank.

"She gets to live in the family home plus a one million dollars allowance, to be paid annually, but only at my discretion" corrected Yasmin.

"Phew," was Frank's response. "I bet she's spitting bloody feathers," he said, after he'd thought about how he himself would have felt in her situation. "Is she a danger to us?" asked Frank, more serious now.

"My mother has always been dangerous Frank, probably more-so now that she has had the rug pulled from under her feet," Yasmin admitted coldly.

"How does this affect us? Business wise I mean," asked Frank.

Yasmin thought about that for a while trying to frame

her thoughts, before answering, "Well as I understand it, I either try to run the business side of it myself, or get someone else in to run it in my stead, or sell it off piece-meal," she finished with a flourish.

Frank weighed up what his wife just said, he wasn't buying the idea that Yasmin would allow someone else to run the business. Nor was he convinced that she would wish to sell off willy-nilly, something that her father and grand-father had so painstakingly built up over the years. That just left the first option. Yasmin would choose to run the business herself.

She confirmed as much, when she began totting up the likely number of employees, and their immediate dependants, who were probably relying on her to take up the reins of power, and thus fill the vacuum of leadership, left empty by her dead brother.

"It would be a challenge," Yasmin said out loud, for Frank's benefit really. "But I think I could do it, with your help of course," admitted Yasmin. "Otherwise, I wouldn't even contemplate doing it."

"Of course I'll help, you don't have to ask," agreed Frank.

"It would mean leaving Chris in charge of running the club whilst we are abroad," stated Yasmin,

"but that's no problem, he's already doing that anyway. I'Il continue to do the books for him, just to lighten that side of things."

Frank marvelled at his wife's ordered brain, she was clearly on top of what she had to do in order for her plans to work.

"Do you think that Luke could take charge of the club's security whilst we are away?" Yasmin fielded.

"I don't see why not, he's easily the most capable guy

on the whole team, after myself of course,"

Frank said, with mock modesty, "and besides, the whole team look upon Luke as my obvious successor anyway" admitted Frank.

"Well, that's the club sorted then," agreed Yasmin.

"When are you planning on going?" queried Frank.

"As soon as I'm well enough, after the baby's born," said Yasmin, without hesitation.

Obviously, his wife had been giving the matter a great deal of thought in his absence, mused Frank.

Where his wife was concerned, she always seemed to be two steps ahead of his own thought processes. That's what he admired about her, brains as well as beauty. He was a lucky sod, and he knew it.

Chapter 80

The Hussein residence on the outskirts of Amman Jordan.

The heat had been oppressive since early afternoon, ominous black clouds had been steadily building and joining forces with spectacular frequency, directly above the Hussein family residence.

It was only a matter of time before the full force of nature would be unleashed. Owing to the darkness created by the massive thunderclouds over head, most of the lights in the rooms within the compound were lit. Fatima Hussein sat morosely in the family living room, quietly seething, a storm of epic proportions was building within her, that would rival the one from above.

Earlier, she had met with representatives from the bank and the legal profession, who looked after the Hussein family's portfolio. She had been incredulous to learn that her estranged daughter, Yasmin, now owned and controlled the entire Hussein portfolio.

She had screamed and protested her outrage, to no avail. Her westernised daughter, no more than a common harlot in her eyes, had somehow inherited the lot. The final twist of the knife had come when Fatima had learned that she could only continue to live in the family residence, with her daughter's approval.

Afterwards, when the odious bankers and lawyers had left, she sat brooding, the suppressed rage only just kept in check. The pressure was slowly building within her, like a modern-day pressure cooker, about to blow. If anyone entering the room could have seen her face just then, it would not have been a very pleasant sight. Madness lurked behind those eyes.

Ever since her son Ali's murder, she had spent a great deal of money, uselessly as it turned out, on so-called investigators, trying to find out who had assassinated her son. As the reports duly came in, they told her nothing that she didn't already know, the general consensus being, that the Israeli's were behind it. But still she wasn't convinced, it was far too convenient to blame it on the Israeli's for her liking, no ...... she felt that the solution was much simpler, and a lot nearer to home, she just had to keep on digging and see what popped out.

What she really wished for with all her heart, was that she could have Ali's murderers here, in her hands ... she would have them stripped and hanging from meat hooks, just as a foretaste. Then with a scalpel, she would carefully carve thin strips of flesh from their quivering bodies, until they were begging her for death. But this she would not grant them, it would be too soon, no.... when they were begging her for death, she would have them salted, and then after she had savoured their agony for a while, and only if she was in a good mood, would she grant them death. The smile on her lips was not pleasant as she imagined these things, this was a woman clearly on the verge of madness.

Just then the sky was lit with a spectacular display of lightening, followed almost immediately by ear splitting thunder. Nature, had orchestrated the mother and father of all storms. Blessed rain had decided to join in, accompanied by gusts of wind, and anyone caught out in it were either very unfortunate or just plain stupid, for the signs had been clearly visible for all to see.

Within the Hussein residence the storm had tripped the circuit breakers, leaving the rooms in darkness. Fatima's personal maid concerned for her mistress, tentatively knocked and entered the darkened room. She could not see much in the gloom, but some sixth sense had warned her to be careful. Lightening momentarily lit the room coming to her aid just in time, to avoid being hit by a heavy Meissen group of musicians, circa 1770. It shattered against the wall, accompanied by a feral scream to, "Get Ouuut."

The maid took the hint and left the room at speed, slamming the door behind her, she shakily made her way down the corridor, accompanied all the way by thunder and lightening. From then on the destruction within the living room rivalled only that of the storm outside. It was almost Wagnerian in scope, the house-hold servants along with some of the internal security staff, could hear the destruction that the mistress was causing, but no-one was foolish enough to want to intervene. Fatima Hussein's temper was legendary, so they let her get on with it.

Much later, when nature's storm had past, leaving the air much cooler and fresher, Fatima's maid, along with security, opened the door to her living room. With the circuit breakers now reset, the destruction within the room was there for all to see. It would have made an art lover weep just to see the sheer scale of the destruction that a woman of such small stature had done. Priceless objects from around the world, reduced to matchwood and rubble.

As well as various Meissen figurines, a beautiful pair of Arith blue-white baluster tankards circa 1700, were now mere shards. There were vases from Berlin, Bow, Chelsea, Clarice Cliff, as well as various Minton's. Two late nineteenth century, French Ormolu, six light chandeliers -the scrolling- Acanthus chased branches, emanating from a bulbous column, 32 inches high, now both beyond repair. The destruction of the furniture, most of it original, not reproduction, now only fit for firewood. A conservative estimate of the original contents of the room, would probably set you back £100,000. And that was only a conservative evaluation.

They found Fatima Hussein soundly asleep amongst the destruction, laid on an original Persian rug, thought to be priceless and thankfully mostly undamaged. With the help of the security detail the maid helped her mistress to her bedroom. She undressed her and helped her into her night attire, then carefully put her to bed.

The next day she awoke with no knowledge of what she had done. After breakfast had been brought to her room, she went to look at the damage that she had been told, was of her making. After only a cursory look inside the room, she gave orders to get rid of it all.

She had no remorse for what she had done, after all it no longer belonged to her, it belonged to that slut of a daughter she had so foolishly given birth to. So, why should she care?

Chapter 81

At Claire's London home

A couple of days after Yasmin had rung with her seismic earth-shattering news, it suddenly dawned on Claire, that maybe she wouldn't be seeing much of her closest friend in the future. The more Claire thought about it the more miserable it made her feel, they had almost been joined at the hip from the moment that Claire had arrived in the capital, when still a naive young woman. The relationship had developed and become more than sister-hood, it was closer to one of blood.

Claire's son Adam, treated Yasmin as if she was his second mother, it would also be fair to say, that Yasmin looked upon Adam as if he was her son. It would simply be intolerable to Claire and by extension Adam, if they were to lose contact with this beautiful young woman.

Adam must have picked up on his mum's melancholy, because he looked up from his drawing book to check that she was alright.

Claire knew with certainty that her son knew what was going on. "It's alright Adam, I'm just feeling a bit apprehensive about Yasmin going away to run her family's business, it will probably mean her having to spend a lot of time abroad, and if that's the case ...well... I'm going to miss her, that's all."

"But she'll be coming back won't she?" asked Adam.

"Oh! Yes, but to begin with she'll probably have to spend longer abroad. To be honest, she doesn't really know what state her business is in, and that's why she has to go and find out for herself. It will probably take some sorting out, which of course will all take time, and if it takes a long time I'm going to miss her, that's all," explained Claire.

"It will be alright mum, Yasmin won't forget about us," said Adam, sagely.

Not for the first time, Claire thought, Christ! It's like having a conversation with an adult. Just then the telephone rang, Claire made her way towards it and picked up.

"Hello....Oh hello Sheryl, I was only thinking about you the other day, Christ, you must have read my mind, I've been meaning to call you ... What!...You're pregnant, bloody hell...congratulations."

Obviously it was good news thought Adam, as he eavesdropped on his mum's one-sided conversation. He remembered Sheryl and James from when his mum and dad got married, although everyone thought that he was far too young to remember such things. His mum, he knew, would be on the telephone for quite some time .

"Well once again many congratulations I'm so pleased for you both ... I know ... I miss you too ... give my love to

James ... bye."

Claire came back to sit next to Adam, clearly very happy. She noticed that he had finished his drawing, they'd both been trying to draw a horse on a sketch pad, using a photograph in a book as a guide. Adam's finished attempt looked like a passable likeness of a horse, it wasn't up to the standard of George Stubbs, but at least you could tell that it was a horse. Claire's effort ... well let's just say that it was something else. Claire put drawing down to just something else that she wasn't very good at, and left it at that.

But Sheryl ringing to tell her that she was pregnant, was bloody great news, it had lifted Claire's spirits immensely.

Our clan, was growing.

Chapter 82

The next few weeks and months, just a blur now, would be a trying time for all of us. Luke and I would have our own share of troubles to deal with, although it would be Yasmin who suffered the most. Happily, her troubles would end in joy, in the shape of a beautiful little girl, who she named,

Aisha. But I digress, let me explain the circumstances. Yasmin, well known for her ordered mind and not wanting to leave anything to chance, booked herself into a private room in Doctor Cooymans' clinic, two days before her baby's due birth. Being her first child, Yasmin did not want to leave anything to chance, and being uber-wealthy, certainly helped to put the odds of a safe delivery firmly in her favour.

Only for some reason, it didn't quite work out that way, Yasmin went into labour two days after her due date, and twenty four hours later she was still no nearer to giving birth.

Both Dr. Cooymans and Violet the senior head nurse, had strongly recommended to Yasmin that she should opt for a caesarean section.

Yasmin so far had obstinately refused, wanting instead to give birth naturally. Hours later, a very stressed Yasmin had still not managed to give birth. Dr. Cooymans once again recommended that

Yasmin should opt for a c-section birth, as she was getting increasingly worried for the health of the baby and for Yasmin herself.

The doctor's worries had now begun to worry Frank.

Meanwhile I had been home to freshen up, and get my family something to eat, afterwards Adam very seriously asked if he could come back with me to the clinic. I had to explain as tactfully as I could, that it wasn't really somewhere that was suitable for him to be. My reason for this was quite simple, Yasmin was in a very dishevelled state, and obviously in a lot of discomfort and pain. Adam had never before seen Yasmin like this, and I didn't think that it was right for him to see her like that now.

He simply said, " I need to be there, Yasmin needs my help."

I looked at Luke for guidance, and he nodded that it was alright for him to go.

Adam and I arrived back at the clinic via a black cab. Yasmin was still no nearer to giving birth, so I asked Frank, who had stepped out of the room for a breather, if Adam could see Yasmin, just for a moment. I'm sure he was about to tell me that he didn't think that it was appropriate, when Adam put his small hand in Frank's.

Thirty seconds later, Frank led Adam to Yasmin's bed-side. Yasmin, though clearly stressed and in great pain, managed to give Adam a smile through tear-filled eyes. Without asking, Adam took hold of one of Yasmin's hands, holding it for a full minute, and then in a clear voice, heard by Yasmin, Frank, the doctor and myself said, "Your baby will be alright now, mum."

I'd never heard Adam call Yasmin mum before, then he came and got hold of my hand, and led me out of the room.

Ten minutes later, Yasmin gave birth naturally, to a healthy baby girl. They had already picked a name for her Aisha.

A miracle you might think. Maybe! I tend to think not, it was just Adam doing what Adam does.

Days later, when Adam and I were playing, I cautiously asked him how he knew that Yasmin's baby was about to be born.

He simply said, "I told it, that it was time to be born."

And that was it, he wouldn't say any more, and carried on playing. God knows, I knew that my son was different, how could he not be, having Luke as his father. But to be different in such a positive way, that was something else. It eased my mind and gave me comfort, at the same time. I'm sure that he helped Yasmin, in fact, I'm positive that he did.

Chapter 83

Claire was feeling restless, she'd tried laying on her side but couldn't get comfortable, piling up the pillows and punching them into shape had almost resulted in her being in a sitting up position in bed. At six months pregnant, she couldn't remember being this uncomfortable whilst carrying Adam.

She wondered, did having a girl have to be so different.

Adam by contrast, had been a far easier pregnancy, she had still suffered morning sickness for a while, just as most mothers did in early pregnancy, but this one was entirely different, Claire felt uncomfortable most of the time. It had even managed to put her off having sex with Luke, although her body had craved that physical intimacy of the act.

Luke, for his part, had not pressed his attentions on her, instead waiting patiently for Claire to initiate sex. She wished he was here now, perhaps sex was just what she needed, instead he had flown to St. Helier in Jersey, to purchase some letters, supposedly written by Admiral Lord Nelson. They had been in a private collection held by an old acquaintance of Luke's, and he had contacted him quite out of the blue, to see if he was interested in buying them. Of course Luke was interested in buying them, he had clients on his secret list who would happily commit murder to own letters penned by Lord Nelson.

So, with Claire's blessing, he had gone off to the Channel Islands, for two or three days. Whilst he was there, he planned on catching up with an old friend, and that was the reason why she was restless and alone in their bed. Eventually, Claire did manage to get some much-needed sleep, but she woke with a start. It was still dark outside, but something in the room had changed. Looking steadily around the room, Claire tried to see what it was that was different. At first, the dark shadow in the corner hadn't alerted her sleep-fogged brain to the danger, but her eyes must have somehow registered the difference because they came back to it, and stared more intently. After a while her eyes widened fearfully, in the realisation of what she was seeing.

Someone very large was stood watching her from the corner; she tried to speak, but fear had gripped her tongue rendering her speechless. Eventually, anger overcame her fear and restored her speech. "Who the fuck are you? And what do you want?" she shouted in outraged anger.

The shadow spoke calmly, "I mean you no harm Claire, please believe me."

Claire fought down her panic, digesting the shadow's measured words, before asking again. "Who are you, and what do you want?"

"I am Michael. Luke and I are old ...acquaintances."

Claire had noticed the slight pause, realising that it

meant, not exactly friends then. Going on to the attack she still wanted to know, "What do you want Michael?"

"I like to watch Adam sleeping, sometimes I eavesdrop on his dreams, they are quite advanced for someone so young you know," answered Michael matter-of-factly.

The bed-clothes had slipped down slightly, exposing Claire's ample milky white breasts, and in her anger, she hadn't noticed that Michael could see them. "What! You mean that you've been here before?" gaped Claire, incredulous.

"Yes, but as I've already said, I truly mean you no harm. I've been watching over both you and Adam, because the world is a very dangerous place these days Claire. There are certain individuals out there, who would stop at nothing to possess your son, governments too, should they become aware of Adam's abilities, they would do all in their power to wrest him from you. So, I watch and wait, in order to prevent this from happening."

Claire's anger rose once more. "But it's not your place to watch over Adam, or me for that matter, it's Luke's."

"Yes it is," agreed Michael, "but where is he now? And how can he look after his family when he's not here. Be on your guard Claire, there is real evil in this world."

Claire looked down at her exposed breasts, and realised that Michael must have seen them in all their glory. When she'd covered them back up, the shadow had gone. Carefully, she looked around the room for signs of him, but he had gone. Fearing for her son, Claire pulled the bed-clothes to one side, and moving as quickly as her condition would safely allow, went naked to Adam's room.

He was fast asleep in his bed, content and unharmed, he looked so peaceful whilst asleep, it was hard for Claire to imagine that there were people out there, who would use

Adam's abilities, for their own ends, but deep in her heart, she knew that it was true.

Wearily, she made her way back to her own room, and climbed back into bed. It was just as if no-one had ever been here. Then she realised to herself, "How the fuck did he get in or out of here? He didn't use the door or the window, so how the fuck did he do it?"

Strangely, Claire woke surprisingly refreshed and rested from her troubled sleep, and later, whilst washing up the breakfast dishes, Claire wondered if she had imagined the whole thing.

Chapter 84

Luke had arrived in St. Helier just before noon, he had no sooner gotten comfortable in the aircrafts seat, when the pilot announced that they had to fasten seat belts as they were about to land.

Obviously, it had been longer than that, but that's how it seemed to Luke. He had only a duffle-bag with him in the overhead locker, so once they had landed and cleared customs, he made his way to the taxi rank. Going directly to the lead cab, Luke instructed the driver to take him to the Mayfair Hotel in St. Helier. Gone were the days of bed and breakfast accommodation, Luke had decided to splash out. The short cab ride brought Luke to the impressive hotel, whose lobby was quite spacious, although busy with milling guests and staff. Luke patiently waited his turn to have his reservation confirmed using his passport as identification, he was given an electronic key card, for room 216.

Once he'd settled in and freshened up, he rang his

client's home number to let him know that he had arrived, and also to arrange a time to meet in the hotel's comfortable lounge. Once that was done, Luke changed his clothes before going back downstairs, in search of a light lunch. These days he preferred to conduct business after eating.

An hour later, Luke was quietly sipping coffee in the hotel's lounge with his old acquaintance,

Dominic West, of Global West, a high-end tourist company that Dominic's father had originally started. It was still operating, although Luke sensed that it may well be in financial difficulties, hence Dom's eagerness to sell him the Nelson letters.

They had initially agreed on a price over the telephone a couple of days ago, this of course was on the proviso that the letters were proved to be genuine, or had good provenance. Luke had gone through the letters meticulously, much to Dom's obvious irritation, though Luke wasn't going to be rushed. He checked that the provenance, where provided was authentic, thankfully the letters proved to be the real deal. But when Luke mentioned the price, Dom suddenly wanted more. When Luke pointed out, quite rightly, that it was Dom himself who had named the figure that they had both agreed upon, not two days hence, Luke realised that things must have indeed become desperate for Dom to try and roll him over. Two can play this game thought Luke, as he began to return his money to his inside jacket-pocket.

Desperation now clouded Dom's troubled face as he saw his money disappearing before his eyes.

Luke said nothing, and calmly continued to sip his coffee waiting for Dom to break. It wasn't long in coming before Dom relented, finally settling for the original agreed for price. Now the old Luke would have lowered his offer, in retaliation for Dom trying to raise the price. The old Luke would have done it without hesitation, instead, Luke the family man sat there. Since marrying Luke had developed a conscience, a very dangerous thing to acquire, especially when trying to conduct business.

After Dom had hurried away with his money, Luke made another telephone call, this one to an old friend. "Matthew hi it's Luke, look I've been doing a bit of business here in St, Helier but it's done now, would you like to meet up? ...You would! Great give me your address and I'll see you tonight ... okay, got that, about six o'clock, see you then." Luke ended the call, genuinely pleased that he was going to meet up with his old friend. Matthew was the same as Luke and although they hadn't seen each other in quite a while, Luke was looking forward to the reunion.

As it was still early Luke decided to have a leisurely stroll around St. Helier, even taking time out to buy himself a famous Jersey ice-cream. His first taste was delicious, sending his taste-buds into overdrive, damn, it tasted just as good as the last time he was here. It was good to be back.

Later, now shaved and showered, dressed casual but smart he was ready to go and meet his friend.

Walking to the cab rank, Luke gave directions to the lead cab driver, "Rozel Bay please."

Twenty minutes later the cab driver dropped Luke off at the bottom of a steep narrow road, beside a pretty little harbour.

Matthew, accompanied by an attractive looking woman, stepped out from one of the houses lining one side of the harbour. Grinning at one-another, Luke appraised Matthew then like long lost brothers they embraced like it was a home coming. Slightly embarrassed by their open display of affection, Matthew realised that he was forgetting his manners, stepping apart he introduced his companion to

Luke. "Cynthia, this is my good friend Luke, Luke this is Cynthia, Cyn to her friends."

Luke was unsure whether to shake Cyn's hand, or kiss her on the cheek.

Cyn had no such problem with etiquette, standing up on her tiptoes she kissed him on the cheek saying, "Hi! Luke."

Luke responded in kind, kissing her back. "Hi! Cynthia, sorry is it alright if I call you Cyn?"

Smiling back at Luke, Cyn replied, "Yes of course," then led the way back inside the small terraced

house, closely followed by Luke and Matthew.

Luke couldn't help but look around, it was as if he had stepped inside an art gallery, and in a way, he wouldn't have been far wrong. Cyn, it turned out was an artist and a very fine one too. Although her subject matter was limited at the moment to one particular theme, the naked body,

Matthew, Luke couldn't help but notice, featured heavily in quite a few of the paintings hung on display. One didn't have to look too closely at them, to realise that Matthew was sporting a rather impressive erection, in a variety of very explicit poses.

One of Cyn's harshest critics on the island, called her work pornography in the guise of art, according to Matthew. Moving swiftly on, Luke couldn't take his eyes off the other side of the coin, several paintings of a beautiful young woman, hung along-side Matthew's.

Cyn informed Luke that the subject of his scrutiny was called Renley and she was meeting them later on at the hotel's restaurant, back up the hill, where they would be having a meal together.

If Renley looked half as good in the flesh as she did on canvas, then Luke couldn't wait to meet her.

Matthew for his part, had turned his hand to wood

carving, he admitted to Luke that at first, he hadn't been very good at it, his first offerings had been crude at best, but once he had met Cyn she had encouraged him to try a different approach. With Cyn's help he had now become a much sort after wood carver, and his birds, animals, and the odd female nude, were very much in demand. Cyn let Matthew exhibit his work for sale in her studio, and in return, Matthew posed for her. He also shared Cyn's bed.

Luke felt an unusual pang of jealousy, when he also learned that Renley often joined them. He knew that he shouldn't be having these kind of thoughts, as normally he wouldn't even contemplate cheating on Claire, especially now that she was pregnant again. But the thought was there, and it troubled Luke.

Later they all walked back up the hill for their meal. Renley had already arrived and was sat at the bar nursing a drink, she looked to be in deep conversation with the girl serving behind the bar.

Cyn sidled up beside her, pulling Luke in close, and introduced them.

Renley gave a disarming smile at Luke, when she noticed how handsome he was, she said, "Hello," devouring Luke with her eyes, then asked Luke to call her Ren, as everyone else did.

Luke could feel the chemistry between them, but knew in his heart that he couldn't risk going there.

They were shown to a table for four, Ren of course made a point of being seated beside Luke.

Matthew mischievously, smiled across at Luke knowing full well that his friend was definitely out of his comfort zone. Ren tended to send most men stupid when in her company, himself included.

They ordered an enormous seafood platter, deciding

that it was easier to share. When it arrived, they helped themselves to freshly caught local fayre that was delicious, washed down with drinks, brought to them from the bar.

They all talked freely between mouthfuls of food and drink, the conversation was both lively and interesting, and Luke had made a point of telling Ren at the earliest opportunity, that he was happily married with a young son and another one on the way, but that hadn't put Ren off from trying to coax Luke into bedding her. It didn't make matters any easier for Luke, knowing that had he not been married, Ren was exactly the type of woman that he really went for.

After they had polished off the platter, they moved away to the bar area so that people wanting a meal could be seated. Luke ordered them fresh drinks from the bar, Matthew beside him, offering his help to carry.

"How are you finding Ren Luke? Has she managed to wear you down yet" said Matthew, chuckling at the thought.

Luke looked at his friend sideways on, "Honestly Matthew, I've never been more tempted in my life," admitted Luke.

"Well, only you can decide my friend, she's certainly something though isn't she?" said Matthew, not helping to ease the situation in the slightest.

Luke, helped by Matthew brought back the drinks. Handing Ren's to her, she gently took it from him lightly brushing his fingers in the process it was like a jolt of electricity had run up Luke's arm. She smiled at him provocatively, her mouth deliciously inviting.

God, thought Luke this was torture, then a sudden moment of clarity, made Luke realise what was happening here. He was being set up, no doubt about it, and it must have been Matthew's idea, probably aided by Cyn. Ren of course was a willing player, but it was a set-up, none-the-less, now forewarned, Luke was no longer in thrall, to Ren's womanly wiles.

Two more rounds of drinks finally brought the evening to a close. Luke asked at reception on his way back from the restroom, if they could order him a cab, they said that they could, and one would be arriving shortly.

Luke stood outside in the cool night air, the smell of the sea brought inland on the breeze, it was soon accompanied by the unmistakeable smell, of Chanel No.5.

Ren came to stand beside Luke whilst he waited for his ride, she slipped her arm inside his experimentally, and Luke didn't pull away.

Matthew and Cyn came noisily outside, in a gale of laughter to join them. Luke turned to them smiling, "Thanks for this evening," untangling himself from Ren, Luke gave Matthew a friendly bear hug. "Thanks man," said Matthew.

Cyn came up to Luke and again standing on her tiptoes, she kissed his cheek. "Bye Luke," was all that she said.

The taxi pulled up onto the white chippings, crunching to a stop beside them. Luke bent down and hugged Ren lightly, kissing her cheek, "Bye Ren," he said not really wanting to let her go.

"Bye Luke," said Ren then joining her two friends, they linked arms. Her parting words to Luke were, "I almost managed to corrupt you, didn't I Luke?" Said with a cheeky smile.

Luke had to smile at that, as she was a kindred spirit after all. But as the taxi pulled away, leaving them behind in the rear-view mirror, Luke had to admit to himself that yes, she had almost managed to corrupt him. It was a good job that he was going home tomorrow, Luke wearily sighed to himself.

Chapter 85

Within an hour of returning home from St. Helier, Luke had been brutally honest with Claire, admitting to her that he had been sorely tempted into bedding another woman. Claire hadn't known what to say initially to Luke's devastating confession, a sick feeling inside, mainly one of disappointment, had hit her like a ton of bricks. The man that she loved, the one that she valued above all others, had almost been unfaithful to her. Was her man, her rock, just like all other men after all, thought Claire? Her mind was reeling, trying to find answers as to why she wasn't good enough for him anymore. Why would her husband want to stray? Alright , being heavily pregnant could be a turn off, admitted Claire to herself, but to risk ones marriage by wanting to stray, she couldn't understand that.

Luke had fully explained the circumstances surrounding his temptation to stray, but by now Claire was only half listening, she just felt so sick inside, desolate. It had been one of Claire's conditions before they had married that they be totally honest with each other, however much it hurt. Now faced with this tsunami of disappointment, she was beginning to wish that Luke had just bedded the woman and kept it to himself. At least that way, she could have retained the myth of Luke's fidelity alive and intact. Luke's brutal honesty had now destroyed that myth, and Claire really didn't know what to do.

Luke decided to take Adam to the park, Claire needed breathing space, time to think.

Once Luke and Adam were out of the door, Claire rang Yasmin, and fifteen minutes later, Yasmin was curled up on Claire's settee, nursing a mug of tea. It was the first time that Yasmin had been to Claire's since giving birth to her daughter, Aisha.

Frank, Yasmin's husband, had been left at home to look after his daughter unsupervised, for the very first time. Yasmin had told Claire that Frank had practically pushed her out of the door in his eagerness to spend some time alone with his daughter. Yasmin had needed that push, she hadn't left Aisha's side since bringing her home from the clinic.

Claire had tentatively begun telling Yasmin about Luke's admission to meeting and wanting to sleep with another woman whilst in Jersey. When Yasmin failed to say anything, Claire carried on miserably, until the tale was told. It was obvious that Yasmin was carefully digesting the information that she had just been given, and maddeningly, she wouldn't be hurried in her deliberation.

Claire valued Yasmin's advice, so she waited patiently until she could offer some. When at last Yasmin spoke, she pointedly asked Claire, "Are you sure that Luke didn't sleep with this woman?"

After a moment's hesitation, Claire answered, "As sure as I can be, yes, I mean otherwise why would he bother to tell me that he had been tempted, when he could have just fucked her and said nothing at all," said Claire perplexed.

"Mmmm," murmured Yasmin still unsure.

"What! You think that Luke did fuck her, and then just told me that he had been tempted?" Claire thought about this for a few moments, her mind reeling, before deciding. "No! Luke would have told me that he'd fucked her, rather than play games. No! I believe him when he says he was tempted but managed to walk away before something happened."

Yasmin broke into Claire's thoughts at this point, "So, apart from being angry and upset and bitterly disappointed that Luke could be attracted to, and tempted by another woman, what's really bothering you?" asked Yasmin. When Claire failed to respond, she carried on, "I mean, are you disappointed to find out that Luke can be tempted by another woman, just like any other man, I might add, or is it the fact that Luke is so brutally honest that he chose to tell his wife that he had been tempted by another woman, but in the end decided not to go through with it," asked Yasmin.

"I mean, looking at it rationally, and from what you have told me, if he is to be believed, Luke was out with friends who apparently set him up with a good-looking woman. He was having a good time and admits to you that he had been sorely tempted by her, but in the end decided not to go through with it. If indeed that is the truth, then I would say to you you've got a good man there, look after him there's not that many about," finished Yasmin.

Claire looked at her friend, eyes brimming with tears ready to spill, Yasmin offered her a tissue and Claire gratefully accepted, mopping them up. "Thanks" Claire offered, "you give good advice, I think," sniffing.

“What would you do if it had been Frank?” asked Claire.

“I would probably kill him,” said Yasmin without hesitation.

Chapter 86

Ominous black clouds were racing one-another above London's crowded streets, the wind was building in intensity, helping to push them along. It wasn't a day for going to the children's park, but that was where Luke was headed.

Adam, unusually for him, an unwilling captive in his push-chair, would rather have stayed at home with his mum. Alas he was being used as a pawn, he realised in whatever it was that had upset his parents. He wasn't privy to all the facts of course, only what he'd overheard as he'd eavesdropped on his mother and father's argument this morning. Something must have happened on his dad's business trip that must have upset his mum, was all that Adam could understand. That the argument was about someone else, Adam had worked out for himself, just because he was a kid, it didn't mean that he was stupid.

When they arrived at the children's play-park, Adam

could see straight -away that the area was empty of mums and their off-spring. No surprise there, thought Adam, perhaps mums have more sense after- all he mused, especially on a day like today.

Luke negotiated the staggered gate-way, and brought Adam's buggy to rest beside the bench-seat nearest to the swings. Luke let Adam out, and motioned for him to head towards them.

Like the good son that he was, Adam dutifully obliged, and choosing his favourite swing, went through the motions watched all the while by his dad. Adam would probably have enjoyed the experience a lot more, had his friend Lizzie occupied the next swing. Sadly Lizzie's mum had more common sense than to bring her to the park, on a day such as this. Adam's heart wasn't really in it, so bringing the swing to a stop, he headed for the slide. Climbing to the top, Adam noticed that someone had sprayed graffiti on the framework since the last time that he was here. He gave it his best shot, but only managed two descents before coming back to his dad. Climbing up onto the seat beside his dad, Adam decided that it was time for questions. "Is mum cross with you?" asked Adam.

Luke of course, had been expecting something from Adam, not really surprised by his question at all.

"Yes Adam, mum is cross with me, I did something very stupid whilst I was away, and now I've upset her, and made her very angry."

Adam weighed his dad's answer carefully, before asking, "Well can't you tell her that you're sorry, and make it better."

Luke thought for a moment smiling inwardly, if only it was that simple, but his son was waiting for a response and he said, "I've already told your mum how sorry I am Adam, but she's very disappointed with me, and I've hurt her as only grown-ups can do. I'm afraid it's going to be a long time before she can forgive me."

Adam was very quiet for a while, obviously thinking about what his dad had said, "Is it because of the baby," he asked. Taking Luke totally by surprise.

"No Adam! What made you think that?" asked Luke, worried by Adam's question.

"Well, we just seemed a lot happier when it was just the three of us," answered Adam, honestly.

"No Adam, it's not because mum is having a baby, we both want a sister for you, and we'll love her just as much as we do you......... do you believe me?" asked Luke, worried.

Adam didn't answer, looking at his shoes instead and just nodded.

Not fully convinced, Luke tried again, "Look it's not because your mum's having a baby Adam, it's because I broke your mum's trust. We'll be alright again, I promise, but it may take a while before your mum can forgive me. Do you understand?"

Adam, looking up into his dad's face needing reassurance, nodded and said, "Alright."

Satisfied that he'd managed to allay Adam's fears, Luke's own thoughts were less certain. He just hoped that Claire could forgive this one major blip, in an otherwise unblemished relationship. He hoped so anyway, otherwise he was lost.

Chapter 87

On arrival for duty at the club that night, Frank had greeted Luke with the words, "What the fuck have you been up to? Yasmin's been bending my ear ever since getting home from your place, I've never seen her so steamed up. Anyone would think it was me who had been playing around, she even threatened to emasculate me, if she ever caught me at it. For fucks sake," finished Frank, exasperated.

Luke just stood there, waiting for an opening. "For a start I haven't been playing around. If you must know, I went out for dinner with friends, and was introduced to a very attractive woman....... I admit that I was very tempted by her, but I managed to walk away at the eleventh hour. I told Claire all about it when I got home, and needless to say, Claire's very disappointed with me," admitted Luke.

"Disappointed," Frank blurted. "If I'd just admitted that to Yasmin, my balls would have been served up to me on a platter, and I'm rather attached to keeping my balls where they belong, thank-you very much," laughed Frank.

"I'm not proud about it Frank, and that's why I told Claire as soon as I got back," explained Luke.

Frank took a careful look at his friend, just to make sure that he wasn't taking the piss, then realising that Luke was being truthful he said, "You know Luke, for a so called man of the world, you've still got an awful lot to learn about women my friend. Why the fuck didn't you just give this woman what she wanted, no-one would have been any the wiser and you wouldn't now be in the doghouse. Just by admitting to Claire that you fancied this woman, doesn't lessen the crime, in a woman's eyes, you were guilty by thought, if not by deed, so you may as well have done the deed and had some fun. Instead you thought to ease your conscience and come clean, and look where that landed you, still in the dog-house mate, that's where. Either way, you can't fucking win," said Frank smiling.

"Thanks Frank, for those kind words of wisdom, I'm glad to see that you care," said Luke sarcastically. Luke knew that Frank was only trying to ease the situation, but really what difference did it make, as Frank had pointed out, his situation hadn't changed, as he was still in the doghouse. He wasn't sure just how long his punishment was meant to last, maybe he should have fucked Ren and kept it to himself just like Frank had suggested. Thousands of other men in Luke's position wouldn't have thought twice about it, given the opportunity. So why couldn't Luke?

Therein lay the answer, Luke wasn't like other men.

Chapter 88

Claire was sat on the settee wriggling in discomfort, trying to find a comfortable position, and no matter how hard she tried it just wouldn't happen. She had just helped Adam to set up his toy garage near to the patio windows, where there was more natural light. She was only half watching him playing, her mind still pre-occupied, with thinking about the last ten days.

Ever since Luke's confession, she had replayed Yasmin's words of wisdom over and over again in her mind.

Claire's first instincts were to lash out, and somehow punish Luke. But what for? Because he had had the temerity to fancy another woman, or because he had been honest enough to tell her about it.

Either way, it still hurt, and it also didn't help that she was beginning to feel unattractive and more like a beached whale, and now her bloody ankles were swelling up, again.

Adam meanwhile, whizzed one of his cars across the

floor, Claire, only just registering his actions, her eyes were pointing in her son's direction, but weren't really seeing. It was as if her sight was disconnected from her brain, and that's why she failed to notice that the car came back to Adam, unaided.

Adam continued playing with his cars for a while, completely engrossed in what he was doing, and then he decided to park up his cars and reached for an Eddie Stobart truck that his dad had bought for him a couple of months ago. It was a splendid looking vehicle.

Claire had toyed with the idea of making Luke sleep in the other room at first, but then realised that she was being ridiculous. They hadn't resumed being intimate, not since Luke's return from Jersey, but that had mainly been Claire's fault, as it was usually she who initiated sex. Luke would certainly have accommodated her needs, had she made the first move, as evidenced by his almost permanent state of arousal, when lying by her side.

Claire knew that she was being totally unreasonable towards Luke, she could quite easily have done something about Luke's erection, without initiating full intercourse. But somehow, she couldn't quite bring herself to make the first move, so she guessed she was punishing Luke after all, by withholding sex.

She finally came to a decision, enough was enough, the next time they were in bed together she would ask Luke to make love to her, one stupid bump in the road, would not be allowed to ruin their otherwise, solid relationship.

Meanwhile, Adam had backed up the Eddie Stobart truck and parked it in favour of a gleaming black Porsche. He did a couple of circuits around the garage then pushed it towards the middle of the floor. Claire had seen the car's momentum come to a stop fully ten feet away from

Adam. The fine hairs on her arms stood up, as the Porsche came back to him unaided. Claire then realised that she had witnessed Adam do it once before, without it properly registering. This time there had been no distractions, Claire had seen it for herself. Adam had the ability of telekinesis.

As soon as the thought came into her mind, her unborn daughter gave Claire a resounding kick.

Wow thought Claire, that was a good one.

Adam looked over towards Claire just at that moment, to see if his mum was alright, but said nothing.

Seeing that look, Claire wondered if Adam and her daughter were already in communication, it certainly wouldn't have surprised Claire if they were, not one bit, but telekinesis, even Luke didn't have that ability. She would have to tell him of course, and as soon as he got up. It would be alright thought Claire, provided that Adam's newly discovered ability, was kept within the family unit.

But more worryingly, it couldn't be allowed to be seen by anyone else, otherwise the men from the shadows would get involved, and if that happened Claire knew with certainty, that Adam would one day mysteriously disappear.

Claire couldn't bear the thought of losing her son, to the sinister grey men, she and Luke would have to talk to Adam as soon as possible. He had to be protected, at all cost. Christ, thought Claire, why did things have to be so complicated? Just leave us the fuck alone.

Chapter 89

Luke knew that something had changed between him and Claire, from the moment that he had come downstairs. She had greeted him warmly for a start, with a kiss on the mouth at the foot of the stairs saying, quietly, "We need to talk about Adam.

As Luke and Claire headed towards the kitchen, Adam looked up at his dad as he passed and said, "Hi dad," then carried on playing.

"Hi son," said Luke, as Claire mysteriously pulled him into the kitchen behind her. Once there he lifted his eyes in question, then asked, "What's going on?"

Talking quietly so as not to alert Adam, Claire whispered, "Adam has the ability of telekinesis."

Luke only heard half of what Claire said, feeling gut-punched, and not wanting to believe it himself, as the words, "Are you sure," lamely left his mouth. Of course Claire was sure Luke realised, otherwise the subject wouldn't have been mentioned, and as this new bombshell finally hit home and began to take root, Luke just nodded to her wearily, then slid his frame on to one of the high backed kitchen stools. With difficulty, Luke tried to process this unwelcome information.

Claire, also with difficulty, tried comically to perch on the stool opposite Luke. Her condition prevented that from happening, so she came around to Luke's side, and slid her arms around his waist instead. "What are we going to do about Adam?" Claire asked, obviously worried about their son's ability.

"He's probably not even aware that he can do it," said Luke, "but we are going to have to sit down with him, and talk it through and we'll have to be very careful what we say to him. It's going to be very frightening for him." Luke shook his head in disbelief, saying, "Is there no end to this nightmare?"

"You think it's that bad?" Claire asked, worried now by Luke's choice of words.

"It's going to get him noticed," said Luke clearly upset, "he's only a little boy and sooner or later he's bound to slip up, probably in front of someone other than us. It's inevitable," Luke explained.

Meanwhile it hadn't escaped Adam's notice, that his mum and dad were being very quiet in the kitchen. Usually, that meant that they were discussing something that they didn't want Adam to overhear. The partly closed door seemed to reinforce that theory, so he decided that direct action was what was needed. Putting down his battered, though much loved red Ferrari, Adam carefully pushed open the kitchen door. Seeing his mum's arms around his dad, delighted Adam, and he got their attention by asking his mum directly, "Are you and dad friends again?"

Claire loved that about Adam, there was no guile where her son was concerned, he asked exactly what was on his mind.

"Yes Adam, your dad and I are friends again," answered Claire.

"Good," was all that Adam said, clearly delighted with his mum's response, and happily went back to playing with his cars.

Luke looked searchingly into Claire's eyes, and asked her, "Are we good?"

Claire answered huskily, "You'll find out later."

Luke said nothing, just smiled.

Chapter 90

At the club, London

"What the fuck are you grinning about? ..... Oh! Wait don't tell me, she's let you out of the doghouse.....She has, hasn't she? And about time too mate," said Frank. "Mind you, if it had been

Yasmin, I reckon she'd have been a harder nut to crack, and I'd still be out in the wilderness mate, no fucking problem."

"Are you finished?" asked Luke.

"Just saying, if Yasmin had caught me ogling another woman"......

..... "I wasn't ogling another woman," Luke broke in. "I was in the company of a very attractive woman, who I was interested in, that's all."

"If you say so mate, but we both know that you were

thinking of giving her one, until you bottled it at the last minute" Frank laughed. He was in his element, and thoroughly enjoying himself at Luke's expense.

They were the best of mates, but Luke was so easy to wind up, that Frank just couldn't resist it. "Anyway, I'm glad for you mate, it's good to see you happy for a change, that face of yours has been like a smacked arse for far too long," finished Frank.

"Thanks Frank, I think?" replied Luke, not really sure if that last statement was a compliment, or not.

Still, it was good to be able to smile again, even if he had had to put up with Frank's constant ribbing.

He had been worried that his poor judgement in Jersey and its consequences had been irreparable. Hurting Claire had been intolerable to Luke, and by extension, it had had a detrimental effect between him and Adam. As a consequence of which, Luke vowed that it would never happen again.

He hated the feeling of being the bad guy, and it wasn't something that he wished to repeat.

"You alright to partner up Eddie, in the big room Luke?" queried Frank.

"Yeah sure, you expecting trouble?" asked Luke.

"Not sure, but it is a match day, so be on your guard eh. Keep in touch via comms, and I'll see you later," said Frank.

As Luke made his way through the double doors, on his way to find Eddie, his spirits had been lifted by Claire's earlier good-will. Now that his home life was back on track, he could concentrate more effectively on doing his job. He found Eddie talking to Chris, he nodded to them in greeting, not wanting to butt into their conversation.

When Chris went to sort out his playlist, Eddie slapped Luke on the shoulder saying, "You with me mate?" Heartily pleased to have been partnered with Luke.

Luke seemed to have an uncanny knack for both sniffing out and preventing trouble from happening. He had also saved Eddie's bacon on more than one occasion. Luke's coolness in tricky situations, had earned him the nick-name 'The Iceman' behind his back of course. No-one used it to Luke's face, though he was aware of it. So Eddie was stoked to have Luke as a partner as they slowly worked the big room, trying mainly to keep off people's radar. The paying public were here to enjoy themselves, not to feel intimidated by over-zealous security. Wherever possible, Luke and Eddie liked to keep out of sight, just hovering at the fringes, or wherever trouble was likely to flare-up.

Mostly, a few carefully chosen words along with a good sense of humour often did much to defuse a potentially hostile situation. Common sense really, was the magic ingredient.

Later, at the end of yet another busy night, Eddie and Luke had had a mostly uneventful evening.

The only trouble of any note, was dealt with swiftly by members of the female security team, two women had come to blows over a bloke, and had been ejected from the club. It had been fuelled by too much drink of course, but hey, no-one was forcing it down their throats, so they were led out and told to go home. The incident had been dealt with quickly and with a minimum of fuss, so on this occasion, their membership was not revoked. However, they were told that if it happened again it would be, so all-in-all the evening had been deemed a success.

Chapter 91

The Henderson's Home, London

Adam had sat quietly for almost a full minute, trying to understand the importance of what his parents were worried about. He knew that he was different to other people, and could understand that it was mostly to do with his DNA that he had inherited from his dad, but he just couldn't understand why it was so important that he should have to hide his gifts, after-all he had had the ability of telekinesis for a while now, and it was just something that he could do, without really trying. So...he didn't really understand what all the fuss was about.

Claire looked from Adam to Luke, worried that it was all getting too much for her son.

"Sweetie, you're not in any trouble, the gift that you have is a wonderful thing. It's just that, anyone seeing you use telekinesis would be frightened by it, people are afraid of things that they can't explain, or do themselves. If anyone saw you using your ability, they wouldn't rest until they'd put it on the internet, and once it's there our lives would just become a living night-mare," Claire said.

Adam looked up, his brow furrowed with worry for one so young, then asked hopefully, "Can you do it dad?"

"No son, I can't," answered Luke, honestly.

"But we share other gifts between us, so why not this ability as well?" pleaded Adam.

"I don't know son, it could be a combination of mine and your mum's DNA although I'm not really convinced about that, or it could be because of what I am, and the gene pool that you've inherited from us, plus entirely new DNA of your own. It's highly likely that you are the first of you're kind, you're certainly more advanced than I am, and you can already do things that I can't, so that's nearer the mark," Luke said.

Adam thought about that for a while then said, "Like Michael? You mean."

Claire stiffened, at the mention of Michael's name, remembering the dream.

Luke had noticed Claire's reaction, and asked, "What is it?"

"Christ, I had thought that it was just a dream, now I remember. He said his name was Michael and that he meant us no harm, and sometimes he watched over Adam and me, when we were alone," said Claire, fearfully.

Luke reacted angrily to this new information and asked her, "When was this Claire?"

"When you were in Jersey, but I'd thought that I'd just dreamt it," said Claire, bristling slightly at Luke's angry tone.

"What, here in our home?" Luke wanted to know.

"Yes, here in our home," declared Claire. "He also said that if you're not here to watch over us, then someone else has to, because there is real evil in the world and men from governments or the military, would stop at nothing to possess someone with Adam's abilities. Christ, how could I have forgotten this, I thought that it had been a dream," cried Claire, utterly bereft.

"Not your fault," said Luke, with feeling. "Michael will have put it into your mind that it was just a dream, that's what he does, and Adam's abilities, maybe they are much closer to Michael's than my own. Perhaps that's why he's shown a keen interest in our son, he's probably afraid that either the military or the government will one day try to use Adam for their own ends," added Luke.

"How can we prevent that from happening?" said Claire, exasperated.

"Without guarding him around the clock, I honestly have no idea," answered Luke helplessly. "I just wish I knew."

"Am I in trouble?" asked Adam, all this while listening to his parents, a captive audience.

Claire scooped him up protectively, "Nooo sweetie you're not in trouble. Your dad and I are trying to find a way to protect you from the bad guys, that's all."

"Is that why we don't go to play-school now?" asked Adam.

There was no fooling Adam, he was just too damn smart, Claire realised. The teachers and some of the mothers at play-school, had commented on how advanced Adam was for his age, compared to the other kids in the group. It was creating unwelcome attention towards Adam, so Claire had taken him out of play-school and had resumed teaching him herself at home.

Luke also did his bit, Adam was a voracious reader, and now that he could understand written

English, he read anything that he could get his hands on. Just a few weeks ago, Luke had brought home a couple of old books that were filled with colour plates of animals, depicted from the age of the dinosaurs pretty much up to the modern era. The books gave the English name for the animal in question, and then underneath its Latin name.

Well of course Adam being Adam, he wanted to know the animals name in Latin as well as English and so long as Luke was there with him to help him with the pronunciation, he was fine. Luke gave Adam the correct name in Latin, Adam repeated it out loud, and bang, it was safely stored in his brain, for later retrieval. Adam was a dustbin for knowledge, his thirst for it was unquenchable, but his favourite subject was animals, or anything relating to wildlife. His own personal library now had books on a variety of mammals, birds, fish, as well as butterflies and moths. He simply couldn't get enough of the subject, watching anything on TV by David Attenborough, fascinated to learn as much as he could. Frighteningly, he probably had more accumulated knowledge on the subject, than Luke and Claire combined.

They thought that they had found Adam a very good private school, to which at the time, were very happy to send him, but now that they had the added worry of Adam's new-found ability becoming common knowledge, were no longer sure if this was a safe option.

With modern technology being so sophisticated these days, it would be so easy to capture Adam in a momentary lapse of concentration using his powers that they now feared for his safety. Once his abilities were out there for all to see, it would only be a matter of time before he became the object of scrutiny and was taken from them. Once again, they were faced with the worry.

"What are we going to do Luke?" asked Claire, for the umpteenth time.

Luke, just as worried as Claire, sadly shook his head saying, "I really don't know, but I do think that we need to look at home schooling again, I don't think we have any other option, it's just too risky for Adam."

Claire nodded in assent, thinking along the same lines as Luke, but that threw up yet another problem.

How to find a tutor for Adam who they could trust.

Chapter 92

Yasmin's apartment, London

''I'm going to have to go to Jordan, Dubai too," added Yasmin, as an afterthought.

Frank was only half listening whilst cradling his baby daughter in his arms, a silly grin on his face.

He had thought that his love for Yasmin could never be rivalled, but his daughter's birth had put paid to those silly ideas, now he had two women in his life to love. He absolutely doted on his first born, treasuring every moment with her, once he could pry her from his wife's arms. "What, why?" was all he could manage to say.

Exasperated by Frank's ludicrous question, she managed to calm her response just in time. She had realised that it had been said out of worry for her, the last time that she had been to Jordan, was to attend her father's funeral and it had ended badly, with her being confined in the Hussein's family residence under armed guard. Her brother Ali, aided by her estranged mother, had kept her there as a prisoner. Whilst she was incarcerated, they had tried to force her into marrying one of Ali's sycophantic friends, in order to gain control of her wealth and business holdings in the U.K

Months later, a daring rescue attempt carried out by Frank and Luke, had proved successful in freeing her, for which she would be eternally grateful. So it was only natural she realised, that Frank should be worried, about her returning to the land of her birth.

But a lot had happened since her last visit to Jordan, fate had intervened in the most brutal fashion, her brother Ali had been assassinated whilst in Dubai. Weeks later, Yasmin's legal representatives in the U.K. had informed her, that as a consequence, she had inherited the entire Hussein portfolio and it was for this reason that she was trying to gain Frank's attention.

"I need to visit the hotels, both in Amman and in Dubai. I am the new face of the Hussein empire and as such, need to be seen by the people who work for me. They need to know that their jobs and livelihoods are safe, as I am responsible for hundreds of lives and their dependants that's why."

Maddeningly, Frank just said, "Oh."

"Oh, is that all you can say," said Yasmin, obviously disappointed with Frank's response.

"Well, when you explain it like that, of course you're going to have to go, but not without me," Frank said, pointedly.

"Of course you're coming, Aisha too aren't you baby," said Yasmin, prying her daughter from Frank's arms.

Frank watched as mother and daughter were reunited, "When are you planning on going?"

"Probably at the end of this month," answered Yasmin.

Frank realised that his wife had been thinking about this for a while, to have a date so readily in mind. He knew that where business was concerned, Yasmin was way above his league, he was just thankful that his wife was so damned smart. In every other way, they were equals, but when it came to business, Frank wisely took the back seat, content to ride along in her slipstream.

"What sort of time frame are you thinking?" he asked.

"To do it properly, four weeks. I have to meet with both management and staff at each of the hotels, sort out any problems or issues, and most importantly, check the books. God knows what state they will be in, knowing how lax my brother was," said Yasmin wistfully.

"That does not sound like a month's sun and relaxation," mused Frank.

"Don't underestimate me lover, we may still get to spend a week relaxing in Dubai, once I've checked the books of course," added Yasmin.

"Underestimate you, never," said Frank. "Will you be alright, leaving Chris to run the club?"

"Yes, he doesn't need me to nursemaid him, and besides he's been running it okay whilst I've been on maternity leave, so I'm sure he'll be fine. What about security?" She asked.

"I'll ask Luke to step up, the rest of the team look up to him anyway, so I don't see any problems arising from him taking over," added Frank.

"Well I'll set everything in motion from this end, and let Chris know that I'm putting him in sole charge for a month. You talk it over with Luke, and let him know the situation, and see what he says," said Yasmin. It's going to seem strange, arranging for our own jet to be made ready, it still feels like I'm in a dream and expect to wake up by falling out of bed," laughed Yasmin.

Frank watched his wife, smiling, she took things like this so easily in her stride, it was frightening to watch, whereas he wouldn't have a bloody clue where to start.

"That reminds me, I'm going to Claire's tomorrow, it's time we had a catch –up," said Yasmin.

"They're fine," Frank answered, "Luke hasn't stopped smiling since she forgave him, he's been grinning like a demented baboon for days, it's quite nauseating to watch."

"You're just jealous that they're back on track," laughed Yasmin.

"Nonsense, but I'm glad that they made up, looking at his miserable face was beginning to give me the willies. Now that I've got my mate back I can have an intelligent conversation with him." Frank replied.

Yasmin arched her eyebrows, listening to Frank prattle on.

"Honestly Yasmin, if Luke had been any more miserable, I would have offered to take him out back and shoot him myself," finished Frank.

"Well I'm going to wait until tomorrow and I'll see for myself," answered Yasmin.

Chapter 93

At the Henderson's residence, London

"Sooo, Frank tells me your back on track," Yasmin said, carefully watching Claire's reaction. Claire had to smile at her friend, subtlety was not something that she was known for, she much preferred the direct approach. "Yes, we're back on track," admitted Claire, there was a temporary lull in the conversation, whilst Claire made sure that Aisha was comfortable. "God, this baby of yours is a real cutie Yasmin she's certainly got your genes," cooed Claire.

Yasmin had to smile at Claire's compliment, secretly happy to agree with her friend's assessment.

Her daughter certainly took after her for her looks, though her eyes were a shade lighter brown than her own. Yasmin was comfortable with Claire holding her baby, but couldn't say the same when Frank held her, she knew that it wasn't rational for her to think this way, but she couldn't help it, it just didn't seem normal to Yasmin to see a man holding her baby, even if it was her husband, and the father of her child. She simply couldn't explain it, but it just didn't sit well with her.

"And Adam's alright, is he? Now that you're back on track," probed Yasmin.

"See for yourself,"' said Claire, indicating Adam and his dad kicking a soft ball about in the back garden.

Yasmin nodded, smiling at Luke and Adam playing.

Adam whooped with delight at that moment, as he managed to slip the ball between his dad's legs sending him chasing after it.

"We're thinking of home schooling him," blurted out Claire, suddenly.

"Oh! Why?" asked Yasmin. "I thought you'd got his schooling all sorted out, it's not a matter of funding is it?" she asked, obviously concerned. "Because if it is, you know that I'm only too happy to help."

"I know you are, and I'm grateful for the offer, I really am," said Claire, almost on the verge of tears whilst thinking about telling her friend the real reasons behind her dilemma. The burden of knowledge was beginning to prove intolerable to her, she had been carrying it around for so long, that it had become too much for her.

Seeing Claire close to tears and thinking the worst, Yasmin said, "Oh! Adam's not ill is he?"

"No! He's as healthy as any young child, in fact healthier than most, he hardly has any ailments at all," added Claire, in an effort to allay Yasmin's fears.

"What then, surely something's happened, to warrant having him home schooled," Yasmin badgered.

Claire was wrestling with the importance, of what she

was about to reveal to Yasmin about her son.

She just hoped that Luke would forgive her for doing so. Claire desperately needed a woman's perspective on their dilemma, the burden of carrying this secret, was becoming intolerable.

Yasmin could see that her friend was troubled and deep in thought, obviously she had something very important to tell her and was finding it hard to put into words. Wisely Yasmin kept quiet, hoping that her friend trusted her enough to tell her what it was.

After what seemed like an eternity of silence, Claire decided to speak, and although hesitant at first, she began tentatively.

"Do you agree that Adam is very smart?"

"Yes of course, Adam's intelligence is beyond question, I can attest to that," agreed Yasmin.

It was hard for Claire to betray the family secret, but she carried on because after all, Yasmin as far as the Hendersons were concerned was family too. Coming to a decision, Claire said, "Alright then here goes. You've seen how Adam behaves just before the telephone rings?"

"Yes, I witnessed it for myself, on many occasions," agreed Yasmin, "it's uncanny."

"Oh, it's more than that," said Claire. "It's frightening." Pausing to recalibrate, Claire then said, "What if I was to tell you that not only does he know when it's about to ring, he actually knows who's ringing before we pick it up." Claire watched Yasmin's eyes open wide in shocked disbelief, nevertheless she carried on, the genie was only halfway out of the bottle so she couldn't stop now. "Did you know that Luke has pretty much a photographic memory?"

Yasmin's mouth although open, remained mute, she knew that Luke was special, but to have a memory like that was beyond amazing.

As Claire fidgeted uncomfortably on the settee, Yasmin indicated if she wanted to pass over Aisha, Claire settled herself and indicated that she was alright.

"We believe that Adam has inherited the same ability from his dad, he's begun showing signs of it more and more. Incidentally, did you also know that Luke is fluent in seven languages," Claire managed to drop in casually.

"WOW," said Yasmin, her voice finally regained. She herself was tri-lingual, but seven was pretty much phenomenal by anyone's standards. How on earth, Yasmin wondered, had they managed to keep all this knowledge under such tight wraps. She realised that it must have taken tremendous willpower for both Claire and Luke to keep this information to themselves. She couldn't imagine the strain that they must have been under. In an effort to try and lighten the mood, Yasmin said, "Please tell me that Adam hasn't started to speak in tongues."

"I wish that I could," said Claire, "but the truth is, Adam's exhibiting signs of a natural flare for languages as well. Luke's been teaching him Latin from two old zoological books that he purchased from the flea-market a few weeks ago. It was Adam himself, who had noticed the Latin name for the animals, as well as the English name," Claire explained. "Well naturally, Adam wanted to know why they had two names, so his dad explained that all animals, birds etc, were categorised by name in ancient Latin as well as modern English, and of course Adam, on hearing this revelation, wanted to learn the correct name for the subject animal in Latin. So, Luke's been helping him with the correct pronunciation of Latin, Adam listens to his dad, repeats it back until he has pronounced it correctly and voila! It's stored in Adam's brain," Claire said, matter-of-factly.

Yasmin had been listening to Claire, absolutely fascinated by it all, "So, let me get this right, you're saying that if Adam's asked for the name of an animal, providing that he's read about it, he can remember the Latin name for it as well as the English," Yasmin said.

"Yes," said Claire.

"If what you are saying is true, and I don't doubt it for a moment," Yasmin quickly interjected, "then your son must be borderline genius," deduced Yasmin. "And if that is the case, what's the problem? Any school would be only too glad to have Adam in it. And why are you even thinking about home schooling, when it's so glaringly obvious, that he would positively thrive in a school environment," said Yasmin, clearly annoyed.

As Yasmin finished delivering her scathing remarks, she immediately regretted them, wondering if she had overstepped the mark.

Claire had listened patiently to her friend, extolling the virtues of proper schooling, and knew with a certainty, that in such an environment Adam would not only thrive, he would excel. It was Adam's new-found ability that was the real problem, but Claire had travelled this far, she couldn't stop now.

Yasmin was carefully looking at Claire, who she noticed had suddenly gone quiet. Fearing that she had gone too far, and hoping that she hadn't put her foot in it Yasmin said, "I'm sorry if I seem to have come on a bit too strong Claire, I just think that home schooling would hold Adam back, that's all, I didn't mean to offend," apologised Yasmin. The last thing she wanted to do was upset her friend.

"No, it's not that and you didn't offend, you said what needed to be said, and I agree with it wholeheartedly, but that's not the only problem," admitted Claire.

Clearly, there was something else bothering Claire, something so huge that the other revelations were merely a side-show in comparison. Yasmin braced herself waiting for Claire to reveal the big one, she didn't have long to wait.

"The reason that we're thinking of home schooling Adam, is because of his latest ability."

Claire even now, though fully committed, was still struggling to reveal it to Yasmin. Biting the bullet

Claire said, "Adam has the ability of telekinesis," and that was it, someone else now shared their secret.

"You're serious!" Was all that Yasmin could say, for once, lost for words.... But, as the importance of what the word meant began to sink in, Yasmin realised the enormity of the consequences involved.

Should Adam's ability ever be captured on film, as so much of every-day life is these days, should that happen then her friend's lives would be over, their anonymity would be a thing of the past.

Eventually, they would be driven into hiding, trying to evade the media circus, that would surely follow them for the rest of their lives.

Yasmin did not doubt for a moment that what Claire had just told her was the truth, and now that she also shared this knowledge, she was only just realising what a truly great burden it was to carry.

Of course, that was why they were thinking of home-schooling Adam, in case some idiot with a mobile phone captured him unawares, using his ability to move some every-day object with his mind.

Yasmin could well imagine the elation, of some such idiot putting it out there on u-tube, or some such nonsense, not realising by doing so it would destroy Adam's life, and that of his parent's. It made her both angry and sad at the same time, as she couldn't imagine the strain of what her friends must have been going through. "I don't know how you've managed to keep it together," admitted Yasmin, "you both must have been under a tremendous strain."

"I've been sick with worry," Claire confided, "and looking like a hippopotamus, hasn't exactly helped either." Claire laughed, trying to lighten her sombre mood.

"Home schooling in this instance, has its merits," Yasmin offered, obviously still thinking about how best to help her friend. "But then you have the added problem, of finding a tutor that you can trust."

"Yes, that's the fly in the ointment," Claire agreed. "It's the one problem that Luke and I, can't seem to solve, perhaps we're not meant to" said Claire, wistfully.

"You think so?" said Yasmin.

"No, not really, I don't really know what to do," admitted Claire, helplessly.

Yasmin could see how low Claire's spirit had sunk, so in an effort to try and cheer her up, she said "Well don't do anything hasty, is my advice. You've trusted in me, and shared the burden, so let me see if I can come up with something," offered Yasmin.

Claire looked at her friend, a glimmer of hope in her eyes, then asked, "What are you going to tell

Frank? I mean, I don't expect you to keep it from him, and it might actually help us in the long run, if we're all on the same page," offered Claire.

Yasmin had been thinking along those very same lines, thankfully Claire had pre-empted her, and given her her blessing. "Thank-you for trusting us Claire, it means a lot."

"No, thank-you," replied Claire. "It's a relief to finally have it out in the open, I don't think my mind could have contained it for much longer. I feel better already for having told you, it's such a relief."

"What about Luke?" asked Yasmin, "do you think he'll be annoyed at you for having told me about

Adam?"

"Probably, for all of about two minutes, then he'll realise that it's in Adam's best interests that you and Frank know, and then he'll be fine with it." Claire said, with confidence.

"You're sure?" asked Yasmin, not entirely convinced.

"I'm sure," reiterated Claire, "don't worry about it, you leave Luke to me."

Later, when Yasmin and her baby had left and returned home, Claire told Luke that Yasmin, and by extension Frank, now knew about Adam's abilities. She had fully expected Luke to be at least angry with her for not having discussed it with him first. She was greatly relieved to find that he wasn't angry with her at all.

They made love before Luke left for work that night. A glimmer of hope had been awoken in Claire's breast, sharing her troubles with Yasmin, had been a good thing, it had certainly eased her troubled mind, she felt at peace.

For the first time in a long time, Claire felt that hope was finally on the horizon, though she felt a little uneasy that two more people now knew of Adam's abilities.

Chapter 94

The powerful animal bore Claire onwards, at the head of the mighty host. Its coat shimmering in the eerie half-light. The grey horse moved at the slightest touch of its rider's knees, obeying without question. On either side of the grey, two black stallions, both of whom were rider-less, kept pace with the grey, their eyes blood red seemed to shine, as if lit from within. The three animals were sweat streaked, glistening with vitality. The animals were big and weighty with awesome bone breaking power as they thundered over the hard, mist covered ground,

Claire seemed to be part of the horse, in perfect balance. Behind her thundered the army of the dead. The souls of the warriors long since slain followed in her wake, eager to do her bidding in the ceaseless battle between good and evil. In her right hand she gripped a flaming sword. A beacon for the souls of the dead warriors to follow.

Where she was leading them was still unclear--- though

there seemed to be something looming on the horizon, something sinister.

Claire awoke from the dream, heart pounding and covered in a film of nervous sweat.

She sat up in bed anxious and a little out of breath trying to calm herself down.

What had awoken her was the downstairs front door being closed and locked.

Moments later Luke quietly entered the bedroom and noticed Claire sat up in bed obviously awake.

"What's wrong?" Luke quietly asked, concerned.

Claire looked over in his direction still trying to calm herself down in order to speak.

"I've just had the most vivid dream. Quite frightening really and exciting too if I'm honest", Claire managed to say.

"Tell me!" said Luke.

Claire described what she had just dreamt to Luke in vivid detail. It was still so clear in her mind, then Claire asked Luke a question. "What does the flaming sword signify?"

Tight lipped Luke answered. "It's fucking Michael's sword."

Obviously, Luke was very angry, thought Claire. Luke never used the 'f' word or hardly ever, at any rate. "Yes! But what does the flaming sword mean? And why does he want me to,

I mean I've only just dreamt I've been riding a horse. I can still feel the power of it, yet how can that be? I've never even petted a horse let alone fucking ridden one," gasped Claire nervously amused.

"The horse, the grey horse," corrected Luke, "is Michael's. The flaming sword is Michael's weapon of choice. It's a beacon for the souls of the dead warriors to follow him into battle.

Michael fights against the forces of evil. It's a never ending war and it's wearisome," admitted Luke tiredly.

"But why put this into my mind? What can I possibly do Luke? I mean look at me I'm like a fucking whale," Claire said.

"Yes! But you're my fucking whale," said Luke shutting her up with a kiss on the mouth.

Pushing Luke away Claire pressed her point home.

"I mean it Luke, what does Michael really expect me to do?"

"He expects you to keep Adam safe," answered Luke.

"How? I mean we do all that we can as it is, what more can we possibly do?" asked Claire.

Luke got undressed and slid in beside her. "I don't know," admitted Luke, "but Michael and I are going to have a reckoning very soon," said Luke with an edge to his voice that Claire did not like.

She lay back down eyes open and staring ---"don't do anything dangerous Luke. I don't want to lose you," Claire said, with obvious concern in her voice.

"Don't worry Claire, I know that I'm no match for Michael, but he needs to understand that he's crossed a line. He can't come into our home whenever he feels like it, not without there being consequences," said Luke.

Claire reached for him, "Promise me you will be careful."

"I promise," said Luke after a lengthy pause.

Chapter 95

"Where's dad gone mum?" asked Adam.

Claire thought about lying to her son for all of a couple of seconds. Then realised that it would have been pointless to do so, because Adam would have known she was lying.

"He's gone to try and find Michael, Adam....Your dad is very cross with him."

"Is that why you are worried for dad? Because of Michael?"

God! This son of mine thought Claire, there are no secrets in this house.

"Yes! Adam I'm worried for your dad, because of Michael."

"Perhaps dad should have taken me with him," said Adam disarmingly frank for one so young.

Claire had to laugh at her son, he was such a sweetie. Enfolding him in her arms Claire said, "That's very brave of you Adam, but it's because dad is trying to protect you that he's gone on his own."

"No silly! I meant if dad had taken me with him, then Michael wouldn't have hurt dad in case I was hurt too," explained Adam.

The wisdom of her son often astounded Claire. It was just like having a conversation with a grown-up. She hugged him even tighter loving him all the more, "That's a very clever suggestion

Adam, if I'd managed to think of that for myself I would have insisted on him taking you with him."

Meanwhile, Luke had been looking in all the places that he knew Michael often frequented.

The search for Luke's quarry had so far yielded nothing. All it had produced so far was frustration and a growing sense of anger. Michael's usual haunts had come up empty, St. Paul's was the last place on Luke's list to try, but it was a brisk twenty minutes walk away. Gritting his teeth in determination Luke headed in that direction.

When Luke arrived at St. Paul's he was sweating lightly. As usual lots of people, mainly tourists were milling around the Cathedral. Luke knew that Michael would be found concealed somewhere amongst the shadows, where he could observe without being observed himself.

It was amongst the shadows that Luke searched first and eventually he spotted Michael half hidden by one of the columns that were deep in shadow. He headed straight towards Michael, who saw him coming. Stepping clear of the column Michael watched his approach, he failed to notice the air of menace that Luke had brought with him.

At less than arm's length away Luke punched Michael squarely on the jaw. Taken totally by surprise, Michael staggered backwards almost going down. The fact that he hadn't gone down proved that he wasn't human as Luke's punch would probably have killed an ordinary man.

Michael's eyes flashed angrily at Luke's unprovoked attack, it took all of his willpower and a lot of self-control not to retaliate in kind. Eyeing Luke warily Michael's smouldering eyes watched his attacker for signs of further aggression. Only a few witnessed the assault, wisely they quickly moved away.

As Michael regained his senses, he warily checked his jaw for signs of damage, it had been a powerful punch Michael conceded and delivered with perfect precision, perhaps he had under estimated Luke after all, he thought ruefully.

After the punch had time to sink in, Luke said what he had come to say.

"Stay away from my family, and keep away from my home and if you still feel the need to protect my family, do it from a distance." His message delivered, Luke turned his back on Michael and walked away.

Michael said nothing just smiled to himself as he watched Luke walk away.

It took Luke all the while walking home to finally regain control of his emotions, he knew that it had been a gamble to confront Michael in that fashion, yet he knew deep down that it had to be done.

Michael had crossed the line, home invasion and messing with his family, had gone way beyond Michael's remit.

As Luke opened his front door Adam ran to him and he scooped him up.

Worried Adam asked, "You okay dad?"

"Yes son, I am," Luke replied cheerfully.

Claire looked anxiously towards Luke for any signs of trauma. Seeing him smiling with Adam in his arms, helped to calm her fears, she was about to ask if he had managed to find Michael, when Luke pre-empted her. "Michael won't be bothering us again," Luke delivered calmly.

Later when Adam had been put to bed, Luke told Claire what had happened.

"Did you think that was wise Luke?" asked Claire.

"It's the only thing that Michael really understands, but if he'd had any doubts about me protecting my family before, he now knows first hand that I would die before I would let anyone hurt my family.....In a way," Luke said. "I think it was Michael's way of provoking me into action and if that was the case, then he now knows that I am ready."

"Mmm, speaking of action," Claire said, "I think that I could manage a little gentle action myself, bedroom type action," emphasised Claire, just in case Luke was a little slow in her meaning.

Always wanting to oblige his wife's wishes, Luke slowly followed his wife's backside upstairs. Perhaps a little R&R was just what they needed.

Chapter 96

The heavy black Mercedes had been in pristine condition when it had set off from Damascus, the Syrian capital. The once shiny vehicle was now covered in a fine film of dust and a myriad number of dead flying insects. The four occupants of the vehicle were irritable and in need of a comfort stop. The driver of the vehicle was unsure of the exact whereabouts of their destination, but carefully followed the instructions of his boss.

Ashraf Malik, unusually for him, sat in front beside his driver. He issued instructions to him from memory, having been here once before. Here being Amman, the capital of Jordan. They were looking for the Hussein residence and if Ashraf's memory served him correctly, the Hussein family residence was situated on the far outskirts of Amman.

As the buildings slowly began to grow sparser, Ashraf craned his neck sideways looking for signs of their destination. At last Ashraf spotted the Hussein residence ahead and indicated to his driver that he should take the slip road. Ashraf thought idly to himself, it's more like a palace than a family residence, perhaps they had illusions of grandeur, these Husseinis.

As the vehicle approached the security gate, Ashraf couldn't help but notice the beefed up security. There were more guards about for one thing and each of them had an automatic weapon pointing in their direction. The driver upon seeing the weapons sensibly slowed down to almost a crawl, a few yards short of the barrier he came to a stop and sliding down his window, he waited tensely as one of the guards came up beside him.

With no sign of politeness, he asked them the nature of their business.

Ashraf Malik spoke across his driver, answering in his stead, "Ashraf Malik seeks an audience with the head of the Hussein family." Having to use such subservient language to this peasant, almost stuck in Ashraf's throat, but Ashraf really needed to see the head of the Hussein household, so a little subservience was a small price to pay. They had driven a long distance and to be turned away now over some discourtesy either imagined or not, was unthinkable.

The guard relayed Ashraf's words to the guard house, almost word for word. After what looked like a heated discussion within the guard house to someone obviously within the Hussein household, two guards approached the vehicle from either side, the levelled weapons aimed in their direction, left them in no doubt that they meant business. They were asked to exit the vehicle and were thoroughly searched, which led to their concealed weapons being quickly discovered and confiscated. They were then instructed to get back inside the vehicle and once the barrier was lifted, told to follow the road left into the vehicle compound.

When the car had come to a full stop and the heated engine was switched off, two guards, one of whom was very tall approached the vehicle from behind.

Ashraf decided to exit the vehicle first, before being asked, he was beginning to feel very pissed off with his welcome.

The very tall man, turned out to be the Hussein's new head of security, Mahmood Kabir, he was wearing a side arm, but it was holstered, his smaller companion trained his automatic on the vehicle, ready for immediate action.

"Mr. Malik," Mahmood offered, "this way please, follow me sir!"

Not intimidated in the slightest by the guard's automatic weapon now being pointed at his midsection, Ashraf Malik said, "And my men?" indicating them with a sweep of his arm, still sitting motionless in the vehicle.

"Just you I'm afraid sir....they have not been granted an audience," said Mahmood, a tight smile firmly in place.

The play on words was not lost on Ashraf, the exchange although polite for now was meant to insult.

Ashraf was duly insulted. "We have driven a long way and my men are in need of a comfort break," Ashraf pointed out reasonably.

"If the need is urgent they can piss up the wall," Mahmood indicated with a pointed hand.

Unruffled Ashraf persisted. "And if they should require ----the other!"

"Then that would be most unfortunate," Mahmood answered matter of factly.

Ashraf followed the tall man into the main building, closely followed by the other guard. He was smarting from the insults he and his men had so far received, it went against every rule of Arab hospitality. These people were just as bad as the infidel, thought Ashraf to himself. Going up a flight of stairs, Ashraf was asked to wait in the corridor whilst Mahmood knocked on the door.

A voice from within answered,"Come".

After a few moments Mahmood held open the door for Ashraf to enter,

Inside the room Ashraf came almost to attention, before him sat the diminutive form of a woman, she was seated behind a desk, and from what he could see of her was garbed in black clothing.

Ashraf was about to speak, when she rudely forestalled him.

"Mahmood tells me that you requested an audience with me?"

Rude! As well as impolite, thought Ashraf with thinly disguised distaste, nevertheless he was here on important business. "Yes, that's correct."

"Very well, what can I do for you Mr. Malik?"

Looking at Mahmood to see if it was appropriate to speak in front of the hired help, he waited for her to speak.

"You may speak freely Mr. Malik, since my son's assassination Mahmood has been my most trusted advisor."

"Very well, it is to do with your son's death that brings me here unannounced. Since his assassination, shipments from the warehouses in Aqaba have completely stopped, if our struggle against the western powers is to continue, we urgently need those supplies," explained Malik.

Fatima Hussein was well aware that her late son Ali had been financing terrorism for years, ever

since her husband's death in fact, but she had been unaware that the arms shipments were being

shipped out of the Hussein warehouses in Aqaba. Ali

had dealt with the arrangements for that side of the business. Realising that things must indeed be desperate to bring Ashraf Malik personally to her door, suddenly her whole demeaner changed. "How can I help you Mr. Malik?" --- then realising that he was still standing, she indicated for him to sit and asked Mahmood to arrange for ice tea to be brought in for her guest.

Ashraf quickly realised that something significant had just happened, either that or someone else impersonating Fatima Hussein had just taken her place, the change in this woman was extraordinary thought Ashraf wryly, she was now all business.

"First of all, please accept my sincere condolences for the murder of your son." Noting the nod of consent he continued. "May his murderers be swiftly dealt with." Waiting a few moments Ashraf began again. "Since your son's murder, the shipments have stopped being delivered. The warehouse manager in your employ refuses to send the shipments without proper authorisation."

Realising that this was a simple matter to rectify, Fatima Hussein decided to be magnanimous to

Ashraf, when the iced tea had been brought to them, she feigned mock horror to realise that Ahraf's men had been left languishing in the Mercedes to cook, and all without suitable refreshment.

She immediately chastised Mahmood for his tardiness, and apologised to Ashraf for her lack of hospitality, she made a show of arranging for suitable refreshments to be sent to Ashraf's men, that and the full use of the guards' rest room should they require it .

No-one was fooled by this late display of hospitality, everyone knew that nothing happened here unless it was orchestrated by this woman.

Wisely, Ashraf sipped his tea and said nothing, if the shipments started up again then he had achieved what he had come here to do. Ashraf Malik and his men left the Hussein's compound having achieved their goal, the arms shipments would begin arriving shortly, but the way they had been treated on arrival would not easily be forgotten. The insult would have to be re-paid at some future date, honour demanded it.

Chapter 97

Luke had taken his time in getting dressed. He had subconsciously been listening out for signs of life within the house, but so far he hadn't detected any. Making his way downstairs he listened carefully to a rhythmic sound that drew him into the living room and towards the patio windows, it was his son Adam playing football in the garden. This was something he had only just become interested in, but already he was developing some useful skills with the ball.

Claire was sat on the garden seat watching her son, the seat was padded for comfort but Claire looked anything but comfortable, her face he noticed was lined with worry. It hurt Luke to know that he had brought this worry to his wife, and if he could have taken it from her he would have done. Neither of them had realised at the time, the worry and the problems that having a child together would bring. Especially one who had such special gifts like Adam, and it was those that weighed heavily on them both, but more so on Claire, and soon, very soon Luke realised that their daughter would be born, adding to that worry.

Making his way into the kitchen, Luke opened the door that led out onto the decking.

"Would you like some tea?" He asked.

Nodding, Claire smiled at Luke, "Please." Encouraged, Luke began preparations for making tea.

Adam stopped what he was doing and headed for the kitchen door, "Dad can I have some orange juice please?"

"Hi, kiddo," Luke said in greeting, "of course you can, go and sit with Mum and I'll bring it out to you." Obediently Adam went to sit beside his Mum. Through the kitchen window, Luke watched

Claire lovingly put her arm around her son, it made him feel warm inside. A few minutes later he took Claire her tea, and handed a glass of fresh orange juice to Adam, who took it carefully in both hands. Now sitting on the arm of the bench seat, Luke put his arm around Claire.

Sipping her hot tea, Claire said half joking, "I think we need a bigger seat," meaning that their daughter's imminent birth and Claire's girth, left little room to comfortably seat three.

Luke gave her an affectionate squeeze in sympathy, again he had to acknowledge that her condition was of his making. In the beginning neither of them had thought that they could have children, Claire because of what had happened to her in her youth, Luke because of what he was, now they both knew differently, in future they would have to practice birth control. Luke certainly didn't want to put Claire through this again, it was making her thoroughly miserable and he didn't like it.

They sat for a few minutes enjoying the quiet and each

other's company, a bird's call intervened announcing that nature was alive and well in the metropolis. Adam straight away identified the itinerant songster as being a black bird, neither Luke nor Claire questioned Adam's hypothesis, if

Adam identified the bird song as belonging to a blackbird, then it was a blackbird, both of them knew better than to doubt their son's abilities when it came to identifying wild life.

The blackbird called a couple more times then moved on, they were left alone once more with the quiet, the muted traffic noise was always there of course in the back ground, it was just that they had become so used to it, that it no longer registered on their senses.

It was Claire who broke into their reverie, "Has Yasmin decided when they are going yet?" Claire asked.

"Next week I think," Luke answered, " I know they've been trying to find a nanny for Aisha ,but Yasmin is being very careful, so that's holding things up a bit," answered Luke.

"Well! You can't blame Yasmin for being choosy, she is only looking out for her daughter's welfare, and quite right too," said Claire.

"Just saying," added Luke," that's what's holding them up."

"If I hadn't have been pregnant, I would have taken Adam and gone with them", admitted Claire wistfully.

"And Yasmin would have welcomed you," agreed Luke. "Aisha would have been in safe hands."

Claire smiled at Luke's compliment, knowing that it was true, despite everything going on in their lives, Claire was a good mother.

"Have they said anything to you since I told Yasmin about Adam?" Claire asked.

“Frank’s mentioned it but didn’t say too much, just that he didn’t know how he and Yasmin would have coped if it was Aisha, Frank tends to keep his thoughts to himself, but I’m glad that he knows, it’s good to have him on side,” admitted Luke.

Adam sat listening to his Mum and Dad, quietly invisible. He knew that their conversation centred around his latest ability and knowing that Aunt Yasmin and Uncle Frank also knew, was a secret blessing. It was sometimes hard to hide his abilities, especially from people that Adam regarded as family, it made things that bit easier in case he slipped up, that’s how he saw it anyway.

“Has Frank told his security team that he’s leaving you in temporary charge, whilst they’re away in Jordan?” Claire asked.

“Yes! He’s already briefed them, no signs of discord, at least none that I’m aware of,” admitted Luke.

“Good, it’s better if no-one’s nose is put out of joint, especially at the club, we’ve enough problems at home, without adding to them at work,” Claire emphasized.

“Well I’ve worked with all the team at one time or another and I get on with each of them , so I’m not expecting any problems, it’s just a matter of delegating who does what, what rooms they work and then rotating, so that everyone takes their turn, including myself.”

“Sounds like you’ve got things covered mate,” admitted Claire, patting his arm for emphasis.

Chapter 98

The elusive search for a suitable child minder had almost prompted Yasmin into cancelling her proposed trip to Jordan. The so called professional child minding agencies that Yasmin had so far contacted proved totally unsuitable for her needs. The few candidates for the temporary position that she had interviewed so far, were wholly inadequate in her opinion. Maybe in hindsight, she was being too picky, but where her daughter was concerned she not only needed someone who was competent, but also someone she could trust. No-one she had interviewed so far could fit this criteria and time was running out, the end of the month was almost here and still no child minder. Yasmin hated to admit failure, but sooner than settle for second best, she realised that she may have to cancel the trip.

That night, a chance conversation by Frank, was eavesdropped on by one of Frank's female operatives. Brenda had been a solid member of Frank's security team for almost seven years and it was she who had overheard Frank discussing his dilemma with Luke. Stepping into the conversation, Brenda offered Frank a possible solution. Now it just so happened that Brenda's cousin, Amy, had once worked as a child minder/helper at a play school. She had enjoyed the work, but had become dissatisfied with the low pay. Fancying a change, Amy had been attracted by the higher pay on offer at Yasmin's club. It had been Yasmin herself who had interviewed Amy for the position of bar waitress almost three years ago and Amy had fitted in nicely at the club. She had an exemplary work record and was popular, as well as being hard working, all the qualities that Yasmin looked for in an employee.

Frank asked Brenda if she would mind sounding out her cousin, it was worth a shot he thought.

If Amy was interested in the temporary position, then the planned trip to Jordan may still go ahead.

Amy of course when asked, jumped at the chance, four or five weeks in the sun child minding, was just what the doctor ordered.

Now all Frank had to do was to arrange for Amy to go see Yasmin in their home, knowing his wife Yasmin would want to see Amy interacting with their daughter, before offering what amounted to giving a virtual stranger, access to her most cherished possession.

To cut a long story short Amy won Yasmin over. The verbal interview was short, words, in Yasmin's opinion were only words in this instance, but the physical interaction between Aisha and Amy was long, and at the end of it Yasmin was satisfied that Amy was more than adequate, and could be trusted with looking after her daughter.

It looked like the planned business trip could go ahead after all.

Chapter 99

The sleek aircraft had been cutting through the air for a little over three hours, they had all settled into some kind of routine by now. Boredom was offset by Yasmin fussing over her baby's needs. Amy was on board and willing to do any task that was required of her, but motherhood was still hard to abandon and besides Yasmin didn't feel the need to relinquish her maternal duties just yet. Even when they arrived in Jordan, she wasn't sure if she could entrust her baby's welfare in to Amy's capable hands. Yasmin knew she was being irrational, and perhaps a little selfish too she thought in hindsight, after all Amy had proven herself more than capable of looking after baby Aisha, it was what Yasmin was paying for her to do. However the bonds of motherhood were strong in Yasmin unlike her own brief childhood, Aisha had hardly ever left her side.

Yasmin's own mother had dutifully given birth to her as required, then promptly abandoned her to a series of virtual strangers, they had cared for her well enough, but she had never known the love that can only come from one's own mother, it had been left to her father to fill that empty void. That he had truly loved her was never in any doubt, she had embraced her father's love greedily, giving it back in equal measure. He had delighted in his daughter's adulation, secretly wishing that she had been born a boy. His own son Ali had been a bitter disappointment to him, he found him to be both inwardly cruel and mean, traits that probably helped to shape the man he was to become. Ali in turn was guided by his grandfather's teachings, who he openly adored.

That Ali and Yasmin shared the same parents, was the only thing that they had in common, as they were virtual strangers to one another in childhood, but their lives would be irrevocably altered forever when Yasmin's father decided to have his daughter educated in a private boarding school for girl's, in London. Aged only five, Yasmin had been sent to a foreign land and to a school filled with strangers.

At the outset she had been almost paralysed with fear, but soon came to realise that in order to survive she must quickly adapt. Already tutored from birth to speak responsible English and French, within three months, she had mastered the local English and had applied herself academically with zeal.

It was a pleasant change, remarked one of Yasmin's tutors, to find a pupil so willing to learn. Of course this caused Yasmin to stand out, and the local bullies saw her as easy meat. A bloody nose and a couple of black eyes soon taught them the error of their ways. Yasmin could fight, and would do so if provoked, the early days were a testing time for her, but grudgingly she earned her place.

Yasmin had thought mistakenly, that she was somehow

being punished by her father and now in a strange land she thought that she wouldn't see much of the man she so desperately loved. In fact, in this new place, she saw more of him than she had whilst living in Jordan.

Every weekend, providing it didn't interfere with her education, he would arrive with his chauffeur and take her to meet people of influence. Together they would visit the museums and stately homes and walk in the many parks dotted around London and eat delicious ice-cream.

Her father would ask about the subjects she was being taught, but more importantly to Yasmin, he asked what she herself was interested in. This was her happy time, Yasmin had her father exclusively to herself, and it was wonderful. In the school holidays, they would jet off to France, whilst there she would only speak in French, encouraged to do so by her Father, he delighted in showing her off to his friends.

Being so young, it never occurred to Yasmin that her father may have had mistresses both in London and France, it was only in later years that she would suspect him of having affairs both sides of the English channel. Although to his credit, he never paraded them in front of Yasmin, not that she could remember any way, but it did open her eyes to the possibility that her father's god like persona was less than perfect, perhaps like her, sadly, he was just human after all.

All this had been racing through Yasmin's mind as they skipped along the air currents.

Frank had noticed his wife's thoughtfulness, "Worried?" he asked suddenly

Yasmin looked at her husband quizzically, then, "A little, yes!" she admitted.

"You'll be fine," encouraged Frank, "just show them who's boss."

"Oh, I intend to, don't worry," replied Yasmin emphatically, but saying it, didn't make it a foregone conclusion, she was head of the Hussein empire yes! But the part of the world to where she was now heading, was mainly dominated by macho male ugliness and all that that implied. Women in most Arab states were seen as inferior persons, for the most part possessions rather than partners, Yasmin was heading into a world where women were required to be subservient, when in the company of men. That attitude would be extremely difficult to overcome, however Yasmin was their boss, and if they weren't prepared to respect her right to manage her own business affairs, then she would replace them with people who would. She was quite prepared to listen to a person's point of view but only up to a certain point, if it was at odds with her own business sense, she would explain her reasoning behind it, then expect to have her will enacted upon.

One way or another, she intended to run her business her way, there could only be one captain on any ship.

Chapter 100

Doug Simons had showered and shaved with care, taking his time with it. Ever since he'd learned about his former boss' death, Doug had been mulling over what he really thought about it. James Martin, was still very much a mystery to him, apart from Martin's obvious intelligence, what did Doug really know about the man? Not much at all really, he had to admit. James Martin, Doug's former boss and mentor, was still a question mark to him, and as far as Doug knew, he was the only person at M.I.6.who had had any real meaningful dialogue with the man. No-one could even claim friendship with the poor sod, including himself, Doug had to admit.

Yesterday, he had received a note from one of Mary Wallace's minions, with instructions to present himself today at headquarters fit for a military funeral. Upon inquiry as to who's funeral to attend, he was told James Martin's. It hadn't really surprised him to hear of Martin's death, the last time he had seen the man it had shocked Doug to the core, James had looked more dead than alive in that military hospital bed. All Doug's subsequent inquiries as to what had happened to Martin to put him in that bed had so far drawn a blank, it was a puzzle and Doug didn't like puzzles, especially ones that he couldn't solve. He had laid out his clothes on the bed, navy blue suit, crisp white shirt, black tie and socks, Doug's shoes had been meticulously shined so as to pass muster, it was the least he could do for the poor bastard, he owed Martin that much thought Doug. Checking himself one last time in the mirror, Doug nodded his approval to his reflection, it was time to go.

Arriving at M.I.6.Headquarters, Doug signed himself in, he got some quizzical looks from some people, perhaps unaccustomed to seeing him so smartly turned out for work but no-one passed comment about it, at least not within Doug's hearing. That he was to accompany Mary Wallace, the head of M.I.6. to the funeral, had surprised Doug, but upon reflection perhaps Martin had earned the right to have the director at his graveside. After all, it had been Martin's painstaking sifting of intelligence that had pointed M.I.6. to Abdul Rahman in Afghanistan. Doug had merely had to follow his ex -boss's trail of bread crumbs, and with a little logic of his own, and perhaps a sprinkling of luck, had found Rahman's hidden stronghold.

Doug had stuck his neck out when presenting his theory and plan of action to the joint Chiefs of Staff in the director's boardroom. No-one had been more surprised than Doug, when later he had learned that they had approved his findings, and then acted upon them. The rest was history, as they say, but it had cost Doug a few sleepless nights.

Nevertheless, it had earned Doug quick promotion and a modicum of respect within the walls of M.I.6. That it was all due to James Martin's initial intelligence gathering was not lost on Doug, he knew that he owed the man a considerable debt, attending his funeral as a mark of respect was the least he could do.

Doug was stood talking to Alan Parker, Head of Operations, London, when he was approached by Tony Coombes, one of Mary Wallace's personal security detail, Doug felt a prickle of unease underneath his shirt collar, as he broke off his conversation to speak to Coombes.

"Are you looking for me?" Doug said. Coombes replied, "Yes sir, the director's sent me to collect you."

Quickly, following Coombes to the lift, Doug said worriedly, "Christ! I'm not late am I?"

Looking bemused at Doug's worried expression, Coombes said, "No sir, you're not late the director wants to get back on the road, she hates funerals." Doug breathed out an audible sigh of relief, much to Coombes' obvious amusement. That such a diminutive woman could have such an obvious effect on most of the male population, was a mystery to Coombes, he personally found Mary Wallace to be a straight talking, downright decent sort of person, with a wicked sense of humour.

That she was his boss, made no difference to Coombes, there had been other bosses before Mary

Wallace, and there would be bosses after Mary Wallace, just saw his position as a job and nothing more. That he would give his life to protect her's never entered the equation, it was just part of the job description. Coming out of the lift into the underground car park, Coombes led Doug to the second of the two vehicles. Opening the rear door for Doug, he slid in beside the diminutive form of Mary Wallace.

"Ma'am," was all he said in greeting, Coombes got in

front beside the driver. The front vehicle, containing the four silhouettes of Mary's designated security detail, led the way. Keeping at least two cars distance behind them they followed, as they stopped and started, bobbed and weaved their way out of London, Doug finally started to relax, nothing had been said by any of the vehicles occupants, as they headed in a north-easterly direction, towards Colchester. On a whim, Doug broke the silence asking the director if she knew the cause of Martin's death.

Swallowing hard, she nodded in affirmation and after a short pause, she replied to Doug's question. "Pneumonia, I'm told--- they tried to combat it with antibiotics of course, but Mr. Martin's immune system was very low, and as a result he failed to respond to treatment, and sadly, he died."

"Thank you ma'am," Doug replied.

After another pause, she asked Doug," Were you close, you and Mr Martin?"

Doug thought carefully before answering, "No Ma'am, we weren't close," he had to admit.

Mary Wallace just nodded, giving nothing away. Doug had thought for a millisecond whether to claim friendship with Martin, then dismissed the idea, because that would have been a lie, so he chose to tell the truth instead, a dangerous thing to do, when your chosen profession was that of a Spook. Silence once again pervaded the vehicle right up to reaching the entrance gates to Colchester barracks. The lead vehicle came to a stop and was inspected by the guards manning the gate. When the barrier was finally lifted, the director's vehicle was allowed entrance without being stopped, after a circuitous route around the base, the lead car pulled into the side and came to a stop, the director's vehicle came to a stop behind it,

An army chaplain and what appeared to be the C.O. of

Colchester Barracks, stood side by side waiting to welcome the director. Her security detail, fanned out in a protective cordon around Mary

Wallace's vehicle, Tony Coombes opened his boss' door, alert to any sign of threat. Just because they were on a British military base in England, it made no difference, they were trained to protect their boss from enemies either foreign or domestic. Mary Wallace ignored the protective screen around her, as she approached the C.O. first, shaking his hand lightly, he then introduced her to the army chaplain, who in turn shook hands with Mary.

She didn't introduce Doug, who alongside Tony Coombes followed them into the small brick built chapel. Doug was surprised to find that the place was almost full, on closer inspection, he realised it was mostly made up of service personnel, both male and female. Obviously the C.O. had ordered a full turnout for the occasion. The two front pews were left empty, save for two seated officers, Doug recognised the uniforms that they were wearing as belonging to that of the United

States Marine Corps, curiouser and curiouser thought Doug. Mary Wallace must have known who the Americans were, as she joined them on the front pews. Doug sat behind his boss on the second pew, with a couple of her security detail. Tony Coombes, taking a careful look around the room, slid onto the seat beside his boss. Doug idly wondered if he was armed, then admonished himself for being so stupid, of course they were armed, a fat lot of good they'd be, if they weren't.

The wooden coffin was centrally placed and slightly forward of the congregation, it had been draped in the Union flag, as befitting a member of the armed forces. As the service began, Doug's ears pricked up as he learned that

James Martin's career had begun in military intelligence, straight from university. Doug hadn't known that, and as the service continued, he managed to fill in a few more blanks for himself, and it was only now that Doug had come to realise, that Martin, had earned the right of a military funeral. He wished now in hindsight, that had he known more about Martin's background, he would have taken more trouble to get to know the man, perhaps a lot of us regret such things, but in Doug's case it was true.

At the end of the service, the congregation followed the coffin to its final resting place in the small well kept military cemetery, and as Doug looked around at those gathered there, he wondered just how many of them knew the man who had been laid to rest, probably a handful, was Doug's sad estimation. Shots were fired over the coffin, the Union flag was removed and folded, but sadly there were no known relatives to receive it. As the coffin was lowered into the earth the last post was sounded, more than one person had goose-bumps at the graveside, Doug included.

Doug was one of the last to leave the open grave, throwing earth onto the coffin he said his own silent farewell to James Martin, he hadn't expected that the burial would be conducted with full military honours, not in a million years, but he had been glad that it had been. Martin, for all his faults, had deserved one.

Walking away from the graveside, Doug was approached by the senior of the two American officers, he introduced himself to Doug as Colonel Anders U.S.M.C. Doug shook the Colonel's hand warmly, wondering why he had been singled out for the honour. Colonel Anders explained that Mary Wallace had credited Doug as being the one who had pin-pointed Abdul Rahman's likely stronghold in Afghanistan.

This was too much for Doug, he couldn't in all conscience accept the laurels that so rightly belonged to another man, he quickly told the Colonel of his misconception, rightly attributing the accolade to the hard work of the man that they had just buried.

Anders immediately warmed to this young man, realising that he was genuinely unused to being singled out for praise. "Don't be so modest son, I'm well aware of James Martin's contribution in our fight against terrorism, but you've earned my thanks and my praise, you've helped to rid the world of a monster." Faced with a full Colonel's appreciation, Doug accepted the praise with a shy smile, they walked back to Mary Wallace's small gathering together. She was just saying her farewells to the C.O. who had been trying his best to coax her into meeting his fellow officers in the officer's mess, but Mary was having none of it, and politely declined his invitation. She was eager to return to the capital.

Sadly, as a guest of the British Government, Colonel Anders couldn't escape so easily. He and his fellow officer as Americans, would have to endure the tedious military protocol that was required of them. There was no getting out of it for them, sadly they would have to perform for their British hosts.

On the way back to London Doug broke the silence once more, "I wasn't aware that James Martin's background came from the military ma'am," ventured Doug.

Turning to him, Mary said, "It's not that surprising surely," wondering where this was leading, "most of our recruits come from some sort of military background."

"I just wasn't aware that James Martin had a military background ma'am, that's why I asked," explained Doug.

"Well rest assured Doug, we recruit intelligent people

from all sorts of backgrounds and walks of life, not just the military. Intelligent people are in short supply, that's why we recruited you," finished Mary.

Doug realised that he had just been paid a compliment by the director of M.I.6., that made two in one day, if he wasn't careful, he was liable to become swell headed.

Chapter 101

Claire had made herself as comfortable as possible, in the circumstances. Being pregnant didn't leave much room to manoeuvre, but being surrounded by cushions certainly helped. Adam had somehow managed to wriggle himself tight against his Mum's abdomen and the back of the settee.

It was a rare glimpse of domesticated bliss. Claire was fondly stroking Adam's hair, and he was milking it for all his worth, enjoying the experience immensely. Though Adam was the first to break the spell, "When will my sister be born, Mum?" he suddenly asked.

"Soon," was all Claire said, unhelpfully Adam pondered her answer before asking ,"Does it hurt?"

When faced with Adam's questions, Claire had to be careful what she said, both her and Luke had always been as honest as possible when answering their son's questions. "Yes Adam, it does hurt," she admitted. Adam remained silent for a while, thinking about what she had just said, then out of the blue he said-----"My sister will come early." Claire stiffened at Adam's words knowing that he was rarely wrong about such things.

"Do you know this for a fact Adam, or are you just guessing?" she asked.

"She will be two weeks early," declared Adam, with a certainty that defied logic.

As Claire digested this latest information, she quietly did the maths in her head, counting back from the due date that she had been given, then realised, that two weeks here or there, wasn't that big a deal. Calmly, she said, "I'll just have to have my suitcase packed a little bit earlier then, won't I?"

Adam didn't answer her, but she felt his head nod, under her ministrations, if in fact Adam was correct and Claire had no reason to doubt her son's prediction, she would be happy to give birth to her daughter earlier than expected. Claire had always been pragmatic when given a due date for delivery, maintaining that a baby would come when it was good and ready, but if it should come early, all well and good, so be it, this may have sounded brutal to a stranger's ear, but she was tired of carrying it around, both her and Luke had decided that this baby would be their last, two was enough. This had been a most uncomfortable pregnancy throughout for Claire, that her unborn daughter was wanted, was never in any doubt, it was just all the unwanted side effects of being pregnant, that had made Claire want it to be over. She just wanted to feel-normal again. Then Claire threw in a question of her own, for her son.

"Are you ready for a sister Adam?"

"I don't know," said Adam, disarmingly honest for one so young, then after thinking about it, he said brightly,

"If she's like Lizzie, that would be good."

Claire thought for a while, trying to conjure up a picture of Lizzie in her mind, then remembered, Lizzie from the park. Of course, Christ! Thought Claire, it seemed ages ago since she was in the park, but to Adam it was like yesterday, Claire idly wondered what Lizzie was doing now, probably started school she thought, which sadly brought back to her, the problem of what to do about

Adam's schooling. Adam must have picked up on what his Mum was thinking, because as usual he jumped straight in, "I would like to go to that school we picked out Mum, I think it would be good for me."

"I'm certain that it would Adam, but we've spoken about this haven't we? It only takes one person to see you using your gifts, and we are toast, we would have to leave this place and try to find somewhere safe."

It was heart- breaking for Claire, to dash her son's hopes in this way, but it was necessary, until they could solve this impasse, they were faced with an impossible dilemma.

"But I promise I will be careful," pleaded Adam.

"I know Adam and I sympathise with you, please believe me, but the problem is, you're only a child and it would be a huge responsibility on your shoulders, besides, it's not just you that would be affected, it would be the whole family. Just one person witnessing your gifts, would make our lives impossible."

These truths clearly upset Adam, as they were hard to hear, but they needed saying, neither Claire nor Luke shirked their responsibilities when it came to Adam's welfare and not until they were absolutely certain that Adam could control his abilities, would they risk sending him to school. That it was blindingly obvious that it was the right place to send him was a no-brainer, but the school yard was a viper's nest, full of traps and pitfalls for the unwary, an innocent, like Adam would be eaten alive. No, Adam would have to be home schooled by Claire and Luke if necessary, or until he could safely control his abilities. In fairness to Adam, Claire had to admit that he had been trying hard to hide his gifts, this gave her and Luke a modicum of hope for the future. Perhaps one day they may be able to send him to school, but not yet, he just wasn't ready. Trying to be positive and to cheer Adam up, Claire said, "Perhaps when your sister is born, you could try to help teach her some of the things you've learned yourself."

Adam looked up at his Mum, clearly interested in this new possibility, "Really, could I?" he asked, hopefully.

"Of course, it's how we learn-but not the mischievous things," finished Claire, tweaking his nose.

This made Adam laugh, which was Claire's intention all along, her son had enough seriousness in his life, without adding to it. Claire had to smile, when Adam started speaking to his unborn sister, as if she was already here.

"I will teach you all that I know Ruth, I promise," said Adam.

Adam, using Ruth's name, made it more real for Claire, she hoped with all her heart that her son and daughter would at least be good friends, there was no guarantee for these things of course, but that's what she hoped. Claire knew, from Yasmin's own experience, that sibling rivalry wasn't always a harmonious affair. Claire was sorry to break up this endearing little scene, but she had to go and pee, again.

Chapter 102

Ever since the Hussein's family jet had come to a stop and the steps had been lowered, Frank had stood by, idly watching, whilst others did the heavy lifting. The sleek aircraft had been met by a large black people carrier that bore the Hussein family logo, a desert palm tree. The driver of the vehicle had been accompanied by the head of security based at the hotel where they would be staying.

Yasmin had made herself known to both the driver and security man, then introduced them to

Frank, naming him as her husband, watching their reactions as they all formally shook hands. In an effort to help, Frank offered to lend a hand with loading the baggage, it was as if Frank had slapped them, it was simply beyond their understanding that their employer should have to stoop to such a lowly task as manual labour. So Frank had had to step back and watch with his thumb up his arse, whilst all the baggage was loaded into the people carrier. Yasmin by comparison, had no such qualms about watching other people doing the heavy lifting. It had been engraved into her skin from the moment of her birth and besides, she was the one who was paying their wages. But Frank had always toted his own kit, first whilst in the army and then again as a private citizen so it still made him feel uncomfortable, having to watch whilst others laboured on his behalf.

Amy, Aisha's temporary guardian, had no such scruples watching others stow her luggage, she decided that she could get used to this type of lifestyle very easily, thank-you very much. Once Aisha was safely aboard, they made their way to the Western Palms Hotel, Amman. It was obvious that the driver was in touch with someone at the hotel, as he was giving them constant updates on their estimated time of arrival, clearly, there was a reception committee of some kind awaiting them thought Yasmin, she had to smile to herself as the thought crossed her mind, that they seemed very nervous, perhaps that was a good thing, as she was feeling slightly nervous herself. As with all journeys, it had to come to an end and their driver pulled into a space, large enough to accommodate three vehicles. A dozen or so people, most of them decked out in the hotel's livery, awaited them, all that it lacked was a rolled out red carpet. A very tall, handsome bearded man stepped forward to welcome them, he looked to be, thought Yasmin, in his early fifties and was impeccably dressed in a light grey pinstriped suit. The driver of the vehicle had already alighted in order to open Yasmin's door, the pinstriped gentleman, immediately stepped forward in order to greet her.

Bowing his head slightly, he offered her his hand, "Welcome, Miss Hussein."

Yasmin took his hand, smiling, "Thank-you Mr Malik," as she read his name from the name tag visible on his breast pocket.

Meanwhile Frank had let himself out of the vehicle and came to stand beside his wife. "But, it's Mrs Hussein now," Yasmin explained, "and this is my husband Frank."

Once again, Mr Malik offered his hand, this time to Frank and it was warmly shaken, as the introductions continued. Next came baby Aisha, safely supported by Amy. Looking down into the baby's wide awake eyes caused Mr. Malik to audibly gasp, "Oh! You have been truly blessed Mrs Hussein." Yasmin, of course, was genuinely delighted by Mr Malik's observation. "Yes Mr. Malik, I think you're right, we have."

They were all a little tired from the journey and sorely in need of a shower and change of clothing, but protocol and good manners demanded that they be formally introduced to the people who were standing in line, waiting to greet them.

Mr. Malik, it turned out, had been the hotel's manager for almost thirty years and had aligned the various heads of department directly in front of the main entrance, in order to greet with the new head of the Hussein Empire personally. Everyone who was anyone, knew of course that a proper meeting of the various heads of department, was scheduled to take place tomorrow, at ten o'clock in the hotel's boardroom. Still, it had been a nice touch of Mr Malik's and Yasmin appreciated it.

After introductions had been concluded, Mr. Malik ushered them into the lift, and they rode up to the corridor that housed the Penthouse Suite. As the lift doors opened, he walked briskly ahead and had the Penthouse Suite's door open to coincide with their arrival. Standing to one side, Mr Malik allowed them access, then crossed the threshold himself, handing the door key personally into Yasmin's hand. He then said, "I hope that you will find everything to your satisfaction Mrs Hussein, but if you require anything further, please do not hesitate to let reception know, and it will be taken care of."

Meanwhile Amy, who had crossed the Hussein's threshold still holding tight to baby Aisha, looked a little lost. Mr Malik saw Amy's confusion and came gallantly to her rescue. "Forgive me miss, we have put you in the room just down the corridor, so that you will be close to your mistress," explained Mr Malik. Amy relinquished hold of her charge to Yasmin, who readily received her, then followed the hotel manager to what was to be her room for the duration of their stay.

Again, Mr Malik opened Amy's door for her, but this time stayed out in the corridor. He handed the room key over to her and told her that if she required anything, she only had to contact reception and an army of helpers would be only too happy to help. With that, he turned and headed to the lift.

Once Amy had closed the door, she couldn't help but smile to herself. The room, even though it was clearly meant for the owner's hired help, was absolutely luxurious, and was far superior to anything and anywhere that she had ever stayed before. She experimentally tested the firmness of the mattress whilst waiting for her cases to arrive, it certainly met with her approval, idly she thought, this just gets better and better.

Meanwhile back at the Penthouse Suite, Yasmin's first priorities were for the welfare of her daughter; a wash first, change of clothes and food for her in that order. Once the luggage had been delivered, Frank immediately sought out his toiletry bag for his shaving kit, he was mindful of his new position of husband to the new head of the Hussein Empire, but had to admit that it was taking some getting used to. The least he could do, whilst he was here at any rate, was to portray himself as a well groomed smartly dressed man and one worthy of such a good looking woman.

Frank was under no illusions at all, that he was married to a very wealthy and powerful woman, yes, but in the eyes of most Arabs, he was still a westerner, an unbeliever, Infidel. Everything that went against their way of thinking. So, whilst he was here, he was going to have to be a model husband so as not to embarrass his wife. Frank knew that it wasn't going to be easy. Once he had shaved, showered and changed, he minded his daughter while Yasmin showered away the grime and weariness of travel. Later, once she had dressed, Yasmin went to see Amy. Knocking lightly on Amy's door, she was ushered inside and Yasmin was secretly pleased to see that Amy had dressed appropriately, as per her guidelines. She had taken great pains to stress to Amy, the importance of being aware, that the culture here, was far different to that of the west,

Although, Jordan was a reasonably tolerant country, it was still an Arab country. Alcohol abuse, inappropriate dress away from the swimming pool and lewd behaviour, could well land you in a prison cell. Yasmin had told Amy that her duties towards her daughter would be conducted as a business arrangement between the hours of 9am to 5pm on a daily basis, excepting Sundays. Which were to be her days off. Her duties were to see to her daughter's needs; changing, feeding and minding her between those hours. She could take her meals in the hotel's restaurant if she so wished, as it was child friendly and catered for them accordingly, or she could order her meals to be taken in her room, if she preferred, it really wasn't a problem.

Yasmin stressed that if she decided to spend her day

beside the pool, Amy was to inform reception, who would then detail a security man to discreetly watch over them.

This, Yasmin told her was none negotiable, she then explained to a wide eyed Amy, that as the new head of the Hussein Empire, the threat of her daughter being abducted, was very , very real. Amy had only just begun to realise that far from it being the holiday she had envisaged, it was turning out to be a very responsible position to which she had been appointed.

Yasmin wasn't quite finished. She also insisted, that on no account, was she to leave the safety of the hotel, whilst in charge of her daughter. She could venture outside in her own time of course, but she was to be mindful that she was in an Islamic country and bound by its strict laws.

Once this had had time to sink in, Yasmin told her that she was to bring her daughter back to her suite, at 5 o'clock each day, after which, Yasmin handed her a mobile phone. It already had

Yasmin's number in on speed dial, and reminded Amy that should she need to contact her for any reason regarding her daughter, she should not hesitate to do so. Then as an afterthought and totally unnecessary, she reminded Amy to have it with her at all times. Not wanting to overwhelm

Amy further, Yasmin tried to ease her obvious tension, by saying, "I'm sure that all these precautions will prove unnecessary, but please take care of my daughter, there are evil men in this world Amy."

After Yasmin had gone, a very worried Amy sat on the bed, reflecting back on everything that she had just been told. She had only just begun to realise the enormity of her newly appointed position.

"Fuck! What the hell have I got myself into?" she said out loud.

Chapter 103

The Western Palm's Hotel

Yasmin had reluctantly relinquished hold of her daughter into Amy's more than capable hands.

Even now, only twenty minutes after watching her leave the Penthouse Suite, she kept anxiously looking at her mobile phone expecting it to ring. It was now the only link that kept her in touch with Amy and by extension with her daughter Aisha.

Frank had watched his wife very closely, he knew that she was struggling in letting go of her daughter, for what was the very first time. Coming up behind her, he clasped his hands around his wife's middle to try and reassure her that their daughter was in safe hands. "She'll be fine, put the phone in your bag, and let's go," he whispered in her ear.

Yasmin smiled back at him nervously, realising that he

was right. She was being totally ridiculous,

Amy had proven herself more than capable of looking after their daughter. Pulling herself together, she reached for her bag and dropped the phone inside. Then spinning in Frank's arms to face him, she steeled herself, "Right, let's go," she said with renewed authority.

Frank had to smile, Yasmin when in business mode could be pretty scary. Hell, she even managed to frighten him and that took some doing.

Yasmin entered the boardroom first, closely followed by Frank. She was pleased to see that the manager and all the heads of department were already there, awaiting their arrival. As one, all of those seated, stood to properly welcome the new face of the Hussein Empire, clapping enthusiastically.

Yasmin, whose outward appearance was both elegant and assured, breathed in an inner sigh of relief at this unexpected show of courtesy, especially as most of the heads of department were male. This certainly exceeded her expectations and boded well for a happy transition of power. Taking her place at the head of the highly polished table, she paused whilst trying to frame a suitable response. Yasmin couldn't help but notice the vacant chair immediately to her right, obviously it had been left for her husband Frank. That small thing definitely made a favourable impression on Yasmin and the room lit up when she smiled her approval.

"Thank-you for your warm welcome," she began, "for those of you who don't already know, this is my husband Frank," who she indicated to by hand. "He speaks with my authority, in all things."

Looking around the room, Yasmin quietly waited whilst those words sank in, "Now, as we have much to discuss, please be seated and we'll begin."

The meeting went well, so well in fact, that it overran into the lunch break. Mr Malik the hotel manager, had contributed greatly to the meeting's success. He had quietly commented on the fact, to Yasmin, that not since her late father's death, had they had such a harmonious meeting, with the owner sat at the head of the table.

Yasmin was incredulous to hear such a thing.

"You mean to say, that my brother never chaired a meeting Mr Malik---how is that possible?" Yasmin asked, as much to herself, as to Mr Malik.

Then coming to her own conclusion, she asked him, "How on earth did anything manage to get done?"

Not sure if it was prudent for him to speak freely, he took a risk, and did so anyway. "I contacted your brother personally by email, telling him what the problem was and what was needed and he basically just threw money at the problem," explained Malik.

Yasmin nodded her head, "Typical of my brother," she let slip, in a rare unguarded moment. Realising that she had spoken her thoughts out loud, she said, "Please forgive me Mr Malik, one should not speak ill of the dead."

"Nothing to forgive Mrs Hussein, then if I may speak freely."

"Please do," Yasmin encouraged.

"For a long time we have managed to keep this hotel afloat, although at times I have to admit, that it seemed to be like a rudderless ship. Finally, now I think we have a good captain," admitted Malik.

Taken aback for a moment by Mr Malik's praise, Yasmin took a breath, "Thank you Mr Malik, I will do my best to prove your good faith in me. Now, as the meeting is concluded and everyone else seems to have left us, I think we should go and get some lunch, don't you?"

“Yes of course, will you be ordering it to be sent to your suite,” enquired Mr Malik.

“No, Frank and I will eat in the restaurant, with the hotel guests,” she replied.

Malik was secretly pleased by Yasmin’s answer. He believed at long last, that here was someone he could work with. “In that case, Mr and Mrs Hussein, bon appetite,” he said, before leaving them alone in the boardroom.

After he had left, Yasmin turned to Frank for his input, “How do you think it went?”

“You were bloody magnificent, you had them practically eating out of your hand, especially Mr Malik. You do know, that he has a serious hard-on for you, don’t you,” teased Frank.

“He does not!” groaned Yasmin, with feigned embarrassment.

“Does too,” insisted Frank, still teasing, “but seeing you, I can’t say as I really blame him,” Frank winked for emphasis.

Yasmin couldn’t help smiling, “Come on, let’s go and see what the foods like.”

As they turned to go, Yasmin saw the three, large framed photographs that hung on the end wall. Her grand-father’s stood central, in pride of place. He seemed to stare right through Yasmin, as though disapproving of her right to be here. He was dressed in traditional Arab clothing, and had the look of a man forged and tempered on the anvil that was the desert.

His clothing, reminded her of Omar Sharif, in Lawrence of Arabia, but there the resemblance ended.

Yasmin’s grand-father was nothing like Omar Sharif, his face was hard and lined from his life spent out in the desert.

Frank, breaking into her thoughts asked, "Do you remember him?"

She simply answered, "No." Her father's photograph was hung below and to one side, it was totally different, of course, Yasmin's father was handsome by comparison. That and the fact he favoured western clothing. The photograph spoke volumes for anyone who cared to look, as he was nothing like her grandfather. Then, there was her brother AIi, he hung on a level beside her father. Ali too, favoured traditional Arab dress, and was more like his grandfather in looks.

Yasmin felt only bitterness when confronted by his image, it brought back bad memories---not content, with having had a hand in her father's murder, he had also tried to have Yasmin and Frank murdered in London. She had more than a fleeting suspicion that their own mother had also been complicit in her father's murder. Going one step further, Yasmin reasoned that she wouldn't have been entirely surprised, if her own mother hadn't been privy to Ali's attempt on her life. In fact she was almost certain of it.

Frank broke into her thoughts once more, "Ready?"

She just nodded in response, and left the portraits in peace.

Chapter 104

Claire's Residence

Claire, on a whim, had invited Chris over for dinner. It wasn't anything fancy, just pork chops and a few vegetables. Simple fare, but good wholesome food, besides it was a bit better than beans on toast and takeaways, which was probably what Chris was surviving on. Today it was Luke's turn to cook, carefully watched over by Claire. This wasn't really necessary, as he was quite a capable cook and knew what he was doing, although it was proving to be a hard habit for her to break.

Luke really didn't mind her fussing as he quite liked her company and besides he thought it made her feel useful.

Chris hadn't seen Adam in a while and was truly amazed to see how much he had grown. No sooner had he arrived and hung up his coat, when Adam was eagerly leading him outside so that he could show off his footballing skills. In the end, Chris enjoyed kicking the ball around just as much as Adam.

After dinner, they watched a little television, in companionable ease, just chatting about everyday things without being interested in the programme when the telephone rang. Claire eased her way over towards it and picked up. It was Sheryl, so Claire knew that she was in for a lengthy chat. They caught up on many things in the next twenty minutes or so. Claire asked how her pregnancy was going, and she also enquired about Claire's. The only difference in their situations being, that she was enjoying the experience, and Claire wasn't. In fact, all the usual questions that one asks, when friends are separated by distance, yet Claire had an uneasy feeling that Sheryl had something important to tell her, but was reluctant to give it voice.

In the end impatience got the better of Claire and she asked her outright if she was holding something back. There was an audible gap in the conversation whilst Sheryl wrestled over whether to spill the beans. In the end, friendship trumped caution and she told Claire what she had been so reluctant to say.

She had seen Daniel McFee, his appearance had obviously changed over the years, but she was certain that it was him. He was a little fatter in the face and had grown a full face beard and a moustache, but apart from that it was the same Daniel McFee. Sheryl said that it made sense for him to be back in Lincoln, as the family had just buried Seamus McFee, Daniel's father.

Claire listened to Sheryl's news with mixed feelings and wondered how she really felt about it.

The last time that anyone had seen McFee, was after he

had attacked Claire and a warrant had been made out for his arrest. As far as they knew, that warrant, although made out years ago, was still valid. Obviously, his father's death had made him risk coming back to Lincoln. It was a gamble, as criminal family funerals often attracted the attention of the police, just to see who turned up. Claire thanked Sheryl for her call, wished her well and told her to be careful.

Later when Chris had said goodbye, Claire told Luke the gist of Sheryl's conversation and he asked if she thought she was in any kind of danger, she didn't think so.

It seemed more likely that he was here on family business. Now that his father was dead and buried, he was effectively the head of the McFee criminal enterprise. After Adam had been put to bed, Claire went to have a long soak in the bathtub. Sheryl's phone call had brought back a lot of long forgotten memories. The whole sequence of events that had happened all those years ago had come flooding back with crystal clarity. She ticked them off in her mind, one by one.

The brutal attack by McFee, Luke's fortuitous arrival just as she was kicked into unconsciousness, meaning that she neither saw Luke's arrival, nor what happened next, but James and Sheryl did. Days later they had told her that Luke had given McFee the mother and father of a beating that had left him bleeding and unconscious, in the Legion Club's car park. Then of course it was down to James and Luke's quick thinking that probably helped to save her life.

Instead of ringing and waiting for an ambulance to arrive, they took her to A&E themselves in James' car. Further quick thinking by the doctors and nurses in A&E had assessed her injuries as being potentially life threatening and then there was the inescapable fact that a surgical team had been already on site, prepped and ready to go. How likely was that? Claire had never really thought about it logically until now. It was as if all the ducks in the shooting gallery had been neatly aligned.

Things like that just didn't happen, not in the real world anyway. She had later learned, when she was considered to be well enough to take in the information, that at the time of the attack, she had been pregnant. She had lost the baby as a result of the kicking received, as well as one of her ovaries and was told that it was unlikely that she would be able to have children in the future. Happily, she thought, we had proved that hypothesis, to be wrong too. No, there were just too many lucky coincidences at play here, she honestly believed that what happened all those years ago was meant to happen and she was meant to spend her life as Luke's companion. It would probably sound fanciful saying this to someone else, but that's what she chose to believe. The coincidences that fell into place that night, were just too fantastic for her to think otherwise.

Chapter 105

The Western Palms Hotel, Amman

Their time spent at the Western Palms Hotel, passed all too quickly. It wasn't meant to be a holiday, it was primarily a fact finding mission for Yasmin to determine whether the hotel was being managed and run properly, but more importantly, whether it was profitable. A close scrutiny of the books had revealed that they were in order, the hotel had been making a profit, in spite of Ali, Yasmin's late brother, having spent a considerable sum of money both refurbishing and up-grading the Hussein hotel chain.

Yasmin was satisfied that the staff at the hotel had more than earned the raise of two and a half percent that she proposed to award them. It was after all, they who had put in all the hard work, so it was only right and fair that they should be rewarded for their effort. Yasmin was of the opinion that in order to see how things were done, she needed to see them for herself. She had accompanied a very uneasy catering manager, unannounced into the kitchens. Without fear, Yasmin checked inside the food lockers and storage areas. Then unafraid, she checked every utensil and work surface, in relation to hygiene and the preparation of food. Finally, she watched some of the dishes being prepared and cooked. The heat in the kitchen was quite intense, but if anyone objected to Yasmin's intrusive presence, no-one gave voice to it, at least not within her hearing. In the end, Yasmin gave the kitchens and its staff her solid seal of approval. The food wasn't bad either. The chefs at the Western catered for European and Middle Eastern tastes. Yasmin's only adverse comment to the catering manager wasn't so much a criticism, but as perhaps a helpful suggestion.

She merely pointed out, that as more and more Chinese tourists were choosing to stay at the hotel, perhaps they might try and put some Chinese dishes on the menu. Hopefully, it was taken in the spirit that it was given, and as merely a helpful suggestion.

Yasmin liked to be unpredictable, choosing to latch onto one of the managers, unannounced. And so it was, with the domestic cleaning staff, that one day she arrived armed with a master door key. She let herself into the guest's rooms, usually right after the domestic cleaning staff had just finished cleaning them. Mostly Yasmin found everything satisfactory, but if not, she wasn't afraid to go and get the cleaner who was responsible for that room and point out to her, what it was that she wasn't happy about. Often a quiet word, spoken in a reasonable manner, sorted out the problem. After a day or two, word must have gotten around the hotel, because standards improved.

Frank for his part wasn't idle either. He had taken the trouble of getting to know the security staff by name and not just the ones on the day shift, the ones on the night shift as well. He cast a critical eye over where the security cameras were sited and if he thought that they would better serve in a more favourable position, he pointed it out to the head of security. For the most part, Frank was happy with the hotel's security arrangements. The only real criticism he had was a short-fall in the number of security staff employed, particularly on the night shift. Frank felt that another security man or woman was needed to better serve the hotel's needs. Also a side gate, close to the swimming pool area, was vulnerable to incursion by outsiders not staying at the hotel. An electronic gate lock could be easily installed and then the hotel's guests could use it to either gain entry or exit by using their own room key card. It was just common sense really, thought Frank, but other than that, the security at the hotel was in reasonably good shape.

The other thing on Frank's mind was one that he could easily solve, although he had to do it without Yasmin's knowledge. Asking Mr Malik if he knew of a decent photographer's shop close by was a rather obvious thing to do, of course he did.

A young Japanese woman had opened a studio not far from the hotel and it was Mr Malik himself who arranged for her to come to the hotel to meet with Frank. He had the devil of a job keeping this assignation with the young woman secret from his wife. He could almost feel his testicles being surgically removed by Yasmin, should she jump to the wrong conclusion.

Now standing in the boardroom with the young Japanese woman by his side, Frank showed her Yasmin's family portraits. "I need a framed photograph of my wife, roughly the same size as these," he indicated.

"And do you wish me to take a photograph of your wife? Or do you have some of your own?" she asked him.

Frank said that he had some on his phone, and clumsily tried to bring them up for her to view.

Watching him struggling for a few seconds must have seemed like an eternity for the young woman thought Frank. Wordlessly, she indicated that he should hand it over, then using just one hand, she deftly brought up the stored photographs, enlarged them, then went through the images one by one.

Frank looked carefully at each picture, trying to decide which one to choose. He liked one in particular, but the young woman had a critical eye and carried on viewing them all, until she stopped at one of Yasmin in a more defined pose. In the end Frank had to admit that the young woman's choice was much better than his own. She transferred it onto something that looked like it belonged on the bridge of the Star Ship Enterprise and said, "I will have this ready for you by noon tomorrow, will that be okay?"

"Yes fine," said Frank---Then remembering, he said, "Oh, I've just realised something, my wife owns three hotels, so I will require three identical portraits, not one."

"No problem, you will have them by noon tomorrow, thank-you for your custom."

"You're welcome," Frank said. Then nervously rode down with her to the lobby in the same lift. He let her get out before him, looking carefully all around, just in case Yasmin saw them come out of it together and got the wrong idea. He breathed a sigh of relief when Yasmin was nowhere in sight, mission accomplished. Then purely on a whim, he decided to go and check on Amy and his daughter.

It wasn't at all necessary that he need do so of course, but hell he was going to check on them anyway. Frank knew roughly the pool area favoured by Amy and headed over in that direction. He arrived at the swimming pool only to find that Yasmin had already beaten him to it. She was sat side-saddle and fully clothed on a sun lounger talking to Amy. Baby Aisha was close by, safely ensconced in the shade. Near by, Frank was pleased to see that the young security guard assigned to their protection, was sat in the shade watchful and vigilant of his charges. That was all that Frank had asked for and wandered over to see him.

The young guard's name was Amir and upon seeing Frank's approach, hastily stood up as if he had been caught in the act of doing something wrong. Frank motioned with his hands in a friendly gesture that conveyed to him that everything was fine and for him to sit back down. Nevertheless he asked Amir,"Is everything alright?"

Amir replied, "Yes sir, everything is fine." Then, on a whim, Frank asked, "Do you need anything?" Taken aback, Amir suddenly blurted out that he could do with a toilet break, then added Sir, as an afterthought in apology.

Relieved that it was such a simple request, Frank said, "Go now Amir, I will watch them." As Amir hastily rushed off, Frank couldn't help smiling to himself, thinking, I bet the poor bugger was desperate to go, but daren't risk leaving his charges. He remembered back to his days, whilst still in the regiment, when he had found himself in similar situations, ruefully he surmised, buggered if you go, in the shit if you don't.

Yasmin had seen Frank swap places with Amir and came over, "New job?" she asked, smiling.

"Just giving Amir a comfort break-----everything alright your end?" Frank asked.

Yasmin nodded in ascent, "Amy's getting nicely brown," indicating with a glance over in her direction," and our daughter, is fast asleep. I thought that the heat would make her irritable, but strangely, it hasn't bothered her at all."

"Well that's something to be thankful for," agreed Frank.

"I'm really pleased with the way everything has progressed whilst we've been here," Yasmin admitted. "I think we can move on to the Eastern Palms Hotel on Sunday."

"Well that puts us ahead of schedule, you must have worked some magic of your own to have achieved that," Frank admitted proudly.

"Not really," replied Yasmin. "Mr Malik and his staff have worked the real magic, not me."

Frank silently agreed that the hotel was well run and from his own field of expertise, he had to admit that the security staff were well trained.

The following afternoon, Frank sought out his wife and mysteriously told her that she was needed in the board room, but was tight-lipped when Yasmin asked him why? Feigning annoyance at first, she reluctantly played along, indulging her husband's vague request.

Arriving at the boardroom, Yasmin could see that the Hussein family portraits had been re-arranged, but with one extra portrait added, hers. Her own father's portrait, now hung below that of her grandfather's, her own portrait now hung below that of her father, to his right. Her brother Ali's now hung to their father's left. The original portraits were black and white, but Yasmin's was full colour. She remembered Frank taking it some time ago, and stepped closer to view it better.

"Why have you done this?" looking at Frank sideways, for an answer. "I mean it's wonderful, don't get me wrong, but I wasn't expecting my portrait to be hung here," she explained.

"Why not? You have every right to be on display here," he replied, "as the new head of the Hussein Empire, people need to see the person that they are working for. Besides, as our daughter gets older, she needs to be able to see her mother's portrait on the wall beside her mother's kin," Frank replied.

Yasmin had to confess that she hadn't even thought about that, she had been so wrapped up in putting her own business affairs in order that she had forgotten that one day, all this would pass to her daughter. Frank had not only been looking out for Yasmin's interest, but for their daughter's as well. Leaning towards him, she kissed him full on the lips and once they had parted she simply said, "Thank you."

Frank merely replied, "You're welcome," grinning from ear to ear.

Chapter 106

Claire's residence, London

Claire was doing a little light dusting in the living room, whilst Adam lay sprawled out on the carpet, reading from one of his books about nature. The radio was on but turned down low so as not to disturb Luke, who was asleep upstairs. The music on the radio was suddenly interrupted by a news bulletin, announcing that some sort of incident had just happened in the capital. The details were still sketchy, but further bulletins were promised as and when more information became available.

Claire hardly faltered in her cleaning duties. Usually, in her understanding, incident meant some sort of terrorist attack had either just been committed, or was under way. Whichever it turned out to be, it was becoming so common that it hardly registered to her any more. As she carried on with her cleaning, the music was interrupted at regular intervals by bulletins that added further information to what was now being referred to as a terror related incident. It was now known for certain that people had died and that others had been injured in this latest attack. Other than that, nothing else was known at this time.

Turning off the radio, Claire now switched on the television set, tuning in to the BBC news channel.

Live pictures, from the area of the attack were now being beamed direct into people's homes. Police cars and ambulances could be clearly seen parked haphazardly in the road. A white van was visible, highlighted by a helicopter T.V. crew, hovering above. It appeared to have crashed into the side of a building, with a black cab embedded, pinning it in place. As the story began to emerge, it was now known for certain that two people had died in the incident, a young mother and her eighteen-month old daughter. Several other people were known to have been injured in the incident, but their injuries or condition, were not known at this time.

The driver of the white van, who was thought to be the sole perpetrator behind the attack, was known to have injured at least one police officer whilst trying to remove him from the vehicle. Armed police officers, who quickly arrived on scene, fired two shots and it was now confirmed that the suspect driver had been pronounced dead.

As the afternoon wore on, more and more information was gathered and collated by the authorities, then slowly released to the media. By the time the six o'clock news was ready to air, a comprehensive account of the incident, was ready for broadcast.

A London cab driver, Harry Beech, was being hailed as a hero, he had witnessed the whole thing from his driver's seat, whilst dropping off his fare. Harry claimed that he'd seen a white van mount the pavement and plough into a group of people who were gathered there. At first Harry had thought that the driver of the van had simply lost control of his vehicle, but when he saw the driver deliberately backing away from the injured party and back onto the road, he knew that the collision had been deliberate. As the van came towards Harry, it became clear that the driver was trying to inflict further casualties, by trying to hit cyclists and pedestrians along the way. With hardly any time to think, Harry floored the gas pedal of his cab and aimed it at the oncoming vehicle. The impact of the collision drove the van back up onto the pavement, wedging it tightly against the wall of a building. The airbags in both vehicles had deployed, but other than that, both drivers appeared uninjured. Harry got out of his cab, perhaps a bit shakily, but the driver of the white van was unable to get out because both his doors were obstructed.

Ambulances and police cars, had arrived on the scene within minutes, Harry flagged down the nearest police car, quickly telling them what had happened. Moments later, armed police officers suddenly appeared, as if by magic. Whilst ambulance personnel were already bravely treating the injured, further up the road armed response officers steadily approached the pinned white van. First attempts to remove the driver of the vehicle peacefully, were soon rebuffed when a police officer was slashed across his arms whilst trying to wrestle him through his mangled door. Suddenly, two shots rang out from one of the armed response officers on scene, quickly ending the issue. The driver of the van could be clearly seen slumped forward whilst still in his seat, apparently lifeless. This incident had all taken place in Queen Victoria Street close to Blackfriars.

The driver of the white van was later identified as

Mustafa Begum and was thought to be of Somali origin, other than that, little was known about him. The woman killed in the attack, had been identified, but her name was being withheld until her next of kin had been informed. It was believed that the eighteen- month old infant recovered at the scene, was her daughter. Other persons injured in the attack had been treated at the scene and transferred to neighbouring hospitals. As yet their condition was unknown.

Claire, who had been listening to the bulletins then watching for several hours as the incident played out on T.V. asked Luke, "Why do they do these things, I mean, what did he possibly think that he would have to gain by killing a young mother and her baby daughter?"

It clearly angered Claire, as it seemed so senseless.

Luke agreed with the sentiment, but refused to be drawn into the conversation; politics and religion were subjects that he refused to get embroiled in.

"Are you listening to me Luke?" Claire badgered, trying to get some sort of response from him.

Sighing with resignation, Luke knew that Claire just wouldn't let it go and tried to think of a suitable answer.

"The guy who committed the attack has probably been thinking of doing something like it for several weeks. Today was the day for whatever reason that he decided to carry it out, it was totally random and because it was random, there was no way of preventing it from happening. The act of murdering innocent people had probably been bothering him for a while, so he simply eased his conscience, by convincing himself that he was somehow doing it for the glorification of god.

That's how he rationalised it, and that's how he justified his actions," explained Luke.

"You think he did it for god?" gasped Claire, not

wanting to believe Luke's answer.

"Yes, why not," answered Luke.

"Because, it's too easy to blame it on god," Claire shot back, angrily, "A young mother and her daughter are dead and he justifies it by blaming it on god. It makes life so meaningless if you can trivialize it like that."

"I'm not trying to trivialize anything," shot back Luke, "and that's why I try not to get involved in politics or religion. Besides you probably wouldn't like my answer anyway," explained Luke.

"Well I'm sorry Luke, but that's not good enough. So why wouldn't I like your answer?"

Luke felt like a cornered rat under Claire's agitated scrutiny, "Leave it Claire you really wouldn't like my answer," Luke said, in a more modified tone.

"Bullshit," retorted Claire angrily, with a hint of sarcasm, "tell me."

After a few moments, Luke turned to face his wife. "You really want me to tell you what I think?" ----When Claire remained silent Luke pressed on, surprising her with his next question, "What's the biggest killer of the human population?"

Claire, taken aback by Luke's random question, paused to think, "Disease, probably--- perhaps malaria," she finally answered.

Luke nodded slowly in agreement, then surprised her again by saying, "Wrong. Religion," puzzled by Luke's answer, she asked him to explain.

"Throughout the centuries of war and strife, perpetuated by the human race, what's the one thing that we all agree on?"

Intrigued by Luke's question, Claire remained silent whilst trying to think of a common link.

"Religion," Luke finally said, when Claire didn't answer. He explained his reasoning in the following manner. "Throughout history, every conflict fought between man had them all believing that god was on their side. Irrespective of skin colour, creed, or faith, no matter what religion, they all totally believed that they were in the right and that god was on their side, even right up to the Second World War. Men and women from all nations and from all sides, firmly believed that what they were doing, was justified, and that god had their back," continued Luke.

"And you disagree with that," interrupted Claire.

"You're damned right I disagree with that," laughed out Luke. "I bet during World War Two, god pulled up his armchair to ringside so he could get a better view, whilst the human race slaughtered one another. Then when it was almost over, he did what he's always done, nothing," spat Luke in disgust.

"You really believe that don't you Luke?" Claire said sadly.

"Yes I do," confirmed Luke. "The mistake that mankind made and continues to make," pointed out Luke, "is thinking that god cares about them, when in reality, he doesn't give a fuck! And that's why I don't get involved in either politics or religion," finished Luke.

After an uncomfortable silence, Claire finally said, "Thank-you for answering my question Luke, it must have been very difficult for you, but I'm afraid I'll have to disagree with you, in this instance."

"I'm sorry to have upset you Claire, but I did warn you that you wouldn't like my answer."

"Yes you did Luke," clearly saddened by having to admit it.

Chapter 107

The Eastern, a totally different animal.

After a leisurely Sunday morning breakfast taken in their room, Yasmin organised the packing of her family's belongings with military precision. Frank shamefully left it to her, just packing his own bits and pieces as he saw fit. His only excuse was that he would have been in the way, even though that sounded lame, he admitted to himself. However the truth being that Yasmin was so self-reliant and efficient in everything she did, that perhaps, he was almost surplus to requirements. Except of course when he was needed to help with their daughter, like now for instance. Aisha, whose eyes were looking up at Frank, were a full shade lighter than those of her mother's. They were trusting eyes and when they looked at Frank, it gave him a funny warm feeling inside. She was clean, changed, fed and smelt-well, she smelt just like a baby should smell and he loved her to bits.

Casting a momentary glance over in Yasmin's direction, Frank shook his head in amazement. Yasmin was just closing the lid on the last of their cases, ready for collection. He had not only married a beautiful woman, he'd married wonder woman. Smiling over at Frank, she said, "That's it, all set." Job done, she called down to reception to let them know that their cases were ready for collection, then reaching for Aisha, she relieved Frank of their precious burden. Now, free of his charge, Frank headed for the door and looked down the corridor to see if Amy had put out her own cases as requested. Frank could see that she had, so decided to knock to let her know that they were ready to go down.

Five minutes later they were saying their goodbyes to all who were in attendance upon them. Mr Malik, Frank noticed, held on to his wife's hand overly long in his opinion, as if reluctant to let her go, but then again when your wife was a looker like Yasmin, it was perfectly understandable. So in the end, Frank couldn't really blame Mr Malik and when it came down to it, he had a sneaky liking for the man and they shook hands warmly, on parting.

The driver of the people carrier, as unobtrusively as possible, gave Frank a thumbs up signal to let him know that the bags were safely aboard. All that was left now, was for them to leave the hotel and climb aboard themselves. While Frank safely secured Aisha's carry-cot, Yasmin and Amy found their own seats and waited for Frank to board too. Amid a final flurry of goodbyes and frenzied waving, the vehicle eased away from the kerb and into traffic. Their destination, the Eastern Palms Hotel, just a short ten minute drive away. The Eastern was built virtually to the same blue print as its sister hotel, the Western. It had the same general layout, with more or less the same amenities, but sadly, that's where the similarity ended.

Ominously, when the people -carrier pulled up outside The Eastern's main entrance, the hotel was shrouded in deep, dark shadow. That could simply have been because the other hotels surrounding the Eastern were so much taller and simply blocking out the sunlight. Or if you chose to look for something more sinister, as superstitious people are sometimes wont to do, you could have simply said that the hotel felt cursed, depending on your point of view. Either way, they arrived unannounced and in dark shadow.

At the Western, they had been welcomed like royalty, all bells and whistles. The Eastern was a different animal entirely. Frank and Yasmin had thought that perhaps a smartly dressed doorman or even a lonely porter would have been on view by now, but sadly nothing, nada.

Whilst Frank set about settling Aisha's carry-cot onto its own fold up wheels, the driver began unloading their baggage. With baby Aisha now fully mobile, they ventured through the doors and headed towards reception, leaving their driver behind to guard the luggage. As they approached the desk they looked around for signs of life, but failed miserably.

Frank said sideways to Yasmin, "I know it's Sunday, but where is everyone?"

"Let's find out," she said on arriving at the reception desk. A shiny brass bell was on the counter just aching to be hit, Yasmin did the honours. They waited, Frank could see the tell tale signs that Yasmin was becoming agitated and obviously contemplating whether to hit the bell once more.

Just as she was about to do so, a smartly dressed young woman, probably in her early twenties, thought Frank, came through a door from behind the reception looking hot and slightly flustered.

"Yes. Can I help you?" She asked almost apologetically.

Yasmin merely asked her, "Where is every one?" indicating the cavernous space that was devoid of human presence with a wave of her hand.

"Oh! We've been conducting a fire drill, but it's almost done now," she said, by way of explanation. Then asked, "Do you have a reservation?"

Yasmin's whole demeanor had visibly changed when realising the circumstances of why no-one was on duty. Now conciliatory, she replied, "Yes we have a reservation, but I'm afraid that we are a day early."

The receptionist, although obviously surprised by Yasmin's statement, gamely went through the computer for their reservation, "Name please."

"Mr and Mrs Hussein," Yasmin said half smiling to herself. Then as it became painfully obvious that the receptionist would find no pre-booked room for Mr and Mrs. Hussein on her computer, Yasmin took pity on her.

"You will find that we are booked into the Penthouse Suite, my child minder, indicating Amy, will be staying in the end room on the same corridor- I trust that the rooms are ready for immediate occupation," Yasmin asked, matter-of-factly.

The receptionist, now only just realising who she was dealing with, tried not to panic, but her eyes betrayed her.

Frank observed her quite closely and had to admit, that for someone surprised by the owner and a day early, she got onto internal comms., and within three minutes an army of porters, management, and general arse lickers, were vying for Yasmin's attention.

Thankfully Yasmin wasn't having any of it, she had the key to the Penthouse Suite safely in her hand, Amy had hers and now that the fire drill was over, they headed for the lifts. They rode up to their floor, Yasmin going on ahead of Frank to open the door. Standing aside she held it open whilst he deftly wheeled in their daughter. Yasmin did a quick check of the rooms to make sure that everything wasin order. Thankfully she gave it her seal of approval, thought Frank. Now they were just waiting for the luggage to arrive.

Later, once everything that needed to be hung, was hung and the drawers were filled to bursting,

Yasmin began to settle. Frank sat on the balcony with Aisha on his lap. The view from the balcony of the Penthouse Suite overlooked the swimming pool and Frank noticed that the sun, absent when they had arrived, now chose to show itself through a gap between the neighbouring hotels. Frank could see that some sun worshippers had known just when and where the sun would make its appearance and were positioned on sun loungers, strategically placed for maximum exposure.

Nothing changes, he murmured to his daughter.

"What are you whispering to our daughter?" Yasmin asked, as she crept up on Frank unawares.

"Just taking in the view," he replied, indicating the few sun worshippers, lined up below.

A knock at the door, announced someone wanting their attention. "It's probably Amy," Yasmin said, already going to see who it was. It wasn't Amy. Instead it was a tall, painfully thin young man dressed in western style clothing.

"Excuse me for disturbing you, Mrs. Hussein," he

began, “I am Kabir Khan junior assistant manager of the Eastern Palms Hotel, at your service. I am sorry, that we were not available to welcome you properly on your arrival, but we were conducting,”-- -a fire drill,” Yasmin finished for him. “Yes Mr

Khan, I know. Please, come in.” Taking him to the balcony, Yasmin introduced him to Frank.

Frank remained seated whilst still holding his daughter, but shook the man’s hand.

Then she said, with undisguised affection, “And this is our daughter Aisha.” Then without missing a beat, Yasmin continued, “You say that you are the assistant manager Mr Khan. Where is the general manager then? Mr Faisal, I believe is it?” she questioned.

“Yes, Mr Faisal,” agreed Khan, “he is visiting with his family today, as it is his day off,” Khan said by way of explanation.

“I see,” was all that Yasmin said. Mr Khan obviously thinking that Yasmin was somehow dis-pleased, tried gamely to smooth things over, “Had we known that you would be arriving today, we would of course have welcomed you properly,” Khan said by way of apology.

“No apology necessary Mr Khan, I assure you,” said Yasmin, in an effort to placate any misconceptions. “Please make sure that everyone is made aware of our planned heads of department meeting, scheduled for ten o’ clock, Tuesday morning.”

“We received your instructions Mrs Hussein and everyone has been notified,” Khan answered, somewhat less defensive now. Then as an afterthought, he said, “If you require anything at all, please do not hesitate to call reception and it will be taken care of.”

Once Mr Khan had left, Yasmin came to stand beside

Frank's chair, then snaking an arm tenderly across his shoulders, she said, "Well, as officially we're not meant to be here until tomorrow and seeing as its Amy's day off, what would you like to do?" Yasmin purred.

"Well, as Aisha seems to have fallen asleep," said Frank, in the same vein as Yasmin, "perhaps we could," -"Yes please," was all that Yasmin said.

Chapter 108

The Henderson residence. London

The elephant in the room was still getting in the way of normality, at home. Claire and Luke were careful to remain civil towards one-another, if only for Adam's sake, as they didn't want him to be caught in the middle of any verbal crossfire. So, at least on the surface they were managing to put on a neutral face, if only for appearances sake. Adam of course was no fool and tried to remain impartial to whatever it was that his parents were disagreeing about. He was becoming quite adept at it lately, managing to steer himself a clear course between his parents more frequent of late, fallings out.

Claire, by comparison, felt the atmosphere weighing down on her shoulders more heavily than usual. The tension in the room of late was of her own making and she had to acknowledge her part in it, although at times it seemed that she just couldn't help herself and seemed to be hell bent on spoiling things between her and Luke. Politics and religion were no go areas, as far as Luke was concerned. Yet Claire had been inexorably drawn like a moth to a flame, unable to resist, goading Luke into answering a question about the one subject that he was loathe to discuss. Religion, as far as Luke was concerned, was considered a dirty word. He had told Claire quite categorically, that he wouldn't discuss religion with her because she wouldn't like his answer, but of course Claire hadn't listened and had badgered and bullied Luke into a corner from which he couldn't escape. His answer, when it came, had been truly shocking for Claire to hear.

Claire was not a religious person, not in the truest sense of the word, but she had always harboured a hope and a belief, in the existence of god and that had never wavered. What had shattered Claire's hopes and dreams of a benevolent god and therefore perhaps a promise of an after-life, was Luke's insistence that the human race held no special place in god's great scheme of things. In fact, according to Luke, it had been man's idea to worship god in the first place and just because they chose to do so, it didn't necessarily follow that god would hold a special place for them in his own heart. Claire had been carrying this heavy burden around for the last few days, ever since Luke's shocking revelation and it had hit her hard.

Whatever Claire's hopes had been for the future, or even for an after-life before, they were now seriously damaged and broken. It had made her doubt and question everything that she thought and knew, about life. Why are we here? What is our purpose and if Luke was to be believed, what's the fucking point. Claire knew, without a shadow of a doubt that he loved her and his children, he was fiercely protective of both his family and friends and loyal beyond compare. But in the last few days, she couldn't shake off the awful feeling, that he had destroyed the one thing in life, that she had so stubbornly clung onto, hope.

Chapter 109

Getting to grips, with the Eastern

After breakfast on Monday morning, Yasmin was fired up to get to work. Her first priority of the day was a meeting with the Eastern's general manager, an encounter that as it turned out, did not begin at all well. As a general rule for Yasmin, when meeting people for the first time, she was of the opinion that one should never judge someone by their appearance alone, as most people she had found, had the ability to surprise you. On this particular occasion, she should have listened more closely to her gut. Yasmin had left repeated messages with reception, and with junior manager Khan, that she was looking for the general manager Mr Faisal. It soon became abundantly clear, that the said Mr Faisal was doing his level best to avoid meeting with her. Yasmin had already wasted a precious hour of her time, in trying to track down this very slippery manager, when alarm bells began to sound in her head. Usually in her experience, when someone was trying to avoid you, it meant that they had something to hide.

It was Mr Khan who finally tracked down her elusive quarry, and spilled the beans as to where he was hiding, in the hotel's restaurant. Now, with nowhere left to hide, and finally confronted by the hotel's new owner, Mr Faisal brazenly lied that he had been searching high and low for her in order to affect a meeting.

Yasmin wasn't fooled in the slightest by this blatant lie, but managed to mask any hostility that she now felt, admirably. She tentatively shook Mr Faisal's proffered hand, then in a firm voice she demanded that he deliver the hotel's books for inspection to the Penthouse Suite, within the hour.

Mr Faisal's face darkened visibly at what he perceived to be an assault on his integrity, then he tried bluff and bluster, in that order, in an effort to forestall on delivering Yasmin's lawful request.

But by this time, Yasmin was fast running out of patience with Mr Faisal, so she threatened to have security seize them by force, should he fail to comply with her wishes.

Mr Faisal's anger was now clearly written across his face, his body language alone betrayed the fact that he seriously wanted to do this upstart young woman physical harm, his clenched fists alone were solid proof of that.

If Yasmin was intimidated at all by this obvious show of hostility and anger directed towards her, she failed to show it. Instead she said in a commanding voice, "One hour Mr Faisal, no longer," then she turned and walked away, as she got nearer to the lifts, she let out an audible sigh of relief.

She hadn't realised that she had been holding her breath, the tension of the confrontation finally leaving her body on the ride up. Although she had to admit to herself that the whole horrible encounter had seriously frightened her.

Frank was with Amy and his daughter when Yasmin let herself back in, one look at her face was enough for him to recognise trouble when he saw it, "What's wrong?"

Composing herself, Yasmin said," I've just had a very unpleasant confrontation with Mr Faisal the hotel manager. I knew that he had been avoiding me, so when I finally cornered him, I demanded that he surrender the hotel's books to me. I gave him one hour to comply, threatening him with hotel security if he failed to deliver." Yasmin blurted out in a rush.

Missing nothing, and knowing his wife, Frank asked, "Did he threaten you at all?"

"No, but if we hadn't have been in full view of the people in the restaurant, then I think he would have," admitted Yasmin.

Frank was all for going down and ripping Mr Faisal a new arse-hole.

It took a lot of persuasion from Yasmin, to finally calm him down and help him to see sense. Talking it through, they agreed to wait the hour that Yasmin had so generously given Mr Faisal.

The hour came and went and the books had still not arrived. Yasmin had been generous, in fact more than generous, and now it was time to act. Ringing down to reception, Yasmin asked that the head of hotel security, along with Mr Khan meet her there. Leaving Amy alone with Aisha in the penthouse, Frank and Yasmin rode down to reception. Meeting puzzled looks from both Mr Khan and Mr Bashir, Yasmin said, "Please accompany us to the hotel manager's office."

They didn't have far to go as it was just across the foyer opposite the reception, but on trying to open the door Yasmin found it to be locked. Frustrated Yasmin asked, "Is there a spare key?"

"Yes of course," said Mr Khan, "I have one." Stepping forward to unlock the door, he stood aside to allow Yasmin access. Just a glance was all that it took to confirm, that the bird had flown.

"Has anyone seen Mr Faisal?" Yasmin asked, to no-one in particular.

"He said that he had to go out," offered Mr Khan helpfully.

"When was this?" Yasmin snapped, uncharacteristically.

"About thirty minutes ago," replied a wounded Mr Khan.

"I see, of course he has," mouthed Yasmin quietly to herself. Then she took charge, "Mr Khan, where are the books for the hotel kept?"

"In the safe," he answered, pointing to it.

"And can we open it?" she asked him, starting to lose patience.

Now in his eagerness to help, he almost tripped himself up trying to impress Yasmin. Fifteen seconds later, the safe doors stood open. They all leaned forward, eager to see what was inside.

Yasmin lifted out several large leather bound ledgers and placed them in a pile on the manager's desk. She asked Mr Khan, "Is this all of them?"

"I'm not sure," he admitted, a bit sheepishly, "but I think so."

"Very well, you are both my witnesses and I am going to take these ledgers with me up to my room to go through them." When Yasmin had given the safe a cursory inspection, she had the head of security Mr Bashir and then Mr Khan both look, to confirm that the safe was devoid of any money. They both did so and then Yasmin had Mr Khan re-Iock the safe.

Her last instructions to Mr Bashir were thus, "I don't expect that we'll see Mr Faisal again Mr Bashir, but should we do so, please place him into custody." Then, remembering that the hotel was now without a general manager, she addressed Mr Khan directly. "Mr Khan do you think that you can run the hotel until I can appoint a replacement manager?"

Standing taller now at being asked, he beamed, "I'm certain that I can Mrs Hussein."

Looking up into his eyes she said, "Alright then please do so, and don't forget that we have a meeting scheduled for ten o'clock tomorrow morning."

Frank hefted the ledgers for Yasmin and accompanied her back to the penthouse, he knew that she would require a number of hours, if not days, to go through the ledgers and that it would be best served if she had peace and quiet. Frank quickly appraised Amy of the current situation and helped her to bundle up Aisha's things, and then helped her down to her own room.

Yasmin was already into the ledgers when Frank let himself back in, he made her a coffee just the way she liked it, and then went to sit out on the balcony so as not to disturb her concentration. Frank kept out of Yasmin's way for a good few hours, which allowed her time to crunch the numbers, without any distraction. Then he quietly as possible ordered a couple of plates of sandwiches to be brought up to the room, knowing full well that Yasmin would skip lunch otherwise.

Five hours later, Frank spied his wife stretching and trying to ease the tension out of her aching muscles after sitting and concentrating so long. Finally she leaned on the door-frame of the balcony for support.

Looking at her, Frank asked, "How bad is it?"

"At least two million, probably more. It seems that Mr Faisal has been embezzling from the hotel for years," Yasmin admitted.

"Surely your brother Ali would have spotted it," Frank queried.

"My brother, to quote an old British witticism Frank, wouldn't know his own arse from his elbow," Yasmin said, tiredly.

He had to admire his wife's fortitude, she had just discovered that someone in her employ had been stealing from her family, probably for years and yet, she could still find the humour to smile about it.

It was also highly unlikely that the said Mr Faisal, would ever be apprehended, or the money recovered.

"So. What now?" Frank asked.

"Now, I need a long hot soak in the tub, while you go and get our daughter," decided Yasmin," I need time to think."

Frank had to smile as he went to relieve Amy of their daughter. He knew that Yasmin would already have the workings of a plan in mind and by the time she had finished towelling off, it would be cooked and ready to go.

The following morning, after breakfast and Frank had once again left Amy in charge of their daughter, Yasmin steeled herself outside the boardroom door. Frank and Yasmin could both hear the hubbub coming from within. No doubt the rumour mill at the hotel had been working over-time since yesterday's bombshell. Yasmin took a deep breath before entering the room closely followed by Frank. Taking her place at the head of the table, she was once again pleased to see that the chair on her right, had been left vacant for Frank, nodding appreciatively to Mr Khan seated to her left, Yasmin remained standing.

The room was now hushed and all eyes were fixed intensely on Yasmin, using a clear voice she introduced herself to the seated gathering, using the same formula as before at the Western, she introduced Frank as her husband. Then just like before, she left them in no doubt that he had her authority in all things. Whilst she had been delivering this message, she had been listening for any signs of dissent.

This time, Frank thought that she held the pause a tad too long, and it made him feel...a little uncomfortable.

Yasmin remained standing as she needed to address the situation of the disappearance of the former general manager, of the Eastern Palms Hotel. It was important that Yasmin give them the facts, and she did so in typical Yasmin fashion, leaving nothing out. Finally, she had Mr Khan and Mr Bashir both attest to the accuracy and truth of her account, to the assembled people.

Everyone tried to speak at once when they finally realised the real reason behind Mr Faisal's sudden departure.

Yasmin allowed them a few brief moments to air their feelings on the matter and then she asked them for their attention. "As we are now short of a general manager, I've placed Mr Khan," whom she indicated by hand, "in temporary charge."

Some of them looked on in obvious dismay, incredulous at Yasmin's choice of manager, they clearly disagreed with her that someone so young and lacking in experience, should be raised to such lofty heights.

Even Frank had his own doubts as to Khan's competence

or ability, but chose to hold his tongue, now was not the time to question his wife's decisions. Besides, Frank thought, Yasmin was no fool, she must have had her own reasons for appointing Khan, and now that she had delivered the facts Yasmin finally took her seat. Everyone's eyes looked in Yasmin's direction, "Please let's begin, there is much to discuss and we have a hotel to run," was all that she said.

Frank had to admire that about his wife, she was the consummate professional when it came to running a business. The meeting over-ran at the Eastern, just as it had done at the Western, but that's where the similarities ended. The fact that the Eastern was only just about scraping by, was glaringly obvious to everyone. The hotel's poor position had a lot to do with it, so there was nothing that could be done about that, but Yasmin was faced with a very serious problem, either somehow get more paying guests to use the Eastern, or face having to close it down. It was a stark choice and one that she didn't relish making. However, that was the reality of the situation. Of course Yasmin wanted the hotel to flourish as she had hundreds of people relying on her for a living, so she desperately needed to find a solution. Mr Faisal hadn't exactly helped ease the situation, Yasmin mused, but at least now that he had done a runner, the books would gradually improve, if only by a small margin.

No, this problem was all hers now, so it was up to her to somehow bring the hotel back into profit.

The next day Yasmin tasked herself with checking how efficiently the various departments were being managed. Not knowing the capabilities of Mr Khan, she had the new (temporary) general manager accompany her on her rounds.

As it turned out Mr Khan was no fool, he knew that his competence was being assessed by Yasmin, but instead of being resentful of the fact that his managerial qualities were being tested, he actually began to enjoy her company and after a while, it became patently obvious to Mr Khan, that Yasmin Hussein knew what she was doing. He quickly came to realise that if he chose to do so, he could actually learn a great deal from this woman. Thankfully Mr Khan wanted to learn, and once he'd overcome his initial shyness, he began to contribute some useful ideas of his own.

Frank for his part re-appraised his role as security adviser, but this time ever mindful that the hotel's finances were balanced on a knife edge, he had to use whatever assets were available to him.

Just as at the Western, the security staff at the Eastern, were one member short on the night shift.

Frank recommended that one of the day shift be rotated in turn to fill the gap, also with having no money to invest in surveillance cameras, he recommended having some of them moved to where they would be more useful. Mr Bashir for his part, listened to Frank's suggestions and agreed with them, whole-heartedly. The cameras indicated by Frank were re-installed and activated and would soon prove their worth.

Amy meanwhile, had her own hands full with baby Aisha, however, it hadn't taken her too long to work out that the sun made its appearance over the pool area, between twelve and three. So being the professional sunbather that she was, Amy had soon staked out a prime spot to indulge in her favourite occupation, sun worship. That soon led to Frank having to ask Mr Bashir to provide security both for Amy and his daughter, explaining that the threat of kidnap or worse, was very real. Mr Bashir took Frank's concerns to heart, sometimes filling in those few hours himself.

Six days later, Yasmin had arranged for a face to face

meeting with the representatives of the various travel companies that used the hotel. She had put together a package of deals in an effort to try and entice holiday makers into choosing the Eastern. It had been a bold move by Yasmin and the reps went away happy, pleased that they finally had someone that they could do business with.

Yasmin knew that it wouldn't provide a miracle cure over-night, but it was a start and a way forward.

Mr Khan was becoming increasingly smitten with Yasmin's work ethic, if he thought he could only attain half of her work ethos then he would be very satisfied. In the few days that he had been at her side, he had learnt more about running a hotel than he had under Mr Faisal's tutelage during the last eighteen months.

They had been at the Eastern for a full week now. Sadly there was still much to do, but on a happier note, Frank had had Yasmin's portrait hung up in the boardroom, how long it would hang there was still to be decided.

Frank had arranged to meet up with his wife for lunch, in the Eastern's restaurant, one good thing in the hotels favour, was the quality of its food, it was excellent. He spied his wife unobtrusively over in the corner, the ever present Mr Khan hanging on her every word. Frank bent to kiss his wife on the cheek by way of greeting, then sat down opposite her, he simply said, "Mr Khan," to acknowledge his presence.

Mr Khan just nodded between mouthfuls of food, choosing to remain silent.

It was obvious to Frank that Mr Khan felt somehow intimidated by him, and that's probably why he chose to remain silent, it didn't really bother Frank how he felt about him, as there wasn't really much he could do about it. Excusing himself from the table, Frank went to choose something from the buffet. He came back with pieces of snapper, done in some type of sauce and a few boiled potatoes. Once he'd sat down, he carefully chewed his way through the fish, and it was a good job that he did, as there were several large fish-bones to work his way around. Carefully arranging the bones around the edge of his plate, he idly thought, if they'd been any bigger, I could have had them made up into a necklace.

Just then Yasmin's phone rang, within seconds Yasmin was hurriedly pushing out of her chair,

"Amy's in trouble," was all that she said.

Frank, followed by Mr Khan tried to keep pace with his wife, they were taking the quickest route to the pool area, where Amy had last been seen.

Amy could be clearly seen holding baby Aisha in a defensive posture, whilst the Eastern's security man was having trouble protecting Amy from three suited men and a diminutive woman, dressed in a black burka.

Yasmin burst on scene like a veritable tigress, placing herself in front of Amy and placing her own body between her and the woman in the burka. Frank stood beside his wife ready to commit murder, should the need arise, comically Mr Khan's reed like frame came to stand beside Frank's.

"What are you doing here mother?" Spat Yasmin, with undisguised loathing.

"Daughter! What else would I be doing here? I have come to see my grand-daughter, nothing more - a grand-daughter who I knew nothing about, I hasten to add, no thanks to you," she spat back with venom.

Frank, though listening to what was being said, never took his eyes away from the three goons, assessing which one to take down first. They in turn were awaiting orders to attack.

"Well now that you've seen her, you can leave," Yasmin fired off verbally.

The burka-clad woman stepped in closer, looking up into Yasmin's eyes, "You haven't changed much daughter. Not content in shunning your own family, you choose to rut with a non-believer, bringing forth this devil's spawn. You will burn in hell daughter," she finally hissed.

"Not before you mother," spat Yasmin with all the vehemence that she could muster. She saw her mother's eyes flash with something like genuine hatred, before she slowly turned and walked away surrounded by her bodyguards.

Mr Bashir, who had only just arrived with added security, was asked by Yasmin to make sure that they were escorted from the hotel. Yasmin meanwhile had taken hold of baby Aisha. She had been visibly shocked by the confrontation with her mother.

Amy was trying to apologise to Yasmin without result, for whatever it was that she thought that she had done wrong. When all of a sudden Yasmin convulsed into heartfelt sobbing, tears of relief streaming down her face, the realisation at what she could have lost if Amy hadn't had the presence of mind to hold onto her daughter.

Turning to Amy she said, "Thank-you for saving my daughter, I won't forget this."

Mystified, Amy replied, "Surely your mother wouldn't have harmed Aisha, would she?"

"Unfortunately Amy, yes she would," answered Yasmin.

For the remainder of their time at the Eastern, Amy's sun-bathing ritual was abandoned. The encounter with Yasmin's mother and her goons had scared her shitless, although she still looked after Aisha while Yasmin worked, she did so either in her own room or within sight of security inside the hotel. The security staff had been put on full alert with orders that on no account was Yasmin's mother, or her henchmen to be allowed inside the hotel, and for all intents and purposes, the former head of the Hussein Empire, was to be considered persona-non-grata.

Chapter 110

"It sounds like Yasmin and Frank have been having a bit of excitement whilst staying in Jordan," Claire told Luke.

Lifting his head off the pillow to listen better, he asked, "What sort of excitement?"

"She says that the hotel manager has been cooking the books and has done a runner with the takings from the safe and as a bonus, her mother paid her an unofficial visit at the hotel and tried to snatch baby Aisha."

Easing himself into a sitting up position Luke said, "Wow! They don't do things by halves do they, are they okay?"

"Yasmin's a bit shaken up by the experience, but thankful that Amy, their baby minder, had the presence of mind to hold on tight to Aisha, or who knows what might have happened," Claire responded.

"Nothing good I'm sure," echoed Luke, "and what about the crooked manager, have they caught up with him yet?"

"Not as far as I know. Yasmin thinks he's long gone by now anyway, probably safely hidden in the south of France, or some such place," Claire guessed.

"Did they say when they would be coming home?" Luke asked.

"Not yet, they are flying on to Dubai next, so they're not sure when they will be coming home," Claire said, stifling a yawn.

Seeing that Claire was tired, Luke eased his frame back down into bed beside her. Before he closed his eyes he told her once again that he was sorry.

"Don't be," she said, sleepily. "I'm the one who should be sorry, go to sleep." Adam, who had been tuning in to his parents conversation in the next room, turned over in bed half smiling to himself. This latest quarrel between his mom and dad had been going on much too long for his liking, but it looked like the thaw had finally set in.

Later, they had a light lunch together and Luke brought up their daughter's imminent birth in conversation, "I'm thinking of asking Chris for time off, I don't like leaving you on your own now that your time is near."

"Do you think that that's wise, I mean that would leave the club's security two men short."

"I know, but I don't like leaving you and Adam alone, if you go into labour while I'm at work," explained Luke.

"Well, leave it for another week or so, Adam assures me that I am not about to give birth to his sister just yet, don't you sweetie," Claire said, ruffling his hair. Adam looked up at his dad, with old eyes, "Mum's right dad, Ruth's not ready to come just yet."

"Why thanks son, I'll bear that in mind when I next see your Uncle Chris," winked Luke.

Although Luke tried to make light of it, this was a worrying situation, as he was genuinely concerned for Claire's health and the safety of their baby. This pregnancy had been anything but pleasant for Claire, Adam's birth had been almost textbook perfection, but who was to say that Ruth's would be the same.

If Frank had been here in London to pick up the slack, Luke would not have hesitated to put in for some overdue time off. Luke decided that he would give it another week or two tops, then that was it, he would take some time off. The club would either sink or swim without him.

Chapter 111

Farewell to the Eastern. Hello Dubai.

For the next three days at the Eastern, it was as if they were tiptoeing around each other on eggshells.

Fatima Hussein's incursion at the hotel, had everyone constantly looking over their shoulders expecting to see her lurking somewhere in the shadows. To say that she had put everyone on edge was a gross understatement and the trouble was, although they desperately needed to leave the place in order to put their daughter in a safer environment, Yasmin needed the extra three days to fully implement her plans to try and make the Eastern profitable.

Frank had seen at first hand the vile creature that was Yasmin's mother. He personally thought that she was slightly unhinged, probably due to the murder of her son Ali, though if he was mistaken, then the only other alternative was that she had finally flipped into madness and if that was the case, then that made her truly dangerous. Either way, Frank kept his opinions to himself. Yasmin had enough on her plate without him adding to it.

On the day that they were due to leave the Eastern, it was just as if the clouds had finally parted allowing them all a collective sigh of relief. The former general manager, Mr Faisal, was probably safely installed somewhere abroad, although he would have to make a life for himself with the money that he had already stolen from the Hussein family. Happily, one of the first things that Yasmin had done, when discovering his criminality, was to cancel his monthly pay check. Mr Faisal's hasty departure had left her with another unforeseen problem, who to put in his place. She had put Mr Khan in temporary charge of the hotel until a more suitably qualified general manager, could be appointed.

Unfortunately, this had proved impossible to achieve, given the limited amount of time that was available to her, so for better or worse the fate of the Eastern, would rest on Mr Khan's very spindly shoulders.

Eager to leave, they finally said their good-byes, Yasmin's plans had now been put in place and everyone now knew what was expected of them, the success or failure of the hotel, now rested with them.

As they pulled away from the Eastern no-one bothered to look back. Frank felt that everyone, himself included, was heartily sick of the place.

Hours later, they all seemed to finally relax as they rode the air currents towards their final destination, Dubai.

Jordan was hot, Dubai was hotter. Both Frank and Amy's necks were constantly on swivel, marvelling at the modernity of Dubai's sky-line. It was as if every building was screaming, look at me, look at me. The place simply oozed wealth, each building in turn vying to be noticed, reaching ever sky-wards in an effort to out-do its nearest neighbour. Neither Frank nor Amy had been here before, so it was perfectly understandable that they were impressed by the buildings. Yasmin of course, had been there several times before with her late father, although even she had to admit that some of the buildings were new to her. Aisha, quietly asleep in her carry-cot, hadn't even been thought of back then.

As they arrived at the Desert Palms Hotel, Frank immediately fell in love with its imitation, art deco era building. That it belonged to a by-gone age yes, but strangely, it didn't seem out of place nestled as it was between those monstrosities of a so-called modern age, it was a thing of beauty, in Frank's eyes at any rate. The trees and shrubs, planted at the time of the hotel's completion, had had the requisite amount of time to both grow and mature. The resulting gardens now provided an oasis set amongst a concrete and steel jungle, a place of quiet and shade, should it be required. Although its beach front position offered an alternative, sand and sun burn. Bordered by an azure and diamond sparkling sea, the hotel in Frank's view, was simply perfect.

Yasmin and her party were received like royalty upon entering the hotel's foyer, it was as if everyone had shed the worry and troubles beset by the Eastern and left them at the door. It was pleasantly cool, inside the hotel seemed to have a life-force of its own and breathed: 'You are welcome here'.

Once formalities were completed, they headed up to the Penthouse Suite. Frank had been worried that perhaps Yasmin wouldn't want to stay in that particular suite, after all, its last occupant,

Yasmin's brother Ali, had been murdered there. She seemed unconcerned by Frank's worries, as she automatically checked out the rooms, although he did notice that she paid particular attention to the bedroom. It was, after all, the room in which he had been murdered. The bed, of course had long been disposed of and replaced with a new one, but she checked anyway, just to make sure. Now satisfied that the room harboured no malevolent spirits, Yasmin and Frank began to relax.

The patterns set out by Yasmin at both the Western and Eastern Palms hotels we repeated here, at the Desert Palms, although it was plain for all to see, that this hotel was being expertly managed and run by the hotel's general manager Mr Assad. Even Frank could find no fault with the hotel's security arrangements, he quickly allayed any fears of a repetition of Yasmin's mother making a surprise visit to Amy, though he still arranged for security to watch over her and his daughter, just in case.

Being almost redundant from work duties, led Frank to have Yasmin's remaining portrait put up in the hotel's boardroom. Even Yasmin, business woman extraordinaire, was impressed with the way that the hotel was being managed and run.

The hotel had gained an impressive reputation over the years, and it had managed to retain an impressive guest list, who continued to come back time after time, after time. Just like Frank they must have fallen in love with the hotel.

Three nights a week the hotel provided live music and dancing, very good singers were regularly featured, ranging in musical tastes, from Frank Sinatra's rat pack era, to Roy Orbison, Barbra

Streisand to Shirley Bassey. Not the real artistes of course, but nevertheless, top class entertainment with a live band thrown in. Just what the paying guest wanted.

It also gave Yasmin and Frank the opportunity to finally have the honeymoon that had so far eluded them. Ever mindful that Amy wasn't to be exploited, Yasmin arranged for baby Aisha to be looked after by one of the female security staff in the evenings. Amy far from being excluded, was invited to join them in the evenings at table, whilst they wined and dined. Afterwards, Amy's eyes were out on stalks, as she watched both her boss and Frank dance. She had never seen Yasmin, or Frank for that matter in such a relaxed mood and it soon became clear, not only to Amy, but to other guests watching, that Frank and Yasmin were hosting a master class.

As she watched them glide effortlessly around the dance floor, she jealously thought to herself, I wish I could fucking dance like that. It was uncharitable of her to think like that she knew, but that's the way it was. After all, Amy thought, Yasmin did have the looks, the money and the handsome prince, so why the fuck shouldn't she be jealous.

The group spent five idyllic days at the hotel, just blending in with the guests, everything seemed to run like clockwork, and they actually began to feel like they were officially on holiday. Frank liaised with the head of security Mr Asif, on a daily basis. So far everything had been running smoothly, and there had been nothing out of the ordinary to warrant Frank's attention, that is, until Mr Asif casually mentioned something about a wild party aboard a yacht. Frank's ears pricked up immediately, and he had to admit that he had totally forgotten that Yasmin was the proud owner of a yacht berthed nearby. Neither of them had had cause to think about the yacht, so it never came up in conversation.

Ringing her mobile he asked about it now, "Hi Yasmin

I'm with Mr Asif, head of security, I've just had an interesting conversation with him, concerning talk about wild parties aboard a yacht, am I correct in assuming that your yacht's name is The Falcon?·· It is, no leave it with me, I'll go check it out. Yes, okay see you later," Frank said as he ended the call.

Meanwhile, Mr Asif had listened patiently to Frank's one-sided conversation waiting for instructions.

Frank asked him if he knew where The Falcon was moored.

"Yes of course" he answered, "it's moored close by."

"Let's go and have a quiet look-see, lead the way Mr Asif." Frank said, pleasantly.

It was obvious that Frank was eager to check out the falcon for himself, he had never owned a yacht before, and couldn't wait to see what she looked like. He realised then that he had referred to the yacht as a she, he wasn't sure if that was the correct term of address or not, but it felt right to Frank, so in future the yacht would be referred to as a she. They soon came upon a sleek looking craft secured at its moorings, a boarding gang-plank led down from it to a small pier. A muscle-bound man, dressed in some sort of sailor's uniform, was diligently mopping down the deck.

Seeing Frank and Mr Asif staring up at him he asked, "Can I help you?" in reasonably good English.

Mr Asif said nothing, leaving it up to Frank to reply, "Permission to come aboard?" Frank asked.

The crew man, taken aback by Frank's request, was momentarily stymied as what to do. Then standing up straight, the crew man politely, but firmly, denied Frank's request. "I'm afraid that won't be possible, the captain and crew are ashore, and I'm under orders to let no-one on board."

“Not even the owner,” Frank fired back.

The crew man was like a gaffed fish, hooked, but unable to respond, finally he found the words he was searching for, “Can you prove that you are the owner of this craft?”

“No not really,” Frank admitted, “but Mr Asif can vouch for who I am.”

Stepping forward, Mr Asif did indeed attest to Frank being the yacht’s owner, but the only problem was, that the crew man didn’t really know who Mr Asif was either, and could have been anybody.

Now he was faced with a real dilemma, allow them on board and disobey his captain’s orders, or deny them entry and thus antagonising the owner, should his claim prove to be genuine.

Frank could see the imaginary machinery working inside the crew man’s head whilst he pondered the problem, thankfully he chose to allow them to come on board.

Once on board, Frank was like a kid in a sweet shop, he didn’t know where to look first. Eventually, he decided to head down and into the yacht’s spacious interior. Frank soon found evidence of discarded empty champagne bottles, as well as expensive bottles of brand-named spirits scattered around the floor. A pair of ripped red knickers adorned a lamp-shade, to one side of a very comfortable looking chair. It was obvious to Frank that the rumours of a party were well founded, but other than that, Frank thought that the yacht though small in comparison to others berthed along-side, was beautiful. Frank now having seen enough, thanked the crew man and left, with Mr Asif in tow. Frank thought that Yasmin would be very interested in what he had to tell her and once back at the hotel, Frank wasted no time in giving Yasmin his report.

“And you say that there was evidence of wild parties

having taken place on the yacht?" questioned Yasmin.

"Yes no doubt of it," affirmed Frank, "empty champagne and liquor bottles were strewn all over the place, as well as some rather skimpy red knickers that had been left behind," added Frank for good measure.

Yasmin's mouth was turned down in obvious displeasure, "This could land us in serious trouble with the authorities," Yasmin admitted, clearly worried by Frank's report. "As the owner of the yacht the authorities could claim me to be responsible for any excess alcohol abuse, or prostitution carried out on board. It could even lead to a prison term," admitted Yasmin.

Now that Frank realised just how serious the repercussions for his wife could be, he wanted to shut this thing down. "What do you want me to do?" Frank asked simply.

Yasmin paced for a while trying to order her thoughts, then coming to an abrupt halt she turned to face Frank.

"I'm going to let the crew go with immediate effect," she said, thinking aloud while she resumed pacing. Then said, "I'll pay them until the end of the month, but only on condition that they leave the yacht today," she finally decided,

"What about the yacht?" Frank asked, tentatively,

"I'll put it on the market," Yasmin said decisively.

Frank was disappointed with Yasmin's decision, it had been nice to think of himself as the owner of a sea-going yacht, if only for a short while, but he knew that it was the right decision and would rather lose everything, than see his wife go to prison.

Later in the day, Frank accompanied by his wife and most of the hotel's security personnel, arrived at the yacht's mooring. It was lit up like a Christmas tree when they arrived, advertising to all that it was open for business,

A crew man stood on board at the head of the gang-plank, this time Frank didn't ask for permission to come on board and was closely followed by Yasmin and her security detail.

The crew man was openly hostile to what he perceived to be an unwarranted invasion, foolishly trying to physically restrain Frank from boarding, was a serious error of judgement on the crew man's part. Frank easily evaded the crew man's clumsy efforts, and instead took hold of the poor man and threw him overboard. Then without missing a step Frank carried on until he was confronted by an immaculately clad first officer, who barred his way.

"Who are you? And what is the meaning of this outrageous behaviour," he boomed with obvious distaste,

Now it was left to Yasmin to step in front of Frank, to give an answer, "I am Yasmin Hussein the owner of this vessel, and you are?" Yasmin questioned with authority.

After only a moment's hesitation, the man replied, "Karim Begum, first officer of The Falcon, Miss

Hussein."

"Mrs," corrected Yasmin, indicating Frank to her left and saying, "and this is my husband."

"I see," replied a now suitably chastened Mr Begum, "in that case, welcome aboard Mrs Hussein."

Yasmin, all business now, instructed the first officer as to why she was here, "Please inform the captain and crew, yourself included, that your services aboard The Falcon are no longer required. If you carry out my lawful instructions and leave the yacht as requested, you will all receive full pay until the end of the month, but if you decide to challenge my wishes, then I'm afraid that I will have no alternative, than to inform the authorities about the illegal activities that have been conducted aboard this vessel. Please be so good as to inform the captain and crew of my intentions, you have twenty minutes to remove yourselves and your belongings from The Falcon, before I take over control, is that clear?" Yasmin finished.

The first officer realising perhaps that the good life aboard the yacht was now well and truly over, merely nodded, then left to go and deliver Yasmin's ultimatum. Meanwhile, a thoroughly soaked crew man, had just managed to climb back on board.

Frank eyed the crew man warily as he trudged passed them, leaving behind a stream of water in his wake. Quarter of an hour later, the captain , first officer, the chief engineer and five crew members filed past them with their belongings and made their way off The Falcon for the very last time.

Yasmin had a quick look around the interior of the falcon, curious to see what it looked like, and once her curiosity was satisfied she had Frank shut it down. Now, once again shrouded in darkness, Frank secured the yacht hoping that a new owner for her could be quickly found, as he thought it would be a shame to see her go to waste. Frank felt a little saddened to be losing The Falcon so soon, it had felt good to be the owner of an ocean-going yacht, if only for a little while. Slipping the chain across the gang-plank, Frank had to walk quickly to catch up with his wife and the rest of the team.

Yasmin, looking a little sadly across at her husband, placed an arm comfortably in his and quietly asked if he was alright. Frank nodded without speaking, but Yasmin was no fool and asked him "Sad to see her go?"

"Yes," Frank answered honestly, "but if it means keeping you out of jail then it's worth it."

"Thank-you, I'll make it up to you," promised Yasmin.

In the space of just a few short weeks, they had achieved a great deal, in Jordan they had been welcomed at the Western Palms like royalty, at the Eastern Yasmin had uncovered a thief, foiled a would be kidnapper from abducting their daughter, even if it was only her mother, and formulated a plan of action designed to bring the hotel back into profitability. In Dubai, they had managed to squeeze in a long overdue honey moon that they so richly deserved, then to top it all, they had discovered the illicit shenanigans carried out by the crew of The Falcon, and which Yasmin soon put a stop to, by making them walk the plank. So, even though it had taken longer than the four weeks that they'd originally allowed, a great deal of good had been accomplished in a relatively short space of time.

It was no secret to Frank that his wife was a bit of a workaholic; give her a task to perform or a job to do and Yasmin was happy, leave her with nothing to do work wise and she soon became restless.

Frank had noticed the tell-tale signs days ago, even though they had both agreed to take the extra days off for a belated honeymoon. Frank also suspected, that Claire, back home in London, must be very close to giving birth by now, and that would obviously be a major factor for Yasmin wanting to return home.

If he was honest with himself, Frank was ready to go home as well, he was a Londoner and he was missing the place. Two days later, they were on their way home.

Chapter 112

Ruth in a hurry.

Ever since Luke had come in from work Claire had been restless and unable to get comfortable in bed. Luke had asked her if she was alright, but Claire had brushed away his concerns, by saying that she just couldn't sleep and in the end she had got up and gone downstairs to make herself some herbal tea.

Uncharacteristically for Luke, he fell into a deep and troubled sleep beset by dreams of warring Angels in a nightmare world of intermittent darkness and fire.

Lightning constantly lit the molten coloured skies all around them as the warrior's advanced. In his dream, Luke saw Michael in the vanguard of a shining host, his flaming sword clearly visible for his followers to see, leading them ever onwards against the forces of evil. Luke had a sword of his own gripped tightly in his hand and was with Michael in the vanguard, but behind and to his right. He recognised his nearest companion as Mathew his friend, who a

lso wielded a sword of his own. The ground beneath their feet seemed to move and smoke as they advanced, the air was uncomfortably hot and was filled with foul smelling smoke and menace, making it hard to both see and breathe.

As the vanguard came to the brow of the hill overlooking a valley, lightning lit up the sky before them, revealing a vast plane below. Lucifer's army and his fallen Angels, as well as all manner of demons and monstrous creatures, were arrayed before them like an endless sea stretching from horizon to horizon, and beyond. Lucifer's army came on, unstoppable and eager to do his bidding.

The host behind Michael was out-numbered fifty to one, yet still he rallied them on, his battle-cry even outdoing the constant thunder that rolled all around them, even Lord Lucifer must have approved of Michael's bravado, as he favoured them with a hideous smile. Just as Lucifer was about to unleash his forces, Luke felt a small hand grip his own, looking down in horror, Luke saw Adam looking up at him, small and naked. What are you doing here son he tried to shout in anguish, fearful that his son should be here in this awful place, you must leave here, he tried to tell him but the words just wouldn't form, as he had lost the power of speech.

"Dad, dad," Adam repeated in an effort to rouse his father, "wake up mum needs you," Adam pleaded. Slowly, Luke's sleep fogged brain came back from Lucifer's nightmare world, seeing his son stood beside the bed finally registered with Luke's sleep addled confusion.

"What is it son?" he asked.

"Mum needs you, I think the baby's coming," said

Adam, excitedly.

"Alright son I'm coming, go and be with your mum make sure she's alright."

Luke had returned from one kind of battlefield only to be faced with another, he had no doubt in his mind that Michael had sent him the dream, but was unsure as to why, but as of this moment, his wife was facing a battle of her own, and he needed to step up and help her through it. Going quickly downstairs, Luke found Claire in the kitchen, arms out stretched, leaning on a worktop for support.

When she saw Luke she asked him to ring doctor Cooymans' clinic, to let them know that her contractions had started, and that they would shortly be on their way.

Luke did what his wife had asked, and then managed to order a cab at the second attempt, from a list of numbers that they had written down. He then helped Adam to get dressed, and had Claire's small suitcase to hand, just as the front doorbell rang. Bundling everyone inside the cab, Luke went through the motions of checking if he had everything; house keys, money for the cab fare, mobile phone, check.

The journey to Doctor Cooymans' clinic, was quick and without incident. Luke paid the cab driver his fare, stuffing notes into his hand, not bothered about the change, then he helped his wife as best as he could, whilst holding on to her case, and making sure that Adam kept pace with them.

They were met at the door by two nurses, who immediately took charge of Claire, helping her into an examination room. Meanwhile, a receptionist led Luke and Adam into a small but comfortable waiting room and asked him to fill in some forms as far as he could, for the doctor. Ten minutes later she popped back into the waiting room to check on Luke, and to inform him that Claire had indeed gone into labour. Not long afterwards a nurse came to find

Luke and to tell him that his wife would like him in the delivery room. Luke quietly asked her if there was someone available to watch Adam, if he left him. She surprised him by telling him that Claire had asked for Adam to be present as well.

Luke asked Adam, "What about it son do you want to be there when your sister is born? It's up to you." Adam just nodded that he did.

They followed the nurse into the delivery room and they positioned themselves to either side of the bed. Claire was now dressed in a hospital gown, trying hard to manage the pain, smiling through tears as Adam gripped tightly to her hand, she was grateful that he had come. Turning to Luke, Claire gripped his hand harder as yet another contraction racked her body. She vaguely heard one of the nurses tell her companion that this baby was in a hurry, as she tried to stifle the pain.

Five minutes later Claire's baby was born, and whilst one of the nurses made sure that the baby was healthy and fine, the other one concentrated on Claire. All through the delivery, Adam had never let go of his mother's hand, he only did so now when the nurse came back with his new born sister wrapped in a clean white fluffy towel, and handed her over to his mum. Claire looked down at her daughter in wonder, she was beautiful just like Adam had been when he was born, she was neither shrieking, crying or making a fuss, but lying content in her mother's arms. Claire showed Adam his sister. "Say hello to your sister Adam."

Gently reaching out to touch her Adam said, "Hello Ruth."

Hearing Adam using Ruth's name for the first time, seemed surreal to Claire, as she now had a son and a daughter to complete her family, it was everything that she had ever hoped for, and more.

Her children were now her future and she would do everything in her power to make sure that it was a good one. Luke squeezed Claire's hand reminding her that he was still there and just as invested in his children's future, as she was. Turning to face him, she lifted Ruth a little higher for him to see her. "She's beautiful," was all that Luke could manage to say, overcome with feeling.

Later, now moved to a private room, Claire was nursing Ruth with Adam close beside her, watching his sister's every move, she had secretly hoped that Adam and Ruth would bond, and so far her hopes were proving to be well founded.

Meanwhile, Luke had stepped out to telephone Chris with the news of Ruth's arrival, and to let him know that he would be taking some time off to be with his family. While he was at it, he left a message on Frank and Yasmin's answer-phone, informing them of his daughter's birth, and letting them know that both mother and daughter were fine. When Luke came back inside, he mentioned that he'd let Chris know of Ruth's birth, and that he would be taking some time off, then let Claire know that he had left a message for Frank and Yasmin.

Claire had to smile when he told her, "Yasmin will be really annoyed, she wanted to be here for

Ruth's birth."

"Well there's not much we can do about that now, and besides, Ruth was in such a hurry to be born, I doubt that she would have been able to get here in time anyway," reasoned Luke.

"Yes, that's true," agreed Claire. "Look, there's not much that you can do here for a while, and as we're well taken care of by the nurses, why don't you take Adam off home, get your selves freshened up and maybe have something to eat, before coming back later," suggested Claire.

Luke agreed that it sounded like a good plan and got the receptionist to ring for a cab for him and

Adam. Twenty minutes later they were on their way home.

When Dr Cooymans arrived at the clinic the staff quickly informed her of Claire's admission and subsequent birth of her daughter. It was a complete surprise to the doctor, as Claire's due date was not for another two weeks. However, seeing is believing and the proof was now right before her eyes and being nursed by her mum. "How are you feeling?" Dr Cooymans asked.

"I'm fine, the birth was really quick and I managed the pain fairly well," admitted Claire.

"The nurses tell me that you asked for Adam to be present in the delivery room," queried the doctor.

"Yes, do you disapprove?" asked Claire.

"Not exactly disapprove," the doctor considered, "but it's not something that perhaps children should have to witness, childbirth is a pretty traumatic experience when seen for the first time."

"Well, Adam wasn't really in a position to view that end of the delivery properly, and it gave me great comfort to have him hold my hand."

"Where is he now?" the doctor asked.

"Luke's taken him home for a few hours rest, he'll be back later," Claire said.

"Speaking of rest, I'd like you to get a few hours rest yourself, I'll have one of the nurses come and collect Ruth for you, so you can try and sleep," ordered Dr Cooymans.

Claire was too tired to argue, and after Ruth had been

whisked away from her, she did indeed manage to sleep.

Claire spent two idyllic days being looked after in Dr Cooymans' care, then it was time to get back to reality and introduce Ruth to the Henderson family home.

Chapter 113

Frank pulled up outside their apartment block in late afternoon. Now came the small matter of transferring baby Aisha and seven heavy suitcases of differing sizes, in through the outside door, whilst trying not to attract the eagle-eyed attentions of a traffic warden. His daughter was the easy part, as she was the lightest. Carrying her up to the second floor, Frank waited whilst Yasmin unlocked their door then handed the baby over to his wife. Going back down stairs, two at a time Frank left the cases where they were in the apartment blocks front entrance, whilst concentrating on moving the car quickly from the front of the building, and driving it around the back into their designated parking spot. Mission accomplished, he said to himself with satisfaction, now it was just a small matter of humping the bloody suitcases upstairs he thought with dismay.

Yasmin thoughtfully left the door to the apartment

open so Frank just had to wheel them inside as he brought them upstairs. He left the heaviest case until last, which just happened to be Yasmin's, pushing it inside, he mopped his brow with his handkerchief and wondered if he was out of condition.

Five years ago he could have run 10K without hardly breaking sweat.

Yasmin informed him that Claire had had a daughter, as the first thing that she had done upon entering the apartment was check her messages.

"Wait, I thought that she wasn't due for another couple of weeks?" Frank queried.

"Well Luke says, mum and daughter Ruth, are both doing well," said Yasmin, sounding slightly miffed.

Frank had to smile,"Surely you're not annoyed that Claire has already given birth."

"Yes I am, I wanted to be here for it," admitted Yasmin quite unreasonably.

"Sorry, I didn't mean to make fun of you," apologised Frank.

Looking at Frank, Yasmin realised how annoyed she had sounded, "I'm being ridiculous aren't I?" she admitted. " Claire has always maintained that a baby would come when it was damn well good and ready and she was right."

"Well give her a ring and see if she is home from the clinic yet, perhaps we'll be able to go and see them tomorrow," offered Frank.

Ten minutes later Yasmin came back all smiles, "They can't wait to see us, Luke's cooking," Yasmin said, happily.

"Bloody hell, I'll make sure to pack my heartburn tablets," Frank joked in mock horror.

Looking past Frank, Yasmin groaned when she realised

that the suitcases still needed unpacking. The realities of travel were not all pleasant ones, there was always the unpacking to do and a load of washing to put on at the end of it. Thinking ahead, Yasmin remembered that in three months' time they would have to do it all over again. The measures that she had put in place, at the Eastern Palms Hotel, would have to be thoroughly vetted when she returned, to see if there had been any improvements in its fortunes. She hoped with all of her heart, that she could turn the hotel around, because the alternative would mean letting go of something that had been in her family's ownership for decades. Still, enough of this maudlin sentiment, tomorrow she was looking forward to seeing Claire and her new baby.

Chapter 114

Claire let Yasmin in first, hugging her tightly in a sisterly embrace. Adam tried to get in on the act as well, holding on to Yasmin's thighs. It had been almost six weeks since they had been in one another's company, a lifetime in Adam's opinion. They broke up the reunion temporarily, to allow

Frank inside with Aisha's carry-cot, Claire managed to peck Frank on the cheek in greeting, whilst noticing that Aisha was fast asleep in the cot.

Yasmin went ahead into the living room almost joined at the hip with Adam, (clearly the boy had missed her) and headed over towards an almost identical looking carry-cot in the corner of the room, which held another sleeping babe, Ruth. Looking down in wonder at her, Yasmin nodded then said, "Just as I suspected, she's beautiful, like her mum."

Frank brought Aisha's carry-cot up beside Ruth's and put them together, side by side. Looking in at Ruth's sleeping face, he declared her to be beautiful also, then promptly left the women-folk, to go and torment Luke in the kitchen.

Yasmin, shucking off her jacket for Claire to go and hang up, claimed one end of the settee drawing her feet up underneath her, and getting comfortable. Adam went to sit beside her, limpet close, wanting to get closer. Yasmin pulled him in tight beside her and asked him, "Miss me?"

"Yes," replied Adam, "you were gone a long time."

"I know I'm sorry, but I had a lot of work to do and I'm back now," she cooed.

"But you'll be going away again soon," Adam said, knowingly.

How Adam knew this without being told, would have unsettled most people, but not Yasmin, she was well used to Adam by now and simply answered, "Yes I know, but it won't be for a while, and I will only be gone for a week or so next time," Yasmin promised.

Moments later Claire came in from the kitchen bearing a tray, coffee for Yasmin, tea for her and juice for Adam, placing them within reach on the coffee table, Claire sat to the other side of Adam, who became the pea in the pod.

"So Mrs. Henderson, you decided to go ahead and have the baby without me," chided Yasmin in mock rebuke.

Finishing a healthy slurp of tea, Claire responded in the same vein as Yasmin, "Well I'm afraid that

Ruth didn't give me much choice in the matter and it was over so quickly it was touch and go whether we'd get to the clinic in time," responded Claire.

Sitting up straighter, Yasmin asked, "Really, it was that quick?"

"Yes it was," admitted Claire, "but I wasn't frightened, I had my men folk with me, didn't I Adam?"

Yasmin felt Adam's head nod in reply, still tight beside her. "And what do you think of your baby sister Adam?" Yasmin asked.

"She's lovely," responded Adam. "I'm going to teach her about the animals when she's older."

"Well that's nice, I'm glad that you like your sister Adam," then changing tack, Yasmin asked Claire if Ruth was settling down alright.

Claire remarked, "She's as good as gold really, feeding well, sleeps fine and hardly cries at all, but that reminds me, how did Aisha take to the heat out there?"

"Surprisingly good, the heat hardly bothered her at all," admitted Yasmin. "Amy took good care of her and made sure that she was out of the sun mostly, and in the shade. I was very pleased with how she stepped up," Yasmin said, obviously very satisfied with her.

"And the other incident?" Claire casually dropped into the conversation.

Breathing out audibly, Yasmin said, "It frightened the life out of me Claire, it really did, if Amy hadn't have clung on to Aisha the way that she did, my mother could have had her away in seconds, then who knows what would have happened. I still shudder to think of the consequences if that had happened," Yasmin said, obviously reliving the awful experience.

"So what do you intend on doing with Aisha when you have to go back, leave her here or take her with you?" Claire asked.

"I'd like to keep her with me," admitted Yasmin, "but I don't know if that would be wise."

After a suitable pause Claire said, "Well don't worry about it now, if you need her to stay safe you can always leave her here with me," offered Claire.

"Thank you, it may well come to that, but we'll see how things go," Yasmin said, happily.

Meanwhile in the kitchen, Frank was necking a bottle of beer whilst watching Luke preparing their meal. He had been telling him about the crooked manager, uncovered by Yasmin at the Eastern Palms Hotel.

"Two point three million, give or take a hundred thousand or so," answered Frank. "That's what the toe-rag got away with, probably won't get caught either," Frank surmised.

Luke whistled at the eye watering sum, "And how did Yasmin take that?" Luke asked.

"Surprisingly well," admitted Frank, "it just needed someone with brains to join the dots, and once

Yasmin was on board, his days were well and truly numbered mate," Frank said, with genuine affection for his wife.

Changing the subject, whilst he chopped up onions, Luke asked, "And what about the yacht? You mentioned something shady about the crew."

"Oh mate, my heart bleeds, that yacht, The Falcon was

a thing of beauty," Frank tailed off, obviously still seeing her in his mind's eye, before he remembered he was telling the tale."The crew had been idle for months with the yacht still tied up at its moorings, and still drawing their pay, someone, either the captain or the first officer, must have got the bright idea of using the yacht to host illicit sex and booze parties aboard. I only got word of it by accident from the head of security at the hotel, we confirmed it when we went to go and check it out."

"So what did Yasmin do about it?" Luke wanted to know.

"Oh, we went back in the evening mob-handed, and Yasmin introduced herself to the first officer,"

Frank said, nonchalantly.

"What and there wasn't any trouble?" Luke prompted.

"Not really," Frank confessed, "one of the crewmen got a bit wet when I threw him overboard, but the rest of the crew quickly abandoned ship when Yasmin explained what would happen to them if they didn't leave quietly."

"It sounds like the pair of you had quite an adventure," Luke said, appreciatively.

"Yes, it was an interesting few weeks," he agreed, "but I still regret not taking the yacht out, just the once," Frank said sadly.

Back in the living room, signs of life were emanating from the carry-cots, which prompted a twin response from both mother's, Yasmin asked Claire if it was alright for her to go and heat up her baby's bottle in the kitchen, already taking it for granted that she could. Meanwhile, Claire whisked

Ruth away upstairs, to breast feed her daughter and to see if she needed changing.

Fifteen minutes later Claire was back on the settee

holding Aisha, whilst Yasmin was holding Ruth, both babies were quiet, but wide eyed looking up at a woman who wasn't their natural mother, without fear.

Frank and Luke did a double take when they stuck their heads in to see if anyone wanted anything to drink, but seeing Yasmin and Claire holding each other's babies, seemed so natural to them, that it hardly warranted mentioning. Realising that their women folk found them surplus to requirements, they retreated back into the kitchen, and out of sight.

"I had a word with Chris last night, he tells me that you've taken some time off to be with your family," Frank queried.

"And," Luke said, defensively.

"And nothing, don't get your knickers in a twist, I was just asking that's all." said Frank.

Luke carried on slicing and dicing peppers while waiting for the rest of whatever was on Frank's mind to surface, he didn't have long to wait.

"I wondered if you wanted your temporary status as head of security, to become more permanent, it would mean you becoming management of course, and with that comes more responsibility, but you've proven that you're more than capable of doing the job, so how about it?" Frank offered.

"Where does that leave you?" Luke wanted to know. "I mean, you are the head of security after all, so does that mean that you will be leaving the club?"

"No mate, but I will be doing a lot more travelling with Yasmin, so it wouldn't be fair of me to keep to-ing and fro-ing with the job. I really need someone solid in charge, and if that's you, I'll just fill in as your number two, as and when

I'm available," Frank explained.

It sounded reasonable to Luke, as he carefully considered Frank's offer, then taking the bull by the horns he said, "I'll take the job, provided that we recruit another security man or woman to make up the numbers," decided Luke.

"Done mate, welcome to management," Frank said, slapping Luke heartily on the back.

"Was it your idea or Yasmin's?" asked Luke.

"Mine, but Yasmin approved it straight away, so it's all good mate. My wife will continue to do the club's books as usual but Chris will be effectively be managing the club on his own from now on," Frank explained.

Luke mulled this over before asking, "So what's next on your's and Yasmin's bucket list?"

"Re-charge our batteries I suppose, then in three months-time we have to return to the Eastern Hotel, to see if Yasmin's measures are starting to bear fruit," Frank said, obviously jaded and not looking forward to it.

"Is it that bad?" asked Luke.

Frank pulled a face whilst thinking of a suitable reply, "There are some good people in charge of the hotel," Frank had to admit, "but it's situated in totally the wrong place, and there's nothing that can be done about that. Yasmin's put in place some package deals with the travel companies, to try and tempt new customers, but for now it's a matter of wait and see."

"Well if anyone can turn it around, it's Yasmin," Luke said, encouragingly.

"Thanks mate that's helpful. Oh, there is one more thing," Frank remembered, "Yasmin's decided that our apartment is no longer suitable to raise a family," Frank dropped in, casually.

"Well that's hardly surprising is it," Luke said, whilst

looking him squarely in the eye. "Claire realised that soon enough, when Adam was born. Got anywhere particular in mind?" Luke asked, interested.

"Not yet, but somewhere detached, preferably set back from the road, and reasonably secure," Frank replied.

"Sounds expensive," quipped Luke.

"I think, that we can safely say that Yasmin can afford it," Frank replied glibly.

Luke said nothing, whilst preparing the chicken breasts, waiting for Frank to continue.

"That sounded arrogant didn't it," Frank realised, "something I've always hated in other people,

Christ, I hope I'm not becoming one of them," Frank said, defensively. "The truth is mate, I'm beginning to feel like a kept man, living off of Yasmin's wealth," admitted Frank.

Luke banged the knife down on the chopping board, making Frank look up sharply, "Now you look here, you've more than earned your place, so don't go feeling guilty now about reaping the rewards. You have a wife who loves you, unconditionally, and a young daughter whose life will be guided by you, so don't start saying that you don't deserve your place, because that's simply not true," Luke said, angrily.

Frank stayed silent for a moment, whilst thinking about what Luke had just said, "Thanks Luke for what you just said, I guess I just needed to hear someone else say it," admitted Frank.

"You're welcome, now get yourself another beer, and get me one while you're about it," ordered

Luke.

Back in the living room, Claire busied herself laying

out the placings at the dining table, whilst Yasmin and Adam watched the babies on the settee both interacting with them. Suddenly out of the blue, Yasmin mentioned that she was buying a house. Claire stopped what she was doing momentarily pole-axed, with what her friend had just told her, "And you've only just decided to mention this now" Claire said, exasperated.

"I've had other things on my mind," Yasmin said in her defence. "Anyway, I've only just realised how impractical it is living in an apartment on the second floor without a lift, and having a young child to look after. You were right to move into a house when you had Adam, it was a sensible thing to do," Yasmin said, placatory.

Feeling guilty now, Claire modified her tone, "Have you got anywhere in mind?"

"I've arranged with an agent to view the Almeda's old house, it's still for sale and I've been there once before," said Yasmin, surprising Claire.

"And you're not put off by the circumstances of why the house is still for sale?" Claire wanted to know.

"Oh goodness no, ghosts you mean?" Yasmin asked.

"Well yes, the Almeda's were murdered there after all," said Claire, for emphasis.

"I'm not worried about that, the Almeda's were my friends in life, so I don't imagine that they would wish me harm now that they are dead," said Yasmin practically.

Claire had to smile, Yasmin was a tour-de-force, and someone you just couldn't help but admire.

"What's the house like?" Claire wanted to know.

Thinking back from memory Yasmin said, "A large detached property that stands well back from the main road, gardens to both front and rear with mature trees and shrubs, fully enclosed at the rear if I remember rightly, four or five bedrooms I think, but I'm not quite sure, and ample off-road parking with a large detached garage," Yasmin finished.

"Are you sure four or five bedrooms will be enough?" Claire said, half joking.

"Oh yes," Yasmin said, missing the joke entirely.

Claire carried on setting the table while trying hard not to laugh, but had to turn her head away in the end, so that her friend couldn't see her face. "When's the viewing?" Claire asked.

"Friday," Yasmin answered.

"Frank doesn't know that it belonged to the Almeda's I haven't told him yet," Yasmin confided. Then in the next breath, she asked Claire, "Would you like to come?"

Taken aback momentarily by the offer, Claire said, "Yes alright."

Later, after a meal consisting of tender pieces of chicken breast, cooked on an oven tray with onions, peppers, and a hint of garlic, along -side thinly sliced oven browned potatoes immersed in a thick creamy sauce, served on a bed of egg-fried rice, had all been consumed, Frank smacked his lips appreciatively, his heartburn tablets not needed, and now consigned to memory.

Luke began clearing the dining room table whilst everyone else relaxed comfortably. Claire's offer to help was politely waived away by him, allowing her free time to remain with her guests.

"Thanks for dinner," Yasmin said to Claire, "it was very nice."

"You're welcome, but I had nothing to do with it," Claire confessed, "it was all Luke's doing."

Adam was sat with Frank amazing him by reciting the names of long dead animals from his old encyclopedia opened at the Jurassic period. Frank couldn't help but be impressed by the youngster's knowledge, he was reeling the names off with such confidence, that it put his own understanding of the subject to shame.

Claire waited until Luke had completely cleared the kitchen table before following him into the kitchen, to make a pot of coffee. She sidled passed him, patting him on the back with affection and offers of help, which he declined, just as she knew that he would. Then she set about preparing the cups and saucers onto a tray, whilst the coffee was percolating, then carried it through into the living room placing it onto the coffee table before them. Claire felt comfortable enough to allow them to help themselves, before asking Adam if he would like some juice, he just shook his head in answer, indicating that he didn't, then sitting back down on the settee she poured herself a rare cup of coffee, whilst waiting for Luke to finish the pots and come to join them.

Ten minutes later, Luke joined his wife and Yasmin on the settee, finally allowing himself time to relax. Adam was happily reciting the names of animals to Frank in the background, whilst Yasmin and Claire were still finding things to talk about, both babies were quiet and back in their carry-cots and all was as it should be.

Later, when their friends had gone home, Luke told Claire about being made up to management level when he returns back to work, which both surprised and delighted her. Claire in turn, surprised Luke by knowing whose house it was that Yasmin had her sights on. She swore him to secrecy when telling him that it was the Almeda's old property, just in case he let it slip to Frank before Yasmin had had time to work on him, then casually told him that she was going with them on Friday, for a viewing. Not because she was nosey, Claire insisted, but because she was genuinely interested where her friends were going to live.

Yeah right, thought Luke, contemplating that when god made woman, he wondered if he realised what sort of monster he had created.

Chapter 115

Old Friends

When Frank picked Claire up at her home on Friday, Yasmin asked her to sit in the front alongside her husband, so that she could keep hands on Aisha on the back seat. The baby was safely fastened in her own seat and perfectly happy at the moment, but Yasmin wanted to be close just in case.

Frank knew roughly the area in which they were heading, but Yasmin gave him verbal directions as they got closer to the house. Slowing down, they turned into a tree and shrub lined drive-way, the for sale sign sticking out from the undergrowth, said Burns & Crabbe, which Claire read out.

Frank immediately quipped, "Sounds nasty," which prompted both him and Claire to laughter, but sadly Yasmin failed to find any humour in it. Pulling his Audi in further, Frank parked beside an old cream coloured, dimple topped Mercedes.

A youngish looking woman got out, ready to greet them, quickly introducing herself to Frank as

Caroline Shaw, automatically reaching out to shake his hand, and correctly addressing him by name as Mr White. Claire tried to distance herself from Miss Shaw, who assumed, because of a noticeable absence of any type of ring, but failed to escape Miss Shaw's earnest attentions, because she was impeded by Frank's Audi. Wrongly assuming that she was Mrs White, Claire quickly straightened Miss Shaw out by indicating that she should address herself to Yasmin, who was now holding Aisha in her arms and bringing up the rear. Indeed, when Frank and Yasmin got married, she took his surname which is White, but retained her family name Hussein, for conducting her business. Temporary confusion over, Miss Shaw expertly side-stepped Claire and fastened herself onto Yasmin.

The former home of the Almeda's, was an impressive looking building built entirely of brick, more brown than traditional red, it looked old but was probably built after World War II. Following closely on Miss Shaw's heels, she let them in by the front door and into an entrance hall.

Once inside, Claire offered to hold Aisha for Yasmin to free up her arms, which she graciously allowed her to do. As they were directed from room to room, Claire couldn't help but notice that the house was still fully furnished, it retained the cabinets and furniture that the Almeda's had lovingly collected over a life-time of memories. A lump came into Claire's throat thinking how callously their lives had been snatched away, by someone else's evil intentions.

They were now in the spacious living room where the

Almeda's lives had been so cruelly ended, but of course the group were unaware of that. The expensive Persian rug, on which the Almeda's were murdered, had been removed to a warehouse months ago; the blood, brains and other bodily fluids that had stained the carpet, had proved impossible to remove when it was sent to a specialist cleaning company. It now languished in a warehouse, waiting for some future wonder cleaning product to be invented, to bring it back to life.

The Almeda's blood had not only stained the carpet, but had soaked through onto the floorboards underneath, a cleaning company had been brought in to try and remove the stains by conventional means, but the blood stubbornly refused to budge. It was as if it was saying, this is our home and we're not going to leave. In the end a specialist company in wooden flooring was brought in to rectify the problem, but first they had to remove all the furniture from the living room before they could sand back the floorboards to bare wood. The re-staining, sealing and waxing that followed, took almost two weeks to complete, and had cost a small fortune. All traces of the Almeda's were now removed from sight, yet still they remained, trapped in the droplets of blood that had seeped onto the tongue and groove joints of the floor boards, where the sanding machines couldn't quite reach.

No the Almeda's came from tough stock, and they intended to stay for as long as the house, remained standing.

Upstairs, Yasmin was pleased by the fact that the property did indeed have five bedrooms, although one of them had been used as a makeshift office or store room. The master bedroom was en-suite, but there was also a separate family size bathroom at the far end of the building that was tastefully fitted out. There was a loft space opening on the landing ceiling, but no-one felt inclined to visit it.

Back downstairs in the kitchen, Yasmin and Claire marvelled at the range of gadgets and utensils that appeared to be mostly unused and in pristine condition. Claire quietly commented to Yasmin, that not much cooking seemed to have been carried out in it.

Frank was mainly interested in the view from the kitchen windows, they showed a very well maintained lawn and garden, that had been obviously lavished with great care and attention. When asked who did the gardening, Miss Shaw commented that a garden maintenance company visited once a week, to tend to the lawn and flower beds. Frank was pleased with the garden, but was more interested in how secure the perimeter was, and from what he could see of it, how high the fence was and in what condition. He also noticed a decent sized shed that was partly hidden by shrubs, over in one corner.

Just off from the kitchen was a utility room, which held a plumbed in washer-dryer, several mops and brushes, various sized buckets and an assortment of cleaning products. They all just gave it a cursory look, not really interested ·in what the room contained, then dismissed it from mind. That was a big mistake on their part, because the room held a secret. Skilfully concealed at the end of the room was a hidden door, which covered a stairway that led down to a large basement room. In this room, was a great treasure that Mr Almeda had painstakingly added to, over the years.

Frank would eventually be the beneficiary of this great treasure, but only after several months had passed, and then only by accident.

As we said our good-byes to Miss Shaw, and turned the car around in the Almeda's drive-way, Claire asked Yasmin what she thought of the house.

"Oh, we've decided to put in an offer," she said, non-committedly.

Claire didn't say anything to her reply, but secretly thought that she would be mad not to, as the place was ready to move straight into.

In the weeks following their visit, Yasmin's offer would be reluctantly accepted by Burns & Crabbe, her business sense was never clouded by sentiment or friendship, and when necessary,Yasmin could be utterly ruthless.

Chapter 116

Friday. back at the Henderson's.

After Frank dropped Claire back home, she found Luke on the settee reading with Adam. Ruth was swaddled in a blanket beside them, wide eyed and seemingly taking an interest in her surroundings, a scene of domestic harmony. Before hanging up her coat in the hall, she just said, "Hi guys," in greeting.

Luke replied, "How was it?" meaning the house visit.

"Perfect, in every way," replied Claire.

Luke could sense somehow that there was more to it than that, but stalled at the point of asking and instead, swapped places with Claire to go and make them a brew. Claire made funny faces at Ruth, who wasn't much impressed, before changing tack and putting her arm affectionately around Adam, "What's today's reading lesson, son?"

"Thoughts on how the dinosaurs became extinct," he answered, like a thirty-year-old.

"Hmm, heavy duty stuff,"' Claire said, seriously, "not exactly Rupert Bear then," she added, only half joking.

Mention of Rupert Bear got Adam's attention, "What's Rupert Bear?" he asked, in all seriousness.

It was sad to realise, but nevertheless it was perfectly true, that Adam had never been bought a children's book, instead he had been thrust into the world of adult reading from day one. Claire planned to rectify that criminal oversight tomorrow, with a trip to the local flea market. It was unforgivable of them to deprive Adam of children's books, what the hell was wrong with them?

Luke came back with a mug of tea for Claire and an orange juice for Adam, before going back to the kitchen to collect his own tea. When he came back, he asked what the house was like.

Thinking from memory, Claire repeated, "Like I said before, perfect," then realising that that meant absolutely nothing to Luke, she attempted to describe the property in more detail. "Brick built, detached with five bedrooms, the master bedroom en-suite, and a separate family bathroom. Front entrance hall downstairs, a large living room with a separate dining room, a humungous sized kitchen and a small utility room. Outside, the gardens have mature trees and shrubs growing all around the property, lawned area at the rear, but with acres of off-road parking at the front, all crowned with a brick built double garage at the side, like I said, perfect."

"But?" said Luke, knowing that there was more.

"It was so depressing Luke, all the Almeda's furniture was still there, I kept looking over my shoulder expecting them to pop out from one of the rooms, it was so eerie," she said trying to explain her feelings to Luke, but making a hash of it.

More practically, Luke asked, "What did Yasmin think of it?"

"Oh, she thinks the house is lovely, and quite rightly too," said Claire, "she's putting an offer in today, with the vendor."

"So, she's not put off by the Almeda's passing there then?" queried Luke.

"No, quite the opposite in fact, and to quote Yasmin, the Almeda's were her friends in life, so why should she fear them now that they are dead," Claire said almost verbatim.

Luke took that on board, thinking philosophically about it, "I think that Yasmin makes a valid point, most houses with any age attached to them, have had at least one of the occupant's death connected to them, one way or another."

"You wouldn't be worried about living there then?" Claire asked.

"No, I think that Yasmin wants a nice house and sees the Almeda's property as being a sound future investment, especially if it comes fully furnished. You imagine trying to fill a house of that size today with modern furniture, it would cost you a small fortune."

"Well, when you look at it like that I suppose it does make sense for Yasmin to put an offer in, she'd be a fool not to," Claire had to agree, then thinking aloud, "she'll probably have her offer accepted too, which would mean a longer commute for us when we go to visit."

"Does it bother you?" Luke suddenly asked. "Her moving to a bigger house, I mean."

Looking at her husband obliquely, trying to discern his reasoning behind the question, Claire said

"God no, I'm not jealous of Yasmin moving on, if that's what you're asking, good luck to her she deserves it," Claire said with conviction. Then realising that Luke still seemed to doubt her sincerity, it began to annoy her that he would question her honesty, "I'm not jealous of Yasmin Luke, she was born into wealth and is now one of the uber rich, so, it's only natural that she would eventually move on to somewhere that reflects that wealth, and why am I having to convince you of this all of a sudden," said Claire, raising her voice angrily.

"I'm just making sure that what we have here, is enough for you," Luke said, in a more conciliatory tone.

Checking her anger now, Claire responded in kind with, "Of course it's enough for me, we've built a home together and I'm more than satisfied with it."

Adam had stopped reading during his parents altercation and raised voices, whilst Ruth, who was normally placid and quietly content, suddenly became irritable and began to cry for attention.

Claire picked her up and took her off upstairs to see if she needed changing, thankful to have an excuse to escape Luke's cross-examination.

The bickering in the Henderson's household, which had seemed to dissipate before Ruth's birth, was never really far from the surface, anything trivial seemed to trigger it off. Neither Luke nor Claire wished to disagree in this fashion or so openly, especially in front of the kids, but both of them seemed powerless to refrain from repeating it. That it was affecting Adam, was quite notIceable to both parents, at the first signs of a disagreement or raised voices, he would immediately go quiet and afterwards would refuse to speak to either of them, sometimes for hours.

Later that evening after the kids were put to bed, they

talked it all through, both deciding that the bickering had to stop, especially in front of Adam. Neither of them could understand why this was happening, when there seemed to be no rhyme or reason for it. They both loved each other, the kids were loved in turn and were most definitely wanted, they were financially secure, and the house was paid for, so why was this happening.

They just couldn't quite put their finger on it, but something or someone was causing this to happen and it was upsetting for the kids.

Chapter 117

Chris had taken his time shaving, designer stubble though fashionable to some, was not his style, hot shower soon followed washing away any tell-tale odours that mIght have still lingered from his latest liaison. Normally, he would wake and have sex again with whoever it was that happened to occupy the space beside him, in his king-size bed.

Reluctantly, when Sarah or Sadie, or something S, he wasn't quite sure, was most rudely woken up and packed off home with cab fare in hand, wondering self consciously if her performance in the bedroom Olympics had somehow fallen short of a podium finish, it was left to Chris to assure her that her stamina and technique in the art of fucking, was more than adequate to satisfy most of the world's male population. Still unsure as to her performance in bed, Chris had to promise a re-match at some future date to be determined, before he could shove her out the door. Now that Miss S was safely on the other side of the door, he could plan the rest of his day without any distractions.

Towelling himself dry, he appraised himself in the fogged -up mirror, having to use the damp towel as a cloth, in order to clear the surface cloud. Now in his late thirties Chris's body was in reasonably good shape, but he went to the gym twice a week in order to maintain an adequate six pack and to help fight off any signs of premature ageing. His numerous lady friends took care of any other muscles that the gym couldn't quite fix.

Now dressed in clean boxer shorts and nothing else, Chris slipped a slice of bread in the toaster, and plugged in the kettle to make a mug of tea. He ate sparingly and nothing really fancy, Claire would take pity on him occasionally and invite him over for the odd meal, which if he was really honest, was the only time that he ate properly. Working in a night club and surrounded by drinkers and drink, didn't really affect him either, he would have the odd pint of lager just to be sociable, but never drank to excess. The only time that he had let himself down through drink, was when he had fallen under Seline's feminine spell. That particular liaison had hurt him badly, and he had briefly turned to drink as a consequence in order to try and get over her. Thankfully he had bounced back from that bruising encounter, and had tried to bed the rest of the female population in an effort to try to forget her. He still saw her in the club from time to time, but would never allow her to hurt him again.

Toast and tea now consumed, Chris brushed away the remnants down the bathroom sink, then dressed in casual but smart clothing. He had a meeting arranged for later with his bar manager,

Jimmy Small on the premises, but first, he had to meet his co-manager Yasmin, who also happened to be his boss.

Chris now buffed and very presentable, walked the few paces along the landing which separated their apartments, and knocked on Yasmin's door.

It was Frank who opened it, stepping aside to let him in.

"Lady friend gone Chris?" Frank enquired.

"You been spying on me Frank?" Chris parried, smiling thinly.

"Me, spying, as if I would Chris," he replied feigning offence.

Yasmin must have been waiting for Chris to arrive because she appeared from the kitchen area, laden with a tray full of crockery, ready for making coffee. The unmistakable aroma of rich ground coffee soon filled Chris's nostrils, bidding him welcome. They all sat without ceremony, long used to one-another's company by now. Yasmin poured them all coffee, black for her, cream and one sugar for Frank and Chris.

Both men stirred in unison, then drank deeply at the same time like some well-rehearsed double act, then clinked their cups back down onto saucers.

Not really one for small talk, Chris barged straight in, "Okay I'm all ears what would you like to talk about?"

"I'd like you to manage the club from now on, you've been virtually doing that anyway, ever since I went on maternity leave, but I'd now like to make it official," Yasmin replied.

Chris was not entirely surprised by the offer, he had thought that this was coming, in fact ever since Yasmin had taken up the mantle as head of the Hussein portfolio he had thought that it was inevitable. Running the club solo wasn't particularly worrying for Chris, as far as he was concerned, he had effectively been doing the job ever since opening night, all those years ago.

"Okay, but what about the books?" he wanted to know.

"I'll continue to do the books, just like I've always done, and see to the wages as well, you just make sure that I have receipts for everything," Yasmin emphasised.

"What's my remit?" Chris asked.

Thinking carefully before answering, Yasmin thought about that, "Just do what you've always done, you have free reign to manage the club your way, so long as there are no radical changes involved. Jimmy has autonomy over running the bars and ordering the drink from the brewery, but otherwise, do basically what you've been doing, just don't do anything silly like trying to book the Rolling Stones, or something stupid like that," Yasmin said, in an effort to lighten the mood.

"Alright agreed, any other business?" Chris asked.

"Yes," Frank interjected, "Luke will be taking over my role as head of security at the club, I will still be involved of course, but only when Yasmin and I are not travelling. Luke will be stepping up to management when he returns from maternity leave, do you think that that will be a problem?"

Thinking about it before answering, Chris replied, "No, I don't have a problem with Luke, we get along fine."

They made small talk out of politeness for a while, but it was obvious that Chris was eager to get to the club, he had a meeting already arranged with big Jimmy Small, the man responsible for ordering the beer and running the club's bars. Arguably the most important man in charge, if asked by the members and guests.

When Chris had gone Yasmin asked Frank if he had any misgivings about putting Chris in sole charge.

"I don't think so, but just to be sure I'll keep a close eye on him when I'm working, we don't want him developing a Napoleon complex, you know what they say about a little power and what it does to one's head," Frank offered.

"Well don't go clipping his wings," Yasmin suggested, "but please make sure that he doesn't change the club too much, as I've become rather fond of it."

"Rest easy my beauty," Frank said, in Treasure Island mode, "I'll make sure that the scurvy knave leaves the club untouched."

Chapter 118

Chris inched forward a couple more spaces before coming stationary once more, the traffic in all directions was going nowhere anytime soon, as there was some kind of demonstration going on up ahead that involved a great many police officers. The crowd was deliberately disrupting the flow of traffic, spilling across the major roads, waving flags and banners in all directions. Tempers were beginning to fray, and scuffles were breaking out between police officers and demonstrators alike.

Seeing a black cab driver suddenly break away from Chris's front, he latched onto it and gained another precious fifty yards of tarmac, before becoming grid-locked once again.

This brought the demonstrators up close and personal with Chris's car, several of the mob began banging on Chris' bonnet and roof in anger, before police officers dragged them off, and none too gently.

The cab driver leaned on his horn and began to drive forward aggressively, Chris once again latched on to his rear bumper following closely, and greatly admiring the man's tenacity, eventually they came through the other side of the melee and into clear roadway, enjoying the sight of the open road.

Chris had a moment to swiftly glance at the time, "Fuck, I'm late, Jimmy will be going spare," he swore loudly to himself.

Chris pulled into the car-park at the rear of the club to see that the brewery lorry was already backed up to the rear doors, and being unloaded by Jimmy and the lorry driver. "Sorry I'm late Jimmy, the roads were gridlocked," Chris tried to explain.

"Don't be sorry, go get the wheels out of the storeroom and start shifting those crates inside," said Jimmy, pointing angrily at a mountain of work. That Jimmy was pissed off with him was obvious, but he went meekly to get the set of wheels without any complaint, Jimmy needed his help not excuses.

Once Chris had stacked enough crates on the set of wheels to just be able to see over the top, he started to move them inside and behind the bar area, Jimmy would take over from there. After two more trips inside, Chris removed his jacket and draped it across a chair, sweat was beginning to flow freely across his brow now, but he gamely went outside once more and loaded up some more crates. After another half a dozen trips he could see that he was making some headway, when

Jimmy came to give him a hand.

"That's all the kegs inside now, the driver's just finishing loading up the empties, then he's away,"

Jimmy said, "I've checked the order and it tallies with

what's been delivered, it just needs your moniker on the docket, and we're all good," Jimmy said, cheerily.

Chris broke off from loading the crates momentarily, to sign the delivery driver's sheet, who handed him the top copy. Chris thanked him for helping Jimmy with the beer barrels.

Once the driver had secured his load he started up the lorry, leaving Chris and Jimmy with the stacks of crates, still left to move inside.

Trying to wind Chris up, he said, "Get a move on with those crates while I go and put the kettle on."

Chris good naturedly told Jimmy to politely, "Fuck-off,' then began loading up more crates. Three more loads later, Chris parked the set of wheels back in the storeroom, before going to the gents toilet to wash his hands and face in cold water, towelling himself dry he went to find Jimmy.

Sitting down he allowed him to pour him a mug of tea strong enough to stand a spoon up in, then

Jimmy asked him sweetly, "AII done?"

Chris just looked at him scornfully, not bothering to answer.

"So, what was that load of bollocks you were spouting, when you finally decided to show up," Jimmy now wanted to know.

Taking a healthy swig of tea, strong enough to strip paint off a door, Chris answered, "Extinction rebels, or some such shite and that reminds me, I need to check the car roof for dents, I bet the fuckers have put a few in it," he remembered.

"Well good luck with the insurance mate, I bet they refuse to pay out," Jimmy said, cheerfully.

"Thanks for your concern Jimmy, it's good to know that you care," Chris said sarcastically.

"You're welcome mate," enjoying Chris's discomfort.

They sat in companionable silence for a while, wincing every time they took a sip of the paint stripper, disguised as tea.

"Yasmin's stood down from minding the club," Chris suddenly announced, "she's put me in charge."

"Well it was on the cards, wasn't it?" Jimmy replied, "ever since she took over her father's business, she was bound to move on to bigger things, and of course she has the little one to look after now as well," he said. On a lighter note he remembered, "Just don't go ordering any more shite beer without running it past me first, I had to pour the last lot down the drain in the end."

Chris had to laugh at remembering his folly with ordering some piss poor beer, and had to admit to Jimmy, "It was shit wasn't it."

"Oh yes mate, it really was. So have you got any changes you want to make to the club now that you're finally in charge?" Jimmy asked, interested.

"No Jimmy not really, we've got a winning formula going for now, so let's just see how we go and let things settle down for a while," said Chris, content for now.

"Well, I for one am glad to hear it, I've got about five good years left in me before I decide to bow out, so you might want to think about scouting around for my replacement," said Jimmy sombrely.

"Don't say that Jimmy, who the fucks going to fill your boots?" Chris said, genuinely worried by Jimmy's candour.

"Just giving you a heads up Chris, it's the least I can do seeing as it was you that gave me a lifeline when I needed it, when the club first opened up," Jimmy answered.

"Well I'll be sorry to see you go mate, I truly will," Chris said sadly.

"For fucks sake, I haven't gone yet. I said in about five years' time," Jimmy spat.

"Well, keep your own eyes and ears open for a suitable replacement, you've got a better idea of a decent candidate than I would have," admitted Chris.

Jimmy took that on board but didn't bother to answer, quietly finishing the rest of his paint stripper.

Chris and Jimmy had had their fair share of disagreements over the years, but nothing serious. The only time that Jimmy really lost his temper, was when anyone tried to interfere in the running of his bars, Jimmy was bar manager, end of. Anyone tried to encroach on his way of running things, it was war. Finishing up their tea, Chris would have offered to help jimmy stack the crates of bottles wherever he wanted them stacking, but knew from experience that the offer was pointless, Jimmy already knew where everything needed to be stacked, and liked to do it himself.

Instead, Chris unlocked what was now technically his manager's office, and put the latest receipt from the delivery driver into the desk drawer with the others. He had a quick look around the office, just to make sure that all was in order, then backed out, re-locking it afterwards. Then he had a walk through the club, checking first the toilets for cleanliness and any signs of a leak, before checking the V.I.P. areas. The dance floor looked particularly good, but he wanted to check on one of the sound decks, as it had been giving him a bit of trouble lately, and may well need replacing at some future date. Switching on the power he donned his head -phones and ran a playlist quickly through them, checking for anomalies. Satisfied with the sound for now, Chris decided that the decks were good for a while longer yet, but reminded himself to keep an eye on them, as the club would only remain successful so long as the music kept pounding out and filling up the dance floor. Checking back with Jimmy, Chris asked how long he was going to be?

"Another ten minutes and I'm good to go," affirmed Jimmy.

"I'll go and secure the fire doors then Jimmy, we can go out the front way together," Chris offered. Jimmy now satisfied that the bars were in shipshape condition once more, secured them with a flourish and walked out with Chris. Alarm's re-set, and doors now re-Iocked they walked out to their respective cars.

Jimmy had to smile when he heard Chris curse, "Fuckers have dented the roof, fuck." Chris swore.

Chapter 119

A series of unfortunate events, re-visited.

The rumours that had been circulating around the corridors of the Eastern Palms Hotel, were that

Fatima Hussein had been deposed as acting head of the Hussein Empire, and had been succeeded by her daughter Yasmin. The rumour had been treated as mis-information at first, pedalled by some rival hotel chain in order to cause uncertainty and confusion amongst the management. Mohamed Faisal, acting manager of the Eastern Palms hotel, treated the information as scurrilous dribble and carried on running the hotel as if Mrs Hussein senior was still in sole charge.

A few weeks later Faisal's worst fears became reality, when it was confirmed by e-mail that Yasmin Hussein was now acting head of the Hussein Empire and would be visiting the hotel in the very near future. If Mr Faisal had had any real sense at all, he would have at least made some sort of attempt to try to sort out the hotel's books. Unfortunately, Mr Faisal had become complacent in the last few years, believing wrongly as it turned out, that Yasmin Hussein would prove to be just as lazy and stupid, as her brother Ali had been. However he had found out to his cost, that Yasmin Hussein was neither lazy nor stupid and he had only just evaded being captured by his own security by about thirty minutes. Nevertheless, Faisal had succeeded in absconding with the contents of the safe, as well as over 2.3 million dollars that he had managed to steal over the years.

As a final act of betrayal to his employer, and knowing of the enmity that existed between mother and daughter, Faisal, before escaping, fired off an e-mail to Fatima Hussein, telling her that her daughter and grand-daughter were currently staying as guests at the hotel. That e-mail had almost resulted in the kid-napping of Yasmin's daughter Aisha, and if it hadn't have been for the tenacity of Aisha's minder Amy, it would have been the work of seconds to have spirited her away.

Fatima Hussein had left the Eastern Hotel in a black rage, vowing vengeance on that person, she loosely termed her daughter. A chance for vengeance arrived in the form of an e-mail several weeks later requesting shipment of supplies, numbered 359, from commercial warehouse number 2, in Aqaba. Request made, by Masud Fazel and marked urgent.

Now it just so happened that Fatima had heard of Masud Fazel, but had never met him in person, she knew that he was Iranian by birth, and that her late son Ali had been both funding and sending him supplies direct from warehouse 2, in Aqaba. She also knew that the designated numbers 359 meant that the crates actually contained munitions and explosives and not the machine parts that they were purported to hold.

Fatima couldn't care less that her son had been funding and supplying terrorist organisations for years and had been openly complicit with him doing so. But she did now see a way of gaining just a little bit of revenge on that wayward daughter of hers.

For some reason unbeknown to her, Fatima Hussein still had influence and control over the contents housed in warehouses land 2 in Aqaba. Why her daughter had not asserted herself and made it known to the warehouse managers that she was now in sole control of the Hussein franchise, was a mystery to Fatima, but she saw Yasmin's indecisiveness as a perfect opportunity to pull the rug from out under her daughter's feet. It was all about timing Fatima realised, so she sent a message to warehouse 2, authorising the entire shipment of the crates marked 359, with immediate effect.

That shipment comprised the last load of not less than thirty tonnes, and would require a decent sized ship, capable of breaking the embargo placed on Iran, by the United Nations.

Just such a ship was already docked at the port of Aqaba, a medium-sized merchantman, flying the Greek flag and named the Aurora. This same ship had been docked here three times in the last year, but the last time she had docked she bore a different name to the one she held now, last time she was known as the Artemis, and the time before that she was known as the Athena. That this ship was a lady of dubious character, was only half the story.

Painted black from bow to stern, she looked ungainly to the naked eye having a medium –sized structure attached central and forward of the bridge, and also one central towards the rear.

Stencilled on these structures was written 'Life Rafts', plausible maybe, but in fact under these structures, which by the way were made of fibreglass and easily removed by two men, was something else entirely. Two twin 40 mm Bofor's guns, one forward and one aft had been bolted on to the deck and been covered over with the fibreglass structures. It was the work of less than a minute for two men to uncover the guns, ready for immediate action. Both weapons although ancient, had been lovingly looked after and were in perfectly good working order.

Everything about the ship was a deception, it wasn't Greek for a start, but belonged instead to a clandestine arm of the Iranian navy, looking sluggish and pedestrian was also a deliberate misconception, if needed, the Aurora could attain speeds that would have left most other ships standing in her wake. Desperate times had called for desperate measures, and the Aurora was one such measure. Once fully loaded with embargo breaking goods and supplies, the Aurora would have to run the risk of stop and search vessels from the U.N. then it would have to travel down the length of the Red Sea and out through the Gulf of Aden, traverse the Arabian Sea and in through the Gulf of Oman, hopefully, to finally reach the safe port of Bandar Abbas, opposite the strait of Hormuz, with its illicit cargo.

The captain of the Aurora well knew the risks he was running by breaking the U.N. embargo, yet chose to do it willingly. However, whatever your views or politics on the matter, bravery, was not an exclusive commodity.

In hindsight, Fatima Hussein in trying to gain her revènge may have instead done her daughter a great service. With the contents of the boxes marked 359 now safely out of warehouse 2 and on their way to Iran, no further incriminating evidence of munitions would be found on the Hussein's property. So in a way, far from gaining any type of revenge over her daughter, she'd actually saved her bacon.

Chapter 120

Wednesday,at the Henderson's.

"How long do you think you'll be?" Claire asked.

"Hopefully just a couple of hours, there's only seven applicants, and besides I've asked Frank to sit in with me for his own input," Luke replied.

"Does he mind? I mean he's put you in charge, so won't he think that he's holding your hand?" she queried.

"Maybe," admitted Luke, "but he does have a great deal of experience, and when it comes to dealing with people, I'd be a fool not to take advantage of his expertise, besides, he offered to help."

"Well if you're sure," Claire replied, only half convinced. Wednesday afternoon at the club. Luke and Frank had set up in Chris's office, ready to interview the seven applicants, five men and two women, all chasing one position as a member of the club's security team. As promised, Frank had posted the position of security guard on the club's front notice board, as well as running an advertisement in the local recruitment section, of the London Advertiser. Forms had been sent out, dutifully returned and collected, and that's why seven individuals sat out in the corridor, nervously awaiting the summons to enter the office. The only criteria that was really required of the applicants, was that they were legally badged and preferably working, but the second preference was not absolutely necessary, in order to secure the position.

As the first applicant was called in, Frank let Luke lead the interview, mainly to see how he handled himself. He only had to intervene once, but other than that, Frank was happy with Luke's questioning of the applicant.

By the time the fourth person had entered the room, the questioning had become almost repetitive, except that this time the applicant was female, and sporting a lot of facial pins and piercings. The club's official policy, pretty much frowned on staff wearing too much metal, as the club wanted to promote a clean healthy look to the people visiting the premises. Nevertheless, the interview on Susan Jones followed more or less the patte of the previous interviews, except that Miss Jones was very well spoken, and dare I say it, if it wasn't for the amount of metal defacing Miss Jones's face, she would have been quite attractive. Luke touched on the thorny subject of the face piercings, by telling her that it was the club's policy that employee's should not be seen to have too many face piercings, as it gave out a false image of what the club represented. When asked if she was willing to remove the metal when working, she became quite angry and point blank refused to compromise, which promptly ended her interview.

The next person up was Peter Walker, who was also wearing metal but only a gold stud in one ear lobe, which was deemed perfectly acceptable. Peter's interview was carried out in tandem by Frank and Luke, who both sensed that this applicant had the requisite skills that were required by the club.

That left just two applicants to interview, one male and one female.

The male's interview did not go well at all, as he had lied on his application form. One of the questions on the form specifically asked if the applicant had a criminal record, this particular individual had written 'No' beside it, which was a blatant lie. Frank had recognised the man, and knew for a fact that he'd been charged and fined for assault, which resulted in his application being rejected. If he had answered the question correctly, his record would have been taken into account, but lying at the interview stage, disqualified him outright.

Last up, was Erica Grey, a blonde haired, blue eyed Amazon of a woman, six foot two tall and quite intimidating to look at. She answered all of Luke and Frank's questions clearly and confidently, and by the end of the interview, Luke had wanted to offer her the job on a month's trial.

Frank was strongly in favour of Peter Walker, pointing out that until Erica's interview, both of them had agreed that he had the requisite skills required by the club, this led to a temporary impasse as

Erica also had the same set of skills, and experience. In the end Frank could not budge Luke's logic or reasoning for favouring Erica. He advocated giving a month's trial to Erica, because the women were short-handed, which was perfectly true. In the end Frank changed the rules completely, because Luke wouldn't change his mind he suggested hiring both Peter and Erica on a month's trial, to see how they got along with the rest of the team. That decided, they agreed to trial them both.

Once Luke was back working again after his maternity leave, he had the perfect opportunity to observe Peter and Erica interacting with the other members of the security team. It was clear from the word go that both new recruits had slotted into their positions seamlessly, and worked well with the others. After the month's trial was up, both probationers were surprisingly offered contracts, which they duly signed. So instead of one extra member of security being hired, we now had two.

Frank continued to work at the club just as before, but made sure that he didn't stand on Luke's toes, always asking him at the beginning of his shift where he would like him to police. It worked well, and now that they had the extra bodies, everyone had less area to cover. Luke had continued with Frank's former regime of alternating the team members so that everyone teamed up with each other. This particular night it fell that Luke was partnered with Erica. Both observed each other in action, quietly assessing each other's interaction with the members and guests. Erica didn't say much, but was very impressed by Luke's confidence and calm polite manner, when sorting out any problems.

She knew that he was married and had two children, because she had made it her business to ask around, not because she was attracted to him sexually, but solely because he interested her. Her own sexual orientation was her own business, but if she was pressed on the matter she would probably admit to favouring female company, over male. However, that said she had experimented with men who intrigued her, so perhaps she couldn't be pigeon holed.

Peter Walker, or Pete, as he soon became known to his colleagues, was pretty much an open book. He was unmarried but had an on, off sort of relationship with a young woman who had trouble with the unsociable hours that Pete had to work. The unsociable hours and a jealous nature often led to the relationship being more off than on. Still that was the nature of the beast, and probably why most of the security team had failed relationships behind them.

Since Chris had been appointed as sole manager, everything had continued to run smoothly without any slackening of footfall, through the club's doors. The only fly in the ointment was the need to renew the decks, as it was only a matter of time before they failed. He had made subsequent enquiries as to pricing up the replacements and had made Yasmin aware of what was needed, and more importantly, how much it was going to cost her.

Yasmin was no fool, realising quickly that the club only survived through Chris's good management and the music coming through the speakers. She authorised the purchase straight away, only asking that he provide receipts to account for the expenditure. It was a harmonious working relationship that Chris had with Yasmin, and he was thankful for it. However, lately he was feeling like something was missing in his life. He wondered, as he got older, whether he was starting to get worried about missing out on his life. Claire and Luke were married and already had two kids, Yasmin and Frank had jumped the broom and now had Aisha to show for it. Perhaps he needed to settle down himself he thought worryingly, and start a family of his own. God, Chris thought to himself, how fucking depressing, but the thought wouldn't go away, that little voice just kept on repeating ,like a metronome, perhaps it's time.

Shortly after Ruth's blrth, I personally rang my sister to let her know that the birth had gone well, and that we were both doing fine. The only way that I can describe the conversation that we had, was that it was like talking to a complete stranger. Maureen had become just an anonymous voice on the other end of the line. There was no real warmth in what we both chose to share, and sadly, I came to realise that the close bond we had shared as a family was now broken. We had promised each other at my wedding that we would both keep in touch, sadly neither of us kept that promise as the weeks and months turned into long years of silence. I don't think that either of us was to blame, or maybe that was just an excuse, and we were both equally to blame, either way, the gap had grown ever wider and I think as a family, we were done. To underline it, I sent a recent photograph of Adam, and one of Ruth, along with a brief note in a letter expressing sentiments that I didn't really feel, and left it up to the mailman to deliver.

On a brighter note, I had kept in touch with Uncle Tony, Chris's dad, as he was my last link with my mum, he surprised me when he told me that he was coming down for the week-end, to stay at Chris's. At least he was a constant in my life, and he had made me feel much better about myself when I finally ended the call. I told Luke about it and he said that he looked forward to catching up with him, Ruth would finally get to know her great uncle, and Uncle Tony would be astonished to see the changes in young Adam. Just one positive telephone call, had made all the difference to what normally would have amounted to another uneventful day.

Since Luke had returned to work we had fallen into some kind of routine that seemed to be broken only by nights, when Luke worked, followed by days when he was at home. Ruth continued to be a pleasant happy little girl, raising my hopes and expectations ever higher, that she would turn out to be just a normal happy little soul. Adam was still trying hard to master his gifts and was just about succeeding. I had every hope, fingers crossed that it would continue and we would after all, be able to send him to school.

No sooner had I sat back down, when the telephone rang for my attention once more. It was Sheryl, so I cut a very long one-sided conversation down into just a few short sentences that were worthy of mention. After the preliminary introductions were got out of the way, I asked Sheryl how her pregnancy was progressing. Her answer was as follows, "Apart from looking as big as a house, I'm happy and feeling like the proverbial pig in shit." That sentence alone, apart from making me laugh out loud, told me that Sheryl was doing just fine. Good old Sheryl. Eventually, I brought up the subject that had been giving me the most concern, had she seen any more of Daniel Mcfee? She assured me that she hadn't, so hopefully he had slithered back into the hole from which he had crawled out of, never to be seen again. The rest was just catch-up, until we said our good-byes, I was both cheered and saddened by Sheryl's telephone call, cheered because distance had not affected our friendship, saddened, because I just couldn't put Ruth in the buggy and stroll around to visit her with Adam. I missed my friend.

Three telephone calls, two good, one not so good, but in the words of the song, two out of three ain't bad, so I was content.

Chapter 122

I got up more or less as Luke came in from work, he looked concerned to see me in the kitchen, asking if the kids were alright. I kissed away his fears and told him I would be up to join him shortly.

Yesterday, I had bought a beautiful joint of beef, and now I wanted to start slow cooking it in the oven, so that by the time it was ready for eating, it would hopefully just fall apart. Uncle Tony and

Chris would be joining us and I was looking forward to it, once satisfied that the oven was doing its job, I went up to join Luke before he went to sleep.

Later, when I'd got the kids up, cleaned and fed, I spent some quality time with my son. Ruth was in her carry-cot, looking out through the patio windows watching the odd cloud formation floating on by. She must have enjoyed watching them, because she sounded cheerful and was making happy sounds. Adam was watching me peeling vegetables, and helping me to eat the odd piece of carrot, whilst questioning me about my family. I remember thinking back, that's how I learned things about my family, through asking my mother whilst preparing the family meal. I expect most families are the same the world over, you learn about the family by asking your parents.

"So, your Uncle Tony was your mum's brother," Adam repeated, "and Chris is Uncle Tony's son."

"Yes! That's right," I smiled, "my mum, had she lived, would have been your grandma and my Uncle Tony is your grand-uncle."

"But you don't mention Chris's mum," Adam wanted to know.

Now things were heading into unchartered waters, and I have to admit I was feeling a little uncomfortable about it. The truth was, I didn't know too much about what had happened with

Chris's mum, the only information that I had gleaned at all, was learned second hand from my sister Maureen. Apparently, Uncle Tony had walked in on his then wife and best friend as was, whilst they were in an obvious state of undress. I don't know what happened after that, but Chris's mother was no longer around for Chris, and neither was the best friend. Uncle Tony brought Chris up alone after that, but of course I couldn't tell my son this sort of thing, so I simply told him that Chris's mum and dad had split up, which wasn't technically a lie. This seemed to satisfy Adam, as I broke off the conversation to check on Ruth. She was as happy as Larry, we had recently bought a garden bird feeder and it had attracted a couple of tits to it, and she was watching them going through various contortions to get at the food, this seemed to please her no end.

Going back in to Adam, he asked me about Sheffield,

"Well, I don't really know too much about

Sheffield," I had to admit, "but mum and Uncle Tony were both born there, and their parents both ran a butcher's shop, and I believe their grand-parents too. Of course, the original shop no longer exists now, as it's been long since demolished, along-side a lot of other old buildings. But there is still a Booth's butcher's in Sheffield, and Uncle Tony still keeps one up and running to help maintain the family tradition."

"But you weren't born in Sheffield," Adam correctly assessed.

"No, I was born in Lincoln. When mum met and married my father, they moved from Sheffield and settled in Lincoln to live, and that's where your Aunt Maureen and then of course I, were born."

"So, Lincoln is really your home then," Adam had worked out for himself.

"Yes! Well it was, but I suppose now that I live in London, you could say that this is my home too.

You and Ruth were both born here, so your birthplace is London. In the end, I don't think it really matters where you live, it's a matter of where your family lives and what makes you happy, that determines where you live."

Adam seemed to take that on board, and took his time about coming to his own conclusions. Once the dinner was prepared, the question and answer session was adjourned, for some future date. I relieved Ruth of her confinement and plonked her on the settee beside me, now it was time for a little mother and daughter one on one.

Adam, predictably went to browse through his book shelf and came back with a full colour book of native British birds. He'd looked at the book so often, that he probably knew it off by heart, yet it was still one of his favourites,

I'm afraid that Rupert Bear, only recently introduced to him, didn't hold much attention in my son's imagination. If it didn't exist in the real world, then Adam wasn't really interested in it, children's stories sadly, were not exciting enough for him.

Later when Uncle Tony and Chris arrived, he asked me what I'd been feeding young Adam to make him grow so much. I simply replied, "Meat and plenty of veg."

Then Tony asked me, joking, "Are you sure you haven't been putting horse muck in his boots?"

It was an old saying for someone who seemed to grow abnormally quickly, and for no good reason. I just smiled, saying that I was sure.

Adam of course, wanted to know the reasoning behind Uncle Tony's words, so I had to tell him that there was no real truth in the saying, and that it was just an old wives tale. That seemed to disappoint Adam at first, but he accepted it readily enough when he realised that it had no basis in fact.

When Luke got up he cracked a couple of beers with Uncle Tony, then went out into the back garden and watched Adam run rings around his Uncle Chris with his ball control.

Later, at the dinner table, Adam was interested to know that Tony supported the Blades Football Club. When asked why he didn't support the Owls instead, he pompously replied, "Because the Owls are not a proper football club lad."

Not wanting my son caught up in some sort of club rivalry, I put a halt to all talk of football at the dining table. Adam seemed disappointed to be overruled by his mother at meal time, but sensibly kept quiet.

After dinner, Luke helped me with the washing up, whilst Uncle Tony played with young Ruth on the living room carpet. Kids, for whatever reason, seemed to take naturally to Uncle Tony and it was just a shame that he'd only had Chris. We had a lovely peaceful afternoon together, it was sad when it had to end and Chris and Uncle Tony finally headed off. At least Adam had got to spend quality time with his Grand-Uncle Tony and I just hoped that it wouldn't be too long before the next time. Adam was growing up and Uncle Tony wasn't getting any younger.

Chapter 123

During the days and weeks that followed my daughter's birth, I looked for outward signs that she had followed in Adam's footsteps, and was showing early symptoms of his abilities. Each day that passed uneventful, allowed me to breathe a little easier. Ruth was a beautiful little girl, I know that most mothers say that, but in Ruth's case it was true. She had taken readily to the bottle and was now sleeping well, through most of the night. Just like Adam, Ruth hardly ever cried and was a pleasant happy little girl. Now that her eyes were settled and focusing well, they missed nothing and followed us everywhere. She favoured Luke's eyes in colour, the deepest of blue which I was quite happy about and I made a joke about it to Luke, saying that she would grow into a real babe magnet in the future, and that he would be beating the boys off with a stick. Luke didn't really want to think that far ahead as he was happy for her to remain a baby for a little while longer.

I must admit that having been so miserable whilst carrying Ruth, I was a little bit afraid that some of that misery might somehow have rubbed off and been transferred onto her, happily this was not the case. Ruth had bonded with us all effortlessly and readily went to both Luke and myself. Adam had a slightly different type of relationship with his sister, just as I suspected that they would have, their bond was much closer now, and had begun even before Ruth's birth. Nothing since her birth had altered my opinion, it was uncanny to watch them interact with one-another, Adam only had to look over in Ruth's direction, and she would immediately turn to seek him out. I didn't know how well developed a babies brain was supposed to be at this early stage, but I'm sure that Adam and Ruth were already communicating on some hidden level. It was lovely to see how well he'd taken to his baby sister, I had thought that there might be some sort of sibling jealousy involved in the beginning, but up to now, that hadn't been the case.

Luckily, we had kept Adam's old crib from when he was a baby, and now it was Ruth who got to sleep in it. Looking in the attic for more treasures, Luke came down with Adam's old solar system mobile. Adam clearly remembered it with fondness, and suggested to Luke, that he should set it up for Ruth. After we had given it a good clean, she seemed delighted with it, so in hindsight I'm glad that we'd kept Adam's old things, instead of throwing them out like we intended.

As soon as I felt able, I began a fitness regime in earnest. I wanted my old body back, and in a hurry.

Luke tried to coax me into taking things slowly, and tried to make light of it by suggesting that he didn't mind me having a little extra flesh on board, as he enjoyed having something to get hold of.

I thought, bugger that, he's had more than enough to get hold of for the last nine months, and I wanted it gone. I exercised at home, usually watched over by an amused Adam, who tried to copy my regime, and an indifferent Ruth who didn't seem to be too impressed by my fat-busting efforts.

When Luke was available to watch the kids, I took to power walking and then light jogging. I ate healthily, and as I did most of the cooking and was in control of what we ate, so did everyone else.

Pretty soon, miracle of miracles my old body began to re-appear.

Our love-making had already resumed, but this time we were taking precautions, no more babies for me, two was enough. Gradually we eased back into a kind of domestic harmony, there was still the problem of Adam's schooling to solve, but even on that front there was a glimmer of hope. Adam had been making a serious effort to rein in his abilities and control them, so all in all things were looking good.

It was while I was doing a spot of house cleaning, that that particular bubble burst, but from a surprisingly different quarter. I was hoovering and dusting my bedroom whilst Adam was reading, and watching over his sister, who was lying wide-awake in her crib. With the hoover now switched off everything returned to peace and quiet, although that didn't last long, as all of a sudden Adam shouted, "Mummm come and see!"

It didn't sound urgent, as in urgent, but I went to see what he wanted, just to be sure. Adam was looking towards Ruth's crib wide-eyed and smiling.

Above Ruth's crib, the solar system mobile was

spinning like an out of control fairground ride on acid.

Ruth was giggling whilst watching it, clearly delighted.

Annoyed, I looked over at Adam, and crossly said to him, "Stop it Adam, I thought that you said you had it under control."

Clearly upset by my tone, he replied, "But mum, it's not me honest, it's Ruth."

Realising the enormity of what that meant, I slumped against the wall as if gut-punched, and simply said, "Oh, fuck."

AUTHOR'S NOTE.

For those of you who are still curious to know more, I can tell you this.

Memhet Yafai returned from Switzerland successfully with the money. It was equally divided amongst his men without the customary squabbles and failings out, usually associated with money, and then they went their separate ways.

Memhet returned to his first love, civil engineering and is currently overseeing a huge hydro-electric scheme in Egypt.

Yasmin's baby Aisha, will grow up to be a future rival for her mother's beauty, whilst the

Hussein Empire will continue to grow from strength to strength, with Yasmin at the helm.

Luke and Claire will remain strong through the rocky times ahead. As for young Adam...his powers and intellect will only grow stronger and continue to amaze you. Ruth, though still only a baby will be the one to watch, as her powers will turn out to be, simply earth shattering.

But what of the future? Well.... I suppose we will just have to wait and see.

Also available, the first in the series.

CLAIRE'S ANGEL

David Simpson

Luke Henderson, seller of antiquarian and rare books in York's Micklegate, is not what he seems.

The bookshop is a front. Part human, part angel, Luke protects the weak, dealing out swift vengeance against evil-doers, meting out his own, often bloody justice.

The more he lives among humans, the more his supernatural powers come into conflict with his humanity, and his angel superiors become concerned that he is exceeding his remit. Unless he is careful, he will be withdrawn.

But in the meantime, Luke is falling in love with a young nightclub worker, Claire, and she becomes caught up in a terrifying power struggle between the club's Jordanian co-owners.

THIS THRILLER WILL KEEP YOU ENTHRALLED UNTIL THE FINAL HEARTSTOPPING PAGE.